MW01592896

THREE WISE MEN

By
Robert L. Fenton

A Bestselling Author

Also by Robert L. Fenton,
published under the name,
Julia Fenton

Black Tie Only
Blue Orchids
Royal Invitation

THREE WISE MEN

By

Robert L. Fenton

Copyright © 2007 by Robert L. Fenton

ISBN: 978-1-60145-347-1

Published by arrangement with BookLocker.com, Inc.

All rights reserved. No part of this publication may be reproduced, stored in a retrieval system, or transmitted in any form or by any means, electronic, mechanical, recording or otherwise, without the prior written permission of the author.

This book is a work of fiction. Names, characters, places and incidents are products of the author's imagination or are used fictitiously. Any resemblance to actual events or locales or persons living or dead is entirely coincidental.

Manufactured in the United States of America.

BookLocker.com, Inc.
P.O. Box 2399
Bangor, ME 04402
http://ww.BookLocker.com

To my one and only… Karen, the best woman I've ever known.
She's been my total inspiration for everything I am,
or ever have been.
Here's to you, Sweetheart!

Big hugs to the Fenton kids: Cynthia, Robert Jr., Aileen,
Robert III, Hallie Marie, and Olivia Paige.
I love you all beyond measure.

Acknowledgments

I'd like to acknowledge the superb efforts of Tom Morrisey in editing the manuscript. Also, I would be remiss if I didn't acknowledge the efforts of the folks at Hiram Walker over in Walkerville, Canada; also Judith Fisher, my former secretary and personal assistant, as well as Deborah Lee Watson, my Executive Assistant. Deborah Lee has been a formidable force in getting things done for almost two years now, and was a great help in finalizing the manuscript. Thanks Deborah Lee!

Then there are all the members of the Franklin Fitness Club that have continuously offered their support and interest, i.e. Mitch, Russ, Rozie, George (both of them), Larry, Jeff, Ira, Sy and Tim, and many more guys and gals who are too numerous to mention individually.

Also, a close buddy, Jerry Lewis, who listens to my prattle just about every morning over breakfast.

How could I not mention another dear friend, Ernie Harwell, who is a proud author himself, as well as a Hall of Fame baseball announcer. Thanks Ernie for all your interest.

Norma & Gil Kleiff, Frankie & Carole Lewis, and the Oakland Six Gang have been great as well. And a special thanks to Norma Kleiff for her invaluable help in sorting out the Yiddish words. Also, thanks to Jonathan Brateman who was always there for me.

Enter not into the path of the wicked,
and go not in the way of evil men.

Avoid it, pass not by it, turn from it,
and pass away.

For they sleep not, except they have done
mischief; and their sleep is taken away,
unless they cause some to fall.

For they eat the bread of wickedness,
and drink the wine of violence.

– *The Book of Proverbs*

THREE WISE MEN

Prologue
New York City – March 1915

Punch-drunk and battered, the two men circled one another warily, their eyes hooded shadows under the glare of the harsh arena lights. A pall of cigar smoke hung over the arena like a low fog, and both men gleamed with sweat, their dark, matted chests beaded with perspiration, despite the near freezing temperatures outside of the Garden on 26th and Madison Avenue.

Their naked chests... Miriam Baker stared at them without flinching at the sight of blood. She had never seen men bare-chested in public before. Even the time Irving had taken her to the beach at Coney Island without her parent's permission, the men had worn bathing tank tops that covered their chests, like the white cotton sleeveless shirts worn by the stevedores down on the docks.

She looked closely at their nipples, pale brown in the incandescent lighting, and felt her own nipples harden at the sight. The area between her legs grew moist. Just then, one of the men threw a punch, a hard right cross that caught his opponent on the side of the chin, sending a spray of sweat fanning out into the ringside seats. A few drops landed on Miriam's arm as she and Irving stood in the aisle cheering on the fighter in black trunks.

She touched her finger to the spot and then to her mouth; it tasted of salt and she shivered as she licked her lips.

She turned to twenty-year old Irving Lowenstein, a law school freshman, dapper and slim in his neatly pressed, pin-striped suit and spats, brown hair parted on the side, blue eyes sparkling intelligently, his moustache neatly trimmed and full. "So go ahead and sit, darling," she told him, kissing him on the cheek. "I'll be right back. I have to go powder my nose." She walked up the aisle to the arena entrance and looked back at the ring. The man in black trunks was working away at his opponent's mid-section, head down, biceps flexed as he landed punch after punch. Despite the shouts and noise of the crowd, she could hear the men in the ring both grunting with tremendous physical exertion.

Half-naked men, hitting each other... Madison Square Garden. Miriam was so glad Irving had brought her here rather than down to the theater district to see Serge Diaghilev's Ballets Russe. That's where she told her parents they were going because proper, young ladies didn't go to prizefights at Madison Square Garden. *That's what they think!*

Her father, he was so old fashioned. Miriam smirked at herself in the ladies room mirror as she thought of him, her green eyes flashing under the shimmering helmet of golden-blonde, bobbed hair held neatly off her forehead by a black headband. She moved her shoulders to and fro, and the fringe of tassels that ran across the front of the dress, just at chest level, undulated seductively. She had a better figure, she knew, than Mary Pickford, Ruby Keeler or any of the other girls she'd seen in the silent motion picture shows. And, if her father had his way, she'd be hiding it under some lumpy, shapeless dress that fell all the way to the floor and hid the exquisite shape of her long, silk-stockinged legs.

Her father, hiding the Jewishness from his Park Avenue patients, went to a schul all the way across town, on Delancey Street, where none of his fancy uptown friends could see him worshipping Judaism. During the holidays, their Menorah was kept well away from the windows, and she and her brothers would be asked to wish their neighbors a "Merry Christmas" rather than a "Happy Chanukah."

But inside the Park Avenue apartment, her father, Benjamin B. Baker, honored the religion he'd been raised in. The kitchen was kosher, with both a meat and milk side, and a glass of wine carefully filled with Mogen David before each meal. And tonight, Saturday night, he had made her wait inside the apartment until sundown before he would allow Irv Lowenstein to pick her up in his Chevrolet coupe.

She finished smoothing her hair. How many half-naked men hitting one another had they already missed by being almost an hour late, she thought. Taking off her bloomers, she tightly folded them and stuffed them into her handbag. She attached the garters to her nylons, smoothed her dress, and stepped back outside the stall. She finished brushing her hair, touched some tinted powder onto each cheek and smiled back from her reflection in the mirror. Straightening her pearls, she left the restroom and headed back to her seat.

Madison Square Garden was flushed with noise and smoke, cries of "Hit him, Paddy!" and "Finish him off!" screamed out from the crowd as the black man, Lightning Jones, backed Paddy Finnegan into the corner.

Miriam walked down the aisle, aware of hundreds of male eyes following her well-formed bottom as she made her way back to where they were sitting. Irv had gotten them ringside seats, and she didn't know how he'd managed that, as the New York City Golden Gloves Championships had been sold out for weeks. Then again, Irving seemed to have ways of getting things done, when he wanted to.

He smiled and stood as she got to their seats, and Miriam deliberately let her fingers trail across his crotch as she edged past him, smiling at the flicker of surprise on his face. She looked around the rows near her before she took her seat; it was mostly men in the audience, all in suits, some in hats, most yelling or booing; some holding fists in the air full of five dollar bills, as if to show the boxers in the ring what was riding on the outcome of the fight.

"I'm a little cold." she told Irving as she sat down, speaking directly into his ear so he could hear her over the crowd. "Would you mind putting your topcoat over my lap?"

"Are you kidding?" Irving replied. "With all these people in here, it's got to be over seventy degrees."

Then he saw the look in her eyes, and he nodded, putting the silk-lined camel hair coat over her legs, covering her bare knees, everything to her waist. In a moment, his hand was on her knee, keeping it there under his topcoat, as the fighter in red trunks slumped heavily to the canvas in exhaustion. The bout was over as she rubbed Irv's fingers with her own, a languid promise of what was to follow after the fight. The crowd was in a frenzy as the winner was announced by the referee using the public address system.

Two new fighters entered the ring through the ropes. These men were bigger, their muscles even more pronounced, the heavy pectorals heaving slowly as they touched gloves during the introduction. The referee, in his white shirt and bow-tie, reminded them that they would be competing under strict Marquis of Queensbury Rules, ordered them to their corners, and rang the bell to bring them out fighting.

Fresh and strong, the men danced around each other, flicking out hard quick jabs with their left while the right hand was cocked waiting for the right opportunity to connect to the body or even better, the jaw. Miriam guided Irving's hand under the hem of her dress, past the turned tops of her silk stockings, and up to where the blonde silky down that covered her sex was already damp with anticipation of good things to come. She looked out of the corner of her eye and smiled at the surprise on his face.

"You're enjoying the fights, I see," he said over the growing noise of the crowd around them.

"Oh yes. Very much!" Miriam replied, and she parted her legs slightly, feeling his finger stroke gently at the edge of her damp, hungry lips.

At the far side of the Garden, high up in the cheap seats, Milton Blackman glared down at Irving Lowenstein and the young goddess sitting next to him. Milton thought of his own Ruth, the love of his hard-fought life; compared her to the magazine picture-perfect woman sitting next to Irving, and had to admit that the two were not even in the same class. That Lowenstein would have the nerve to bring a woman to an event like this appalled Blackman. To think that he would bring such a raving beauty was absolutely outrageous, it was almost sacrilegious.

Ringside seats. Milton had been grateful when his uncle had come through with one back row seat for himself to this sold-out event. Now his ticket seemed bush league compared to Lowenstein down there in the second row where all the swells were sitting with their friends, definitely in the limelight, the smug look on his face visible even at this distance.

Then again, that was Lowenstein's way. Every time Milton had clawed his way to some kind of recognition at law school, Irving

Lowenstein seemed to get there first, with something even better, and made it look easy as he did it.

The first day Milton got off the streetcar at Columbia Law School, the very first person he saw was Irving Lowenstein parking his shiny new Chevrolet, taking care as he got out not to scuff the shine on his perfectly polished Florsheim shoes. They took most of their classes together, and although Milton burned the midnight oil to get honor grades, Irv was consistently top of his class, even though reports came through regularly that he was out 'til all hours at some jazz club or another. And it didn't help matters any that, as Milton added paunch and lost hair, Irv Lowenstein seemed to grow more handsome by the year.

The most irritating thing of all to Milton Blackman was the way that Irv Lowenstein treated him – with deprecation, always polite, but polite with a certain disdain, as if the both of them weren't from the same Jewish neighborhood clawing their way uptown.

The trouble was, Irv Lowenstein seemingly appeared to have made it years ago. Milton Blackman, from the back of the arena, looked down at him, and saw the blonde beauty next to Lowenstein whisper something in his ear that made him laugh. They looked like a million dollars together. Irv acted as if he had a million dollars, and Milton Blackman wondered for the hundredth time where a supposedly unemployed law school freshman got the money to dress and act the way Irving Lowenstein did. Squinting through the haze, Milton Blackman glared down at Lowenstein and his girlfriend from his distant, smoke-choked seat.

Miriam panted through slightly parted lips as Irv Lowenstein touched her, shivered as she watched the two men, not ten feet away from where they sat, exchanging blows with the power of titans. She watched the men stagger around the ring, could smell the sweat rising from their hardened bodies, and could see it running down their rugged, angular faces. Irving rubbed her mons in just the right way, and she nearly jumped with a quiver that ran from her scalp to the soles of her feet. Under the heavy topcoat, she put her hand on his, helping him, guiding him, stroking herself with his fingers.

Now the fighters in the ring picked up the pace, pummeling one another harder and harder, the white-trunked man trying to duck under the blows of the man in the gold, and getting knocked sideways for his effort. That was all it took. The gold-trunked man worked his way in, raining blows on his opponent's body, staggering him until the referee separated the two. And then the boxer moved back in again, knocking the other fighter's head back with two quick jabs to the chin. Blood began to flow down the weaker fighter's chin, and Miriam parted her knees further, guiding Irving's strong fingers deep inside her.

Her breath became ragged as gold trunks began alternating blows: head, then stomach, then head again on the other fighter. By the time white trunks dropped to his knees, Miriam was pressing Irv's hand in deeper, and feeling the warm waves of pleasure beginning to radiate out from where he rubbed, the rising crescendo of the orgasm imminent in every fiber of her being.

Then white trunks fell sideways, like a toppled oak, and the other fighter was having his arm raised high by the referee, as Irving's hand was suddenly gone, slipped out from under her own.

"What... what's wrong?" Miriam asked, her voice thick and husky with lust.

"This is it," Irv replied excitedly. "He's up next. Barney Green. This is the guy, Miriam – the guy we came to see. Could be the next light heavyweight champion of the world in a couple of years."

Miriam pouted.

* * *

The only good thing Miriam had ever seen in the Friday evening trips down to the Delancey Street Schul had been Irving Lowenstein. While their families were members, her father and mother had enlisted the help of a business associate, their personal Shabbas goy, to drive them there and back on Saturday. This way her father would not have to drive his Cadillac on the Sabbath.

And, while Irving had not been in Schul for a few years prior to this Yom Kippur, just as Miriam had not been since she'd begun college, they had met each other on the steps outside, after the services, and she had then decided that there was one thing worth getting to know better on Delancey Street, namely, Irving Lowenstein.

But it was just as her mother had warned her, "You can take some of these Jewish boys out of the neighborhood, but you can never take the neighborhood out of the boys."

"Bruiser" Barney Green was well-known in the Jewish neighborhood as a local hero, a real up-and-comer in the boxing world. The name Green came about through the courtesy of an Ellis Island immigration inspector who couldn't spell "Gruen," the German name which his father had when he arrived in the United States several years ago. He was from the Bronx but the fame of this rising young Jewish boxer had spread in the city from one Jewish neighborhood to the next like a raging fire. They talked about him in the kosher butcher shops, bakeries and produce markets, even the candy stores, after all he was one of their own.

Even Miriam's father had talked about Barney Green. One didn't hear much about Jewish athletes except in New York City, where they dominated basketball to the point that guys had taken to calling it a "kike game."

But boxing, that was the sport of Englishmen in Europe, and Irishmen and Italians over here. Jewish prizefighters were unknown, until Barney Green. And now he had a record of twenty-four wins and no losses in the local circuit, twenty of those by knockouts. Her father, a real sports fan, had explained all this to her several weeks ago when the sports section of the New York Daily News had featured a story about Barney Green in the Sunday paper.

* * *

Finally, it was the main event. The men around Miriam rose to their feet as the light heavyweight Barney Green and his opponent entered the ring, knee-length silk robes draped over them, towels covering their heads and shoulders to keep their muscles warm.

Miriam looked up as Bruiser Green took off his bright red robe. He was well built at 175 pounds, with thick ropes of muscle running around his arms and legs, but by no means stocky. His hair was thick, curly, jet-black, with more than a hint of five o'clock shadow running down a sturdy jaw. Green shadowboxed, lightly moving around his corner getting rid of nervous tension by keeping himself loose. Except he didn't look nervous. He looked calm, and his eyes were... kind, Miriam decided. Not the look she'd expect from anyone the press had tagged with the nickname Bruiser.

"That's Green?" Miriam asked in Irving's ear. "He sure doesn't look like a bruiser to me."

"You wait," Irving laughed. "Wait'll you see Barney Green fight. I've got five hundred dollars riding on this big bruiser tonight. He's great!"

"Five hundred?" Miriam said it so loud that the people next to them looked her way. Five hundred dollars was more than her father made in a month, and he was one of the most expensive dentists in New York City.

Now Green's opponent, a stocky, red-headed Irishman in green trunks was taking off his robe with a shamrock emblazoned on the back. Miriam looked at the two muscular boxers, as they faced one another for the pre-fight instructions from the referee, then she thought about the fact that Irv Lowenstein had five hundred dollars to gamble on a fight that looked like anything but a sure thing.

"Good luck, Barney," Irv yelled up to the ring, and the Jewish fighter nodded his way. Then the bell rang.

Miriam looked at Irv as the two men charged out at one another at the sound of the bell. Lowenstein was thoroughly absorbed in the fight as she pulled the topcoat back up over her lap. This time, it was her own hand that she slid underneath.

It was clear to the crowd that these two fighters were much better than those boxers who had fought before them. One was a sleek thoroughbred racehorse, the other, a powerful raging bull. Barney Green was a slick boxer while Mick Fitzpatrick was more of a slugger. They didn't windmill or throw roundhouse punches. They didn't plow into one another with reckless abandon. They feinted, boxed carefully and waited patiently for the right moment.

And then – pow – a lightning-like fist would shoot out and land somewhere vulnerable, hurting the other boxer a great deal. There was no wasted motion or ring theatrics, like dancing around unnecessarily. Fitz went for the head with crushing blows that sometimes landed but frequently missed, while Barney was all over him with jabs that rocked Fitz's head back or landed with regularity in the mid-section. In the clinches, Green would hammer away at the kidneys while the referee would break them apart.

Miriam leaned forward, both hands atop the topcoat now, intently watching the two boxers warily pursuing each other, waiting for an opening. The heat she felt within herself was as much admiration for their skill, as it was the raw lust from the sight of two half-clothed men skillfully hitting one another.

They circled each other until Green snapped off two rapid jabs – one-two – that banged his opponent's head back and forced him to retreat. Then Green began a steady tattoo of body blows that softened his opponent up before landing a right cross that whipped the man's head around. The bell rang and the Irishman stumbled to his corner.

The second round was more of the same. The Mick could land nothing but body blows, which Green seemed to absorb without much harm. Barney concentrated on his opponent's head, landing punch after punch on the seemingly bewildered Fitzpatrick. The Irishman's right eye was almost swollen closed now, but he kept up a spirited attack, although none of it seemed to affect Green, who shuffled and danced confidently around the ring with a killer look in his eyes.

When the third round started, Green threw his whole weight behind a right hook that sent the Irishman down to the canvas for a count of eight. The referee stopped the fight as Mick rose groggily to his feet. He said a few words to the Irishman, who shook his head, and the fight started again. This time, it was a left jab to the head and a vicious right uppercut to the chin that sent the Mick backpedaling all the way to a neutral corner, and Green looked at the referee inquiringly. The ref held up one hand, and said something to the Irishman's corner manager. Amid a chorus of boos and catcalls, the Irishman's manager crossed his arms over his chest and shook his head vehemently.

Shrugging, the referee motioned for the fight to continue, Barney Green, head bobbing, leaned away from his opponent's job, retaliated with an uppercut to the chin, landed two body blows and then another uppercut, then two jabs and a third uppercut. He was stalking his opponent backwards, across the ring, keeping him on his feet with the intermittent uppercuts, knocking him senseless with the blows in between. When they reached the Irishman's corner, Green connected with a right cross that whipped the man's head around until it seemed almost to face backwards; a dull, wood-like crack echoing across the crowded arena. The Irishman fell at his manager's feet and the referee chanted a quick ten-count and hoisted Barney Green's arm.

"The bookies wouldn't give even odds on Green unless you gave them the first three rounds," Irving yelled above the din into Miriam's ear. Fitzpatrick's manager was trying to stretch the fight into the fourth round. We've got five hundred extra dollars for dinner!"

But up in the ring, something was wrong. The Irishman's manager was splashing water into his face, the referee down on his knees as well, both of them yelling the Irish fighter's name. After what seemed like an eternity, the man moved one finger, and then two, but when they tried to get him to his feet, his legs collapsed like a marionette's.

"My legs," Miriam could hear the Irishman groan. "I can't feel nothin' in my damn legs."

Men came running with a stretcher from somewhere near the entrance, and the Irish boxer moaned as they lifted him onto it. Green, meanwhile stood off to the side, his head bowed, lips moving noiselessly in prayer.

Madison Square Garden was alive with cheers, yells and catcalls. Behind them, someone shoved a handful of bills into Irv Lowenstein's hand, patted him on the back and congratulated him.

Miriam looked around and she was conscious of several pairs of eyes, each with a different look. Irv's eyes, gleaming in victory; the Irishman's eyes, round with fear; Barney Green's eyes, heavy with remorse. The ones she could not see were the eyes high up in the loft on the far side of the arena, eyes that glared down through a ceiling of smoke and sweat. They were Milton Blackman's eyes, and it was just as well that Miriam could not see them…

…because those eyes were full of hate.

Chapter One
Lower East Side – November 1915

Irving Lowenstein was always punctual, a trait that he owed not to any dedication to self-improvement, of which he had plenty, but to his mother, who set dinner on the table every night punctually at 5:30 by the carved wooden Bavarian mantle clock she had brought from Germany in her youth. And, she expected all four of her children to be there, freshly scrubbed, presentable and in their places, especially on Friday night, for the Shabbas dinner. She enforced this sense of promptness, not with threats, but with the greatest of a Jewish mother's weapons … guilt. She had an ability to inflict pangs of guilt that could penetrate to the very depths of one's soul. Even now, when Irving was almost twenty-one and making plans for an apartment of his own after he finished law school, pleasing his mother was still important to him, and to disappoint either her or his father was utterly inconceivable.

And so, after taking his law classes in the morning, and having made certain that he was in a study group that would meet only in the afternoons, Irving pulled his Chevrolet to the curb, a few feet from his house on Delancey Street. He grabbed his black leather Gladstone bag full of law books and bounded up the steep front steps bursting into the weathered brownstone with enthusiasm. "I smelled Shabbas dinner all the way down the hall. Smells great, Momma," he exclaimed, stepping into the steamy kitchen, wafting delicious smells of cooking food.

"Nu, this is what a mother gets now?" Esther Lowenstein asked with a hidden smile. "A 'smells great'? No kiss? My son has become what? All stomach?"

"Come here," he said, spinning the good-looking portly, apron-draped woman around like a ballerina and kissing her warmly on the cheek. "Smells great, and I love you. How's that, Momma?"

Music from Beethoven's "5th Symphony" wafted softly into the kitchen from the upright piano in the Lowenstein's immaculate front parlor. Hearing the perfectly played music, Irving smiled. He had bought the Steinway piano for his brother, Seymour, at a second-hand dealer sale in Queens only three weeks ago.

"Well," Irving said, looking around. "I can hear Seymour, but where is everyone else?"

"Your sister is going out after dinner to learn to crochet over at the Schumacher girl's house. And Rebecca Schumacher has a handsome brother, Harold, who works at the brewery; and maybe the brother will be home and answer the door and be smitten by Sarah's charm; or walk through the house and suddenly notice our Sarah for the first time; or maybe he will pass her by on the street and suddenly realize how pretty she is. So Sarah is presently upstairs trying to make herself look like a moving-picture star," she said with a wry smile. "Meanwhile your dear Poppa is making deliveries but, God willing, he'll be here by five. And your two brothers? Who knows where those little muhziks are? School was over at three. It's like they don't know where they live anymore."

Irv glanced at his watch. It was half past four: "There's plenty of time, Momma. Don't worry, Herbie and Seymour will be home in time for dinner." *They'd better be or else*, Irving thought, but he didn't want to say it aloud.

He took the stairs two at a time and carried his books up to the room where he'd slept since he was five-years-old. Like all of the bedrooms in the house, it was tiny, but it had electric lights, which was more than one could say for most of the homes on Delancey Street. And, their present house, even though not new anymore, was a great improvement over the two rooms that he and Sarah and his parents had once shared at the back of his father's leather good shop. Back then, his mother had cooked meals by chopping up meat and vegetables for stews, and then Sarah and he had carried the cold pot over to the bakery, where a penny got you the right to set the pot in a hot oven for three hours. These ovens were kept going fifteen hours, every day except Shabbas. Some of the neighbor boys would play pitch-penny with the family cooking money; the losers got a cold dinner, or no dinner at all, that night. Irving would never have dreamed of doing that with the meal money because he knew that Morris (Moishe) Lowenstein, his father, really looked forward to his dinner after a hard day in the shop.

But he had noticed that gambling attracted even young 15 and 16-year-old boys. It was a desperate attempt to make money but with only little at risk. The fast buck appealed to most everyone. When boys grew to be men, the attraction was even stronger, and with a boost from cheap whiskey, it would not be hard for them to lose, in less than an hour, their entire paycheck for the week.

Back then, Irv's home smelled like polishing wax and leather. It was a rich heady smell that he would forever associate with his father. But, it was also a scent that, for as long as he lived, every time he walked into a luggage shop or bought a new belt, would remind him of how hard the family had struggled in the early years. Those that had no ambition would remain on the Lower East Side with nothing to look forward to except despair... and, desperation.

Irv took the law books out of his bag and set them on the rough, wooden bookshelf above his narrow bed. He always admired the black Gladstone with a blue-silk lining, polished brass clasp for opening and closing, and waxed black stitching so precise that no one could believe the stitches had been put in by hand. He ran his hand over the butter-soft leather. It was known as a doctor's bag and he could carry it with pride into any classroom, hotel or law office in New York City. But better still, it was the work of his father's hand, the bag that Morris Lowenstein had tearfully presented to his son on the evening that Irving had graduated from high school – a feat that, to the best of anyone's memory, had never been accomplished before by a Lowenstein. Irving hoped when he graduated from Columbia Law School that his Poppa would give him a hand-tooled briefcase for courtroom appearances.

You could search the length of Fifth Avenue and never find a Gladstone bag of such fine quality. In his heart, Irving knew this, even though he had only made his first trip uptown after his Bar Mitzvah because Jewish boys from Delancey or Orchid Streets were not welcome in the better shops, generally because they had no money to buy, they could only look.

The beautifully crafted hand luggage was his father's art, the leather-worker's equivalent of a fine painting or a wonderful piece of music. The bag, generally black, consisted of two equally-sized, hinged compartments and was extremely popular with doctors. Even here in a city the size of New York, there were only a handful of men who could turn out such finely finished work. But it was not the type of item Morris Lowenstein usually made; his stock in trade was stout workmen's belts, or the tough leather aprons worn by the blacksmiths and ferriers who could still be found, despite the enormous popularity of automobiles, on just about every street in the city. And he made the straps that children used to carry their books to and from school – those who were well-off enough to afford to go to a school that used books instead of slates – and the tack used by the hansom cabs that still flooded the downtown streets of New York, and suitcases for those who were tired of looking for success here on the streets of New York and were giving up to seek a business in other large cities. He made the big, heavy wallets that tradesmen carried to protect their daily cash, and the patent leather visors that bookkeepers wore to protect their eyes from the bright light necessary to read their own spidery entries. If it was leather, Morris Lowenstein made it, everything except shoes, because being a cobbler was a thankless trade with not much profit.

But Gladstone bags such as the one Irving carried were Morris Lowenstein's dream. More work than an apron or a belt, certainly, and far more costly to make, but if you sold just one of these, your family could eat like royalty for an entire week, which was why Morris and Guiseppe Lucci, the cheerful Italian who tanned and sold him his hides, had come up with their grand scheme to lift themselves by their bootstraps out of the pushcart ghetto.

Lucci, whose hands were hard and as brown as coffee beans from the tanning solution he worked with daily, turned out hides that were second to none on this side of the Atlantic. And Morris Lowenstein, he knew, was one of the best leather workers in New York. So why, they reasoned, did the big shops uptown buy their leather goods from London and Rome, when they could have bought them from right here in New York, and at the same time, save themselves the shipping charges?

For half a year, they had worked on this scheme, Lucci tanning some especially fine hides for the project, and Irving's father working nights to make up the samples after he had finished his customers' work for the day. He made handbags, and fine, slim gentlemen's wallets. He made a squat black leather bag suitable for a banker, and a Gladstone bag, the same one Irving carried his law books in each day, for other businessmen. The luggage could be made in other colors such as tan, and dark brown but Irving liked black the best – like a real professional man. And he made gentlemen's garter straps, and fine leather spats, supple shaving kits, and soft kid gloves and more. Then he talked to a friend who knew a man who had connections, and Lucci and he had made an appointment with who he called "the big momzer", a buyer down at Macy's. Irving, who had been twelve at the time, had gone with them, along with Aldo, Francisco and Guido, the three Lucci boys and his only goy playmates for as long as he could remember, to help carry the carefully wrapped goods up to the buyer's office.

That meeting, Irving remembered, had been pitifully brief. He and the Lucci boys had waited outside, but they remembered how their fathers, confident and cheerful in their coarse woolen suits, proud of the fine bag that they would present to the buyer as a gift, a token of their esteem, had walked into the man's office with its frosted glass partition, and how they had come out fewer than ten minutes later, dejected and disappointed.

The buyer, the boys learned by bits and pieces on the wagon ride home, had admired the work, even had praise for it. But he had told the men that no one in Manhattan wanted to buy leather goods made on the Lower East Side. Customers expected these things to come from Europe, and paid a premium because they had. He hadn't even asked prices He'd just thanked them for their effort, and advised them to go home and "sell your things to your own people." And on top of all that, he'd had the chutzpah, balls, to keep the gift.

It was all right, the men had told one another. There were other stores downtown; maybe none as big as Macy's, but big stores, nonetheless. They would find someone willing to listen, someone who could recognize a bargain when he saw one, maybe even Gimbel's.

Except they hadn't. And finally, after months of making appointments, and making trips downtown, and eating countless meals of cabbage and potatoes to scrimp up the money to pay for the bags that they left as samples, Morris Lowenstein and Guiseppe Lucci came to the conclusion that Lower East Side Jews and Italians were still a joke as far as uptown stores were concerned. They went back to what they'd always been doing; they just worked longer and harder at it to better make ends meet. And the handbags and wallets and garters and gloves had been given away as wedding and birthday gifts to relatives.

Irv would always remember that experience, always think of it every time somebody mentioned taking the high road, trying to make an honest living by working hard. Thinking that way kept you in a rented flat on Orchard or Delancey Street with one day's food in the cupboard and no hope of anything better down the road. Irving had other ideas. Real wealth and power came by different means.

He thought about the nickel-and-dime card games he had started quite sometime ago, and he had made some good monies, but nothing like the neighborhood craps games over the past six months. He shifted the loose board in his bedroom floor and took out the money hidden there. He smiled. Stacks of greenbacks, fifty to a stack, and rolls of silver dollars went into the bag until they covered the bottom of it. And, he hadn't even started with goyische-run games yet. Irv then put a small note pad into his pocket which recorded what went where and how much went to each place: "Greenbaum's - $150; Rosen's - $175; Levy's - $100; and so forth."

He was just putting the board back in the floor when his mother called up the stairs, her voice frantic, "Irvie! Irvie, come quick! The police! Oy vey, the police are at the door! Whadda those momzers want with us?"

Irving glanced frantically around. There was no time to put the monies back in the floor. What to do? He pitched the bag underneath his bed, knowing that it would be the first place the cops would look if they shook the place down, and hoped that he could keep them downstairs. Suddenly feeling warm beneath the dark blue suit and tie he'd worn to his law classes at Columbia and wondering how he'd ever find work as a lawyer with a police record, he went down the stairs to where his mother moaned and was wringing her hands. Irving looked at her troubled face and promised, "It's okay, Momma. I'll take care of it. You finish making dinner so Poppa can eat on time."

Irving glanced out the narrow sidelights next to the heavy oak front door and relaxed. It was Houlihan, a beat cop he knew well from the 12th Precinct. He had Irving's younger brother, Herbie, gripped by the collar in a ham-like fist, squirming and defiant. Drawing in a deep breath as he opened the door, Irv stared for one long second at his kid brother and then nodded to the cop, saying, "Come on in, Patrick."

The cop came in, taking his hat off as he crossed the threshold, and released his grip on Herbie, who stood, arms crossed, his face fixed in a sneer. Irv closed the door, blocking off the view from the neighbors staring out their windows across the street. "How's law school, Irvie?" the cop asked pleasantly.

"It's good, Patrick. Thanks for asking. What do we have here?"

"Old man Fleischman caught him pinching a bag of candy off the shelf in his store. He probably woulda just whacked him with a broom and chased him outta there, but I was walking my beat, and he saw me, so he gave the kid to me. I figgered I'd better bring him home."

"I was gonna pay!" Herbie protested.

The words were hardly out of his mouth when Irving shoved the thirteen-year old into a chair. Herbie scrambled to his feet, fists balled, but dropped them to his side after one look at his brother's face. In the parlor, the piano music suddenly stopped. Seymour yelled, "What's all the noise out there? I'm trying to practice and you guys aren't making it any easier for me."

Mrs. Lowenstein yelled from the kitchen. "Be quiet, sonny boy. There's a little problem, but Irving's in the hallway and he'll take care of it. You finish your practicing and then get ready for dinner."

"Turn out your pockets," Irving said looking at Herbie with cold eyes...

"Irv! I swear to God I was gonna pay for it. I swear!"

"Turn out your pockets," Irv repeated firmly without much compassion for his younger brother's anxiety attack.

Herbie did as he was told and a rubber band and three paper clips dropped to the immaculately polished front hallway floor.

"There!" Herbie cried. "Ya see? I didn't pinch nothin'. These are from school."

"And how were you going to pay for the candy you had in your hand?" Irving asked him.

The kid said nothing, the color draining from his face.

"Thanks for bringing him home, Patrick," Irv told the cop. "I appreciate it. I really do."

"Aw, that's all right," the big Irish cop grinned. "If we ran in every kid that pinched tobacco or sweets off the store shelves, we wouldn't have no room left down at the station for us cops."

He stood there, glancing out the window at the street, while Irv fished in his pocket and came up with two dollars. "Here," Irv said. "Get yourself a beer and a sandwich for your trouble in coming so far out of your way."

"Naw, 'tis not a'tall necessary, Irv," Houlihan said in a thick Irish brogue, quickly pocketing the two green bills. It was enough money to buy him beer and sandwiches for a week. "But try to keep him off the streets, okay? We can't have him be actin' like that, at least not on my beat."

"You have my word on it, Patrick," Irv promised, gently herding the big cop out the front door.

"Stinkin' copper," Herbie sneered as the door closed. In an instant, Irv had smacked him on the shoulder and Herbie had fallen to the floor. He stared up at his older brother.

"No, stay there," Irv warned him as he tried to get up. "What the hell is wrong with you? Coming home like this, where all the neighbors can see Houlihan, and embarrassing the whole family, but especially Momma and Poppa. They sure don't need any trombeniks around here."

"And, the whole family?" Herbie returned. "Does that include you too, Irvie? God, with all those craps games you run, I ain't doin' nothin' you don't do."

Irving yanked his thirteen-year-old brother up off the linoleum kitchen floor. Herbie felt himself dangling in mid-air, his toes just barely touching the ground. Both of his leather jacket lapels were tightly gripped in his older brother's hands, the tips of their noses only inches apart. "I never stole from anyone, ever in my whole life, swear to God. Do you understand me?" Irv shook Herbie until the kid nodded. "And as for my craps games, don't you ever mention them again, not in this house, not on the street. Do you understand that?"

Herbie nodded and Irv drew a hand back, as if to slap him, but lowered it after a second. Shoving was one thing, but he had never struck his brother and he never would.

"Can I go with you tonight, Irvie?" Herbie pleaded. "Can I help you carry the pushke, the bank, out to the..." He didn't say the word "games," not after what Irving had just told him.

"No," Irving said forcefully. "You are going to stay home tonight with your brother, Seymour, and you guys are going to study. One Lowenstein brother on the street is enough. Now go get washed up for dinner, for God's sake. It's almost five. And, tell your sister, Sarah, to get cleaned up too."

In the parlor, the piano music started up again, as Seymour, the middle son, skillfully played the "Overture" from William Tell. Seymour was all smiles again.

The mantle clock was just beginning to toll for the fifth time when Morris Lowenstein came through the front door, wrapped warmly in a blue woolen overcoat, reeking of cherry pipe tobacco. Morris removed his overcoat and scarf, hanging them up on the peg left for him in Esther Lowenstein's neat front closet. He had worked exceptionally hard today on a number of customer orders and was weary.

But, he was also excited that it was Friday night and that made him feel better. Next came his hat, replaced with his black yarmulke, which he wore for dinner only on this day of the week because he was not an Orthodox Jew, but more or less Conservative rather than Reform. But Shabbas was the seventh day, God's day, and Morris Lowenstein wore a yarmulke on this evening to show, as he often said, "I'm God's Jew."

Sarah, who was just now coming down from her room, hair combed and brushed in the new pageboy fashion with a brown headband, ran to greet her Poppa and threw her arms around him in welcome. The boys, hearing their father open the front door, each left their rooms and greeted him with a kiss. Esther Lowenstein gave him a wifely peck on the cheek and went back into the kitchen to finish preparing the Friday night Shabbas dinner.

And, Seymour, his slender frame seasonably dressed in a clean white shirt, sweater vest and navy blue, pressed pleated pants, his black hair neatly combed, reluctantly left the piano and kissed his father on the cheek with a hearty, "Good Shabbas, Poppa."

Irving looked forward to joining in the blessing of the wine and also the broche over the freshly baked challah. Only Herbie appeared worried that the conversation would include the visit of Police Officer Houlihan. Irving and his mother had already decided that they would not trouble Morris with the news of Herbie's arrival in Houlihan's custody, that is, not unless he heard it from one of the neighbors first. Seymour was in the den practicing his piano and really knew nothing about Herbie's problem.

Moving slowly into the bathroom, Morris carefully washed his hands, and then put on a clean white shirt and dark blue tie. He was ready for dinner. His family was all there at the table anxiously waiting for him and he again greeted them with a "good Shabbas." He sat down, looked around the table at the scrubbed faces of his children and nodded approvingly at Esther. She had done a good job in raising the family, and he thought that he was a lucky man. Morris poured sweet red Mogen David wine into the small silver cup that he had first brought from Germany, then to London, England and finally to America almost twenty years ago. Morris filled their glasses with the same dark burgundy wine. He recited the blessing, the evening broche, in singsong Hebrew, rocking on his heels as he prayed for probably ten minutes. After he finished the prayer, Morris took a sip of wine, inviting the other members of the family to join him with their own glasses. The broche over the fresh challah bread was recited by the oldest male child of the family. Irving loved this part of the Shabbas dinner, the tradition of over five thousand years, performed at each Friday night dinner. It made the whole evening feel special, and as Irving finished the broche, each member of the family ate a small crust of the bread for good luck.

That done, Morris accepted the first plate of gefilte fish and the next of roasted chicken with browned potatoes. Beaming as they ate, he asked each child about their day. He didn't seem to notice that Herbie was unusually quiet about his day's activities.

Irv, the eldest son, responded first: he was working on a paper for his Tort class, and he explained a few of the details, none of which his father understood, but which Morris still nodded and kvelled with pride at Irving's patient explanation.

Then, his mother nodded to Seymour. The middle son slowly stood up and grinned. "Well Poppa, the letter finally came today. I've been accepted at Julliard."

As Seymour told everyone about the new song he had written out at the piano, Esther passed around the table a salad of tomatoes, cucumbers and onions in olive oil and vinegar. This evening she had also made a delicious carrot and prune casserole called Tsimmis, one of Morris's favorites.

Like many Jews living in America, Morris Lowenstein's observation of Jewish custom was a peculiar mixture of observation and neglect. He thought some rules were ridiculous, such as the one that prohibited writing during daylight hours on the Sabbath day, but no force on earth could have compelled him to open the doors of his shop on Saturday. And he had scrimped and saved to set aside enough money for each of his sons' Bar Mitzvah on their 13th birthday. At that age, a boy becomes a young man according to the Torah. Like many households on Delancey Street, the Lowenstein's lacked a kosher kitchen, a costly extravagance requiring two of almost everything in a kitchen, including china and silverware. But some things to Morris Lowenstein were important to him such as his family and the music of their chatter around the dinner table discussing each other's day before he told them about his own. After Sarah told everyone about her day's activities, Morris tucked his napkin in a little tighter under his chin and began to talk.

"Our friend, Lucci, thinks he may know an important man," he explained, taking a second helping of the Tsimmis, "with the Department of the Army this time who may be able to help us," he continued. "They are buying leather holsters and ammunition belts for their officers, and he thinks we might be able to reduce the price."

"They'd have no trouble buying from someone with a German name?" Irving asked keeping in mind the war raging in Europe.

"Lucci thinks not," Morris shrugged. "We sell to a man who sells to a man who sells to the Army. A Smith or a Jones, nu? Anyhow, it won't take much to make the sample, and Lucci gave me the pattern, so I'll try, and we'll see. Maybe God will bless our efforts."

That God might be hesitant to bless the making of goods used for a war between countries was a fact on which no one commented. Irving wondered how much money his father could make, being a supplier three times removed in a government contract. Not much, he imagined; the lion's share would probably go to the one making the final sale. But he knew Lucci would give his father the hides on credit, payment due only when the money came through, and his father was obviously pleased with the prospect of making a few extra dollars, even though it offered no large financial gain for his family. Maybe, Irving thought, his father was content to live on Delancey Street for the rest of his life. But one thing was for sure, Irving Lowenstein was not!

People like his parents couldn't imagine anything better than they already had, but Irving could, and Irving had already resolved to get it – for himself and for those that he loved. He hoped and prayed that he could see his mother and father settled comfortably at a better address, maybe even Park Avenue, God willing. He didn't even care if he had to rent the apartment under an assumed name, one acceptable to the goyische landlord. Irving was going to do this on his own, and the proof that he was on his way was sitting upstairs in his room, in the Gladstone bag that his father had given him.

After dinner, Sarah helped her mother with the dishes before setting out for her crochet lesson, two pennies tied into the corner of her handkerchief for carfare if she needed it coming home, although she had carried the same two pennies around for many months and never used them. Seymour kissed his father on the cheek and said that he was taking the bus uptown to listen to a private concert with a friend.

Patting Seymour's cheek, Morris retired to the little parlor to sit in his lounge chair and read, ostensibly from the Talmud, although everyone in the household knew that, within fifteen minutes, he would turn to the newspaper, a morning edition of the Herald Tribune or the Yiddish paper, the Daily Forward, that he picked up each day, second-hand, from Wasserman, the greengrocer. Herbie went upstairs to his room to study, under pain of promised death from his older brother. And Irving went up to his room to retrieve the bag from under his bed.

* * *

Half a mile away, having missed his own Shabbas dinner, settling instead for a chicken sandwich eaten on the run, Mendel Goldblatt stood at the corner of the alley, his body hidden mostly by a large telephone pole, and gazed out at the street in front of the Orchard Street Social Hall. He pulled out his Elgin pocket watch and checked the time, thirty minutes to go before Local 22 of the International Garment Workers' Union would meet for their strike vote against Braun's Apparel. Goldblatt was not Reform, he was not Orthodox, he was not even all that religious, but a Jew was a Jew. And even though he rarely stuck his head in a synagogue, it still offended him somewhat that the union, his client, would hold their meeting on a Friday night. Then again, Braun's was a Jewish business, but it still operated sixteen hours a day, every day of the week. The union, hoping to get enough votes for a strike, had to hold the meeting when most of the girls were off work and could attend; and, that meant Shabbas or nothing. A strike vote meant higher wages and that translated into larger donations for the synagogues which then filtered down into the Rabbi's pocket.

So hold it on Shabbas they did, and the Rabbis didn't openly complain. There was another reason too. Braun's working conditions were widely known to be the worst on the street, but he provided hundreds of jobs for those living on the Lower East Side, and the economics of those wages were important to the community. A third reason was, if the Rabbis approved the union organization, that would mean speaking out against an important member of the Jewish community. Therefore, the Rabbis said nothing, and because they said nothing, the Shabbas meeting was going forward, and it would start in just thirty minutes.

By the light of the street lamp, he could clearly see the Ford Model T paddy wagon parked at the curb next to the side of the hall where five cops gathered around its doors, talking to two more cops in the front seat. Some of them were smoking cigars, all of them obviously killing time, waiting for the start of the meeting.

Mendel turned to a short fireplug of a man next to him, all sweater, baggy pants and workingman's cap, and cleared his throat. "Jake," he said quietly. "Braun has paid off the police and he'll have Riccolo and his boys here to bust things up just as soon as the meeting starts. If we put up a fight, the cops'll run us in on disorderly conduct charges."

Jake listened and said nothing, because he knew exactly what his boss was thinking.

"I want the boys to move up now so I can give them final orders and tell them not to worry about the police," Mendy said. "I can fix this."

A few minutes later, a ragtag group of street toughs, most not yet out of their teens, were gathered around Goldblatt. A wind was picking up, and he turned up the collar of his pea jacket against the cold and blew on his hands to warm them before he spoke. "Jake, you got a watch?"

The little man in the sweater shook his head, and Mendel unclipped his Elgin from his own pocket and handed it to him.

"Okay," Mendy continued. "Run over to your cousin Bennie's house, and get some of those firecrackers he bought last month to sell the goys for New Year's Eve. Get a bunch of 'em too... tell him I'll pay him tomorrow. Then I want you to run down to the 12th precinct house... you know the downspout by the washroom? Shinny up it, and just wait for a few minutes until you hear the police whistle. They always leave the window open in there, even in weather like this, because the Micks are always plugging up the damn shitters."

This got some guffaws from the group of rowdies listening to him closely for instructions.

"At exactly seven, I want you to light five or six strings of the `crackers, and toss 'em into the washroom. See if you can hit the trash can with `em, maybe it'll set it on fire."

Jake nodded, pocketed the watch and set off down the alley in a trot.

"Okay," Goldblatt continued. "Moe, I want you and these two other guys to go over to the jewelry store on the corner of Orchard, and, at the same time, seven o'clock sharp, I want you to bust in the front windows. You won't need a watch cuz they got a clock in da store window." He paused, took out a nickel-plated policeman's whistle, and handed it to a bowler-hatted tough. "Moe, just as soon as you bust the windows, start blowin' on this, and keep blowin' hard for about a minute. When you can hear the cops on their beat blowin' their own whistle, then get the hell out of there fast. Don't take nothin' out of the store, cuz you wanna be clean if they catch you."

Led by Moe Greenbaum, the bowler-hatted kid, three of the gang sauntered briskly down the street, staying well clear of the police gathered around their paddy wagon.

"Okay," Mendel said. "The rest of you guys just hang around here with me. Riccolo and his boys will be along any minute."

The lights were all on in the Social Hall and people, young women mostly, walking in groups of three or four began arriving. Pretty soon, the hum of forty or fifty conversations going on at once began to spill out onto the street every time the doors opened. At five minutes to seven, a long, dark green Auburn sedan pulled up behind the police wagon and sat there, idling.

"That's Riccolo," Mendel said, stamping to keep his feet warm. "Won't be long now."

Minutes later, they began to hear the faint trill of police whistles sounding from two different directions. Over by the hall, the cops heard it too and began talking with one another agitatedly. The shrill whistles continued, more insistent, and a distant siren sounded.

That was it. One of the cops ran to the front of the paddy wagon and turned the crank, starting it up. The rest bustled into the back and it began to pull away from the curb, but then stopped as a stocky wop in a slouch cap jumped out of the Auburn and ran in front of the wagon. Angry words issued from the driver's seat and the cop on the passenger's side waved a billy club. The stocky man jumped back to the curb and the paddy wagon roared off, its siren wailing as it turned the corner.

Three more Italian men climbed out of the Auburn, two carrying wooden axe handles.

They talked loud, waving their hands in excitement, and then somebody from the passenger's side of the sedan barked an order, and they began walking up the front steps to the Hall.

When Mendel saw them, he yelled, "Let's go guys." He picked up a crowbar and trotted across the street, followed by six of his men, all carrying chains, hammers, and shortened baseball bats. The Italians had just reached the door of the hall when one of his cronies spotted the Jewboys crossing the street. He spat out a dark Sicilian curse and turned away from the door, patting the axe handle against his hand. Then three more Jews came running out of the alley; followed by a fourth from down the street. That made eleven against four – bad odds. He yelled something in Italian to his men, and they began racing back to the parked Auburn.

"Take `em down," Mendy ordered, and his boys raced in to block their retreat.

Gangs, Mendel knew, were like packs of wolves, if you just let them go they'd come back, only next time, they'd be more aggressive. He would let them escape, but he'd have to punish them some first.

Most of Riccolo's men were big, swarthy and muscular guys with low brows and thick necks, heavy through the shoulders. But since most were straight off the boat from Sicily, they'd never played stickball, and they swung the axe handles awkwardly, like the kids you saw over in Little Mexico, trying to knock down a piñata at Christmastime. Worse yet, the big thugs couldn't run worth a damn; the best they could do was sort of a fast shuffle. So they had to fight, and it was three-to-one odds, against street-smart

Jews who'd grown up playing stickball, Johnny-come-over and kick-the-can.

One of the Italians swung his axe-handle, only to have it snatched out of his hands by one of Mendel's boys. Another one, with a baseball bat, cracked it over the thug's head. One of the Jews came running up behind the big Sicilian, jabbed him in the kidneys with the bat, and then smashed his arm. Amazingly enough, the Italian didn't go down, but rather staggered off into the alley moaning, clutching his right arm, the fight all gone out of him. Similar skirmishes were taking place all over the street corner. Mendel raced to the parked Auburn and got there just as a sawed-off double-barreled shotgun was leveled out the passenger side window. Mendel swung his crowbar and struck the gunman just above the wrist, sending the shotgun clattering to the ground. Snatching up the weapon, the Jewish gang leader pointed it in the open window. It was Riccolo himself, face twisted in pain, contempt in his hard eyes looking directly at Mendy. "Well, go ahead," Riccolo said, "shoot me, you little Jew boy prick. What's the matter? Ain't ya got the balls?"

Mendel slammed him in the face with the butt of the shotgun, knocking the Italian's bloody head back, sending his brown derby flying into the driver's lap. Mendel thought of firing the gun into the Auburn's hood, messing up the smooth coach work with its slick lacquer finish, but he decided against it; the noise might bring the police back, and it'd panic the girls in the hall, some of whom were already crowding the windows to watch the fight. He broke the shotgun open, tossed the shells into the gutter, and swung it by the barrels against the Auburn's back door, shattering the window and giving the Italians a seat full of glass to ride home on. "That's good," Mendel yelled. "Let's go." He ran back across the street and his boys immediately broke off and followed him, one of them kicking a fallen Italian in the ribs for good measure before he left.

Two of Riccolo's men picked up the unconscious thug and dragged him to the Auburn, tossing him in the back. The big car's lights came on and the driver gunned its engine and raced away around the corner, heading downtown.

Mendel's boys yelled, whooped and watched them go. A couple of guys wiped bloody noses; one held his wrist. But for the most part, they'd come through the battle with only a few minor bruises.

"Yes sir," the kid in the heavy sweater said, slapping a comrade on the back. "We showed them! Whatcha think, Mendy? Didn't we show them?"

"Yes," Mendel said quietly. "We did, but don't get too cocky. They'll be back, and they'll want lotsa Jewish blood. Riccolo can't let this stand the way it is now. He'll lose too much respect. If word gets out that we beat the piss outta 'em and ran him off, nobody'll hire him again, and he can't afford that. He could lose big bucks. So watch yourselves boys, those guys will be back, but not tonight. And no more than two of you guys walking together on the way home, you hear? More than that, and you'll draw some suspicious cops. I'll see ya tomorrow."

"Sure will, Mendy."

"See ya later, Mendy. Let them come back, we'll give 'em more of the same."

The gang split up, setting off down the darkened streets. Mendel watched them go, then jammed his hands deep down into his pockets, turned up his collar in the chilled night air, and casually walked home as if he hadn't a care in the world. He started to whistle the new Tin Pan Alley tune, "Yes sir, that's my baby, no sir, don't mean maybe."

* * *

Across town, Irving Lowenstein was at the wheel of his Chevrolet, passing a bar where a couple of drunks had come out to urinate in the alley, heading down toward the warehouse district. He smiled because Morris Lowenstein had asked him, as he always did, why it was that his oldest son had to go out on the Shabbas evening. Couldn't he stay home and read the Talmud with his old Poppa... maybe even have a glass of tea with lemon and a sugar cube?

And Irving always told the same story, a fib. He held up the Gladstone bag, hoping his father would believe it was full of schoolbooks, rather than money. "I gotta study, Poppa. School's tough and the library's only open 'til 11 p.m. on Friday nights.

And the old man's face softened, as he nodded, his yarmulke bobbing slowly. "Then come kiss your Poppa before you go."

So Irving, after again lying to his father, drove away towards downtown. The night was foggy, but the street was still fairly well lit since lights burned in every family parlor celebrating the weekly holiday.

It made him feel like a goy, driving on Shabbas like this. And it made him feel like a putz lying to his father and his mother. But it was for their own good, he told himself. If he ever got caught running the games and word got out that they knew about it, that would probably be the end of Morris and Esther Lowenstein in the neighborhood because it would be a disgrace they couldn't soon get over. They'd be shunned in synagogue and people would stop coming into his shop. Friends would no longer drop in on Morris at home for a Schnapps and a little conversation.

This way, if Irving got nabbed, his parents could honestly say that they'd never suspected a thing, a real shanda for them. His parents would be shamed, but he would just be the son from a good Jewish family that went bad and that, people would understand. You heard the old ones, talking all the time about how America makes some young men do foolish things, and it's always the fault of a few meshugenehs in this brash new country. Why? Because a good Jewish family could not raise a bad boy.

Still, as Irving drove, he knew perfectly well that he was gambling with a lot more than the six or seven hundred bucks, half a year's wage for a middle-class working man, that he left the house with every Friday and Saturday night. He was rolling the dice on his family's future, as well. There was lots that could go wrong here and maybe even put him in jail. This would shame Momma and Poppa and that would kill him, if that happened. But chances were he'd be okay if he could only stack the deck favorably.

Irving had learned early about house odds, how to use the percentages to his own advantage, or stack the deck favorably. And, that included paying off the beat cops and the desk sergeants who worked the precinct on the weekend, getting them to look the other way while his games went on. He paid kids a quarter an evening to stand on the street corner with a whistle, and blow it if a paddy wagon rolled up out front. He also hired dealers to run the games for him, never so much as touching the dice himself. He was fairly insulated from the games by several layers of people. House odds; you rigged things a little in your favor, and over time, they all added up to a big win.

He thought of his father at home, reading his Talmud and his newspapers, lips moving while he did it, because he never learned to read all that well. But on Shabbas, he read because that was what a man did on God's holy day, read and study. More than once, Irving had wished that he could be there with him, making his father happy, but he couldn't do that, and he knew it. Friday was when everybody got paid; pay envelopes fat with greenbacks from all over the city, the Bronx, Brownsville and Brooklyn. And Irv couldn't let those pay envelopes get home because if he did, the homes had wives, and wives had mason jars, flower pots and enameled tins where the money went. And once the bills were in the till, there was simply no getting it out for something like playing the numbers or dice games. You might as well try to rob Chase Manhattan.

Some of the more lenient wives, the younger ones mostly, might let their husbands have fifty cents or a dollar to go down to the bar or to gamble in one of Irving's games, but fifty cents or a dollar was not nearly enough to satisfy Irving's dreams. So he fibbed to his Poppa and drove his car like a goy on the Shabbas and moved furtively around the boroughs with his Gladstone bag of cash. He didn't like it, but he did it. It was the price he paid for his ambitions.

He got to his last drop-off, a stable in the Bronx. The owner gladly took the five dollars Irving game him each week to use the empty tack room; horses were on their way out, and stables were becoming a thing of the past. Parking in front, glancing up and down the street and feeling nervous because the Bronx was not his part of town, Irving hurried down the alley and stepped into a side door where the smell of oats and hay and horseshit surrounded him.

The light of a single kerosene lamp spilled through the open tack room doorway as Irv walked in, glancing over his shoulder, as he always did, making sure no one was behind him. He was also careful once he entered the room that no one was lurking behind him because Irving always carried large sums of money to bank the games.

"Jesus Christ, ya had me worried," the dealer said, smoothing out a blanket on a table set against the wall. "Game starts in twenty minutes. The boys will be here soon."

"Have I ever been late?" Irving asked as he set the bag on the table. He counted out the cash; two hundred dollars for this joint, because men stopped from three different factories, and slid over his notebook with the stub of a pencil. The dealer counted the cash slowly, signed the chit, and then Irving closed the bag, nodding.

"All right, then," he told the dealer. "I'll see you around midnight."

"Midnight," the dealer said, putting his dice and their cup on the blanketed table, not even bothering to look up as Irving left.

Sorta cocky. That bothered Irving because a man didn't get cocky with you if you were all he had. Cocky meant he was getting something else going, or at least he thought he was. Maybe he'd been skimming, setting up a nice little nest egg for himself, something with which to start his own game? Maybe he had just been saving his own money? Or maybe he'd found somebody else that would give him a better cut? But whatever way you looked at it, Irving couldn't help but think the dealer was on his way out. Unless he continually did something to put the fear of God into his dealers, something to make them think twice about taking advantage of him, they could lose respect for the boss.

So how did he do that? Irving wasn't sure, since there were many different ways, depending on the dealer. Irv wanted to think about it for an hour or so. He got back into the Chevrolet and headed for a goyische bar down on Orchard Street. You weren't supposed to be out drinking on Shabbas either but somehow after all the tummel, activity and excitement of the last few hours, it didn't seem to matter much.

* * *

It was getting late, and Sarah Lowenstein walked quickly down the darkened street in her stiff dress shoes, her coat buttoned, and her hat fashionably low over her ears. In her gloved hands she carried a doily that she'd crocheted with her own two hands. It didn't look like much right now, but Mrs. Schumacher had said that after she starched and ironed it, it would come out just lovely.

"Just lovely!" Those had been her very words. And Harold Schumacher, her son, said it "looked nice." She was thinking of ironing it and giving it to him as a small gift, but that might be too forward.

Sarah was in a hurry, because she stayed later than she'd intended at the Schumacher's. Harold hadn't gotten home until after nine. Now the streets were mostly deserted, families going to bed early so they could wake up refreshed for the Saturday morning services. And she didn't want to go anywhere near the Social Hall. Her brothers had all warned her that the union meeting was going on there tonight. "On Shabbas-oy, oy, oy," her mother had added. Such things sometimes got so rough, it was no place for a young lady.

And yet the hall was between the Schumachers' and her house. She thought for a moment and knew there was an alley coming up; if she cut down it, she could miss the hall by a block. She walked up, stopped, peeked down the deserted corridor. Dark, but it was only a block. And Poppa had reminded her not to walk past the hall. Shrugging, she turned down the dark, garbage filled passageway.

She'd not gone twenty feet when she heard it, a faint sound like water running. She looked in the shadows and blushed in the darkness when she saw a man relieving himself against a wall. Blushing again, she tried to continue as quickly and as quietly as she could down the alley.

"Hey, you!"

The accent was Italian, and he sounded as if he'd been drinking. Heart pounding, Sarah tried to run, but the dress shoes rocked unevenly on the cobblestones of the alleyway, causing her to stumble. She tried to scream, but a rough, grimy hand covered her mouth, pulled her off her feet and threw her, kicking and fighting, to the ground. Her head struck rock, and she was dazed for a second, stars dancing in her vision.

"You're one of those kike cunts from down at the union hall," the toughie grunted, and Sarah tried to shake her head, but he pulled a stiletto out of his boot top and held the tip pressed against her throat. "I'll bet you laughed your stinkin' ass off when you saw Goldblatt and his gang jump on us, didn't you?" He didn't wait for an answer, just prodded her chin up with the knife tip. "What were you looking at back there? Trying to see what a real man has between his legs? Whaddaya say I show you, huh?"

Pressing the knife tip more insistently against Sarah's throat, Riccolo's thug put his hand up under her dress and ripped the bloomers away, causing Sarah to gasp as the band cut into her waist. He probed with his finger, forcing his knee between hers, trying to get his hand between her legs. "Don't fight me, damn you," he hissed. "I'd just as soon cut your face as fuck ya."

That's when he heard the sound of glass breaking behind him.

* * *

Warmed by the two Scotches he'd lingered over for the last two hours, Irving drove the Chevrolet slowly through the back streets of the Lower East Side. In the noisy bar, with its ragtime piano and half-naked floozies hustling drinks, he hadn't thought much about business. He had no solution to his dilemma. Some men married to seamstresses came in and talked about what had happened down at the union hall, the diversions that had drawn the police away, and the klopping a bunch of Jews had given the Italians. Irving wished he'd known who the Jews were, they sounded like the right kind of people to know in his line of work.

He drove on into the warehouse district, and pulled into a side street. As soon as he'd shut the car off, a noise caught his attention. It was coming from upstairs, the back office – the sound of two men yelling.

"Schmucks," Irv muttered to himself as he grabbed the bag and made his way quietly up the outside stairs to the office entrance. He stepped into the entry cloakroom and waited, sizing up the situation, letting his eyes get adjusted to the yellow light of the single bare bulb burning in the next room.

"Fuck you, you palmed them damn dice," said a whiskey-thick voice in the back office. "I seen you."

"Ain't nobody palming nothin', Arnie," said a calmer second voice. "You threw the snake eyes yerself. Ya crapped out."

Irv sighed. Arnie Fleigelmann, drunk again and blowing his entire pay envelope from the barrel factory. When would his wife wise up and stop letting him put their rent money on the dice?

Irv reached into his inside breast pocket and pulled out a thick leather sap.

"I didn't crap out nothin'," Fleigelmann shouted. "I wanna throw again."

"You're done," the dealer insisted. "That was all you had."

Irv stepped quietly through the doorway. He could see Fleigelmann's back now. The man was huge, built like the oak barrels he made six days a week.

"I'll show you what I got left," Fleigelmann snarled. His hand darted into his jacket pocket and came out with a wicked, long-bladed knife.

Gladstone bag still in his left hand, Irv covered the six feet between him and Fleigelmann in two quick steps, swinging the heavy leaded sap with a quick practiced motion that caught the big barrel-maker on the base of his skull. There was a dull crack, and the big man turned, as if to see who had done it. Then his eyes rolled back in their sockets and he dropped heavily to the floor.

"The House is closed," Irv said to the half dozen other men still in the room. He flipped a half dollar to each of the two largest craps players, and said, "Take Arnie home, will you? And tell his wife that she's got to start meeting him down at work on paydays, take the grocery and the rent money off of him before he heads for the bar or comes down here."

The gang of men left and Irv could hear the heavy thump-thump-thump of Fleigelmann's boots as his friends dragged him down the wooden stairs. Irv looked up at the dealer still wearing his gartered sleeves and eyeshade, and Irv motioned for the cash box. "Give it here."

The dealer handed over a pasteboard cigar box. "I could have handled Fleigelmann myself, you know," the dealer finally said with restrained irritation.

"Didn't look like you were," Irv muttered as he counted out the take, nearly five hundred dollars. He looked up at the dealer. "This all of it?"

"Sure, Irv!" The dealer nodded earnestly. "You know I wouldn't hold back on ya."

Irv looked at the man and thought *why wouldn't he cheat?* Maybe that's why he was so cocky, figuring he was skimming the House, and getting away with it. Irv had other games going all around the borough, he couldn't be everywhere at once. And it wasn't as if he had anybody checking up on the dealers. As far as he knew, they could be stealing him blind. It had been bad enough a couple of years before, but now that he was in law school, it was getting harder and harder to keep a handle on the games.

True, he was still raking in more each week than his old man made in a year. And he barely had to lift a finger to do it. But this guy was too cocky. He had to find a way of putting his dealers on a shorter leash. He shrugged. "Here's your cut, Ozzie," he said, dealing out ten five dollar bills. He paused, and added another five. "Take your girl out for dinner, okay?"

The dealer grinned, showing' a gap where a tooth had vanished a few months ago in a fistfight. "Hey, Irv, thanks! You're all right."

Irv nodded and put the take in his Gladstone bag. Tipping the dealer was more than generosity on his part. If he couldn't keep these guys with him through fear, maybe money would make them stick around, at least a little while longer. He had to hire him some heavy muscle, some guy that would stay loyal and bust heads without thinking twice about it. The problem was, he didn't know anybody with those qualities.

He closed the Gladstone bag, pulled up the collar of his topcoat and headed down the stairs. Just as he put his foot on the running board of his Chevy car, he felt something sharp at the small of his back, and in an Irish accent brogue growl, "Okay, Hymie, the bag. Hand it over."

Irv froze and stole a careful glance over his shoulder. There was just one guy, short and stocky with an ice pick in his right hand. His brimmed hat, pulled down low on his brow, and the dim light in the alley made it impossible to make out his face.

"Hey," Irv said, deliberately putting a shake in his voice. "My old man made this bag for me. Would it be alright with you if I just gave ya what was inside? Bag means a lot to me, ya know."

"I don't give a fuck," the Mike snarled back. "Don't wanna Chrisskiller's bag anyhow. Just give me the dough, eh kike?"

Irv nodded, set the bag on the running board and undid the clasp. Reaching inside, he wrapped his hand around the handle of the big Webley .44 caliber revolver and pulled it out in one swift motion, stepping aside, outside the reach of the pick. The little Irishman straightened up, stunned.

"Drop the sticker," Irv ordered. The ice pick clattered to the ground, and he stepped forward and kicked it back under the car. "Okay! Now turn around slowly and put your hands up on that wall. Spread your feet out. I gotta see what else you're carrying."

The thug complied, and Irv kicked out and up, burying the tip of his Florsheim shoe in the thug's open crotch. Transferring the gun from his right hand to his left, he grabbed the gasping Irishman by the jacket collar and smashed his face into the brick wall. The sound of breaking bone and cartilage echoed in the small, dark lane.

"Okay, you Paddy dreck," Irv said quietly. "You get this, and get it good. And then tell your friends. You fuck with me and I will not only kill you, I will burn your pissant house down with your potato-grubbing family still inside of it. You hear me? You'll all be toast."

The little man nodded and choked back a moan.

"Well, make sure you remember," Irv said. And with that, he smashed the man's face against the cold bricks two more times. When he released his hold on the Irishman's collar, the thug dropped to the gravel alley like a sack of flour.

There was a noise on the stairway, and Irv looked up. It was Ozzie, the craps dealer, bundled up in a Mackinaw and a muffler.

"Hey…" Ozzie looked at the mick lying faced down in the alley, blood pooling under his chin. "I thought I heard somethin'. I was comin' to see if ya needed help."

"Sure you were," Irv muttered. For all he knew, Ozzie and the mick were in cahoots. If that was the case, or even if it wasn't, it was good for him to see that Irv could get tough when necessary. If nothing else, it bought him some respect. But he knew that the Paddies would be back, and that they wouldn't come alone next time. No doubt about it, time to hire himself some muscle, a real klopper, some guy that could take care of the rough stuff for him, kill if he had to.

He threw the Gladstone bag in the passenger's side, stepped to the front of the Chevrolet, cranked it, and got in. Putting the car in reverse, he backed away, hearing a low moan as he ran over the Irishman's foot.

Irv put the revolver back into the Gladstone bag as he drove off. He'd won the piece off a Limey sailor in a poker game up in Queens the year before. Tonight was the first time he'd ever had to pull it. *Guess that means it's about time I found some bullets to fit the damn thing*, Irv thought to himself as he made the turn at the end of the block. It had been a heck of a night, and he still had four more games to go.

By the time he got home, it was midnight. He cut his lights at the end of the alley and then switched off the engine, letting the Chevrolet coupe coast into the old stables behind the Delancey Street house. But when he stepped out of the rickety wooden building into the small vegetable garden in their backyard, the hair went up on the back of his neck. The family should be asleep by now, but every light was burning in the old Brownstone house. Nervously, he shifted the bag under his left arm and let himself into the house. From the pantry, he could hear crying in the kitchen. His mother. *Oh shit!* Irv thought. *It's the old man.*

But it wasn't. His father was sitting there at the table, a bottle of Mogen David at his elbow, and two untouched water glasses of the Concord grape kosher wine on the table. And the old man was patting Irv's mother's hand, making soothing noises.

"Momma? Poppa? What is it?" Irv asked. "Whattsa matter? Who died?"

"It's your sister," his mother sobbed.

"What?" Irv felt his knees weaken. "Sarah's dead?"

"Nobody's dead," Morris Lowenstein said calmly. "But some boy brought her home two hours ago, her dress all torn and her face scraped. She said something about some Italians, Braun's hired strikebreakers. Then she ran up and locked herself in her room. She's been there ever since."

"A boy brought her home," Irv's mother sobbed. "Now he knows. She's ruined. Who will marry our tochter now?" she said looking at Morris.

"Who brought her home?" Irving asked, still confused. "Now he knows what, Momma?"

But Esther Lowenstein only sobbed a few moments more. Then, suddenly she stopped and looked at her oldest son with tears streaming down her face. "Go talk to her," she moaned. "To you Irving, she would always talk. Maybe it's not the worst. Go. Talk."

"Sure, Momma. I'll go now. She'll be just fine," Irving said encouragingly for his parents' sake, but wasn't at all sure he was right.

He hung his coat up in the hallway and hefted the Gladstone bag. It had more than twenty-five hundred dollars in it, and while he had plenty of payoffs to make – the cops, the warehouse and shop owners whose space he used, the kids who watched the corners, the neighbors who heard the noise from the games – better than half of it was his… a good chunk for an evening's work. He usually stashed the money down in the basement, but that'd mean going back through the kitchen. Shrugging, he carried the bag upstairs and stuck it under his bed. Then creeping to his sister's room across the hall, he rapped softly on the door.

"Go away," sobbed a feminine voice within. "Leave me alone. I want to die in peace."

"Sarie," Irv whispered. "It's me. Open up, it's brother Irving."

There was the sound of a key being turned and the door flew open. Sarah, in her nightshirt, threw herself into his arms and buried her face against his neck. She was well into her teens now and had quite the figure, and he could feel her firm, young breasts pressing against his chest, a feeling that made him uncomfortable. She was, after all, his sister.

"Hey," he said, stepping into her room and peeling her away from him.

"What's up? Why the tears?"

She sniffed and they sat on her bed together.

"I was walking home from Rebecca Schumacher's," Sarah began tentatively. Then it began to pour out of her how she'd been afraid to walk past the Union Hall, the short cut down the alley, the Italian grabbing her, wrestling her to the ground. She threw herself into his arms again, sobbing, and he held her, rocking her to calm her down.

"Sis..." Irv whispered. "I've gotta know. Did he do anything to you, you know, touch you – down... there?"

Sarah nodded. "Yes," she said. "Well, he tried. He ripped my bloomers, and he had his hand up under my dress, trying to put his..." She looked at the closed door and whispered, "...you know. But I was fighting him, kicking and scratching. And that's when Mendel showed up."

Irv sat up. "Mendel?" he asked. "Mendel who?"

"Goldblatt," Sarah said. "You know, his father owns the candy store."

Irv nodded. The Goldblatts had moved into the neighborhood about five years before, but he didn't know much about them. They had a German name, but they'd come from Russia.

"He's the boss of the gang of men that works for the union," Sarah said. "And I don't know where he came from; it was as if all of a sudden, he was just there. And he... Oh, Irv, it happened so fast..." She looked at the door as if someone was outside listening and whispered again. "Mendel broke the bottom off a bottle, and he pulled the man off me and shoved the broken bottle in his throat... just like that. Swear to God... I couldn't believe my eyes... it happened so fast," she gushed. "The blood just poured out of him... it was a terrible sight. And then, ya know what, he tried to get up, but Mendel kicked him in the head, and he fell back down and didn't move again. Can ya believe it, Irvie? It all happened so fast, you wouldn't believe it, honestly," she continued in a rapid-fire manner, not even stopping to take a breath. "I kept telling him I wasn't a union girl, but he wouldn't listen. And that's when Mendel looked at me and said, 'You told him right. You're not one of my union girls. You're much too pretty to be a seamstress.'"

Irv's eyes narrowed. "Did he touch you?" he asked hesitantly.

"Only to wipe the blood off my forehead with his handkerchief," Sarah said. "And then he put his coat over my shoulders and brought me home, and I ran up to my room, and I've been here ever since. He was really kind to me. He's a nice guy, Irvie. He's really a nice guy." She paused. "It's my fault, isn't it?" Sarah asked. "I shouldn't have been in that alley."

Irv held her closer and looked directly into her eyes, wide with fright. "No, Sis," he said. "This isn't your fault. It's that stinking wop's fault. And it sounds like he got what's coming to him. Now, tell me again, where'd this happen?"

She described the alley, and he nodded. The block was all stables and warehouse space. Nobody lived there. No one would have heard a thing after six o'clock, and that was good. If word got out that Sarah had been attacked, never mind that the attacker had been stopped, the wagging tongues of Delancey Street would have her gang-raped and pregnant by noon the next day.

Irv got up, went to his room, took ten dollars out of the Gladstone bag, and came back. "Listen," he said. "I want you to buy another dress tomorrow, just like the one that got torn tonight and make sure you wear it a couple of times in the next week, okay? Get yourself some other clothes too, but do it uptown, not around here. And Sunday morning when you go get the milk off the stoop, I want you to slip on the steps and get up holding your head and crying, and make sure Mrs. Lederman sees you do it, okay? Can you do that?"

She nodded and smiled, understandingly. Mrs. Lederman couldn't keep anything to herself. Within an hour, the whole street would have heard how Sarah had bumped her head going out to get the milk. "Sucha klutz," she would add with her wagging tongue.

"Okay," Irv said. "You didn't do anything bad, Sarah. You're a good girl. Now get to bed. I gotta take care of a few things."

He went downstairs and told his parents that everything was fine, that the attack had not been a rape, and the story was that Sarah slipped and fell on Sunday morning, bumping her head getting the milk. That's what the family would tell the nosey neighbors He said the wop had been so scared that he would never talk. His father had frowned at that shaking his head, but Irv put his arm around his father's shoulder and quieted him down. The fewer people that knew about a dead Italian, he thought, the better.

The family kept a carbide bull's-eye lantern down in the basement, where Morris could use it for changing fuses and shaking clinkers out of the furnace. Irving found the lantern, slipped it under his overcoat, and set out on foot for the alley Sarah had just described.

It was bitterly cold in the dark alley, the gravel crunching underfoot, his breath hanging white-grayish in the air before him like steam from a locomotive. He lit the carbide lantern, adjusted the flame and reflector to get a narrow, bright beam, and swept it back and forth, checking the ground. He found a spot where the gravel had been raked, and he dug down with his heel, exposing a red-brown patch of frozen blood. Kicking the gravel back in place, he found a few shards of broken glass – nothing that anyone would look at twice in a New York City alley. He walked the length of the alley, looking for drag marks where a body had been pulled and there were none. Then he found a single rutted track that looked like a wheelbarrow track. *Holy shit!* Irv thought to himself. *This Goldblatt fellow takes Sarah home, gets a wheelbarrow and a rake, comes back here and puts the body in the wheelbarrow. Then he picks up the busted bottle, rakes the gravel so nobody will see the blood, and walks off pushin' the barrow, looking like some street sweeper on an ordinary night. And, five will get you a hundred that the body, the wheelbarrow and the broken bottle are all on the bottom of the East River by now. That's one cool customer.*

Dousing the lantern, Irv set out for home and smiled. He had two reasons to feel good. First, this Goldblatt was a careful guy. There wasn't anybody going to hear about some Dago trying to rape a Jewish girl, so Sarah's reputation was safe. And second, Irv thought, there's a bright side to this as well. It looked as if he'd definitely found his klopper.

Chapter Two
November 1915

"Of course he's liable for it! It's a valid contract. There was mutual consideration and a date certain. What's the problem?" Milton Blackman folded his arms, as if what he'd just said was the final word.

His two table companions, bathed in the shaded light from the table reading lamp, didn't look so certain.

"But the defendant in this case is a minor," objected a young, dark-haired man in a brown plaid sport jacket, speaking in whispered tones, respecting the other students in the library. "Minors can't enter into binding contracts."

"Ah, but they can if..."

"Look!" Peter Haas, the third young law student half rose from his seat. "Here's Lowenstein. He'll know what's the latest law on New York contracts."

Dapper, his blue suit neatly pressed and his shoes shined until they gleamed, Irving Lowenstein took an empty seat at the library table. Setting his Gladstone bag on the chair next to him, he smiled revealing a row of perfect white teeth under a barber-trimmed moustache.

"What's up, gents?" he asked.

Blackman glowered. *Wasn't this just typical? It was enough to frost your balls, he thought to himself.* The rest of the study group toadied up to Lowenstein as if he'd already graduated from Columbia Law School and passed the Bar which, of course, he hadn't. But he sure acted like it. He even had his briefcase already, the traditional gift for a law school graduate. The rest of the guys carried their books with leather straps, like schoolboys. Not Lowenstein.

"We're looking at Andrews versus Mendelson," Haas, the frail-looking first young student said. "And Mendelson, the defendant, is a minor..."

"Which is neither here nor there in this case," Blackman interrupted him impatiently. "The contract was a lease for a room in a boarding house; a lease provides shelter, and minors are liable for contracts regarding food, clothing and shelter. The precedent is – is…

"The Innkeeper's Statute under the English Common Law?" Irv Lowenstein prompted helpfully.

Blackman nodded.

"Correct, to a point," Lowenstein agreed tentatively. "But, if you'd read the depositions carefully, Blackman, you would have learned that Mendelson already had a room in his stepmother's home, just one block from the boarding house, when he signed the lease. That room was still available to him; he just didn't like living there because his stepmother enforced a curfew. And the Innkeeper's Statute doesn't protect the provider of a necessity if that necessity is already available to the minor defendant through another source. The contract is null and void."

"There!" The Plaid Jacket laughed. "I knew Lowenstein would have it."

"Well!" Milton Blackman scowled, "if you hadn't been late for this study group, Lowenstein, you might have saved us some time."

"I'm sorry, Blackman," Lowenstein grinned. "I guess you'll just have to settle for me saving your tuchas in our next Contracts class discussion instead."

Blackman worked his jaw, but no words came out. Finally, he scooped up his books in total frustration and stood up from the table. "I... I need to get going," he stammered. "I have several cases to brief for tomorrow's classes in Constitutional Law and Restitution"

He stormed away from the table and Lowenstein chuckled. "There goes a tempest in an ugly little teapot," he commented. "Our boy, Schwartzah Man."

His study companions, both Jewish like Lowenstein and Blackman, howled at the Yiddish translation of Blackman's name. Several people at neighboring tables in the Columbia Law Library looked up at the outburst, and Blackman, already near the exit also turned and looked back. Lowenstein waved at him; even at a distance, all three law students could see Blackman's face redden.

"Okay, that's it for Contracts," Irv Lowenstein said, looking back at his loose-leaf book full of briefs. "What's next, Torts?"

The three hit the books and argued precedents for certain negligence cases in Tort law, especially the Palsgraf Case, for another hour before Irv looked at his stylish new Cartier watch that that had been created for tank commanders in the Allied forces, over in Europe during WWI. He clucked his tongue and began packing his books. "Gentlemen, I'll see you tomorrow at the usual time for our study session." He smiled, throwing on a camel hair topcoat.

The other two students half-rose as he left the table, then with Gladstone bag in hand, he walked with a jaunty air out into the cold November air.

Lowenstein's Chevrolet started with the first crank, and he jumped into the driver's seat, thumping his gloves together for warmth. The new Cadillacs had just come out with electric starters, and he could easily afford one, but that would raise too many eyebrows around the law school. He'd just have to keep a low profile until he'd graduated and passed the Bar exam.

Irv smiled, wiping the inside of the steamed windshield with the back of his calfskin glove. As it was, half the guys in his class thought that he had been born into money, the son of some rich industrialist or something like that. He wondered what they'd think if they knew that his father was a simple tradesman who made and sold leather goods for a living, and that he'd made the very bag in which Irv carried his law books. For as long as Irv could remember, the family home on Delancey Street had smelled of oak tannin and leather polish, the smells from his father's clothes.

Well, Irv thought to himself, it won't be long now before I'm out of there. And I'll get Momma and Poppa a new place too, some place just for them, maybe even on Park Avenue. It won't be long now.

He drove down into Brooklyn, where the street lights became dim, and the traffic dropped off to a few rag pickers in their horse-drawn carts, their kerosene lanterns held high as they checked the waste bins for usable blankets and clothing. As he waited for a wagon to get out of his way in front of a brewery, Irv took his books out of the Gladstone bag and set them on the rear seat of the car. He needed the bag for something else.

Chapter Three
November 1915

It was a chilly November morning and men worked in their heavy jackets, unloading the dozens of horse-drawn wagons and Model T delivery trucks that struggled for space on Orchard Street. The cacophony of different accents flooded over New York's Lower East side as delivery men wheeled barrels of flour, pickles, herring and soda crackers, and crates of lettuce, tomatoes and other produce into stores down adjoining crowded streets, all the way from Rivington to Houston. Everywhere women, many wearing babushkas over their heads, were strolling with their shopping baskets on their arm, some bargaining at the fruit and vegetable pushcarts that cluttered every street corner.

Flicking his half-smoked cigarette into the gutter, Mendel smiled at the gold lettering on a shop window – GOLDBLATT CANDY STORE & ICE CREAM PARLOR – lettering he'd paid to have painted there only the week before. As he pushed open the oak-framed door, he saw through the window, a slim, attractive 45-year-old blonde woman with a huge apron covering her waist lifting a wooden keg, and in three quick strides, he'd entered the shop.

"Momma, what on earth are you trying to do, hurt yourself?" He took the barrel of gumballs from the struggling woman, setting it up on the shelf she'd been straining to reach. "How much more do you have to put up?" Mendel asked, kissing his mother on the cheek.

"It's okay, I'm almost done," she scolded. "You shoulda been here half hour ago, it woulda been better. Besides you'll ruin your suit. Just talk with me, I'll do," she said, running her words together in a European accent. Her light blue eyes fairly danced with pride looking at her son.

"Talking we'll both do," Mendel smiled, taking off his hat and coat and putting on a white cotton shop apron to keep his mother from worrying about his suit. "But no way does my Momma lift the big wooden kegs, not while I'm here."

"I'm fine," his mother protested smoothing her skirt. But smiling with pride, she sat on the stool behind the counter watching Mendel as he picked up heavy kegs of candy, two at a time, from the large pile the deliverymen had left inside the back door. "If you need help, though, it's the shelf over by the door, where they go."

"Is that my boychick, I hear?" asked a gruff voice from the curtained office. Saul Goldblatt stepped out into the small front room of the shop, saw his son wearing the apron, a keg of candy under each arm, and beamed.

"Look at you," he said approvingly. "Whadda shtarker." He pulled at his neatly trimmed beard like he was trying to remember something.

"Oh yeah! You know the man that you sent here a few days ago? He said that he could come back and paint *"and Son"* on the front glass anytime we want, for only one dollar more."

"Maybe someday, Poppa," Mendel said, stooping to kiss his father. "But not now." The young man quickly stocked the rest of the shelves, putting the contents of the nearly empty kegs atop the freshly opened new ones as his parents looked on. The brass bell rang on the shop door and three young teenage boys came walking in, all knickers, sweaters and elbows, politely doffing their caps as they sat down at the soda fountain counter.

"Come in, come in," Ethel Goldblatt called jovially. "Nu, what can we do for you boys today? Maybe three chocolate sodas?"

"I don't think so, not today, Mrs. Goldblatt. We don't have enough money for all that," said the tallest of the three. Then one of the shorter ones, obviously continuing a conversation that had started out on the street, asked the big one, "So your brother's really gonna let you work some of the games with him? Yeh, I bet."

"Sure," the big one swaggered. "Swear to God, probably next week."

Still straightening the shelves, Mendel kept an eye on the kids. The shop lost a certain amount of candy every month. It wasn't hard to distract two older people with a conversation while a friend filled his pockets on the far side of the shop.

"Ain't no way," said Joey, the other one.

"You callin' me a liar?" the big one asked, arms poised at his side, fists clenched.

"No, no, don't get your bowels in an uproar, Herbie. But, when you goin' with him, tonight?"

"Naw, ya dope." Artie threw up his hands in disgust. "Herbie already toldja... sometime next weekend he thinks, but he's not sure, Herbie could never go with Irving on a school night."

"Oh, sure, maybe next weekend, you'll start working the games with him, huh?" Joey snickered.

"Well," the tall one hesitated. "Maybe we won't start until summer, when school's out."

"Oh, yeah, sure. Irv Lowenstein's gonna take a big-mouth schmuck like you out to work his craps games. You bet."

"Who you callin' a schmuck, Joey?"

"You, Herbie, you schmuck."

The shoving started, and Mendel stepped around the end of the counter and grabbed the two boys in a vice-like grip, one in each arm.

The shoving stopped.

"You're Irv Lowenstein's brother?" Mendel asked the tall one.

"Yeah." The kid looked like he was thinking of asking, *What's it to you?* Then he looked as if he'd thought better of it. Nodding, he said, "I'm Herbie Lowenstein. You know my brother, Irv, don'cha?" he asked Mendel.

"Just by reputation," Mendel said. "I hear he's a pretty smart guy."

"He is, but his sister ain't so smart," piped up Joey, the cocky one who'd been baiting Herbie Lowenstein for the past few minutes. "She's a klutz."

"Who are you callin' a klutz?" demanded the Lowenstein boy.

"Oh come on," said Joey, "She fell down and scraped her head gettin' the milk last Sunday morning, ain't that being a klutz?"

"She fell and scraped her head?" Mendel asked, interested.

"Yeah," said Artie, the other short kid. "Mrs. Lederman saw the whole thing. Said she looked like Charlie Chaplin!"

"Watch it," Herbie Lowenstein warned his friend.

"Hey. I didn't say it," protested Artie, shrugging off the warning. "I'm just telling you what Mrs. Lederman said. You wanna klop somebody, klop her."

"Well, the steps were pretty icy that morning. I almost fell myself," Mendel said, mollifying the situation. "Can I buy you guys a licorice?" he continued to change the subject.

The three kids brightened as Mendel took three Indian-head pennies out of his pocket, dropped them in the till, put three large licorice sticks in a bag, handing it to them. "Maybe next time you'll have enough money for chocolate sodas."

"Gee, thanks, mister," said Herbie. "You know my sister too, maybe?"

"No," Mendel lied. "I don't think I've ever met your sister."

"You'd like her," Artie said with a wink. "She's pretty."

"But a klutz," added Joey.

The shoving match started again. Mendel cleared his throat, and the three kids straightened up, thanked Mendel again, and left the shop. Just before the door closed, Mendel heard the whack of a punch, and the first short kid, Artie, whining, "Hey! What didja go and do that for?"

"Trombeniks," Ethel Goldblatt, Mendel's mother said, shaking her head. "They're just kids. And you buy them candy? Like stray dogs they'll be, hanging around the store all the time waiting for more."

"Now, Ethel," said Saul Goldblatt. "What is a candy store without kids? You tell me that."

The well-built woman shrugged and wiped her hands.

Mendel looked up at the clock ticking steadily on the shop wall. "Momma, Poppa, I love you both," he said. "But I've got to get going. I have a meeting."

"Another meeting down at the union hall?" his mother asked. The young man nodded.

"You can do better than that, sonny boy," Saul Goldblatt grumbled. "These union people, they're using you. Come in with me, we can make a good business together. Something you can have now."

"Maybe someday, Poppa," Mendel smiled, kissing his two favorite people goodbye and waving at them.

"We'll be here for you zohn," the older Goldblatt said as the shop door tinkled shut.

The older couple puttered around the store. Now that the deliveries had all been put away, there wasn't that much for them to do late Monday morning. Sunday was the first day of the week for most of the shops on Delancey Street since Saturday was Shabbas. All of the cleaning, the inventory for special sales stacked on the shelves, and new orders for stock had been completed the day before. After awhile, Ethel retired to the apartment upstairs to make lunch for her husband, leaving him alone in the store, thinking that it was a good day to start a new week.

* * *

Lou Kravitz carried his heavy topcoat over his arm as he walked down the upper end of Orchard Street. It felt strange for him to be part of these jammed, narrow passages with nothing to do specifically except walk around looking at all the people; but, Lou pushed his feelings away. He'd be chained to a desk like most other men come Monday, from 8:30 a.m. to 5:00 p.m., and he was determined to enjoy his leisure time over the weekend. Although the air was chilly, the sun shined brightly and there were fluffy clouds filling the blue sky. Lou Kravitz finally had a job and he felt good. A sign in a shop window caught his eye, GOLDBLATT CANDY STORE & ICE CREAM PARLOR, and Kravitz smiled. Every man had his vice, for some it was liquor or fancy women, and for others, gambling. His was a sweet tooth.

The brass bell on the door tinkled, and the tall good-looking man in a gray suit entered. Like most people, he first stopped for just a moment to savor the different aromas of the shop. He stood for a moment, letting his eyes adjust from the bright sunlight. The strong aroma of cinnamon wafted through the light breeze.

"Yes, sir?" Saul Goldblatt asked from behind the soda fountain, "Are you here for the Karen Roth order?"

"Pardon?" the man asked. Then, "No, I'm not here to pick up the Karen Roth order."

Looking up with a thick head of grayish hair, stocky but powerfully built, Goldblatt wiped some powdered sugar off his hands. "Of course you are not with the Roth family, alov hashalon; may the old man rest in peace. You are much too clean-shaven to come from a house that is sitting shiva. Anyways," he said in a slight accent, "I'm Saul Goldblatt, and what can we do for you today?

"Lou Kravitz," Lou replied, shaking the man's hand. The shopkeeper looked at him curiously, which was nothing new to Lou for at six-foot-three, he towered over most people, and his athletic frame was obvious, even covered by his new gray flannel suit.

"Kravitz," Goldblatt said, "now there is a name I know...no don't tell me..."

He stepped back through the green-curtained doorway and there was the sound of drawers opening and closing, papers being rustled.

"I remember putting it here..." came his voice through the thick curtain. "If my wife, kain ein horeh, hasn't thrown it away with the trash, nu? Here it is, I've found it!"

He emerged from behind the curtain with a successful grin, a tattered newspaper page in his hands. He looked at the photograph on the page, compared it to the man standing at his counter, looked again and beamed. "As God is my witness, it is you," the shop owner proudly exclaimed. He read from the New York Sun sports page, *Lou Kravitz, All-American... Sweet-Shot Kravitz, king of the basketball court... The pride of the University of Pennsylvania.* "And, now he's in my candy store. I can't believe it," he smiled.

Lou felt his face redden much to his embarrassment. "Well, that was a few years ago, Mr. Goldblatt," he said. "Not too many folks still call me 'Sweet Lou'."

"It was exactly three," the storeowner replied, showing Kravitz the date on the newspaper. "And when you get to be my age, three years is like yesterday; it is nothing. Besides, I remember showing this to my son, showing them the proof that a Jewish boy can really be somebody here in America, he can be a mensch." Lou smiled and let the man ramble on. His fame on the court, as captain of the University of Pennsylvania basketball team had certainly opened doors for him, like getting him into the Wharton School of Finance, and had helped land him a job in New York. But, this was the first time it had made him feel welcomed in a candy store.

"Not that many people follow basketball anymore, especially these last few months," Kravitz observed. "Lately, it seems like all the papers want to write about is the war."

"What do you think of that?" Goldblatt asked, suddenly somber. "Do you think America is gonna be drawn into it?"

Kravitz shrugged. "Earlier this year, I would have said that there was no way," he said frankly. "But since the Lusitania was sunk by a German submarine, I don't know. She had a lot of Americans on board."

"The Daily Forward said there was speculation she'd been blown up, rather than torpedoed," Goldblatt added knowingly. "An attempt to make America angry with the Kaiser and help out England and France."

"Same thing they said about the Maine, a few years back," Kravitz agreed. "But I don't think so. A lot of the survivors said they saw the wake from the torpedoes."

"A bad business," Goldblatt observed, and both men nodded somberly.

"So what brings you up here from Philadelphia?" Goldblatt asked with a smile, changing the subject.

"A new job," Kravitz smiled. "I start tomorrow at Solomon & Sons, an investment firm up on Wall Street. I'm staying with my uncle, just down the street from here until I can find an apartment uptown."

"And you come to see us, first thing!" the shop owner beamed. "Again I am honored. What can I fix you? My treat."

"Oh, no, I can't" Lou stammered, bringing out a handful of coins.

"And deny me this mitzvah?" The shopkeeper shook his head. "Please, just to say that you were here..."

"Well, if you could make me a double strawberry malt –"

"You bet," Goldblatt beamed.

With a flourish, the aging shopkeeper poured strawberry syrup into a metal canister with three scoops of strawberry ice cream, topped off with a tablespoon of malt. He then dropped a raw egg and a glass of milk into the mixture, pressing the switch at the same time letting it swirl for a minute or so.

"There you are!" Goldblatt beamed, emptying the canister into a large glass. "One extra special double-strawberry malt, with a straw. Wiping the countertop, Goldblatt continued the conversation. "It's funny how there are different names for the same thing depending on where you're from. Why only last week I had a salesman in here from Detroit. What do you think they call a root beer float out there?"

"A black cow," Kravitz said, sipping his drink and smiling.

"But of course, a man like you, traveling with the college team, you'd know that," Goldblatt said appreciatively. He looked up as two men entered the shop. He smiled a greeting, but they said nothing, just hung around the magazine rack, so he went back to putting some additional cartons of Lucky Strike cigarettes out on display.

"Mr. Goldblatt," Kravitz said. "This is excellent. The best malt I ever tasted. But really you must let me pay for it."

"No, no," the shopkeeper protested. "It's on the house!"

"I dunno, Pops," said a brogue-thick voice behind Kravitz. "If I was you, I'd be charging for your malts. You got plenty of expenses."

"Excuse me?" Kravitz said, turning.

"I ain't talkin' to you, Slim," said a short, red-haired man in a tan plaid jacket. Turning back to the shopkeeper, he said, "I'm here for the payment we talked about last week."

Goldblatt glowered. "This is not right... you people asking us for money all the time like this."

"Yeah?" The little Irishman smirked. "Maybe ya wanna replace a few broken windows, instead? How 'bout wakin' up and findin' the place on fire some night?"

"Now just a minute..." Kravitz started to argue with him. Then he stopped in mid-sentence as the smaller man jabbed an index finger in his chest.

"You, I told to shaddup," the little man snarled. "And before you go balling your fist up like that, you might want to take a look at my friend by the door."

Kravitz turned. A big man stood at the door, holding it open with his foot, as if he and his colleague might want to make a hasty exit. He weighed a good two hundred and seventy-five pounds easily, the top of his bowler hat well above Lou's eye level. As Kravitz looked his way, the man smiled, revealing a missing tooth, and opened his jacket to show him the butt end of a .38 automatic pistol.

"Please," the shop owner pleaded. "No trouble. Mr. Kravitz, don't try to help me. These men will shoot you! If I pay them what they want, they'll leave."

"There you go! That's the spirit Hymie," the Irishman smiled. "Pay us, and we'll be gone like the morning fog."

"How much?" Saul Goldblatt asked in a frightened voice.

"Three dollars will see you through to the end of the month," the Irishman said, holding out his hand for the money. "Actually, we're giving ya a break 'cause it should be five."

Goldblatt glowered and Kravitz gasped at the chutzpah of the little mick. Three dollars had to be almost a day's earnings for a small shop such as this. He bit down on his tongue as the shopkeeper opened the till. But before the three-dollar bills could be placed in the Irishman's greasy hand, there came a loud crash of breaking wood from the doorway, followed by a series of moans.

All three men turned to the doorway where the Irishman's big accomplice lay sprawled on the wooden floor in a sea of multicolored jawbreakers.

Standing above him was someone the big Irish thug had never seen before, a blond, handsome young man with a thin moustache and strange blue, smoldering eyes. He was dressed in a dark blue pinstriped suit, and in his hands were the remains of the candy barrel he had just smashed over the big Irishman's head.

"Mendel, please..." the shop owner began, but the young man cut him off with a curt wave of his hand.

"We have some stock damage here," he said in a low menacing voice. "One barrel of jawbreakers, that's what, Poppa? Two dollars?"

The shopkeeper nodded and the young man stooped, never taking his eyes off the other Irishman, as he removed the brass knuckles and the Colt automatic from the groaning giant on the floor, slipping them into his own coat pocket.

"Poppa... aw shit! You mean this guy's your old man, Mendy?" the young mick stammered apparently confused.

"He's my father, yes," the young man said, still not raising his voice. "And he has better things to do than clean up this mess, so you're going to pay him to hire someone to do it. That's another two dollars. Two for the barrel, two for the mess. Four dollars."

"Sure. Sure." The Irishman jammed his hand into his pocket, came out with four dollar bills and held them out to the young man.

"How much did he ask you for, Poppa?" Mendel asked, ignoring the money.

"Three dollars," the shopkeeper replied.

"Three," the young man repeated, his voice still low. "We have a custom, Paddy, you try to steal from us, you pay back five-fold. It says that in the Tanaach, Old Testament to you, if you can read. Five times three is fifteen, plus the four is nineteen. Call it an even twenty. And don't pay me, pay him. It's his shop."

"Twenty bucks!" the mick whined. "Jesus Christ, Mendy, I was only squeezin' him for three."

The young man took a step closer, his hand sliding toward the gun.

"Okay, okay! It's good! Twenty it is." The Irishman put the four dollar bills back in his pocket and came out with a thick, old-fashion, brass-clasped wallet. He took out three five dollar bills, looked for another, didn't find it, and counted out five more bills, all ones. It didn't leave much in his wallet.

"Jesus, Mary and Joseph, I'm sorry about all this..." he stammered, sliding the money across to the shopkeeper. Turning back to the young man, he explained, "I didn't know it was your Pops, Mendy. Honest to God, I never would have come in here, if I'd a known it was your family's candy store."

"It's not just my store," the young man continued. "It's my street. All of it. All of Orchard Street, you hear me? The length of the Lower East Side, Delancey, Hester, Orchard, Rivington and Houston streets. You go over there, come around here, you're on my turf. You want to shake down shops for a living, you do it across the river in Brooklyn, or in the Bronx, or uptown, or out in Queens. Not here. Not ever. Now get out, and take your friend with you."

"Sure, sure." The little Irishman edged around the muscular young man and roused his groaning comrade from the floor, tugging him to his feet and jamming the dented bowler back on top of his bleeding head. Slipping on jawbreakers, they scrambled out the door into the sunlight and disappeared into the street.

"Mister Kravitz," Goldblatt said, still holding the crumpled wad of bills in his hand, this is my son, Mendel. Mendel meet Mister Lou Kravitz."

"Sweet Lou, the basketball player?" Mendel asked smiling and speaking in a normal voice for the first time since he'd entered the shop.

Lou nodded, blushing again, and shook Mendel's hand.

"You didn't have to do that Mendy," his father said, sadly.

"No? And what would you have done if I hadn't come back for my hat? Give him what he wanted? Poppa, you pay these people now and next week, it's the Italians coming around with their hands out asking for another three dollars. And then after the dagoes, who knows who would come next. Hunkies, maybe even the Polacks. Everybody would come to our neighborhood and squeeze the Jews. This way, we nip it in the bud before it even starts."

"But all this klopping, this hitting," his father shook his head sadly. "It's no good, Mendel. It's not right."

"Poppa, it's the only language they understand. I've got to go right now. Sorry about the mess, but I'll hire a boy to sweep up in here, on my way back down to the Union Hall. I'm already ten minutes late, now, for a meeting."

The young man turned back to Kravitz.

"Nice to meet you, Lou," he said, shaking his hand again. "I have often read about you, would have loved to seen you play, but I don't get to basketball games much."

Then nodding to both men, Mendel put his fedora back on his head. "Sorry, I've gotta run now, but I'll catch ya later.

"With that he stepped outside and started down the street, obviously checking to make sure the Irishmen had left, before turning and walking away.

"The union..." the elder Goldblatt grumbled. "That Garment Worker's Union, or whatever they call it, I don't know. They're socialists, maybe even Communists, like they have now back in Russia. The Czar was bad, but I think maybe they're even worse. And this union work my boy does, you know what it is? Breaking the heads of men sent to break other heads."

Kravitz was silent, not certain exactly how to respond.

"He takes care of his Poppa, though," Kravitz finally said.

"That he does, but still, his mother and I..." Saul Goldblatt came out from behind the counter, the paper candy sack in his hand, as if considering something. Then he smiled. "Did you see the way he looked at you, Mr. Kravitz?"

"Please, Lou."

"Sweet Lou, yes? That's what they called you in the papers. He respects you, Mr. Sweet Lou. You could see it in his eyes. Nu, maybe you could talk to him, a little sense would be good, huh? I mean a boy like that, how much attention does he pay to what his father tells him? I'll tell you how much, not much. But you, a businessman and already famous. To you, he'll listen. Could you have a word with him? I'm sure he's not far away. The hall is just down at the corner."

"Well..." Kravitz started to make an excuse, and then he looked at his empty malted milk glass and smiled. "Sure, I'll talk with him."

"What a mitzvah," Goldblatt beamed, pressing a sack of chocolate peppermints into the tall man's hands. "Please, go in peace, Lou. And mazel tov on your new job."

"Well, let me at least pay for the candy..." Lou stammered.

"Please," Goldblatt insisted, shaking his head. "Don't insult me. Now go, catch up with him before he's gone."

* * *

Sucking on a piece of peppermint, Lou caught up with Mendy as the young man finished talking to a boy with a broom on the sidewalk.

"Looks like you're a handy man to have around," he said, offering Mendy the candy sack.

Shaking his head, Mendy took out a cigarette, a Lucky Strike, and lit it with a wooden kitchen match, squinting through the smoke. "He wants you to talk to me, right?

Lou nodded.

"Then you've kept your promise, Mr. Kravitz. Thank you. I've got to be going now."

"It's Lou," Kravitz said, falling in along side him. "And, Mendy? It's not what you think, because I believe you're doing exactly the right thing."

"Yeah?" Mendy squinted under the brim of his gray snap-brim as the two men walked past a tradesman sharpening scissors on a foot-powered grindstone. "And why's that?"

"I did my Master's dissertation at Wharton on investment opportunities with the new unions. They'll be representing thousands of members with huge amounts of money to invest for their pension funds. It's all a brand new concept," Lou explained. "And, Mendy, unions aren't the political pariahs people make them out to be. They're part of the future of American business, they're necessary, and... well, put it this way, because in this day and age, it's hard to set yourself up as a new captain in industry. The railroads have their barons, and so do the steel companies, lumber mills and the coal mines. You've got some real comers, like that Henry Ford out in Detroit, but not many. But unions?" Kravitz continued, "A bright and energetic fellow who gets set up with the unions, becomes part of the mechanism that runs big industry. He can have just about as much power as the captains of business, Mendy, and damn near as much money, if he plays his cards right."

"Even if he busts heads to get his point across?" Mendy asked, and for the first time Lou saw him smile.

They walked in silence for a few feet, then Lou cleared his throat.

"You know how I made All-American?" Lou asked. "My elbows, Mendy. A guard would get too close when I was trying to shoot and I'd give him an elbow in the ribs. It's the same reason the British ran the world for so long, because they had the biggest Navy, the biggest guns. And it's the same reason Mexico listens when America talks, if they don't, we send General Pershing down there with his cavalry, and he makes them listen. Busting heads is the way the world works. It's what every bully, whether he's some mick hooligan, or Kaiser Wilhelm, or even Andrew Carnegie, understands."

"Yeah?" Mendy looked directly into Lou's eyes again. "They teach you that at the University of Pennsylvania, Lou?"

"Nope," Lou shook his head. "To tell you the truth, I don't think they've figured that out yet at Wharton, but I have since graduating from school. Unions are the coming power, Mendy. Get close with them, and stay close. You'll be glad you did."

"Well..." Mendy paused to flip his cigarette butt out into the street, where a draft horse flattened it with its huge wheels as it passed, pulling a Budweiser beer wagon. "That's good to know... Lou. And this magnificent office building," he waved at the boarded-up storefront they'd stopped in front of, "is the union hall, and I'm late for my meeting, so I'd better go. Nice talking with you."

"You, too." Lou watched as Mendy Goldblatt stepped into the union hall, walking as if he owned the place. And the thing was, Lou didn't think it would be too awfully long before he did.

Inside the hall, in the big office at the back, Joe Polasky was already carrying on with his audience as Mendel came through the door. Polasky was one of those fat guys that tended to sweat when he got worked up, and he was sweating now, waving his hands as he talked. He didn't even introduce Mendel to the two men with him as he entered the office, just nodded to him as Mendy found a seat.

Mendel frowned. One of the guys sitting across from Polasky was Abe Newman, the treasurer of the local, and the other was a hulking, dark-suited guy from downtown, an organizer from the steelworkers' union that he remembered they'd invited in for the meeting. Mendy had already forgotten his name, although he remembered that he was a Polish Jew, like Polasky. And that was the purpose of the meeting, to impress the steelworkers' guy with their organizational efforts. He had been invited, Mendy realized, to make Polasky look good.

Mendy sat down and stared at the steelworkers' guy. The suit he wore was expensive, downtown tailoring. And he had a fresh shine on his Florsheims. Money.

The steelworker union guy said something else, and Polasky started nodding vigorously, as if he'd just heard the gospel. Sweat dropped off the fat man's jowl and rolled down the old-fashion celluloid collar that he wore. Even though he was indoors.

Polasky was wearing his hat, a dusty black bowler because, in addition to being fat, he was halfway bald, and tried to cover his sparse hairline. He talked for five minutes, and then he said something about "emancipation of these poor, downtrodden women" and waved his hands some more.

Mendy didn't know what the hell Polasky was talking about, since he'd stopped paying attention about ten minutes before. The meeting didn't have anything to do with providing protection for their union activities. It didn't have much to do with anything including poorly paid women. Actually only about 20% of the thousand or so of the seamstresses showed up. The steelworkers' guy grunted something and Polasky arched his eyebrows and nodded, like he was hearing revelations straight from the burning bush. Mendy shifted in his seat and fished a cigarette out of his pack, struck a match and lit it, and then sat there pretending to pay attention as Polasky prattled on. Throughout Polasky's entire boring monologue, Mendy had been thinking about how his father believed he was being taken advantage of here, and of what Lou Kravitz had said, that unions were the coming power, and how he should get close with them and stay close. Pretty interesting thoughts for a college man, Mendy thought.

Was this getting close? He wondered. Acting as the toady to some fat man with an ego didn't seem tike a long-term proposition to Mendel. And if unions were the coming power, he didn't want to simply be close with the power, he wanted to be part of the power behind the union movement.

Now Newman was saying something, agreeing with Polasky, and the steelworkers' guy was grunting positively, and Polasky finally looked at Mendy and said, "What about you? Goldblatt, what do you think?"

Mendy looked at him, turned his head and sized up the other two, and then turned back to the fat man behind the desk. "I think," Mendy said softly, using the same tones that he'd used with the mick at his father's candy shop, twenty minutes before, "I think... that I want ten percent."

"Huh?" Polasky looked puzzled. Newman, too. They'd been talking about wage scales for seamstresses.

"Ten percent," Mendy repeated, his voice still low. "Every month, you get fifty cents from each girl in the union. I want a nickel of it."

Polasky chuckled nervously, as if he and Mendy joked all the time.

"But Mendy," he called him. Before it was Goldblatt. "You get more than that now. There are only sixty girls working at Fischbaum's. Sixty times fifty cents is thirty dollars. Ten percent of that is three. We're paying you twelve dollars a week."

He looked to Newman, who nodded in agreement.

"That's Fischbaum's," Mendy said, his voice still low. "I want ten percent of everything – every local the International opens, from this point on."

"Every local?..." Polasky, started, and then glanced at the steelworkers' man, who was watching silently. "Every local in the city, but that could be hundreds?"

"No," Mendel said in that quiet whisper. "Every local in the country that I have anything to do with organizing from here in New York since the main headquarters controls all the locals."

The steelworker guy laughed and spat a thin stream of brown juice into the spittoon near his feet, and Polasky smiled as well.

"C'mon, Mendy," he said, "That could be a lot of green."

"Could be?" Mendy repeated. "If my aunt had balls, she would be my uncle. But she don't. And you don't have any locals outside of Manhattan right now. So who are you trying to shit? If you want to get this thing going, somebody's ass," he almost said tuchas but caught himself, "is going to be on the table, and it's mine. I'm the one taking the heat from the cops. I'm the one out here busting dago heads, traveling all over the country. It's my sweat that's building this union, Joe, and I want mine."

"But ten percent of everything..."

"Or I'm gone," Mendel growled deeper, "I could pull out now, let you guys fight your own battles and lose, and then you'd have ten percent of nothing."

"Mendy," Polasky tried to argue over agreeably, "I don't know if this is the time and the place..."

"Then let me clear up your confusion," Mendy said evenly. "This is the time and the place. You believe in strikes? So do I. Either do it on my terms, or I pull my 20 men and we take a walk."

"But Mendy, we..." Polasky looked at Newman and the man from downtown, and then at Mendel, who was staring him down. Polasky turned back to the union men. "Gentlemen," Polasky finally said to the other two. "Would you mind excusing us for a couple of minutes?"

Newman and the union man looked at one another and stood up, taking their hats with them. They stepped into Polasky's office, a shabby, tired-looking room where the stewards came to meet every month.

Polasky waited until the door was closed, and then he growled, "Are you fuckin' nuts? The steelworkers are thinking of loaning us money, something to tide us over until Fischbaum accepts a union shop."

"Good!" Mendy said, drawing on his cigarette. "Then I want ten percent of that too."

Polasky laughed and settled back in his chair. They still had the desk between them. He took out a cigar, stripped off the cellophane wrapper, bit off the end and spat it into a spittoon next to the desk. Then he searched for a match.

Mendy lit a match and held it out. Smiling, Polasky leaned forward, holding the cigar to his mouth with his thumb and first finger gently turning the stogie between his lips.

Dropping the lighted match onto the desk blotter, Mendy reached out and grabbed Polasky by the shirt collar, hearing the celluloid crack like winter ice. With his free hand, Mendy flicked the bowler off the fat man's head, beads of sweat glistened on the union leader's pasty white scalp.

"You smiled at me?" Mendy whispered hoarsely into the man's face, just inches away. "I tell you my terms and you smile at me?"

"Mendel..." Polasky choked the words out, his face turning red. "Be reasonable."

"I am being reasonable," Mendy said. "If I was unreasonable, I'd want it all."

Smoke began rising from the desk where the match was still burning, scorching the blotter.

Polasky reached to smother it, and Mendy jerked him forward, so only his toes were still on the floor.

"Leave it," Mendy whispered. "Ten percent. What's it going to be? Yes or no?"

"Jesus," Polasky grunted, and Mendy almost laughed – imagine a Jew calling on Jesus for help.

Polasky swallowed hard, trying to regain his composure, even though Mendy had him half-dragged over a smoldering desk. "Why should we pay you that kind of money?" Polasky asked.

"Because, if you don't, I work for whoever pays me the most. If Fischbaum pays for my services, he's got a deal. The next union that comes in and tries to organize these girls, you'll be screaming for me to straighten them out."

"Oh," Mendy added. "And one more thing. One of Fischbaum's dagoes didn't show up at home last night. Messy thing, a broken bottle right in the throat. You start getting prissy with my percentages, and that bottle could turn up at your place. Police might find it, put two and two together."

It was a lie. The bottle was at the bottom of the East River, but Mendy wasn't taking any chances with this guy.

"Mendel..." Polasky now was terrified, whispering, "You killed a man?"

"No," Mendy replied. "You aren't listening? You did. Six of my guys saw you doin' it. They'd swear it on their mothers' graves. Now what's it going to be? Ten percent, or the police?"

"God, Mendy," Polasky stammered, still trying to understand the fact that one of Fischbaum's thugs was dead. "If the police found out about this..."

"They'd be the least of your problems," Mendel said. "Because, we may not have told them yet, but we have gotten word back to Riccolo that you were the one that clipped his man."

"You're bluffing,"

"You think so?" Mendel smiled. "Then fine, walk around the Lower East Side without my protection. See how long you keep breathing."

Mendel let him think about that for a minute, while the smoke curled up from the desk blotter. Then he asked it again, "Ten percent?"

"Ten percent," Polasky said. "Of everything." Polasky nodded, and Mendy dropped him to his feet.

"Good," Mendy said. He picked up his hat and walked out the office door.

"Good meeting," he said agreeably to the other two men in the hall. Then he walked the length of the big open room, went out the big double door, and was gone.

* * *

Outside, Irv Lowenstein had been sitting in his beige Chevrolet parked in front of the union hall for nearly half an hour, smoking, watching the door and flicking a cigarette butt into the street every once in awhile.

Even if Herbie hadn't told him about the conversation in the candy store, it wouldn't have taken him long to figure out where Goldblatt was. Orchard Street was like a big family. Actually the entire area of Orchard, Delancey over to Allen, including Henry Street down to Jake Goodman's pawnshop on Elridge and then over to Canal Street was a Jewish ghetto where most people either knew everyone else, or knew someone who knew them. A nickel to some kids playing kick-the-can in the street would have been enough to get the information that Mendel was "meeting with some big machers down at the hall." Through the doors and windows of the hall, Irv could occasionally see movement; a couple of guys standing out in the hall, talking behind the frosted glass windows. Maybe the meeting was busting up. He slid the side curtain over, lit another cigarette off the butt of the old one, and threw the butt out into the street.

Earlier that morning, he'd had a call from Aldo Lucci, the son of the tanner, who had a business idea and wanted to discuss it with Irv. So Irv had driven over the bridge to Brooklyn and met with him for cappuccinos and brioche, and Aldo laid out his new scheme.

Aldo, it turned out, had no plans for following his father into the family business, either. He and his two brothers, Francisco and Guido, had found a guy in New Jersey who would sell them punchboards at low prices. They were selling punches all over Brooklyn for a nickel a punch, and if the number on your paper matched the number on the board you won. The board had 100 punches on it that cost 5 cents each. There were only four punches on the board that could be redeemed for a quarter. There was a $4 profit on each board if you sold out the board. He expected to place 5,000 boards each week in the next several months, covering the entire metropolitan area of New York City including the Lower Eastside, the Bronx, all over town. It was a perfect set up because you didn't need to rent floor space anywhere, just give the punch boards to shop owners and let them run the boards for you. The shop owners got to keep half the profit or two dollars a card. Easy. But Aldo didn't know the Lower East Side, or the Queens either and barely knew the Bronx. He had no way to make contact with the shopkeepers there, but Irv did. So maybe they could go partners.

It was a good gimmick, but it would spread Irv even thinner than he already was, but you could use dozens of youngsters as runners. Still, if the Lucci brothers didn't partner with him, they'd find someone else, so he'd agreed. He and Aldo Lucci ordered another cappuccino to celebrate their new business arrangement. It wasn't exactly a real "toast", but it would have to do for an early breakfast meeting. Now, Irv was anxious to figure out how he was going to increase the punch board business without letting it get away from him, and he had to figure it out fast.

The union hall's doors opened and Mendy Goldblatt walked out, the same stride of a man who knew he could handle himself. Irv slipped the Chevy into first gear and let it inch forward. Mendel walked with his hands in his overcoat pockets, thinking about what he had just done. He had Polasky covered, but only temporarily, he knew. The fat man would be looking for a way out, maybe hire other muscle to push him out of the way. What Mendel had to do was keep him intimidated, terrified, give him enough to worry about so that he could keep him under his thumb until Mendel could take the Union over himself. But that would take people, an organization and some smart guys, not just the gang of twenty or twenty-five kloppers that Mendel had working for him. And Mendy didn't know that many smart people, only the muscle. He had to think about it some more.

He turned up his collar. A cold wind was coming down from the northwest, somewhere out across the Hudson, engulfing the warmth of the afternoon sun. There was a fresh smell of snow in the air as he put his hands back in his pockets to keep warm. Irv Lowenstein suddenly pulled alongside Mendel, stopped, and opened the passenger's side door as cigarette smoke drifted out into the November afternoon.

"It's getting cold," he said, "Get in."

Mendel looked into the darkened car before making a move.

"I'm Irv Lowenstein," Irv told him. "Sarah's brother."

Mendel nodded and then got in. The car was warm and smelled like new leather.

"So, how's Sarah, feeling okay?" Mendy asked as the car rolled forward.

"She's good," Irv said. "Thanks for asking. Got a nasty scrape on her forehead, though. Slipped and fell getting the milk last Sunday morning. Neighbor lady saw her."

"That's what I heard, too." Mendel smiled.

"Yeah. You know Orchard Street. Word gets around fast."

Mendel looked at Irv, but there was no expression on the law student's face as he drove.

"She told ya, huh?" Goldblatt finally asked him

"Yep," Irv kept his eyes on the street ahead of them, slowed and made a turn towards Manhattan. "Wanna have lunch?"

"Sounds good to me. My stomach is growling because it thinks my throat has been cut."

Irving laughed at his choice of words. "So, whaddja do with the Guinea, Mendy? The river?"

"Yeah, so what," Mendy growled. "Leave it alone, Irv, it's done... there's nothing more to talk about."

"But I'd like to do something for you," Irving pleaded. "The family appreciates your efforts, that's all. Not a big deal, I'd just like to be friends, that's all," Irv replied. "And, maybe I can help you, Mendy, even if you're not looking for it... and no offense intended."

Mendy quickly let him know that he thought Irving was an O.K. guy. "No offense taken, Irv, and we can all use some help from time to time." Mendy's voice was more relaxed now. "Seriously, though, Irving, thanks for the offer but I'm doing okay. I'm always looking for a little more dough than what a guy can make bustin' heads on the Lower East Side, but it'll come, though, I'm not too worried. It just takes time."

"So maybe I can help make it come faster, Mendy. After all, what you did for my sister a few nights ago was... well, you know what I'm talkin' about. She also said you were a perfect gentleman."

Mendy lit a cigarette and took a deep drag before answering. "Sarah's a good girl, Irv." he finally said. "She wouldn't lie to you about something as important as that."

"I know," Irv said. "But a brother has to make sure, that's why I asked you."

"That he does," Mendy agreed. "That he does."

They drove on in silence, and Irv finally pulled up in front of Tim McCarthy's Saloon, a popular neighborhood eatery. Opening the car door, they could hear the sounds of ragtime piano and men's boisterous laughter.

"I owe you a lot, Mendy," Irv said pushing his way through the swinging doors into the saloon.

"You don't owe me nothin'," Mendy said. "You'd have done the same for me, besides we're both Jews and gotta take care of each other. No one else will, that's for sure."

"That's one way to look at it," Irving said.

Mendy looked him right in the eyes after a second or so. "Com'on Irv, so what's really on your mind?"

"I've got some fairly good action going these days," he began slowly.

"So, I've heard," Mendy agreed.

"And it's getting bigger. I've just teamed up with some real smart Italian boys. Their old man sells hides to my Poppa... They have some great ideas, but they've had no experience running this type of operation, you know what I mean?"

Mendy didn't, but he nodded anyways.

"It's getting big enough so that somebody is eventually going to think about steppin' in and trying to take it over from us," Irv continued. "I can't be in two places at the same time, and besides, I'm in law school, and that makes it even more difficult. I need some help from a partner, somebody who people respect and will listen to. Someone who has some muscle."

Mendy took a drag on his cigarette, thinking carefully about Lowenstein's remarks.

"You're in law school..." he repeated. "So what're the craps games, something to tide you over until you're a lawyer?"

"No." Irv turned and looked him directly in the eyes. "I'm learning the law so I can figure the action better than most. Smarter. I figure that if you're going to break the law, you'd better know the law, understand how it works and how to make it work for you. Otherwise, you're just pissin' in the wind."

Mendy grinned at the expression. "And you want a partner, not just a hired hand?" he asked quietly.

"Hired hands will eventually turn on you," Irv replied. "I need someone in business with me as a partner."

"What share?"

"Fifty-fifty."

Mendy let out a low whistle, raising his eyebrows in surprise. He'd heard on the street what kind of money was involved in Irv's craps games. He wasn't expecting a full share but was happy with the offer. At least he knew Irving Lowenstein was a real mensch.

Irv had found himself thinking of Mendy as more than just muscle. The man had a certain presence that Irv knew could be useful; that's why he offered him a 50/50 split.

Mendy finally replied, "Well, I've got this union thing," he said. "I can't drop that."

"I wouldn't expect you to," Irv said nonchalantly. "This is extra. But remember, if we're partners, we're partners in everything including the union and the punch boards... and, that's the way it's gotta be."

Mendy nodded. "I understand and that's fair enough. You're a lawyer, huh?" He then quizzed, "What kind of lawyer you gonna be? A smart one?"

"I've had to work my ass off, but I'm at the top of my class at Columbia Law School which ain't too shabby, eh?"

Mendy's mind drifted back to what he'd been thinking about, how he'd need somebody smart to help him organize the takeover of the union. "You ever hear that expression, 'A good bargain makes two smiles'?" Mendy asked Irving.

"Sure," Irv grinned. "My Poppa uses that all the time."

"I think we've got one of those situations going for us right now," Mendy said, sitting down at an empty table.

McCarthy hurried over to the table to take their order. "Good day, gents. What'll it be this fine afternoon?"

Turning to Irving, Mendy said, dead seriously, "One thing clear, though. I'm buying the beer."

"You see me reaching for my wallet?" Irv asked as the two men gave their order to the burly red-faced owner.

* * *

The boys lost no time in establishing themselves in several different businesses over the next year, all of which were lucrative and some of which were actually legal. Most were not.

* * *

The key to the whole scheme had been the Lucci brothers' punchboard business, which once Irving was in partnership with them, had blossomed in all five boroughs and even a few dozen bars and grocery stores in Newark. Irv, Mendy and the Lucci brothers were operating better than two thousand boards a week around Metropolitan New York City, so that was four thousand dollars from punch boards alone before paying off the runners, and that didn't count the five hundred or so that Irving was netting off his craps games every week or the two hundred dollars each week from the organization of garment unions.

Of course, all of this money had to be collected by a handful of bagmen that Mendy had hired for that purpose, and inevitably some of it went into their pockets. A couple of the runners had faked robberies, but these were easily found out, and the sight of these guys hobbling around the Lower Eastside on crutches had quickly put an end to that. The remaining runners had been convinced to protect their cash even more vigorously.

On one occasion Lefty Yankovitch had been waylaid by five toughs with over four hundred dollars in his paper bag. Mendy had gone to see him in a private room at St. Ignatius Hospital, and Lefty had told him that the gang had been Irish paddies. It was clear that the Irish gangs were getting their courage back, trying to move in on Irving's territory again. After it happened twice more, Irving had sent word that he wanted a meeting with Liam O'Shannon, leader of the Green Hats, New York's leading Irish gang. O'Shannon agreed to a Saturday late afternoon meeting because he knew it was Shabbas, and that it would not only be inconvenient for the Jews, but also would show a lack of respect.

Lowenstein almost cancelled the meeting since he hadn't made a Friday night dinner with his family for the last two weeks, pleading a heavy caseload at the office. But he had always tried to make it up on Saturdays by sitting with them in schul, and then having lunch together at home, spending the rest of the day relaxing with conversation or a good book. But this Saturday, he had picked Mendy up in front of the candy store early in the afternoon in his Chevrolet. The two of them had driven down to the bowery and parked in front of Sullivan's Bar where the Green Hats held court, and then had gone upstairs to the private room where two Irish goons had frisked them. They took the Smith and Wesson.38 out of Mendy's waistband, and then escorted the Jews inside, where Liam O'Shannon and five of his lieutenants were waiting at a table heaped with glasses and a half-empty keg of beer.

Mendy took off his cap and put it on his lap as they all sat around the table, and Sean Corrigan, one of the gang members that Mendy had recognized from the street sneered, "Well, would you look at the sheenies. They're even taking off their caps. Maybe the Jew boys are learning some manners down at the sin-a-gog these days." He purposely mispronounced the word synagogue.

"Shut up, Sean," O'Shannon growled, giving him a hard look. "We've got business to discuss."

"How wouldja care to shut me up, Liam?" Corrigan said, as he laid an old-fashioned Colt revolver on the table in front of him.

O'Shannon sighed in frustration. "You're my wife's brother, and I gotta put up with your shit, Sean," he muttered, ignoring the gun. "But if you push me again, I'll be forced to pound the livin' bejejus outta ya. Do you hear me good, lad?" Now turning to Irv and Mendy, he smiled graciously. "Please forgive the bad manners of Sean, gentlemen. May I offer you a glass of beer?"

Both Irv and Mendy accepted his offer although neither touched their glasses.

"Whattsa matter?" Corrigan asked, his voice thick from the beer he'd already drunk. "Think you're too good to drink with us?"

"Sean!" O'Shannon cautioned, again.

Neither Irv nor Mendy had said anything, although Mendy had kept looking at the window behind Corrigan.

"Now, what can I do for you gentlemen?" O'Shannon had asked pleasantly.

"Gentlemen?" Corrigan interrupted again. "They're just a couple of damn kikes. We shouldn't even be drinkin' with 'em."

Mendy had glanced sharply at the window once again.

O'Shannon had sighed, rolling his eyes, and held a hand out toward Irving inviting him to speak.

"We've had a few of our collections knocked off in recent weeks," Irv said politely.

"Knocked off?" Corrigan had sneered. "Knocked off ya say? Why they went right into my damn pocket."

Mendy looked at the window again.

"So I've heard," O'Shannon had said, ignoring Sean's remarks. "How can my lads and I help you with that?"

"We were hoping an arrangement could be worked out to our mutual satisfaction," Irving said.

"Sure," Corrigan chuckled. "I'll arrange to beat the living shit out of you and your whole Hebe gang. And then maybe you'll arrange to get the hell out of New York."

"Sean..." O'Shannon had warned him once more.

"What, Liam? What now? Are you going to let some dirty, stinking Jews come in and run games right under our noses and do jack shit about it? You're going soft, damn you, and I've said it before."

Mendy looked out at the window again.

"And what the hell are you looking at?" Corrigan finally asked Mendy.

"I'm just trying to see if the sun has gone down yet because then the Shabbas would be over," Mendy had said, his voice low and even.

Corrigan leaned back in his chair and looked out the window himself. "Yeah," he said. "The fuckin' sun has just gone down. Now, what the fuck has that got to do with anyth...?"

And just moments later, the air had been shattered with a sharp report that had sounded like the crack of thunder in the small room. Corrigan had flown backwards as if someone had just taken a coal shovel to his face, landing against the wall behind him where he slid prone, leaving a thick smear of blood on the wall.

And then Mendy leveled the .45 automatic that he'd carried into the meeting, taped inside his leg aimed squarely at Liam O'Shannon's chest, and the Irish thug next to O'Shannon muttered, "Mother of Christ! Did you see that? He whacked him, right here at our own blessed table. He whacked him cold."

"Are we going to have trouble because of that?" Mendy asked O'Shannon.

"Trouble?" O'Shannon had shrugged, sipping his beer. "And would you know how many times in the last two years I would have given my eyeteeth just to do the same thing? No, Mr. Goldblatt. There's no trouble here. Try the beer."

And Mendy had, and so had Irving, and by the end of the evening they had worked out an arrangement by which about 75 members of the Green Hats would join with Irv and Mendy for ten percent of the gross off all the games they'd run. They also had picked up a guarantee of an additional 800 boards placed with Irish businesses. And Mendy had earned a new nickname – "Whacko" – although Irving never heard anyone use it to his face, and he seriously doubted that he ever would.

That had been just after Christmas. Since then, with the Green Hats help, Irving had added two strings of prostitutes to the growing crime empire, after making certain that all of the girls were of majority age, already hookers, and were on the street of their own free will.

Irving Lowenstein was in his office and had just hung up from telling Mendy Goldblatt about his new job as an Assistant District Attorney in Manhattan. Mendy seemed surprised that he was already assigned to the criminal law division because he had just graduated law school some three weeks ago. Irving wasn't surprised though, since he had been heavily recruited by the top firms in the city, including Davis, Polk et al and Sullivan Cromwell. Irving had negotiated a good deal for himself with Patrick Moran, the Chief Assistant D.A. Now Irving Lowenstein was in a big hurry to learn the ropes of criminal law.

Three weeks later, Irving Lowenstein opened his briefcase and took out three Corpus Secundum law books, setting them on the end of the bookshelf farthest from the steam radiator. He was fortunate because he had been assigned an office with a large window and a view of the Superior Court Building. He had already had three jury trials – an illicit solicitation by a prostitute, a shoplifting case, and the other a B & E, breaking and entering case. He had three convictions and had been in the D.A.'s office only a few weeks.

Those early convictions had certainly put him in the spotlight as rookie Assistant District Attorneys were only supposed to do research, warm seats and shuffle paper. Courtroom trials were left to those with at least a year's experience. But Irving's record in moot court competition during his senior year had been outstanding and that, together with an added incentive of a box of Cuban cigars and a bottle of single-malt-scotch, had convinced the senior member of the D.A.'s staff who assigned files to the young attorneys, to give him several simple cases just to get some courtroom experience.

Moot court had taught him the three elements of a successful prosecution: never speak unless necessary; never introduce questionable evidence; and, never ask a question to which you don't already know the answer. His first case was fairly easy. Even with her expensive attorney, it had taken him all of seventy-five minutes to convince the jury to render a verdict of guilty for the accused, a twice-convicted prostitute who'd been moonlighting to supplement her income. Now she was in upstate New York for the next five months, spending her days laundering sheets rather than spending her evenings making a living on them.

Irv's quick victories had been noted by the D.A. himself, and he had lifted the young prosecutor out of the cubbyhole down the hall and had given him his own small office. And the senior assistant D.A. who'd given him his chance had nearly broken his shoulder, slapping him on the back enthusiastically. "Outstanding job, Lowenstein. You've got a real career in this office."

Irv doubted it. Sitting in the wooden swivel chair, he smiled. When he'd gotten into his new office for the first time, the chair squeaked when he sat in it, but he'd told a secretary, and the secretary called the building maintenance department. The chair had been fixed in the next fifteen minutes for a $1.00 tip. He already knew the rules of the game and had started to establish the right connections to get things done outside of the usual routine.

* * *

First in his class at Columbia Law School... that was how he'd finished up his three years. The New York State Bar had done something unprecedented for third-year law students the previous winter. They'd allowed students eligible for military service to take the bar exam early. So Irv had taken and passed the New York Bar two months before he had even graduated. Then he'd sent Lefty Yankovitch, one of Mendy's enforcers, down to the federal building with fake identification to take the army physical for him. Lefty had a talent for breaking other people's legs, but he also was missing two fingers on his right hand – thus the name – so, of course, he had failed the physical. And so in addition to his certificate to practice law, Irving had also picked up a 4-F deferment from the military service on the way to earning his sheepskin.

Irving's mother had wept through the entire graduation ceremony at Columbia University. His father had beamed when he finally understood that his son was the star of the show. Sarah had spent hours fussing over Irving the morning of the ceremony, ironing his shirt for him, picking out his necktie and turning a deaf ear to his protests of, "Sis, would you please just let me get dressed." Both Seymour and Herbie had come to the ceremony with their new Kodak Brownie cameras that they'd acquired for the occasion; Irving didn't want to know how or where Herbie had acquired the camera.

Photographers from the Times and the Daily News got pictures of his big brother receiving his honors from the Dean of the Law School. Herbie lined the family up and asked one of the other grads to get a picture of the six of them, crowded elbow-to-elbow on the steps of the law school.

While Irving, who'd come out at the top of his class, had chosen to work in the D.A.'s office, he had received offers from most of the silk-stocking law firms up on Fifth Avenue that were lined up to recruit such a prospect. Generally, with a last name like Lowenstein, the New York society firms would not dream of offering a Jew a job as an associate. However, they would make an exception for Irving Lowenstein. He would be the token Jew.

It didn't matter, however, because Irving didn't even consider their offers. He wasn't there to launch a brilliant legal career. He was there to make all the right connections in New York City for the next couple of years or so.

* * *

Irving straightened his law books on the office shelf and thought about that night down at the bowery. The fact that he knew about the situation involving Mendy and the Irisher's death had arguably made him an accessory to murder, and he'd often wondered how he would feel about that because he knew he might have to face the situation some day. The thing with Sarah and the Italian guy in the alley had convinced him of that, and besides it came with the territory. He never had to account for Corrigan's murder because his body had been dumped into a bridge caisson that was being poured on the East River by the Green Hats. Corrigan's sister was told by two of the gang members that her dear brother, Sean, had enlisted in the Merchant Marines to lay low until the flap over some of the robberies he'd committed had blown over.

Irving nodded and smoothly rocked in his chair again. Right now, he had other more important things to worry about, like opening up two new speakeasies.

Chapter Six
June 1917

"Please, if I can just speak to the Assistant District Attorney in charge of the case, I'm sure I can straighten this whole thing out."

The New York Police sergeant at the front desk crossed his arms and glowered at the tall, muscular man before him. Dark suit coat, dark trousers, a white shirt with no necktie, his black felt hat in one hand, but he still had a black yarmulke perched atop his head of curly black hair that appeared like a fertile garden that hadn't been tended for years. The man looked like any of a thousand other Jews you might see shuffling in and out of the garment district or the diamond market on 47th Street.

"Listen, mister," the cop began, an Irish Catholic and suspicious of anyone who was not a police officer, "It's like I told ya, I called over to the station across the street for the kid. They just brought him in half an hour ago. He's still in the holdin' cell. They ain't even done bookin' him. There's no A.D.A. assigned to him yet, so I ain't got nobody for ya to talk to. You understand?"

The tall, muscular man scowled. "Well I can go over there and at least speak with the sergeant, can't I?"

"Not until they're done bookin' him."

"But…"

"But nothin', that's the way they do things around here, buddy. Ya gotta follow the rules. Know what I mean?"

The man with the yarmulke took a deep breath in resignation, but said nothing in total frustration.

Two steps past the reception desk on his way to the backroom, walking with Ronnie Pelavin from the D.A.'s office, Irv Lowenstein stooped short. The guy standing in front of the sergeant looked awfully familiar. Irv grabbed Ronnie's arm and then they backpedaled to the front desk.

"Barney?" Irv asked. "Barney Green."

The man in the yarmulke turned and looked at him blankly, like he didn't recognize him. "Do I know you, sir?" he asked cautiously.

"No," Irv grinned. "But you made me a few bucks at the Garden about two years back."

"Oh…that," Barney nodded.

"Name's Irv…Irv Lowenstein," Irv said, shaking his hand. Then turning to the man who'd been walking with him, he called, "Hey Ronnie. C'mon over here and shake hands with Barney Green, the best light heavyweight that ever got in the ring."

"That so?" Irv's gray-suited companion walked over and vigorously pumped Green's hand, smiling.

"So Barney," Irv asked. "Whaddaya now, a Rabbi?"

"Not yet," Barney said, deeply blushing. "I'm a rabbinical student and have about six months to finish up before I'm ordained. I'm just down here trying to help out a neighbor kid."

"Kid from Brooklyn got run in on a misdemeanor," the sergeant explained to Lowenstein. "Had a coffee and doughnut at a diner uptown and skipped without paying. The beat cop heard the owner yelling and collared him."

"He's a yeshiva student, just in from Germany," Barney explained, talking to Irv, and gesturing with his hands. "He said that he left the money for his donut and coffee, plus a little for the waiter, next to his plate. Somebody must have picked it up before the waiter got to the table."

"Not too smart for New York," Irv said, shaking his head, chuckling. Then, turning to the sergeant, he asked, "What's goin' on, Francis? Things so slow at the precinct that we're hauling kids downtown for skippin' on a ten cent tab?"

"You know how it is, Mr. Lowenstein," the big cop said, shrugging. "The owner was right there making the complaint. And I guess he's gotten stiffed a lot lately."

"More likely," Irv mused. "He's got some wisecrackers hangin' around the joint, pocketing the table change when the waiters' backs are turned. Ronnie," he asked his companion, "would it be jake with you if we had lunch tomorrow instead of today?"

"Sure thing. I have to be at my doctor's in about 45 minutes anyway," the gray-suited man replied, shaking Irv's hand and then turning to Barney before taking his leave. "Nice tomeetcha, champ," Ronnie said sticking out his hand.

"So why didn't the kid just pay the guy at the diner again?" Irv asked the rabbinical student.

"He's on a tight monthly budget," Barney explained. "His family sends money over to me from Germany for him every month. That's why he was on this side of the river this morning. He was coming to see me, to pick it up. He had already left all his money on the table. Coffee and a donut was all he could afford."

"I see," Irv nodded. "What's the kid's name?"

"Fritz…Fritz Silverman, but everybody calls him Freddie."

"Okay!" Irv turned back to the desk sergeant. "Francis, is it all right if I use your phone?"

Five minutes later, after placing four calls in a low muffed voice, Irv hung up the phone and turned back to Barney Green, smiling. "Okay, we're all squared away now," Irv said. "I called the booking sergeant and got the restaurant owner's number. Then I called and told him that we'd have somebody watch the place and see if we could catch the momzers that are robbing his tables. Based on that, he's dropping the charges so your boy is clear."

"I'll pay for the restitution," Barney said, nodding.

"Naw, that won't be necessary," Irv assured him. "It's only ten cents." He didn't add that his third call had been to Mendy, who was sending a couple of the Green Hats down to the diner with orders to watch the place and leave a few bruises on whoever was robbing the tables. "Freddie will be about fifteen minutes in getting the charges dropped and processed," Irv told Barney. "I still have to grab some lunch. Wanna join me?"

Ten minutes later, the two men were standing shoulder deep at Stein's Delicatessen, right around the corner from Police Headquarters in a swarm of lawyers, plainclothes detectives and businessmen, most in dress suits, all wearing hats. Cigar smoke hung in the air like a London fog, and the only clear floor space was around each of the six brass spittoons that sat next to the foot rails of the crowded lunch bar. Every once in awhile, one of the detectives rid himself of a wad of chewing tobacco by a direct hit of the closest spittoon.

Irv shouldered up to the bar and ordered two pastramis on rye with cole slaw, a Schlitz beer for him and a cup of tea for Barney.

He laid a silver dollar on the bar top, told the bartender to keep the change and handed Barney his tea. Irving grabbed two thick ceramic plates with over-stuffed sandwiches on them, and then they wound their way around to the back of the restaurant where a group of businessmen was just leaving a corner booth.

"So, Barney," Irv said, first taking a dill pickle out of the wooden bowl placed in the center of both tables. "What's with the change of occupations? You were a shoo-in to be the next light heavyweight champion of the world."

"I don't want to be the world's next light heavyweight champion boxer," Barney said, smiling slightly. "I want to be the world's light heavyweight champion Rabbi, or at least a contender."

"What caused the change of heart?"

"You were there, my friend. At Madison Square Garden, the Golden Gloves Championship Fight with Mick Fitzpatrick. I paralyzed him, Irv. Hit him so hard that when he fell and his head whipped back and hit the floor, it bruised the spinal cord."

"But I thought I read that he recovered from that. Didn't he?" Irv asked.

Barney nodded. "Enough to walk, thank God," he agreed. "Not enough to ever box again though. I went to visit him in the hospital the day after the fight."

"I see," Irv said. "He was pretty bitter, I bet?"

Barney shook his head. "Quite the contrary," he said. "Mick assured me that he'd put himself there, that I was more than a match for him, and his manager should have thrown in the towel. But, he was trying to get enough distance to satisfy the bookies. You said you won money on me. You know how it is?"

Irv nodded.

"And even though Mick didn't know if he'd ever fully recover then," Barney continued, "He told me he wanted me to go on. I remember his exact words; 'You ain't like the rest of the palookas in this game, Barney. You're an okay guy with some class. You got real moxie. Go win yourself the title, you deserve it.'"

"So why not do it?" Irving asked, puzzled.

Barney shrugged. "What Mick said got me thinking," he told his new friend. "That maybe I was different from the rest of the guys in the fight game because I wasn't supposed to be a boxer. Maybe I was just put here on earth to lift heads, rather than bust them. So I thought about it. I prayed about it. And, in the end it was clear. This is what God wanted for me. That's all, nothing more."

"That's it? No angle?"

Barney Green shook his head. "There is no angle in becoming a Rabbi, Mr. Lowenstein," he said smiling.

"Well then mazel tov, Barney," Irv said, lifting his beer in a toast.

"Thank you, Mr. Lowenstein."

"Irv, please."

"Thank you, Irv."

The two men munched their sandwiches while male voices all around them told jokes, laughed, and carried on in all the ways that men carry on during lunch in a delicatessen. Irv looked across the table at his luncheon companion and cleared his throat with a swallow of beer.

"You know, Barney, I don't meet many straight shooters in my line of work."

"I would imagine," Barney said.

You don't know the half of it, Irv thought silently.

"So where are you going once you're ordained?" he asked the rabbinical student.

"That's the question I think about everyday," Barney said. "Most young Rabbis work with the older ones; men of God who are getting on in years, assisting them, helping them. But, I'm several years older than the average rabbinical student. In fact, I'm already older than most young Rabbis. And, I don't think God has called on me to assist an older Rabbi by straightening out his study, as worthy as that service may be. I believe that my calling is to help people...ordinary people, but..." He left the sentence unfinished.

"But a horse can't hardly shit in the Lower Eastside without hitting a Rabbi's leg," Irv said, grinning wryly.

Barney smiled.

"Not exactly the words I would use to express the same sentiment," he said, laughing some. "At least not in schul on Shabbas, but yes. Your general idea is correct. The Lower Eastside does seem to have more than its share of Rabbis."

"So why not move across to Brooklyn or maybe even uptown?"

"Uptown?" Barney shook his head. "No. There are already enough Rabbis for rich people. I wouldn't feel comfortable there."

"Then maybe you should consider staying around here?" Irv said, "Downtown. You'd be different than the other Rabbis already here in the Lower Eastside, just think of it. A Jew gets off the boat, and he usually goes to Brooklyn, but why? Usually because he has family there. He's not looking for a schul. He'll go where his relatives are. But down here, half the people have sold everything they had owned in Europe just to get here, and now that they're here, they don't have a clue what comes next. They go to Delancey Street because some customs officer on Ellis Island told them that's where the Jews live in New York. Jews don't move to the Lower Eastside. The Atlantic Ocean washes them upon the shore, and they go to work in sweatshops, get in financial hock and can't get out, so they stay. They're the true lost tribe, Barney. Come to think of it, they need someone like you, honestly."

Barney nodded, finishing his sandwich, thinking about what Irv Lowenstein had just said. He knew that Lowenstein was from the Lower Eastside, because he could hear it in his accent, even with the Manhattan lawyer's polish and his deliberate attempt to minimize it.

"You might have something there, Irv," he agreed. "I mean, I might not be able to move into an established schul right away, but maybe a storefront, some chairs, a bimah, a place to daven."

"There ya go," Irv said. "Now you're cookin', Rabbi Barney."

"If the rent's not too high."

"If the rent was high, Delancey Street would be a desert," Irv chuckled. "Nobody could afford anything. Don't worry, Barney. I'm sure you'll be able to find something, and the folks there will help you, too. They don't have much, but if it's for God, they'll give until it hurts."

He didn't say it, but in his head he ran through what it would probably cost to put Barney Green in a storefront and run a schul out of it for a year or so. A thousand bucks would probably do it. And he and Mendy probably spent nearly that much every month just taking broads out to dinner and having a few laughs. He didn't know why, but he liked this ex-fighter who'd decided to give his life to God and his people. And who knows, Irv thought to himself, getting Barney going in his own schul might be a good idea, sort of like an insurance policy with the Almighty. He made his mind up right there to do it on his own. It made Irving feel good, thinking about Rabbi Barney Green. It warmed his kiskas, insides, thinking that maybe Irving Lowenstein was an alright guy. Irv finished his sandwich and beer and checked his watch. "They should have had time to finish up the paperwork by now," he told Barney. "Let's go spring your young yeshiveh bocher, your schoolboy from the slammer."

Barney wiped his mouth with a paper napkin and nodded. "Sure," he said, adding, "You're a good man, Irving."

"I wish that were true," Irv replied, laughing off his words. He grabbed his hat and guided the rabbinical student out of the crowded bar and back onto the warm June streets of New York, where they headed for the precinct station.

* * *

Across town, Lou Kravitz was just getting back to his office at Solomon & Sons after his late lunch, one that he'd taken alone walking the streets of the city. In truth, he could have lunched in the office. Lou brought his lunch, a sandwich and an apple wrapped in a cloth napkin in his briefcase every day. He was renting a room from a friend of his uncle's, widow Levine, and she packed it for him each day for an extra five cents, in addition to the two-dollar-a-week rent.

Usually the sandwich was chicken, roast beef or cheese, sometimes salami. Today Lou wasn't really sure what it had been, maybe tuna fish. He'd eaten it, but he couldn't remember. He'd eaten it while he was walking. He'd been heading toward Central Park, a destination that he had never quite reached because the streets of New York City at midday were a constant press of jostling people especially on a warm midweek business day. Men in hats weaving determinedly through the crowd or walking with friends, laughing on the way to or from luncheon appointments, women carrying department store boxes tied with string, vendors pushing carts selling hot buns and flavored shaved ice. The streets had been a constant kaleidoscope of color and action, but he had missed it all, lost in deep thought.

The job at Solomon & Sons had not turned out to be nearly as good as he'd expected it to be initially. Sure, he'd been part of a lot of important meetings and had met several wealthy clients, but it had always been in the company of the senior partners who had introduced him as a former University of Pennsylvania basketball star who'd come to work for their firm. His job was to shake hands, nod his head and smile while the clients told him how they'd seen him make the winning point at this game or that.

The fact that he had an MBA from Wharton, and that his professors had considered his Master's thesis outstanding enough to have it published, didn't seem to be important.

Abe Solomon, the senior partner of the firm, had come to Lou's office only twice since he'd arrived almost two years earlier. Abe had looked around Lou's tiny cubicle, which was just barely a window office, taking in brokerage banks and year-end statements from large companies on the bookshelves, the single green-globed desk lamp and the empty blotter. "Where are your trophies?" he asked, looking surprised. "And some of your game photographs?"

"My trophies?" Lou had responded, confused.

"Sure," Solomon had told him. "You know All American, game balls, player-of-the-year awards, most valuable player, that sort of thing."

"Oh! Well I have some of those at my room where I'm staying, but most of them are back home at my folk's house."

"Well send for them," Solomon had replied. "You don't want to hide those things, Lou. How're people suppose to know who you are if you don't display them in a prominent place?"

"Well, there's that," Lou had replied, proudly nodding at his MBA diploma from Wharton, hanging on the wall in a large black frame.

"Oh sure," Solomon had nodded, barely giving the sheepskin a glance. "Lots of folks have an MBA, but not many were All American basketball players. Send for the trophies, all right, Lou?"

Lou had written to his mother, and she had sent him a few things like the Look Magazine All American Certificate, an autographed game ball, a couple of most valuable player trophies, and the "P" from his letter sweater framed with a couple of photographs of his teammates.

The reason for Abe Solomon's second visit to his office disturbed Lou the most. The old man had been sitting there waiting for him at 8:30 when Lou arrived for work one morning. "Lou," he begun, "We don't like to make a big display of religious items in our office," he said looking at the gold-plated menorah his mother had also recently sent him.

"Religious items?"

"That," Solomon had said, nodding toward the menorah.

"Oh," Lou had smiled. "My father brought it over from Germany to England. It's been in the family for years, and I really like it. The folks gave it to me in college for luck."

"Well I'd like you to put it in your briefcase and take it home when you go tonight."

Lou blinked totally confused.

"It's not that I have anything against being Jewish, Lou," Solomon said somberly. "I'm a Jew, myself, of course. So are several of the partners in the firm, but it's just that we don't want to do anything that might upset our...our gentile clients."

Lou had almost smiled. "Well, it's just a gift from the folks," Lou had begun to explain again.

"All the more reason not to leave it here," Solomon said somberly. "What if something were to happen to it? The firm could not be held responsible, of course."

Lou shook his head again. Here, just a few weeks ago, Mister Solomon had twisted Lou's arm to bring some college basketball mementoes from his senior year at college, but now was going on as if the office had become a synagogue because of one religious item. In fact, Solomon had nodded curtly, risen and left before Lou had realized that what he had just heard had been more than just a strong suggestion, it was an order, to remove the religious artifact from his office.

That was when he'd started noticing it: how when clients invited partners to parties or their homes on Friday evenings, nobody ever said that they couldn't come because they were keeping the Shabbas. If it was a high holiday, they might refuse but say that they had a previous commitment to attend another dinner party.

They were in New York where Yiddish had crept into the everyday language of the city decades before. Even the shiksah secretaries in the office would complain that the weather was schlect or talk about schlepping their packages home after Christmas shopping, maybe even calling someone a putz. But the associates were instructed to use proper English at all times. It was as if, Lou thought to himself, he had entered the Society of Secret Jews. Everybody knew what they were. "Solomon" certainly wasn't a name you'd find in the social blue book, but they all acted as if they had come over on the Mayflower together, or something. Lou thought that they must be ashamed of being Jews in a white Protestant society. It was certainly not what he had in mind when he'd come to New York to join the firm. Lou was lost in this thought, hanging up his hat, when the phone rang. "Good afternoon," he'd said, picking up the phone and putting the receiver to his ear. "This is Lou Kravitz."

"The terror of Sigma Alpha Mu?" asked the voice on the other end of the line.

"Hank!" Lou exclaimed. "Mr. Phi Delta Theta himself. You old dog! How are you?"

Hank was Henry Theodore Van Dyke, Jr. of the Westchester Van Dykes, heir apparent to a considerable fortune in steel mills, lumber, steamship companies and firearm manufacturers. The latter had become, in the wake of the recent war in Europe, something of a license to print money, adding to a fortune that even a playboy such as Henry Van Dyke would be hard-pressed to spend in several lifetimes. Actually, Van Dyke was a former playboy. Hank had met Lou during their freshman year together at Pennsylvania. They were dormitory roommates, Van Dyke having just arrived after flunking out of his freshman class at Harvard. Lou Kravitz had pledged the Sammy House but wasn't eligible to move in until his sophomore year.

"You'll make varsity this year," Hank had told Lou. "And any fraternity house would be crazy not to want you. Don't you see that? You should rush some other fraternity houses like the Sigma Chi, Beta or even the Phi Delta Thetas.

That's when Lou Kravitz decided to pledge a Jewish fraternity. Lou's work ethic and studiousness had been the only thing that had kept the two of them in school for the next four years. He did his own work, tutored Hank through his classes and practiced basketball four hours each day. He spent the evenings before exams quizzing the likeable Hank Van Dyke on subjects for which the latter had not the slightest bit of aptitude.

Van Dyke had only really come into his own after the sun went down. He was a true night person. They would begin the evening with Hank buying rounds at the local bars or clubs and end with Lou helping the stumbling Hank home after he'd emerged from the upstairs window of whatever sorority house or working-girl's rooming house he'd ended up in. His appetite for women had seemingly been insatiable. He even picked up girls for Lou, and when Lou quietly refused, determined to save that part of his life for marriage, Henry generally ended up in bed with both girls.

He could have any girl he wanted, that is, until he met Martha Donovan.

Eighteen years old, she was a freshman in college and supplemented her meager monthly check from her parents by being a barmaid at her uncle's pub, the Shamrock Tavern in downtown Philadelphia. Martha was a stunning auburn-haired Irish beauty with light green eyes, legs like Greek sculpture, firm breasts and a waist that a man could encircle with his hands…if she were to let a man touch her, which she most often did not.

Martha came from working class Irish stock. Her father, a coal miner, had come over on the boat from County Cork, and her mother had grown up on a farm about 20 miles outside the City of Dublin. Neither had been completely literate when they arrived in the United States, but they had worked hard and scraped to provide an education for their only daughter. After they both died from a recent flu epidemic, Martha had moved into her uncle's modest home in a middle-class section of the city. She'd been taking college business school classes in her spare time when Lou and Hank met her at the Shamrock Tavern, and clearly like most women, she had been taken with Hank's good looks and social charm. She even went with him to dinner on more than one occasion, but for months that was all she had done. On their third date, she had allowed him a goodnight kiss at her uncle's door, but she had firmly moved Henry's hand away from her breast. She and Hank had been dating for more than a year; he'd enticed her to the Berkshires for a winter holiday, promising two rooms and feigning surprise when the hotel gave them one suite. Henry had had his way, but when he got back to the fraternity house, rather than bragging of his conquest as he had with every other girl he had ever met, he had simply told anyone who would listen, including Lou, "She's an angel, a genuine Irish angel. I'll never find another like her and that's for sure. I'm gonna marry her."

Eight months later, the inevitable had happened. It was the end of Hank's senior year in college. One Friday night, the boys had gone to the Shamrock where Martha had insisted on keeping her job, despite Hank's offer to support her. Tears had come to her eyes the moment that Henry and Lou entered the crowded, smoky room, and she'd taken Henry into the back room for about ten minutes. The look on his face when he'd emerged had said it all. She'd been to the doctor that morning and was two months pregnant.

They'd gotten married the following weekend. There hadn't been any communication with Hank's parents about their wedding. He'd know that their reaction would have been to pay the girl off, send her to a discrete physician in a private clinic in Vermont, and forbid their son to ever see her again. Hank never even gave that option a second thought because he adored her and was deeply in love with the stunning Irish lass; and, besides, the thought of having children with Marty had thrilled him.

So the ceremony had taken place before a Justice of the Peace in Darien, Connecticut with Lou standing up as the sole witness and best man. They'd had dinner afterwards, and during the toast Henry had said, "You are my true best friend, old sport. So promise me something, eh? If anything ever happens to me, promise to take care of my girl. Okay, Lou," he said holding Marty's hands between his.

And Lou, looking at the most beautiful woman that he had ever seen in his life, had nodded and said that he would.

"Alive and creaking," Hank responded, his voice chuckling on the other end of the phone. "But can you believe that I'll be twenty-three next week, you know?"

"Same as me," Lou said. "How's Martha?"

"She's doing great," Henry said. "You know Marty, she can't stay down for long."

Lou said nothing. He knew what Hank was referring to because Martha was having a difficult pregnancy. She insisted on working at the Shamrock over Hank's strong objections.

"And your family?" Lou asked.

"Oh God!" Henry began. His family had been outraged when they'd discovered that Henry had not only gotten married in secret, but that he was married to an Irish Catholic working girl, miles beneath their social position. They'd pressed for an annulment, but Henry wouldn't hear of it. They'd even tried cutting Henry off from a trust account. But in defiance, he had taken a job as a laborer at a steel mill owned by one of his father's competitors. Horrified, the family had quickly restored his trust funds and given him a job with the family. "They sent my sister to visit us," Hank said. While most of the Van Dykes still lived in Westchester, Henry and Martha lived in a four-room apartment on Park Avenue, just a short walk from his family's offices on Madison Avenue. "Mary Beth finally admitted that she was there to observe Marty's table manners. I told her to go back and tell Mom and Dad that Martha and I are heathens and eat in the nude with our fingers," Hank grinned.

Lou chuckled at the thought.

"How're things with you, old boy?" Hank then asked seriously.

Lou paused. Henry Van Dyke's contacts had everything in the world to do with getting him the job at Solomon & Sons. He debated saying that things were just fine, but he stopped himself. In seven years of friendship, he and Henry Van Dyke had never lied to one another. Not once. Lou was not about to start now.

"Not so great, Hank," Lou began. Keeping his phone voice low since the office door was open and closing it would just attract attention. He told Van Dyke about how the senior partners never used him as anything more than a greeter-window dressing only. He left out the part about the menorah, but made it clear that Solomon & Sons were really not using his business skills to their fullest extent. In fact, his skills weren't being used at all.

"Hmmm," Henry mused. "Well, it sounds as if that's two of us."

"Two of us?" Lou asked.

"My family's offices," Henry said. "Both of my cousins are vice presidents now. One of them is being groomed to take over the steel business, even though father always bragged that it was going to be my job some day. But I'm not even vice president or on any of the boards. It's the Van Dyke way of showing Martha that I'm not going to be part of the dynasty, in hopes that she'll dump me and look elsewhere."

"Then they don't know Martha," Lou said.

"They don't want to know Martha," Henry replied.

"So what are you going to do?"

"Enlist in the military as an officer."

"What?" Lou almost dropped the phone.

"There's a war on, sport. Don't you know?" Hank laughed. "I figure that if I go in the Army in the next week or so as an officer, the family will have more contact with Martha. There won't be any way around it. It's either that or it will look as if they have no interest in their daughter-in-law, which they don't, but you know my family, Lou. Appearances are everything. And you know Marty. Who can be in contact with her, day in and day out, without loving her, especially now that she's pregnant?"

"But Hank, four years in the Army?"

"It won't be four years," Henry interrupted. "It'll be one. Two at the most. They're doing duration-of-conflict enlistments right now, and you read the papers. The Kaiser's running out of steam as we speak. I wouldn't be surprised if it's all over by next July."

"And then what?" Lou asked.

"And then I come home the conquering hero, hunchbacked from all the medals on my chest, and the family's in love with Martha and their new grandchild," Henry told him. "Or even if the old stone faces are not in love with Martha, they'll have to make me president of the steel company or the railroad or something to protect the baby. They won't have a choice. If they keep me down, it'll look as if they're punishing me for signing up to do my duty and again, they'll never do that for appearances sake."

Lou was silent, listening to his friend.

"In fact," Henry continued. "If old Abe Solomon is treating you like some kind of freak show, why don't you come along with me? I'm going in as a first lieutenant. You've got your MBA, and you'll be a captain in no time. I'll make a call and have Mister Solomon hold a place for you, with seniority. When you get back, they'll have to treat you right or they'll look bad to me and my family."

"I don't know," Lou mused.

"What's to know?" Henry asked. "Do you think Abe Solomon's going to risk pissing off the president of Van Dyke Steel? Or the Hudson and Allegheny Railroad?"

Lou said nothing, pondering the possibilities.

"Let's do it," Henry said. "Let's sign up together. Why not?"

Lou looked at the signed, half-deflated basketball and the trophies on his bookshelf, at the bare spot on his desk where the tiny menorah had once stood. As they said their goodbyes and he hung up the phone, Lou thought to himself, *Why not? Why not, indeed?*

Chapter Seven
London – Summer 1917

Big Ben was slowly tolling 7 a.m., as the plain black Model-T stopped before a nondescript brownstone building, the duplicate of hundreds of other buildings lining the streets of London's West End. Lou Kravitz tugged his overseas cap with captain's bars closer to his head and stepped out of the car, smelling the smoke of the city and the faint salty scent of the distant Thames. Thanking the driver, he straightened his Sam Brown belt over his uniform jacket and walked up the steps, where he returned the salute of an armed sentry.

All of the business with saluting and military formality still felt awkward to Kravitz, who even as a star basketball player in college, had taken pains to treat every member of his team as his equal, right down to the water boy. Now he ate at an officer's mess, relaxed at an officer's club and, as an officer, was quartered at the Five-Star Savoy Hotel in fashionable Mayfair, a considerable step up from the drafty barracks where his enlisted men slept. Indeed, he had initially felt uneasy at being put in command over men who had years of service under their cartridge belts after he had completed only ninety days of Officer's Training School in Fort Benning, Georgia. Then, Kravitz discovered that it was the master sergeants who actually ran the army. He was simply a lower rung on the chain of commissioned command and once he had discovered that basic truth, he'd felt better about the whole business.

Business. That's what the Army really was – a business. It ran on supplies and capital, was highly dependent on manpower and morale and, like a business, it prevailed by overcoming its competitors. That an army did this with manpower, shot and shell, rather than sales and market share, mattered not one iota in the long run. As Napoleon had learned in the Russian winter, deftness of command and brilliance of strategy didn't mean a thing if you couldn't match supply and demand, couldn't move the beans and biscuits to where the troops were. Armies rallied on the basis of courage, but they prevailed on the basis of supply and inventory. It was hopelessly unromantic, but it was absolutely true.

And it was especially apparent in this nondescript office in the Old West End, where Kravitz had been assigned to fight the war. Because the uniform of the day required all officers overseas to wear gaiters and puttees, he wore them, and they stayed every bit as spotless as the brilliantly shined boots they protected. And because regulations said he had to, he still carried a sidearm daily – the Colt .45 automatic that the Army had adopted six years earlier, and with which Kravitz had just barely qualified in his training. The only shots he'd heard during his entire month in Europe had been the firing of the daily noonday cannon gun at the King's Own brigade barracks, near Buckingham Palace.

Pulling off his cap, Kravitz took the stairs, two at a time, and heartily greeted the corporal typing a requisition order in the outer office. Lou was glad that at least in the office they would not have to exchange salutes, as they were indoors and neither was wearing a hat.

"Any correspondence come in, Jack?" Kravitz asked the NCO, non-commissioned officer.

The young man nodded, saying, "Yes sir, a stack of them. I've put them all in your basket, sir."

Kravitz nodded back, went in, lit a cigarette, and tossed a smoking match into the empty fireplace. Putting his cap over a bust of Shakespeare left by the office's previous occupant, a faculty member for a nearby public school, he settled into a padded wooden desk chair and noted, as he did every morning, that the office the Army had given him in London was half again as large as the one provided him by Solomon & Sons on Wall Street.

Lou still had trouble believing he'd actually left the firm to take a commission in the Army. He hadn't worried too much about what his aged parents would think about him leaving a Wall Street brokerage house to put on a uniform. The efforts of his uncle, his dad's youngest brother, along with Henry Van Dyke, a former classmate at college, had helped get him the job with the Solomon firm. Lou had thought it would be a good idea to discuss his enlistment with Uncle Harry before going down to talk to the recruiter at Union Station.

Amazingly enough, his uncle had welcomed the news by encouraging his enlistment. The old man's insurance business was losing customers because of the war in Europe. "They hear Kravitz, and they think German," Lou's uncle had told him sadly. And when Lou had asked what he could do, the sharp old New Yorker had replied, "Just what you're thinking of doing, enlist. Give your old Poppa a reason to hang a star in his front window. Show these putzes that the Kravitz's have a young man in the family who is off doing his military duty. This war can't last more than two more years, and then it will all be over. I'll talk to Abe Solomon, too and square it with him. Your same job will be waiting for you after the war."

After both Van Dyke and Harry Kravitz had spoken to Abe Solomon about Lou, Solomon had gone one better and told Lou that he would count his time in service toward his seniority, meaning that he would move closer to a full partnership despite his absence. Lou had jumped at the chance, enlisting the next week in OTS, the army's Officer Training School program.

Lou finished his cigarette, smiled his thanks as the corporal brought in a fresh cup of coffee, and turned his attention to the paperwork that had arrived overnight from the front. Most were weekly updates of battalion food and military supplies. Some were requisitions for fuel allotments. But one caught his eye. He saw the salutation, From: Henry T. Van Dyke, Major, U.S.A., 19 Inf. Bat., and smiled, separating this report from the rest. He reminisced about how he and Henry had been good friends in college. And, as a matter of fact, Henry had introduced Lou to Martha, who was now his wife, almost as soon as he had met her.

Henry and he had gone through training together and then shipped over to Europe together on the RMS Carpathian, the aging passenger liner that had become famous when it picked up survivors the morning after the Titanic disaster. Now it had been converted into a troop ship, albeit one with better accommodations than some of the smoke-belching monstrosities that had been pressed into service to transport young men overseas to their stations and, in many cases, their deaths from German submarine patrols.

Lou and Henry had roomed together at the Savoy Hotel, gone out drinking and carousing with English barmaids together, Henry always finding an excuse to depart early and leave the attractive females to Lou. They even sat together at the officer's mess. It had started to look like a fine war, but then Henry had been sent to the front to coordinate the supply lines.

That had been about six weeks earlier. The two young men had gone on a first-class bender the night before Henry left for the Continent. Staggering past Nelson's monument at two in the morning, Henry had made Lou again promise that he would take care of Martha if anything happened to him in the war, and Lou had agreed before carrying his friend to a hansom cab for the ride back to the Savoy Hotel. Lou had early duty the next morning and hadn't been able to see Henry board the troop carrier to Western Europe.

After Hank left, with communications restricted to priority matters, the two friends had lost contact with one another. But now, here was a communication from Henry from somewhere in Belgium, probably Brussels, because that was one of the centers of activity for the allies. Sipping his coffee in anticipation, Lou broke the envelope seal and read the single page message.

"NEW YORK EXPEDITERS REPORT WINTER UNIFORMS DELAYED DUE TO SEAMSTRESS WORKER'S STRIKE STOP. NEED PRODUCTION NOW IF SHIPMENT TO ARRIVE THROUGH ENGLAND IN TIME FOR COLD WEATHER STOP. WE NEED FOUR MONTH'S TIME STOP. COLONEL BLACKWELL CONCERNED WITH POSSIBLE SHORTAGE STOP. ANYTHING YOU CAN DO FROM YOUR END QUESTION MARK. IF YOU CAN ASSIST MAYBE COMMAND WILL POST ME BACK TO NEW YORK STOP. MARTHA SENDS GOOD NEWS THAT WE NOW HAVE A HEALTHY SON, HENRY THEODORE VAN DYKE, III. WE ARE BOTH VERY EXCITED. APPRECIATE YOUR HELP. STOP. HANK."

Grinning at the good news, Lou wondered how Henry had gotten the signals corps officer to put in the part about Martha having a baby. No doubt a bottle of scotch on the right desk had done the trick.

Lou read the communiqué again and pursed his lips. A seamstress workers' strike – seamstress workers? What was that fellow's name again on Delancey Street back in Brooklyn?

"Jack," he called to his NCO. "Bring your steno pad in here. We need to send a cable to...to a Mister Goldblatt, Mister Mendel Goldblatt, with the, uh...wait...the International Seamstress Worker's Union.

* * *

Mendy tipped the delivery boy with a quarter and left the union hall, heading back out into the cacophony of sounds and smells of a Thursday morning in New York's Lower Eastside. He read the cable twice and then stuffed it back into his pocket. A wagon load of horse manure was being pushed down the street by a white-clad street cleaner. Another man pushed a pushcart of pots and pans in the opposite direction, and children, just freed from school for vacation, already had handball and kick-the-can games going up and down the block.

Mendy left the noise to step into a diner where he ordered coffee and a poppy seed hard roll. The coffee tasted good. He'd not yet been to bed and needed a quick boost. The games were running late into the night now, some didn't break up until near dawn, and Mendy made it a point of staying up until every runner had reported in, and the winnings were safely locked in his office safe back at the Moulin Rouge, the first speakeasy they had purchased about a year ago. It was one of the newest and most popular speakeasies in the city. He'd go back to the club in the afternoon, after a few hours sleep, divide out the monies that each game would need, and take the balance of the cash to five different banks where each account operated under a different business name. But he still had plenty of union action, so he made a point of stopping in at the union hall every morning. Besides, the salary he drew amounted to another $1,000 a week.

Irv arrived at the diner punctually at eight, looking fresh and dapper in his immaculate suit. Unlike Mendy, he'd already had a good night's sleep, or at least five hours of it, but Mendy did not begrudge him this. Irv was due down at the D.A.'s office in about an hour, and he'd do his part with the games that evening; and, even find time to duck into the club for an hour or so just to check things out. And then take over full-time, as was his custom, when the weekend came. This half hour or so at the diner was the time the two men had to brief one another on new developments in the gang's businesses.

"Bad news?" Irv asked, nodding at the yellow cable form sticking out of Mendy's pocket.

"No, not at all." Mendy took the message out and slipped it across the table as the waitress came with Irv's coffee.

"A captain, huh!" Irv grunted as he read the form. "Got a lot of moxie, asking you for a favor like this. You know this guy, Lou Kravitz?"

"Just barely. But you probably recognize the name. Look at it again."

"Sure!" Irv now smiled. "I remember Sweet Lou Kravitz, the University of Pennsylvania basketball star. He's in the service, huh! I thought I read in the paper that he went in as a first lieutenant. He must have gotten himself promoted, but he's still a little low on the totem pole to be asking for a favor, isn't he?"

"I don't think he's in the Army for good," Mendy shrugged. "Met him last year in my pop's candy shop, he was working on Wall Street at the time. My guess is he just went in for the duration of the war."

"Yeah! Being in law school kept me out of the draft. I never did ask you how you avoided it."

Mendy smiled. "You know Dorothy? The girl I see Wednesday afternoons, the one whose husband works second shift at the Ford auto plant in Jersey? Well, she's a secretary down at the draft board, and my file is now somewhere behind a file cabinet, permanently lost for the duration."

Irv grinned. "So, you gonna help this guy?"

"Maybe," Mendy shrugged. "It's not our union that's striking these shops. It's the Teamsters. But if I made a couple of calls, I could probably get them to open up the back doors for a few deliveries just to get this order done for the army. Help the war effort and everything, you know?"

Irv nodded. "It'll look good for the unions too, get 'em a good mention in the papers."

"That's so," Mendy agreed. "And then we'll have us a man down on Wall Street too, once this dreck of a war in Europe is over and done with. Lou's a pretty smart guy, I like him. Hey, Mary Ann," he called to the waitress. "Gimme some change for the phone, please."

* * *

The cable was waiting for Lou the next morning when he got to his office and hung up his dripping raincoat, London being drenched with a torrential downpour. He read it, grinned, and dashed off an encouraging memorandum to Henry, then headed down the hall to the bathroom to clean up some from the rain. He turned the corner and almost ran into a staff sergeant coming in the opposite direction.

"Sorry sir," the older NCO grinned. "But it's good I found you. The Major's been asking for you."

"Really!" Wondering what was up, Lou quickly smoothed his hair with a small pocket comb and followed the sergeant up two flights of stairs to where the commanding officer of this section of the Quartermasters Corp kept his office.

"Captain Kravitz," the portly Major grinned as Lou entered the room. "Good news. You're going to see some action. I've got a TDY, temporary duty, for you at the front for a few weeks, about one hundred miles outside of Brussels."

Lou's heart sank. He had grown to like London. And he knew as well as his commanding officer did that a posting to the Belgium front, even during the comparatively dry summer season, was never good news. Still, this was war, and such things were to be expected. "That's...great, sir," he said, forcing a smile. "Where am I headed?"

"First infantry," the Major said, consulting a form on his massive oak desk. "They have an immediate need for a supply officer."

"The First Infantry Division, but isn't that Major Henry Van Dyke's unit, sir. He's supply officer there, isn't he?"

"Was," the Major shrugged. "Major Van Dyke was killed in action two days ago, artillery fire from what I hear. The casualty report came in this morning. Got the unit commander, as well. So you'll be starting out with a brand new CO...have your work cut out for you. But the good news is the T.O., table of organization, calls for a Major. That means you'll probably be promoted within the next week."

The room seemed to spin. Kravitz steadied himself, putting a hand against the Major's desk.

The officer signed the orders, handed them to Lou, and then noticed the ashen look on Kravitz's face. "Oh, that's right," the Major said, nodding slightly as he spoke. "You and Van Dyke were buddies, weren't you? Well...sorry to break the news to you this way, Captain. It's a dreadful thing, this war."

"Yes, sir," Lou muttered as he accepted the sheaf of transportation orders and left the office, glad that he wasn't required to salute. He headed back to his own office, locked the door and sat down in an oversized lounge chair and, with tears flowing down his cheeks, thought back again to when he first met Henry Van Dyke in college.

While Lou and Henry had remained close, they had bonded even further when they found that they were both stationed in London. They had met at the Savoy and exchanged hugs. Two hours later they had finished a bottle of Haig & Haig scotch, and then another, and by the time the dawn had tinted the horizon, Lou Kravitz and Henry Van Dyke had agreed that it was a stupid excuse for a war, the Kaiser and Queen Victoria were cousins, after all, and a sorry waste of an ocean voyage.

Van Dyke was the son of the New York Van Dykes, and one reason that he had such a deep supply of good whiskey was that his British uncle owned a sizeable chunk of Ballantines. Henry, with his MBA degree from Wharton, had no trouble in obtaining a commission as a captain. It wasn't much of a salary, he admitted, but he lived on the base, and had enough left over to support Martha and keep her in a small Park Avenue apartment. He knew that his parents would eventually come around, especially after she had a baby. All he had to do was hold out long enough, and a two-year wartime plus duration enlistment gave him the perfect means of doing so.

Lou pulled himself together and choked back the bile in his throat. Henry Van Dyke was gone. His beautiful Martha, the one he'd enlisted for, was a widow and probably didn't know it yet. Their baby was without a father, and now Lou was the one going over…over to Belgium where the war was – really was.

He gulped and put the orders into the pocket of his uniform jacket. If his country wanted him to go to war, so be it. He'd go to war, but he'd come back as well. He needed to. Martha needed him, too. He'd given Henry his word, and he was determined to keep it.

Chapter Eight
December 1917

From the snow-whitened apron on the outside plaza, to the magnificently decorated pine tree in the lobby with hundreds of silver lights and the holly with red bows around the windows, the Manhattan District Courthouse was decorated for the holidays. Lawyers and bail bondsmen thronged the corridors with brightly wrapped gifts mostly containing fifths of whiskey for the judges, court officers and members of the District Attorney's staff. Outside, on Broadway, people crowded the stores as they finished their shopping, wishing one another either a Merry Christmas or even a few Happy Chanukahs, since it was the middle of the Jewish holiday season.

Milton Blackman cooled his heels in Joseph P. Murphy's waiting room, as he thought about the stacked deck he faced as a Jew, even in New York, the most cosmopolitan city in the world. Not that he thought of it in exactly those terms because Blackman had never played cards in his life and didn't have the foggiest notion what a stacked deck was. He looked himself over carefully in the long full-view mirror on a sidewall. He was five-feet-ten with 190 pounds fairly well distributed over his big-boned frame. He was quite good-looking; his black curly hair complemented his dark brown eyes and framed his angular face. He didn't have typically Jewish features, but he knew all about religious prejudice and was constantly reminded of it each day by the restrictions placed on Jews in the business world as well as in the social structure of the community. And, he had also noticed that lately he had put on a little weight. He would have to be more careful since both parents were quite heavy.

He'd had a lot of time to think about Jewish quotas for job opportunities here in Murphy's anteroom. He'd already been waiting almost forty-five minutes, but the District Attorney's secretary, Eunice Haggerty, a stern-looking black-haired woman with small eyes, had told him the District Attorney had someone in his office and would be available shortly. He had heard that the Manhattan

D.A.'s office had been looking over a few Jewish job applications because of the growing immigration of Jews from Europe. That was at 9:30 a.m., the exact time of his appointment. It was now 10:05 a.m., and he'd been waiting patiently ever since. He didn't mind though, he was used to waiting.

The secretary picked up a large pile of papers, pleadings or briefs written on yellow legal pads that Blackman used daily at Columbia Law School as a senior. She carried them into the office, leaving the door ajar, and Blackman heard a baritone voice asking, "So where the hell's that Jewish law student that was supposed to come by today?"

"Waiting outside, Mr. Murphy," the woman replied. "He's been here since nine-thirty."

"Well for God's sake, Miss Haggerty, send the poor kid in."

Face still pinched, looking as if she'd just sucked a large lemon, the secretary came to the door and said in Blackman's general direction, but not really looking at him, "The District Attorney will see you now."

Blackman picked up his new Homburg, bought special for the occasion, and carried it self-consciously into the office of the newly elected Manhattan District Attorney. Once inside, Blackman blinked. There was nobody at the desk. Then the brisk metallic snipping of scissors drew his attention to an alcove at the window, where ruddy-complected Joseph P. Murphy covered by a white and black striped sheet, his two-hundred-fifty pound frame sprawled into a barber chair, was having his thatch of thick white hair cut by a swarthy, elderly man. The barber had Murphy's white hair combed forward over his forehead so he could trim it evenly. It made the D.A. look ridiculous, like an overweight Julius Caesar in a Roman toga.

"C'mon over here, kid," Murphy barked, not bothering to introduce himself. Pulling a gold-chained watch from under the sheet, he added, "Wait – it's almost ten-thirty. Get yourself a good, stiff drink. Some fine Irish whiskey is on the table next to my desk. Bring me one too."

Tucking his new hat under his arm, Blackman did as he was told and poured half a glass full for Murphy and then splashed a bit in another tumbler for himself. He wasn't planning on drinking it because he didn't drink, and besides no matter how fancy the glasses were, he didn't know how they had been washed, and Blackman's family kept kosher. As he lifted the decanter, a little bit of the liquor sloshed onto the table, and Blackman, feeling his face redden, looked furtively around for a napkin. There being none available, he wiped up the few drops with the cuff of his suit coat. He carried the tumblers over to the District Attorney who accepted his, looked at the two inches of empty space above the sloshing amber liquid, and said in a slight Irish brogue, "Listen kid, a little light with the booze aren'tcha? It's almost Christmas, and there's gonna be a few dozen bottles of this stuff comin' through our front door in the next week. But, that's okay! I'll get a refill later. Stand over there by the window where I can get a look at you. If I turn my head too quick, Antonio here is likely to cut off one of my ears."

Blackman did as he was told, as Murphy looked him over carefully, noticing his polished but well-worn black shoes, a black suit, shiny at the knees, a navy blue and red-striped tie, and dark gray wool department-store topcoat. The D. A. had a full face that was well on its way from being cherubic to jowly, white bushy eyebrows, and light-blue, dancing eyes. Blackman liked the pleasant Irishman right away.

"You look a little long in the tooth for a law student, Blackman. How old wouldja be, lad?"

"Uh, twenty-six, Mr. Murphy."

"Twenty-six, huh! What'd ya do before law school?"

"Bookkeeper, sir," he smiled nervously. "At Brooklyn Savings and Loan. I had to save enough money for law school."

"Bookkeeper, huh! That's good. Most lawyers can't find their asses with both hands when it comes to numbers," he continued his pleasant Irish brogue. "You're a Columbia boy, right?"

"Yes, sir. That's right. Columbia Law School."

"They gave you much trouble about being a Jew? Naw, don't even answer that. Of course, they give you trouble bein' a Hebe, but you won't have to worry about that around here. We're... what the devil they call it... a meltin' pot? Just like it says out at Ellis Island; 'Give me your poor, your starving, whatever it is you want to throw at me and I'll find a home for them.' Ya know about the Statue of Liberty, eh, lad?"

Blackman nodded.

"Don't mind Antonio, here," Murphy said, waving his hand under the sheet in the general direction of the barber. "He only speaks enough English to find his way across town on the streetcar. Talks dago, but you don't want to call him one. He's from Sicily, and gotta real short fuse. Ain't you, Antonio?"

"That's a right, Meester Murphy. From Sicily."

"Yeah, that's it. Sicily. You know, I went to law school myself almost twenty years ago over at Fordham, not a bad school either. Passed the bar exam on the first try, too. Pretty good for a shanty Irishman like myself, eh." He laughed at himself. "So what're you doin' lookin' to clerk in a D.A.'s office, kid? Why ain't you talkin' to one of those silk-stocking firms over on Fifth Avenue?"

Blackman cleared his throat. "I'm...," he started. "I'm more interested in criminal law, sir."

Murphy nodded, raising another murmur of protest from the barber. "You're interested in prosecution, and besides, the big firms won't touch you. Am I right? The Vanderbilts and the Rockefellers would have a fit if they thought some Jew kid from the Bronx was handlin' their big corporation's law work."

"I'm from Brooklyn, sir."

He nodded his head before continuing. "Hey, I don't care, you can call me either Joe or J.P., kid. Ain't none of them fancy manners around here. Jew, Catholic, Irish or Polack – the Eye-talian crooks don't care who puts 'em in jail. So, let me ask you something, Blackman. Why'd ya think I get my hair cut up here in the office rather than goin' out to the barbershop and shootin' the breeze with the swells?" A streetcar went by on the noisy crowded street below, its brass bell jangling loudly.

"I would imagine it's to save time, sir," Blackman replied.

"There you go," he said, throwing his hands up and agreeing with Blackman.

Behind him, Antonio stopped snipping hair around his ears, stepped back looking over the finished job.

"Don'cha believe that crap the New York Post prints about me bein' afraid to go outside the office on account of the wops sayin' that they're gonna catch up with me for throwin' too many of their dumb asses in the clink. And, then the Daily News comes out saying that more politics is discussed in these offices than at Tammany Hall. The lyin' sons-of-bitches don't know what they're talkin' about. Now the New York Times, that's a classy newspaper, oh yeah? They have no time to be writin' stories like that, no sir. Too busy goin' on about the war in Europe or all the devil's work the Congress is cookin' up in Washington. Buncha blue-blood bastards, runnin' around with their noses in the air and their thumbs up their asses. I got me no use for any of the newspapers. Who cares anyway? They ain't ever gonna support me. Not a mick Irishman like myself. But, you're right, kid. I stay up here to save time. One of my boys comes in here lookin' to get an arrest warrant from a judge for some lawbreaker, they don't have to go huntin' for me. I'm here, and I know all the right judges. You a hard worker, Blackman?"

"Yes, sir," Blackman nodded vigorously, almost dropping his hat. "At least I'd like to think so, sir. Sixty hours minimum a week, that's me."

"Good! We'll see soon enough," the big Irishman smiled knowingly.

"I'm hired then, sir?"

"Hell yes! I need another law clerk and the crooks sure as hell aren't takin' time off."

Blackman agreed and moved to shake the older man's hand, but then thought better of it. "When would you like me to start, sir?" he asked, hoping he wasn't being pushy.

"I toldja once before, kid, call me Joe or J.P. Got it?" Murphy snorted, the noise making the barber start. "You're here, ain't you? So grab yourself a desk. Anything that doesn't have papers on it out there is fair game. And Blackman?"

"Yes sir?"

"Whaddaya think it is that you should be spending your time on around here?"

"Well..." Blackman thought a moment. "Justice, sir. Seeking justice."

Murphy laughed, his massive frame bouncing up and down. "Justice!" He laughed again. "You hear that, Tony? Kid thinks he's here for justice."

The barber grinned but missed the joke.

Murphy shook his head. "Naw, kid. Don't you worry about no justice. Justice is the judges' job, and half the time there are none of them around losin' any sleep over it. No sirree, boy! Your first priority here is doin' what I say. You got that?"

Blackman's face reddened for the umpteenth time during the last twenty minutes.

"And second, be loyal. Be loyal to the boss, and that's me, lad. Always make me look good because that's probably one of your most important jobs around here, as far as I'm concerned."

"Uh sure! Yes sir."

"Good," Murphy nodded. "This here's an elective job, just like a judge, and anything starts to look bad the voters boot me out on my ass. You with me? I may have greased some palms with the local Tammany Hall boys to get in here, but grease only goes so far. Understand? So don't make me look bad in the newspapers with a hung jury or worse. The worse publicity is for the District Attorney's office to lose a big one. The newspapers will kill ya every time."

"Yes, sir. I understand completely."

"Good! And Blackman, if you decide to go after some of the bad boys on your lonesome, you better put together a real doozy of a case, and make sure that we can make it stick. No goin' off half-cocked around here. You follow me?"

"Yes, sir. I surely do." After a few drinks Joseph P. Murphy's brogue seemed to thicken, and Blackman wasn't all that sure he really did understand everything the D. A. was talking about.

"Okay, that's good, kid. Now go get yourself a desk. Miss Haggerty will be along shortly with some papers for you to fill out for payroll. We don't pay jack shit for a law clerk, but we can still keep you in carfare and help pay a few other bills as well until the Bar results are out."

"Yes, sir. I mean no, sir. I just mean, sir. I understand, sir."

The District Attorney howled at the law student's consternation and Blackman, his new Homburg now perched on the back of his head, muttered his thanks again and moved out of Murphy's office into the anteroom, thanking his secretary. Blackman entered the large office space for the assistant prosecutors that was buzzing with activity.

In an open space crowded with desks, perhaps forty attorneys and clerks sat behind desks, all busily engaged in some kind of law work. Mailroom clerks pushed wire baskets up and down the aisles on wooden carts. The whole room smelled faintly of stale sweat and cigarette smoke. Most New Yorkers still bathed only weekly on Saturday nights, except religious Jews like the members of Blackman's family. His mother stressed the importance of cleanliness by making sure that each member of the family bathed daily.

Blackman looked around. There were a couple of desks open near the windows, so he walked slowly around the area until he found a desk with a decent view and then settled down into his new surroundings.

"You new?"

Blackman turned. It was one of the mail clerks, a boy who couldn't have been more than sixteen years old.

"I sure am," he said, not sure about striking up conversation with a mail clerk. "I'm Mister Blackman, Milton Blackman."

"Blackman, huh? Shingle or no shingle?"

"Pardon me?"

"You an attorney or a clerk?"

"Oh, I'm a law clerk. I haven't passed the Bar yet."

"Thought so. Well, welcome aboard, Mister Blackman. I'm Maxie. You need anything, you call me."

"Well?" Blackman looked around, embarrassed to be asking the particular question.

"Oh!" Maxie smiled knowingly. "You lookin' for the men's crapper aincha? It's down the hall on the..."

"No, no!" Blackman protested loudly. "It's just...who do I see to find out what to do?"

"You kiddin' me? You ain't got nothin' to do?"

"Shhh!" Blackman was embarrassed. "I'm sure it will all work out. After all this is an office of the court."

"What?" The kid was genuinely confused. "Hey listen, you've already met Joseph Patrick Murphy, the jovial Irishman, right?"

"Yes." Blackman straightened up. "I just concluded an interview with him, not five minutes ago."

"You did, huh? The kid took out a pouch of tobacco and some cigarette papers and expertly rolled a cigarette with only his right hand. "Well don't worry. Miss Haggerty will be out here in no time flat, and you'll be up to your tuchas in work. Pardon my French. I forgot you're new here. Hey, if you got some spare time, enjoy it, Mister Blackman. Believe me, it won't last long. Well nice to meet you."

"Sure," Blackman said to the boy's back as he seemed to skip around the large room either picking up or handing out letters and packages to the various occupants of the many cubicles. Blackman put his overcoat and Homburg on a coat tree and sat down at the desk, opening the drawers, checking their contents from its former occupant. The center drawer held some thumbtacks and a few erasers. The top drawers had packages of index cards and an unopened box of pencils. The lower drawer on the left hand side was empty. On the right, a wire file basket supported half a dozen green pasteboard file folders, their tarnished brass label-holder tabs empty. Blackman closed the drawers and folded his hands on the green desk blotter. He thought about Murphy's final words of warning. The District Attorney had started out by saying that he didn't expect his law clerks to come up with any original ideas of their own. But then he made it clear that he would welcome new cases from his law clerks, as long as they were willing to gather enough information to make the charges stick...that's how he had put it, "stick." They had to "make them stick." The D. A. wanted to look good.

Blackman, his slightly overweight frame, dark hair and thin face were all working together now because he had some definite ideas. At least, he had one good idea. And if he worked at it long enough, he was sure that he could find enough to make the "charges stick".

He opened the lower drawer, took out a file folder, and then opened the upper drawer and unwrapped a package of index cards. Blackman used the silver Schaeffer Cross fountain pen that his parents had given him for his Bar Mitzvah, his thirteenth birthday. It wasn't the most expensive one, but it was the best pen that his father had been able to afford and it had taken him almost six months to save enough money for it out of his meager weekly earnings. Blackman carried the pen with him all the time and kept it clean and in perfect working order, but even so, he used it very rarely. It was precious to him, and he only used it for things he felt to be really significant, like filling out the application to law school, writing his resignation to the bank and signing the marriage license as a witness at his older brother's wedding. He took it out now and looked at it appreciatively, admiring his name engraved on the side. Blackman wrote out a label tab for a new file, blowing on the ink to dry it. He put the folder back in the drawer and looked at it. The folder was empty now, but he didn't plan on it staying empty very long. He'd fill it with information – facts – whatever it took to make a case that no one could successfully defend against; something that would stick. Blackman looked at the label, Lowenstein, Irving, with contempt for several minutes. Milton Blackman then closed the drawer and smiled. He would make Joseph Patrick Murphy look good. He swore to that, with God as his witness.

A thick file under each arm, Milton Blackman trudged by in the hallway, staring into the office where Irv Lowenstein gazed out the window at the American flag. The smartass had his own office. And he'd won his first few cases in court too. True, he hadn't had much opposition with the first one, a high profile lawyer but public defender with an alcoholic whore for a client. But still, Lowenstein had won his first case. And it wasn't as if he had graduated that much higher in the class than him, Blackman thought to himself. Blackman had been in the upper ten percent of their class, enough to make Order of the Coif, and that wasn't exactly chopped liver, even if Lowenstein had been number one in the class and Editor-in-Chief of the Law Review. Blackman fumed, trudging down the hall to the cluster of cubbyholes set up for assistants like himself who had graduated from law school but not yet passed the State Bar exam.

That was the other thing, Lowenstein was already a lawyer. Blackman wasn't that far away. He was getting ready and even went to court occasionally, but he still couldn't open his mouth when he got there. He couldn't say a word because even though he had taken the Bar exam immediately upon graduation, that had been less than a month ago and the results were still not back yet from the state capital, and until they were, he had not officially passed the Bar and could not be sworn in by a judge.

Lowenstein had enlisted, taken the Army exam for Officer's Candidate School, passed it with flying colors, of course, and then failed the physical. How he had failed was still a mystery. The man appeared healthy as a horse, healthier than most New York horses. But it hadn't occurred to Blackman to use the special exemption to take the Bar exam early. What Blackman overlooked, Lowenstein scooped up to his advantage. And, Lowenstein lived the high life on no visible means of support, certainly not the wages earned by a newly appointed Assistant District Attorney.

Blackman sat behind his ancient desk, the chair groaning in protest as he leaned forward, sorting the files for the cases into piles: misdemeanors into the large pile on his left, felonies into the smaller pile on his right; a stack of papers represented the cases that had yet to be read; and a pile of manila folders and a bottle of India ink told the entire office that this job, the lowest on the totem pole in the D.A.'s office, had fallen to Milton Blackman. He read the first name, dipped a steel-quilted pen into the inkwell, and lettered the file folder in a neat hand. He did this for half an hour until all of the papers, documents and briefs were in their folders and one empty folder, a leftover, remained on his desk.

He heard laughter down the hall. It was Lowenstein laughing with one of the other Assistant D.A.'s. Blackman checked his watch, almost twelve. They were probably stepping out for a bite of lunch. No one had asked Blackman to join them. He fumed a little more.

The Moulin Rouge Club had only been open a few months into the year of 1918, and it was already popular with the sporting crowd-bookies, boxing promoters, and the horseracing players; also Broadway producers, movie stars, and big-name athletes. Smoke hung in the air like a soft cloud over the noisy crowd. Tonight it was packed with wall-to-wall customers struggling for space at the roulette tables.

Some of the patrons wore tuxedos or formal evening dress; others wore suits, but none were without a tie and jacket. The heavyset Italian at the door, a childhood buddy recruited by one of the Lucci brothers, Aldo, Francisco or Guido, carefully scrutinized the players before entering the casino room, making sure they were properly attired and were not from the police. The standards of the Moulin Rouge Club were well-known throughout the city, and a person needed the proper membership card for entrance.

The trendy women who entered the club were already flaunting the shorter dresses that were still years away from general popularity, but fashionably styled in Paris and London and extremely expensive. Most favored bright colors that would call attention to the design. Some had fringes that moved as they danced to a ragtime piano played slightly ahead of tempo. Some wore sequins that sparkled in the light as they danced. A daring few of them had bobbed their hair into short, "Dutch boy" cuts with headbands that would attract open stares on the street outside, but would not collect as much as a second glance in the Moulin Rouge Club. All moved and bobbed rhythmically to the accompaniment of a ragtime piano, playing something Mendy Goldblatt thought he recognized as a Scott Joplin tune, the "Varsity Drag", or something like that.

From his private table on the mezzanine overlooking the dance floor, Mendy gazed out over the crowd, watching the packed house while looking for the slightest trouble. It was only nine in the evening, and already the place was jammed, the laughter creating a constant stream of noise, like the sound of a waterfall welling up from the sea of patrons below. Mendy's tuxedo was tailored and immaculately pressed, his black bow tie pulled just so over a row of pearl studs. His shoes were black patent leather, and when he lit a cigarette, he took it from a Tiffany case and used a solid gold lighter. He always dressed well outside the club – suit, tie and fedora with polished Florsheims, but never in evening attire. Tough guys didn't frequent the streets of the Lower Eastside in bow ties and black dinner jackets. But here, in the private club, well it was his place, his turf, and he was damned if he was going to have anyone better dressed than he was. He wanted everyone to know that Mendel Goldblatt was boss of the Moulin Rouge Club, the classiest joint in Manhattan.

As the players came through the front door, a few glanced up at the mezzanine, like theatergoers checking to see if the presidential box was occupied. Mendy made eye contact, smiled, and nodded, never waving, not even at guests who waved first, because he didn't like it. Waving was, in his eyes, an effeminate gesture, something only a faigallah would do. It made a man look weak, and Mendy knew that in this business, the appearance, even the faintest suggestion of weakness could be fatal.

There was a buzz near the front door and Mendy rose to his feet, looked down and saw Mary Pickford, the stage actress, come walking in with Florenz Ziegfeld, a famous Broadway producer. The posh Moulin Rouge wasn't as big as some of the other nightclubs uptown, nor was it nearly as well-known. But, it was discrete. It was trendy. It was expensive, and it operated to a high standard of luxury. When Irv Lowenstein and Mendy Goldblatt purchased the bar and dance hall and then transformed it into an exclusive private club, they had never dreamed it would become New York City's popular "in spot". Those things appealed to celebrities. Broadway stars, actors and actresses from the film studios that were springing up over in New Jersey, investment bankers from Wall Street, business tycoons and a few important politicians had begun to frequent the place, giving it a reputation as the downtown place to be. Even Jack Dempsey and Babe Ruth were frequent patrons.

Casually, Mendy made his way to the circular staircase, shaking a few hands along the way, and went down to the main floor where he stood for a minute or so, smiling, and then walked over to the show business personalities.

"Welcome, Mary," he said giving her a quick peck on the cheek. "It's good to see you again…Flo." He smiled, taking the handsome impresario's hand into both of his.

"Mendy, I swear that you have more famous people here than our Mayor, Jimmy Walker, had at his dinner party last week," Ziegfeld said with a grin.

Mendy, who had been taking diction lessons to remove traces of his Lower Eastside accent, noticed that Mary Pickford still had more than a little of South Jersey in her speech. It was a good thing, Mendel mused, that the movies were silent, at least for now. He had heard recent rumors that the studios had been working on sound for the past six months but weren't quite there yet. They called them talking movies but who knew whether they'd ever really work or not.

"The Mayor asks for campaign contributions when you go to his parties," Mendy smiled. "I don't and that's the big difference between us."

This got a roar of laughter from the show-packed crowd. Pickford especially seemed amused. He noticed that her eyes sparkled, as she looked him over. He knew that look. He'd seen it first with neighborhood girls over on Delancey Street, then in the seamstresses as he walked past their tables on his way to meetings with garment manufacturers, and then on the faces of the wives of several prominent New York businessmen. It was an intense hunger for something forbidden and exotic. He was about to say more when a tuxedoed Italian, another of the Lucci brothers' relatives, touched his shoulder and whispered in his ear.

Mendy nodded. "Mary, you and Flo enjoy your evening," Mendy said. "Your first bottle of champagne is on the house, and now if you'll excuse me, duty calls." He walked off with the young Italian houseman, looking over the flow of customers in an appreciative manner.

"Hey, I'm sorry," the houseman said. "But the pit boss said for me to come get you right away and tell you that the Vanderbilt kid is losing his ass at the poker table."

"It's okay," Mendy said. "I'll take care of it." Mendy wouldn't let any of the Green Hats – his private army of Irish toughs – into the front part of the club. They were too rough-cut to mix among the swells. He was seriously considering the same policy concerning a few of Lucci's family members as well; some of these dagoes just had too much of the paisano left in them.

They went to the back of the club, through a double set of doors that looked as if they might lead to a kitchen, and then down a short hall to another wooden paneled door guarded by another dark swarthy Italian.

"Good evening, Mr. Goldblatt," Joey Corina said respectfully.

"Hey, Joey. How's your Momma? Feelin' a little better these days?"

"She's good, sir. Thanks for asking." The bouncer opened the door to another noisy den-filled room. This one was slightly smaller than the one up front, but the raucous laughter here was punctuated by occasional loud shouts and hoots, and the voices were mostly male.

Hands in his pockets, Mendy made his way past the roulette wheels, a craps table and several games of blackjack, back into a side parlor where six men sat around a poker table. There was a $500-minimum buy of chips when you sat down to play. Money and chips littered the green felt surface. The green-shaded dealer glanced up as Mendy approached and looked relieved.

"Hey boys," Mendy smiled. "How're the cards running tonight?"

"Not worth a fuck," the effeminate twenty-one year old poker player said, not even looking up.

"I'm not sure that we have a marker written up for you... Lionel, are you?" Mendy asked nonchalantly, the way a person might ask the time of day.

"Fuck if I know," Lionel responded, sipping his drink and practically ignoring Mendy. "But I'm good for it, aren't I?"

"What's Mr. Vanderbilt drinking?" Mendy asked the dealer, ignoring the young man's question.

"Scotch, sir."

Mendy nodded, and a waiter came over.

"Send a fifth of Johnnie Walker over to my office, willya, Tony?"

The waiter nodded and hurried off to the bar.

"Tell you what, Lionel," Mendy asked casually again. "Why don't we step into my office for a few minutes and we'll write up a marker so the books are nice and balanced, shall we?"

Lionel stared at him.

"Drinks are on me," Mendy said. "The rest of you boys take a short break while Lionel and I have a quick business meeting for about ten minutes or so, okay?"

The rest of the men nodded and put their cards face down as another houseman came over to watch the table. The poker players wandered off in the direction of the men's room or the bar as Mendy put his hand lightly on the young man's shoulder.

"What say, Lionel?" Mendy asked quietly. "I'll buy you a drink."

"Why the fuck not," the young man shrugged with indifference as he got up from his chair.

The two of them walked alone into Mendy's office at the far end of the gaming room. Mendy let the young man in first, and Vanderbilt walked over immediately to the bar, where he broke the seal on the fifth of Scotch and poured a healthy slug – neat – into a tumbler. Mendy stood next to him, looking down at the ledger that lay open on his desk.

"Well, Lionel," Mendy mused. "It says here that you still owe us eleven hundred dollars from the last time you were here."

"Shit, Mendy," the kid shrugged, sipping his drink. "Don't worry about it, my old man will cover it."

"I don't know, Lionel," Mendy smiled. "We start extending credit over a few hundred dollars, people might confuse us with the Chase Manhattan Bank, you know. How about paying up last week's marker before you get any further into us?"

The young man looked at Mendy disdainfully, the way a man might look at a broken-down horse. "Fuck you," he said, raising his glass to his lips.

There was an immediate loud slap, followed by the sound of the heavy crystal tumbler shattering against the far side of the room.

Then Lionel Vanderbilt, heir to the Vanderbilt Chemical Empire, inhaled sharply and went wide-eyed with terror as he was lifted onto his toes.

"Who the hell do you think you're talking to, Lionel?" Mendy asked, his right hand lifting the twenty-one year old a fraction of an inch higher by his crotch. Mendy squeezed once hard, and saw with satisfaction that the Princeton boy nearly passed out. "You think you can breeze in here like you own the fuckin' place, run up a marker for eleven hundred dollars, drink my booze and then talk to me that way?" Mendy squeezed hard once, and the kid shook his head hurriedly.

"No, no! Jesus, Mendy, I'm sorry. Really I am!"

Mendy squeezed and twisted, stopping only when the kid's eyes began to roll back.

"It's 'Mister Goldblatt,' Lionel. Deadbeats call me Mister Goldblatt, and that's what you are, Lionel, a deadbeat. No way you can come in this club and piss on a bunch of Jews and dagoes from the Lower Eastside just because your old man owns a few steel mills and you're a Princeton boy. You think you can fuck us?" He jerked upwards, lifted the kid all the way off the floor and then dropped him back down onto the deep carpeting.

By now, Vanderbilt was trembling, truly terrified by Mendy. "You can't do this," the kid gasped. "You can't shove me around. I know too many important people."

Jerking him back up in the air, Mendy slammed the kid back against the desk and still holding a fistful of the kid's crotch, pulled a .45 automatic out from his black cummerbund, and shoved the barrel into the kid's open mouth. "Is that what you think I'm going to do, Lionel, shove you around?" The gangster laughed as the young man choked on the gun barrel. "Naw, kid. For a hundred bucks, I shove you around. For eleven hundred, I fuckin' blow your brains out."

Lionel Vanderbilt's pale skin got two shades lighter.

Mendy felt something, something warm and soft against the knuckles of his hand, while grasping the kid's crotch. He kept the gun in the kid's mouth, but jerked his other hand away. "What the fuck?" Mendy laughed. "What'd you do? Shit your pants?"

Still gasping, the kid shook his head.

"You lying motherfucker!" Mendy pulled the hammer back, cocking the gun.

The kid's eyes went wide in terror.

"Okay," Mendy ordered. "Real quick before you piss on yourself too, empty your pockets."

The kid dug into his trouser pockets, coming up with a money clip and a cigar cutter.

Mendy let go of him, tossed the cigar cutter into the trash, pulled the cash out of the clip and counted it. "Only five hundred, Lionel," Mendy said. "You're six big ones short."

"It's all I got," he said with difficulty, the .45 still in his mouth, pressed against his tongue.

"Seven steel mills in the family and all you've got is five hundred bucks? I don't think so."

The frightened kid grunted something that Mendy couldn't understand.

"What?" Mendy took the gun out of Vanderbilt's mouth, but kept the barrel pointed between the kid's eyes.

"I mean it's all I've got on me."

"Your watch," Mendy decided. "Give me your watch and your ring."

"But that watch is worth eight hundred by itself."

"Not to me. The watch and ring, Lionel."

"You're fuckin' robbing me."

Mendy grabbed a handful of shirtfront and hoisted the kid into the air again, pressing the gun barrel against his forehead. "Listen good, you fuck up," he hissed ominously. "I'm not robbing you. You're robbing me. You come in here and play our games of chance but don't pay, then that's robbery. I'm just getting what's mine, with interest. And besides, I'm letting you live. You're getting a real bargain."

"The ring was a gift from my mother for my 21st birthday, and it cost her almost a thousand dollars." The kid winced at the thought.

"Then she'll buy you another."

A gold ring and a pocket watch with platinum chain clattered onto the desk, and Mendy finally released the kid. "Now you know not to come back here again unless you have enough cash to cover your losses, don't you?" Mendy asked him.

The young man nodded.

"Okay, then get the hell out, and hold your pants while you're leavin'. Any of that crap spills out on the rug, I swear to God I'll make you eat it."

The kid nodded and scooted quickly for the door, both hands holding the back of his pants.

Mendy cleaned his hands in the office washroom, wiping them on a dry towel tastefully embroidered with the Moulin Rouge Club's logo. Then he put the money back into the clip and pocketed it, tried on the ring, found it too small, dropped it into a drawer, and finally slipped the expensive Swiss watch into his pocket.

There was a light rap at the door, and Irv Lowenstein came in. He looked at Mendy and laughed. "I just saw Lionel Vanderbilt in the hallway making a mad dash for the men's room," Irv said. "He looked slightly pale and scared outta his wits. Whaddya do to him?"

"Poker tables got a little too rich for his blood," Mendy said casually. "Gave him the shits."

Irv shrugged. He took off his coat. Irv wore a dark business suit, not a tuxedo like Mendy. As the silent partner in the Moulin Rouge, he spent time at the club only when it was necessary.

"Where you been?" Mendy asked. "It's nearly ten o'clock. You aren't going into the D.A.'s office on a Saturday evening, are you?"

"Naw! I stopped by the schul first for awhile."

Mendy looked up. "The Shabbas services were over a coupla hours ago, weren't they?"

"Yeah, they were but I stayed after anyways, just thinking about a few things."

"What were you thinking about?" Mendy said. "Old Rabbi Kirshfeld already thinks we're monsters. The shame of our families, anyhow, selling booze and gamblin' to the goyim."

"If only he knew," Irv chuckled. "But I wasn't at the old schul. I was at the new one."

"We've got a new synagogue?"

"Not a real synagogue, yet. It's only a storefront now. The place that used to be the dry goods store. It would make a perfect schul."

"Oh yeah," Mendy nodded. "I heard about that last week. Somebody bought it from outside the neighborhood. Brooklyn, right?"

"You know who it was?" Irv asked.

Mendy shook his head.

"Barney Green."

"The fighter?"

"Used-to-be fighter. He's a Rabbi now."

"No shit!" Mendy picked his gun up off the desk, uncocked it, and slipped it in the back of his trousers, under his cummerbund again. "You tell him, he ever wants to go ten rounds with Rabbi Kirshfeld, I'll handle the action and give him half the gate."

Irving laughed at the thought of the old Rabbi and Barney Green in the ring. "I'll do that."

"You know him?"

"We've talked. I sprang a kid out of central lockup for him last month."

"The one you called me about? The restaurant thing?"

"Yeah!" Irv nodded. "That one."

"We caught the little putz that was doing it," Mendy said, sitting down and putting his feet up on the desk. "Get this, it was the owner's nephew."

"You tell the guy that owns the restaurant?"

"Naw! We dealt with it."

"You didn't…" Irving asked worriedly.

"No, no!" Mendy shook his head. "For crying out loud, you think we'd whack some sixteen-year-old kid over pocket change? We shut his hand in a door nice and tight too. He won't be sticking it anywhere but into a plaster cast for the next month or so."

"Okay," Irv nodded. "That's good, that should teach him some respect for his uncle."

"So what's the deal with the schul?" Mendy asked, changing the subject.

"I just went down there," Irv told him. "Found a guy, you know Herman Greenspan's uncle?"

Mendy nodded.

"I gave him a few bucks to put in an envelope for the Rabbi a few days ago."

"Yeah!" Mendy grinned. "How much?"

"One bill."

"A hundred bucks?"

"A thousand."

Mendy dropped his feet off the desk. "A thousand bucks? You gave Barney Green a thousand bucks?"

Irv nodded. "We gave Barney Green a thousand bucks for his schul."

"We? Irv!" Mendy shook his head in surprise. "And, I just made Lionel Vanderbilt shit his pants for eleven hundred."

"Then we're a hundred ahead."

"Yeah!" Mendy laughed. "I guess so, but why have Herman's uncle make the contribution? Why not do it ourselves?"

"I dunno. I guess I thought maybe Green might not accept it from us, you know…about where the money comes from. Plus, he's engaged to Kirshfeld's niece…"

"The one with the big tits and nice ass?"

"Yeah, that's the one."

"Man," Mendy mused. "I always wanted to try some of that."

"You and half the Lower Eastside," Irv pointed out. "Anyhow, her family's pretty straight-laced. I figure it might screw things up if her father ever found out where it came from."

"So why give him anything at all?"

"To help him out. He was a fighter, Mendy. And, now he's trying to do some good work in the community."

Mendy looked at him. "You goin' soft on me?" he said, shaking his head. "And, I'll cut your balls off." Mendy kept a straight face for perhaps ten seconds, then he broke into a grin.

"Not to worry, partner," Irv quipped, putting his arm around his shoulder.

"Okay, so we're now partners in a schul, eh? Maybe it'll keep us in mazel."

"It will help solve our family's problems," Mendy replied. "Your Momma talks to mine. She's sure you're gonna knock up some shiksah one of these days and be forced to marry her."

"If I don't," Irv told him, "It won't be for not trying."

Mendy laughed and poured his friend a scotch, and then poured one for himself. "Seriously though, Irv," he said. "What's with you and this Rabbi?"

"Nothing," Irv told him. "I just figure…well, we cause enough tsouris, you know? For other people, for our families…"

Mendy nodded.

"I just figure," Irv continued, "That maybe we need a little luck now and then, you know, to kinda balance things out for us with the Big Guy."

"Maybe," Mendy shrugged. "It's just that, well, sometimes you worry me, Irv. Getting too religious."

"I'm not religious. We gave Barney some dough to start his schul, that's all."

"Okay," Mendy said. "But you're still with the D.A.'s office, aren'tcha?"

"Yeah, but not for much longer. They're giving me some big cases now, like Arnold Rothstein."

"You're trying a case against Arnold Rothstein, the gambler?"

"Not him, but one of his main bookies, a big one. Some important banker downtown lost a bundle, got pissed and turned him in. The D.A. couldn't turn a deaf ear. So we brought him in, and I'm getting the case."

"And you'll what? Dismiss it?"

"I can't do that," Irv said. "The witness is too credible with a high profile. But I can recommend a light sentence, probation or maybe even a mistrial. Give him a break."

"Do him a favor?" Mendy grinned.

"Exactly," Irv agreed. "Do him a favor and then enter it in our ledger book. I do that for five, six, seven guys, make them believe in me, and then we've got markers we can collect on for the next ten years. I'm gonna get out of the D.A. business in the next few months or so, but don't worry, not until every one important in town owes us."

Mendy looked at him and nodded his approval. "Smart," he said.

"I try! So how're things going with you at the club?"

Mendy shrugged. "Not bad, but that Lucci's cousin, Angelo Cusmano or something like that is somethin' else."

Irving frowned. "Whadda 'bout him?"

"You know the kid I'm talking about, the one with a mole on his chin? Well, he's a real pain in the ass. As a matter of fact, Irv, most of Lucci's relatives are real goombahs, nightmares. They always smell like garlic. They can't say a damned thing without a dem or a dose in it, ya know what I mean? Makes the place look bad."

Irv nodded that he understood. "I'll talk to the Luccis," he said. "Have them clean up their act with their relatives. Enough is enough, but we'll also switch the real bad ones away from the customers, maybe have them pick up the take from the craps games. We'll call it a promotion or something, pay them a little more and get them outta the club. Let me check it out with Frankie, so there's no hard feelings."

"Don't let word get out," Mendy warned. "That gets around, every guinea workin' for us will start eatin' more garlic."

Irv chuckled. "Other than that, everything else okay?"

Mendy nodded. "We've got a blackjack dealer whose bank seems a little light. Maybe he's just unlucky, but we're watching him closely every night for the next week or so. Anything looks funny, we'll break a few of his fingers and toss him out. The rest of them dealers will get the message real fast."

"Why not just get rid of him now?"

"He's Lucci's brother-in-law."

"So what's the big deal?"

"Guido already thinks he's cheating on his sister and is just waiting to catch the schmuck."

Irv rolled his eyes. "Wouldn't want that to be me if it turns out to be true."

"No kidding. The Lucci boys will put him into a smaller pants size – cuttin' off his prick and shovin' it in his mouth."

"How are the clubs doing, generally, now that the Volstead is close to becoming the law?"

"Both the Moulin Rouge and Mirage Clubs are holding their own. The Cavalier Club in Queens though, what can you say? It's fucking Queens."

"Let's hold onto it though," Irv said. "We'll need it once the Volstead is passed; and it is a classy joint."

"You're right, it is classy. But I'm not sure about Prohibition. Maybe it could pass Congress in the next year or so," Mendy said, nodding his head. "I hear that Carrie Nation and those other bitches, they're talkin' like they might really have the clout to outlaw booze in the near future."

"It's still doubtful though," Irv said, "even with all the pressure on the politicians in Washington. But if they do pass it, this town goes from a thousand places where you can get a drink down to just a handful. And if we're one of the handful, we'll be rolling in bucks, Mendy."

"So where we gonna get all the booze?"

"I'm working on it," Irv said. "I think we're gonna be home free – really in good shape – but now I'll have more time to work out the wrinkles of the plan. I'll let you know in a few weeks, but in the meantime, how's the rest of the games comin' along?"

"Got the books right here." Mendy smiled, pushing them over to Irving.

Irv opened the ledger and, pencil in hand, began tallying up the takes from the speakeasies, the unions, a dozen high-stakes poker games, twice as many craps games, more than five hundred punch boards spread around the five boroughs, a loan-shark business tied into the gambling operations, and a couple of whorehouses that the Lucci's had taken over when their former owners welched on bets. He added the figures up twice and whistled softly. The weekly gross was slightly over one hundred thousand dollars. True, they had overhead—an army of Italians and Irishmen didn't come cheap—but it was still more money than he'd ever dreamed of.

"Man!" he said, grinning at Mendy. "Aren't you glad that we decided to go into business together? We've got some sweet deal going for us now, and it's only gonna get better."

Chapter Ten
The Lower Eastside – November 1918

Dapper with a fresh haircut and a tailored suit, Irving Lowenstein stood in the bathroom doorway and smiled as his younger brother scowled into the oak-framed mirror, struggling with the four-in-hand knot on his tie.

"I'll help you, Herbie," Seymour, the middle son said as he walked into the bathroom and started to preen in front of the mirror.

"Better let me give you some help with that, sport." Irv chuckled as he looked at Herbie's frustration growing by the minute even with help from Seymour.

"Naw," Herbie replied, scowling more deeply. "But thanks guys, I tied these before a million times." He undid the necktie, took another shot at it, and wound up with a badly shaped Windsor knot. "Shit," Herbie muttered under his breath. "Okay, Irvie, I'm calling uncle. Help me out here, will ya? I just can't seem to get it right. I'd ask Seymour for help but he's useless when it comes to anything but music."

"That's okay with me."

Seymour went back into the hallway watching his two brothers with interest as Irv smiled and stepped behind his brother, untying the tie and then swiftly retying it into an expertly smoothed knot.

"I thought there was supposed to be a crease in the middle," Herbie said, with real concern as he made a face and squinted into the mirror.

"That's only if you tie a half Windsor knot," Irv told him, straightening his brother's collar. "A cheaper tie, wool or something, you go half Windsor. This is a silk tie from Sulka's that I got you here, and it ties smoother. With a better tie like this you can go with a full Windsor and you don't need any dimple in the middle."

"It looks good," Seymour said looking at Herbie's reflection in the mirror.

"Bull crap," Herbie said, scowling back into the mirror and brushing off Seymour's compliment. "This is all a bunch of dreck, anyhow. I'm too old for a fucking Bar Mitzvah."

Irv dropped his hands to his sides. "Watch your language, sport," he said, his voice suddenly becoming considerably lower. "This is our parent's house, and we should have some respect for the folks."

"Easy for you to say," Herbie shot back to his older brother while at the same time smoothing his hair down once more with his hands. "You been outta here for over a year with your fancy apartment, up on Park Avenue. You ain't gotta be here all the time followin' house rules. It's for the birds."

Irv smiled. "We've all got rules to follow," he said. "Incidentally, how about using better language?"

"Yeah, okay – but how about the rules you follow?" Herbie retorted. "You're a big shooter! You got your nightclubs, unions, craps games and your punchboards. Heck, Stanley Schneider says you even got yourself a whorehouse over in Brooklyn."

"I'm a Manhattan Assistant District Attorney," Irv told his brother, his voice now frigid. "And if you go shooting your mouth off like that, it'll be me going behind bars instead of the fellas that run up against me in court, you got that? And besides, I don't have a whorehouse in Brooklyn because that's Dutch Schultz's territory."

"You got punch boards in Brooklyn though."

"Herbie," Irv sputtered through clenched lips. "Shut up about that kinda shit, will you!"

"Well, I'm too old for a Bar Mitzvah anyhow," Herbie maintained. "For Pete's sake, Irv, I'm sixteen. A Bar Mitzvah is for a little thirteen-year-old pisher."

"Well if you'd gone to cheder and learned a little Hebrew when you were supposed to, it would have happened two years ago," Irv said. "I'm just glad you finally applied yourself and learned your moftir. In fact, I'm proud that you did."

Herbie said nothing in reply.

Irv knew full well that the only reason his younger brother had ever studied for the Bar Mitzvah was that Irv had told him he would give him a hundred dollars if he could memorize enough Hebrew to read his portion of the Torah in schul without making a fool out of himself.

"Well, look at my three fine gentlemen," their sister, Sarah Lowenstein beamed from the bathroom doorway. "My goodness, but you should always look this nice. You're all so handsome."

"Yeah," Irv laughed. "We're regular 'Beau Brummels', that's for sure."

"More like 'Diamond Jim Bradys'," Herbie added with a half sneer.

"You're my dreamboats," Sarah kvelled. "And speaking of dreamboats, Irv, is your good-looking bachelor friend, Mr. Goldblatt, going to be at the schul today?"

"He sure is," Irv said. "He's coming for the Bar Mitzvah ceremony, and he's staying for the kiddish as well. Then he's coming to the dinner party at Rosen's Catering Hall tonight, and he's bringing his girlfriend too."

"He's got a girlfriend?" Sarah frowned.

"From what I hear," Irv told her. "She's a knockout too. And they're almost engaged to be married." It was true. Mendy had been seeing a girl, Elaine Hoffman, for almost five months now, a quiet, shapely young woman who had come into the Moulin Rouge with some of her Jewish girlfriends on a dare. She was a graduate of NYCC, New York City College, and was now a librarian in upper Manhattan. She was exceptionally pretty, and she was Jewish. That was important to Mendy's parents. She lived in Manhattan with two roommates in an apartment now, but originally came from Brooklyn.

And she was, as Mendy put it, "A good steady girl, not like the flashy dames that we see in the club every single goddamn night. And you know what else she is, Irving? She's a way to get my Momma and Poppa off my back about dating a Jewish girl. But marriage? I'm not quite sure it's for me. I really haven't made up my mind yet. Actually, last night, I met someone else who's sort of interesting too, Margie Hauser, but I'm just thinking out loud. She's really not all that special yet," Mendy mused.

Irv had absolutely no illusions about Mendy ever settling down, and he hoped in his heart that Mendy's pretty Brooklyn librarian had no illusions on that account either. Elaine Hoffman may have been the only girl Mendy ever brought home to have Shabbas dinner with his mother and father, but Irv had seen his handsome single partner on plenty of mornings where he showed up for their breakfast meetings unshaven, having just come from a long night and a short sleep at the apartment of some Manhattan nightclub hostess, or even the occasional cocktail waitress or dancer from a Broadway show. He never dated anyone from the Moulin Rouge, however, because he didn't believe in dipping his pen into the company's ink well. It didn't make sense and was too dangerous, especially with all the available good-looking pussy around town.

"So nu?" Sarah smirked. "Who is my gorgeous brother bringing to this family shindig today? Miriam?"

Irv just rolled his eyes and nodded, as if he didn't really want to continue the conversation. "Yes," he said. "Miriam's coming today, and let's just leave it at that. She's a nice date."

Miriam Levine. Her father was an accountant with a respected Madison Avenue firm, while her mother was active in the Hadassah. She was one of those Jewish girls whose parents insisted that the family only attend religious services for Rosh Hashanah, Yom Kippur and other special occasions. She studied piano at Julliard, and Irv had met her through a friend from his law school class.

Miriam also knew Seymour, Irv's middle brother, also a student at Julliard and who played a mean piano and was starting to get fairly well-known around music circles.

Miriam had an idea that Irving was somehow involved in the Moulin Rouge Club because they'd had dinner there several times, but he'd always been careful to keep the gambling and the other businesses away from her, especially since he wasn't sure how serious he was about her. Esther and Morris Lowenstein were openly complaining about their eldest son's bachelorhood just like Mendy's parents and Miriam might just be the one for Irving. But, until he was sure, Irv didn't want her mouthing off to her folks about craps games, punch boards, and how her boyfriend, an Assistant District Attorney, was involved in all sorts of different businesses. And that included using the unions to put the arm on different companies for extortion money around the city in his spare time.

"Well," Sarah pouted. "Looks like everyone's got an escort but me. Guess I'll just have to spend my evening on the arm of the Bar Mitzvah boy." The pretty young girl put her arm around Herbie, who scowled and squirmed away.

"Knock it off," he complained, checking his reflection in the mirror and patting his hair down again for the third time. "You'll mess up my hair."

Half an hour later, Irv had the whole family in his brand new Cadillac touring sedan that he'd just picked up at the dealership on Broadway the week before. Because the family members were Conservative Jews rather than Orthodox, they usually drove to the synagogue instead of walking the thirty-five blocks. Herbie and his older brother, Seymour, were alongside of him in the front seat, and the rest of the family was in back. On the one side sat Morris Lowenstein, who had refused in no uncertain terms the offer Irv made to give him his old Chevrolet. Morris still insisted, ten years after Ford introduced the Model-T, that a car was a rich man's plaything, and what would the neighbors think if he were suddenly to appear on the streets at the wheel of such an extravagance?

On the other side sat Sarah, enjoying the attention that the fine automobile, with its regal blue body and large white sidewalls, was getting from the strapping young men standing on the sidewalks. Carrying sacks of flour and trundling barrels of pickles and beer from wagons drawn by teams of massive draft horses, they stopped what they were doing and nudged one another as if the Mayor himself was passing by on parade. Sneaking sidelong glances at their reactions, Sarah pretended to gaze straight ahead, and tried to look as if she rode to schul in a Cadillac everyday of her life.

And in between her husband and her daughter was Momma Esther Lowenstein who had begun trembling when she'd learned that they were going to the Bar Mitzvah in one of those new motorcars and was certain that, at any minute, the noisy contraption was going to explode.

Irv glanced back over his shoulder and grinned as he drove. He was proud of his family and had told himself many times over that they were the real reason he took the chances that he took.

Indeed, even the Cadillac was something of a risk since an Assistant D.A. made only a modest wage, barely enough to justify owning a car of any sort, let alone the finest automobile made in America. There would be gossip, it was inevitable. But Irv had let it be known around the office that he had been fortunate in a couple of wartime investments, and he had also told the D.A. himself that, thanks to the recent armistice, the Lowenstein family had finally been able to sell some real estate property that they had owned back in Germany and England.

Both stories were bald-faced lies. The Lowenstein family had never owned property in Europe and the house on Delancey was the first real estate that a Lowenstein had owned in more than six centuries. Well, actually the bank owned it, and even when Irv had tried to pay off the mortgage a few months ago, his father would not hear of such a thing. Irv had been contented to hire some contractors to help fix the place up, putting in an extra bathroom and all new heating and plumbing fixtures. That way, with a new furnace, Poppa would not have to get up so early on winter mornings to shovel coal. A year later Irving had convinced his father they should have a modern roof with asbestos shingles. Such things Morris Lowenstein allowed, as long as Irv called them Chanukah, anniversary or birthday presents, or a "little something for Momma because she worries about the roof in the winter." Morris Lowenstein would starve himself before taking charity, even from his own son. But when it came to his beloved Esther, he could deny her nothing.

Irv knew the truth would eventually come out, especially since the putz Blackman was always nosing around for dirt about Lowenstein. One of these days somebody would tell the District Attorney that Germany and England were in the midst of a devastating recession, land values had fallen, and even if there had been a Lowenstein family estate to liquidate, the proceeds would have been too modest to fund one of Henry Ford's Tin Lizzies, let alone a Cadillac.

However, Irv planned to be long gone from the District Attorney's Office by the time that happened. Two years of brilliant prosecution had now given him a conviction record that any lawyer would envy, especially Milton Blackman, who had, since law school, been snapping at Irving Lowenstein's heels in pure jealousy. But regardless of Blackman, Irving had managed to handle his initial cases with such aplomb that the D.A. had quickly elevated him from the basic work of traffic offenses and petty thefts and burglaries to major gang-related crime – the criminal justice system's major leagues. But plenty of other mobsters in the rackets, craps games, numbers, pimps, prostitutes, and loan-shark thugs, had gone to jail from Irv's courtrooms. But, they hadn't gone for long because Irv had always asked for lenient sentences, giving him a reputation as a staunch advocate for rehabilitation. And the gangsters at the very top of the mob hierarchy had never been bothered by the D.A.'s Office, primarily because of Irving's effort. They had enjoyed remarkable freedom from the scrutiny of the law-enforcement community.

So Irv had accomplished what he'd wanted. He'd become both feared and respected in the world of organized crime, gained connections at the very top of New York City's political and social machine, and he'd obligated the heads of some of the most important Jewish and Italian crime families – from Charlie Lucky Luciano to Bugsy Siegel, Meyer Lansky, Salvatore Maranzano and Arnold Rothstein. There were even some out-of-town heavyweights like the Fleisher brothers and Benny and Joe Bernstein from Detroit's Purple Gang. Irv had already accomplished everything he'd wanted in the D.A.'s office. Next month, he planned to submit his resignation, tell the District Attorney that he'd decided to go into private practice. He had even signed a lease for a small office space in the Woolworth Building to complete the charade.

Eventually, Irv knew rumors would come out, would be checked out, and would give rise to questions. But by that time, Irv had plans to be so far along in his plans as to literally be above prosecution.

Already he had just about every important cop in Manhattan's Ninth Precinct on his payroll, and he was also paying off police officers in other precincts around the city, and even Newark. As far as the criminal justice system was concerned, the other side of Irv Lowenstein's life, the side where he made all of his money, was squeaky clean. His boys never got bothered by the police.

* * *

The family schul was on Orchard Street, a little storefront place with a menorah in the curtained front window. The sidewalk was swept clean from the light November snow that had fallen the evening before and old men were already arriving for morning prayer, most of them in worn woolen suits, a few wearing the black suits and forelocks of Chassidim. This part of the Lower Eastside was, as America was, a melting pot with Russian Jews, Lithuanian, Polish, German and Austrian Jews. Even a few English and Irish Jews worshipped together in the same schul, putting aside the religious reform, Conservative and Orthodox differences that had set them apart in Europe for hundreds of years.

Irv pulled up to the front of the synagogue and then helped his mother and Sarah out of the car, escorting them into the women's side of the little schul, while his father, Herbie and Seymour retired to the men's area to put on their yarmulke and tallis, prayer shawls, and prepare Herbie for his Bar Mitzvah, acceptance as a young man into the religious faith of Judaism.

Irv hung up his mother's overcoat and then left everyone while he took the Cadillac and headed up Orchard street south to Broome, to the banquet hall that Irving had arranged to rent for a song. He really wanted to hire a fancy uptown Jewish caterer like Wells Symington. Irv could still remember when he was Wally Singer, but he wasn't quite ready for that yet. Maybe for the next party. He parked on the street out front; since everyone knew whose car it was, no one in his right mind would bother it.

Irv picked his way through the dusting of snow on the sidewalks out front and around to the service entrance where the mingled aromas of lox, salami, corned beef, pastrami and chopped liver, good thick Jewish rye breads from the best bakery in the neighborhood, and a dozen kinds of pastries and cookies made his mouth water. He smiled and walked into the hall, where the plump caterer was supervising the setting of folding chairs and tables. Reading glasses perched on the tip of his aquiline nose, pudgy Sammy Rosen, the caterer, dressed in a tailored suit and hand-made monogrammed shirt, ticked off items on his clipboard with a heavy gold Waterman fountain pen.

"There's snow on the sidewalk out front," Irv told Rosen as he walked up to the man. "Better get somebody to sweep it."

Sammy Rosen looked over his glasses, not bothering to raise his head. "That's a maintenance problem, boychick," he said as he continued to tick off his checklist.

"It's your problem," Irv replied coolly. "I'm paying you good money for this kiddish, and I expect some service and right now. Have one of your people go outside and sweep it now, before the snow gets trampled onto the sidewalk and makes it slick when it freezes later on."

The man peered back over his glasses, considering what Irv had just said. "Certainly, boychick," Rosen said, snapping his fingers and calling over a busboy whom he dispatched outside with an overcoat and a broom. Then looking back to his clipboard and addressing it rather than Lowenstein, he asked, "Would you care to look over our waitstaff now or a little later?"

"Pardon?"

"The staff, boychick," Rosen replied, looking in Irv's general direction this time. "Would you care to have them line up so you can inspect them? I got them all wearing tuxedos just like you requested Mister L."

"Mister L?" Irving Lowenstein wasn't used to being addressed by his initial. He just shook his head in exasperation. "Oh! Sure, line 'em up."

Another snap of Rosen's fingers and a dozen young men, ruddy-faced and barbered, not an Italian or a Semitic face among them, stopped what they were doing and dressed in flawlessly pressed dinner jackets and trousers, they fell into line in front of Irv. All kept their faces somberly neutral, their postures ramrod straight.

Irv took them in, left to right, and then turned back to the caterer. "They look just fine, but make sure they give the people some great service. After all, this is a fancy party, and I want everyone talking 'bout what a swell affair the Lowenstein's put on for their son's Bar Mitzvah."

"Don't worry, boychick, this will be one swell party," Rosen said, winking at Irv with a smile.

"May I see you out in the lobby for a moment Mister Rosen?"

"You've got it, Mr. L, and don't you give it a second thought about the party," he said, wagging his finger in Irving's face as they walked out to the lobby. "The guests will love it. Guaranteed, boychick! It'll be swell!"

When they were in the banquet hall's small entry foyer, Rosen shut the door to the hall, turned and smiled, expecting Mister Lowenstein to be pleased with the arrangements. "If it's about the food, everything's taken care of, and you're in the hands of Sammy Rosen, the best kosher caterer in the entire city. I got the best food for the best prices, boychick."

Before Rosen could say another word, Irv had snatched the fountain pen out of his hand and was holding it vertically about two inches in front of his nose. "Now you listen to me, you fat pompous little fuck," Irv whispered. "If you call me boychick or Mr. L. once more, I'm personally gonna shove this fancy gold pen so far up your ass that you'll have to sit on the desk to sign a check. Do you understand me?"

Ashen, Sammy Rosen nodded.

"Good," Irv said, jamming the pen down into the caterer's breast pocket. Irv took out a twenty-dollar bill and shoved it in after the pen. "Now as soon as your maintenance man gets done sweeping the sidewalks out front, why don't you give him the twenty and send him out to help park any buggies or motorcars that will shortly be arriving? Do you hear me?"

Rosen nodded again, his face white with fright. He had never been spoken to like that before.

"Good," Irv repeated. "So when I get back here after my brother's Bar Mitzvah ceremony at the synagogue, I can expect everything to be smooth as silk, right?"

Another nod.

"Excellent," Irv whispered, slapping the side of the man's face lightly. "And I know that everyone in this hall will be taken great care of by your staff as if they were fuckin' English royalty, right?"

Sammy Rosen nodded again and looked like he was going to faint on the spot.

Straightening his tie, Irv opened the front door and stepped out into the reception area, turning once more to Rosen, "I'm sure your boys will do just fine."

* * *

The caterer stood there for a moment after the door had closed, and then felt a dampness in his pants. He rushed over to the employees' bathroom breathing heavily. He looked down at dark wet spots spread around his crotch. For a minute he felt faint and gasped for breath. Irving Lowenstein was not to be treated lightly. From now on he would know better!

* * *

It was now past twelve noon and Herbie had just finished chanting a perfect moftir, and the whole congregation had moved over to Rosen's. Since the synagogue was too small for the kiddish following the Bar Mitzvah ceremony, the Lowensteins had arranged for the noon kiddish to be catered by Sammy Rosen at his banquet hall down on Orchard Street. The catering staff was all dressed in white aprons folded over at the waists displaying their starched white shirtfronts over black pants. Rosen himself had changed from a gray flannel suit to a pair of chocolate brown pants, a fresh white shirt and camel hair sport jacket with a solid brown tie. His waiters brought several trays over to Esther Lowenstein and urged her to sample the lox, the gefilte fish, the brisket of beef and the rich pastries, also to pinch the shiny twisted freshly baked challah bread to see for herself the freshness.

Irv Lowenstein stood back and watched his mother beam as if she were a queen, which she was on this special day – the queen of the Lower Eastside. She even had her own court – Irv's Miriam and Mendel's Elaine, both who had sat with Esther and Sarah on the women's side of the schul as Herbie had read from the Torah, and attended her now as she smiled at her friends and her family.

"Kain ein horeh," Barney Green told Irv. "What a feast. And this is just the kiddish? I've seen wedding dinners that weren't nearly as wonderful as this."

Irv smiled and squeezed Barney on the shoulder. Barney was the living proof that Esther Lowenstein still ruled her roust. Barney was Irv's first choice as Rabbi to officiate at the Bar Mitzvah, but Esther disagreed. She wanted Rabbi Ashbaum. True, he wasn't the Delancey Street schul, but Rabbi Ashbaum, the youngster who had come to assist and pretty much replace Rabbi Kirshfeld after he had suffered a stroke, could not, in Irv's opinion, pour piss out of a boot with instructions printed on the heel. But, Ashbaum, Momma had insisted, was their Rabbi and besides, that Green fellow was from Brooklyn, and they said that he had been a former prizefighter. And while he was welcome as her son's guest, their own Rabbi would do the honors just fine.

It didn't matter, Irv supposed. A Rabbi didn't do much at a Bar Mitzvah anyhow except announce the next few holy days, meetings of the men's auxiliary and members of the congregation that have recently passed away. He also took out the Torah, put it back, and whispered the right words in the Bar Mitzvah boy's ears if he had forgotten a certain passage because, in the excitement of the moment, his mind went blank. After the moftir was finished, he would also give a twenty to thirty minute sermon praising the Bar Mitzvah boy, the congregation and the most recent large contributors for the synagogue building fund.

Irv straightened his yarmulke, setting it squarely on the back of his head. He often thought that the little black skull caps never really fit anybody, except the old guys who were all bald back there anyhow.

"You're too kind, Barney," Irv smiled with Barney Green's enthusiastic praise for the kiddish, and then thought of something else. "Incidentally, before I forget, Rabbi, that kid you came to bail out of trouble a few months ago, you got him straightened out now? He's okay?"

"More than okay, thanks to you." The young Rabbi Green grinned appreciatively. "Let me know how I can repay you. I owe you a big one, and I won't forget it."

"Hey even a guy like me might need a rebbe to talk to every once in awhile," Irv said resolutely, but with a twinkle in his eyes. "Just be there for me, okay?"

The smile straightened a little and Barney Green suddenly looked serious again. "I will, Irving," he said. "I give you my word. I will."

An awkward silence followed, after which Irv clapped Barney on the shoulder again. "C'mon, Rabbi," he said. "You met my Poppa at the schul, but let me introduce you to the real boss of our family, my Momma. But first, a glass of Mogen David wine, this one's especially good."

* * *

The Delancey Street crowd knew about the Lowenstein Bar Mitzvah and all the important people that had been invited over to the kiddish at Rosen's. It was the largest hall in the neighborhood, and still the two men who had just come into the crowded room turned sideways to pass through the large crowd. Irv was just bringing Barney over to meet his mother when Rabbi Ashbaum stepped up to him.

"Excuse me, Mister Lowenstein," he said. "But there's a gentleman, Mister Guido Lucci, here to see you at the front door."

"Lucci?" Irv's mother turned to him. "One of those Lucci boys came here?" When the invitations were being made out, old Giovanni Lucci, Morris Lowenstein's longtime friend, had of course been on the invitation list for dinner, as had his wife, Isabella. But at mention of the Lucci boys, Esther Lowenstein had put her foot down and said, "No."

"They run around town with their fancy suits, their Chesterfield cigarettes and a different girl every night," Momma had exclaimed. "They are no good, I tell you. Trombeniks... I hear the stories about them. They're no good. I will not have them, not at my Herbie's Bar Mitzvah."

Irv had prayed that his mother would never find out that the Lucci brothers had suits and cigarettes bought with his street money, and the girls on their arms were dancers from his other clubs. And it would have been no treat for three young Italians to get invited to a Bar Mitzvah dinner and sit around and watch the alterkochers, the old men, dance to a five-piece band anyhow. So he hadn't argued.

"And Guido," Momma went on. "The worst one of the bunch, a real hoodlum. Irving, why would you ask him here?"

"I didn't, Momma," Irv began.

"Well get rid of him quick, before people start to talk."

"Sure, Momma. I think you're wrong, but I'll do it if you feel that way."

He shouldered his way through the crowd to the lobby, which was empty. He looked around and saw Lucci's snap-brim hat at a jaunty angle, collar turned up on his topcoat, standing out on the steps. Lucci was a fairly large man with a dark complexion and wasn't hard to spot. Irv pushed the door open. "Guido," Irv beamed. "Get in here before you freeze your ass off. For Chrissake!"

"Oh thanks, Irv." Lucci removed his hat, brushed his coat off, looked around and noticed Irv's yarmulke. He quickly put his hat back on and then crossed himself.

Irv chuckled at the thought of a Catholic genuflecting at a Jewish reception. "It's a banquet hall, Guido, not a church. The beanies are just traditional. Come on in and eat something. You're getting' too skinny so we'll fatten you up a little."

"No, no please. I can't stay. I don' wanna crash your party or anything. It's just…"

"Guido Lucci!" Esther Lowenstein approached with her arms outstretched, as if Lucci was a part of her family. "What a mitzvah! What a treat!" She kissed him leaving red rouge on his cheek. "Come in…come in. Eat with us."

"Oh no, Missus Lowenstein, really. I don't have no invitation…"

"Invitation?" She dismissed his protest with a wave of her hand and gave him a little glass of sweet wine. "This is a kiddish, Guido. Don't you know our ways by now? There are no invitations. You just come. You're part of the family. Now come, nosh with us."

"Well," Guido grinned. "Maybe just a bite."

Irving, completely amazed with his mother's change of attitude, almost laughed out loud, but instead pulled off Guido's coat and hat, shoved a yarmulke on his head, and moved him through the buffet line.

"Irving," the young man whispered. "This is very nice, really. But I gotta tell ya somethin'. You got a place we can talk?" He continued to eat off his plate as they walked to the back of the hall and into a small office between the reception area and the kitchen.

"What's up?" Irv asked, as he put Lucci's coat on a chair.

"Abie Feldman is what's up."

Irv scowled. Abe Feldman was just a snot-nosed kid, not twenty-one years old, and the nephew of Sam Feldman, Morris Lowenstein's best man at his and Esther's wedding. As a favor to Sam, Irv had hired the kid to be a courier, to carry money from the uptown games down to the Lower Eastside warehouse where Irv and Mendy kept their count room. But lately, it looked like the kid was coming in short. Worse yet, he was bragging to his friends about how he was fucking over the big momzers down on Delancey, and they were too dumb to even notice the shortage.

"He's got his hand in the till for sure?" Irv asked.

Lucci nodded.

"We counted when he came in and when he left the game. A hundred."

Irv whistled. The Feldman kid did the weekday runs. Weekends, they used two guys together. Still, at a hundred a run, five nights a week, the kid was stealing almost five hundred dollars a week out of their pocket. "Okay," Irv said. "I've gotta be here awhile more, maybe another hour."

"I unnerstand."

"He ever been to the club?"

"Naw, we don't take him there."

"All right," Irv said. "Blindfold him and drive him around awhile, for about 30 minutes. Then take him over a few bridges, and head over to the Moulin Rouge Club. Put him in the back room where they bring in the booze and the food, okay?"

"You've got it, Irvie."

Irv walked him back to the lobby and Esther Lowenstein waved at them.

"Nu you'll come back for dinner tonight at seven," she said, approaching Guido. "And don't be late Mister Lucci. It's a special day for the Lowensteins."

"Aw, I gotta work Missus Lowenstein, but thanks anyways." Lucci smiled.

"Well if you get the chance, come back for a nosh."

Lucci smiled. Once in the lobby, he stopped and handed Irv an envelope. "For the Bar Mitzvah boy," he grinned. "From me and my brudders."

Irv hefted it. There was a wad of bills in there.

"Now, Guido," he said. "That's not necessary."

"Please!" The Italian raised a hand. "Don't embarrass us."

Irv nodded and pocketed the envelope. "You'll come back for dinner?"

"Are you kidding?" Lucci rolled his eyes. "Your Momma's really not too crazy about us. I know that, and I wouldn't dream of spoiling her night. But thanks anyways, Irving. You're a good friend and besides," he added with a grin. "We've got us some new young dancers to try out tonight."

Irv shook his head, smiling. "One hour," he told the Italian. "I'll see you at the club in exactly one hour," emphasizing the importance of the exact time by pointing at his wristwatch.

* * *

It felt strange to Irv and Mendy, walking into the back door of the Moulin Rouge Club at two in the afternoon. The evening deliveries would not be coming for another two hours, the kitchen opened at six, and the band at eight. The place was quiet, not much activity at all. Guido Lucci had opened the back door in the alley when they knocked. He had his coat off, his sleeves rolled up.

"He here?" Mendel asked, his cold stare piercing the room.

"Oh yeah," Lucci said. "He's here, been waitin' for ya."

They went into a storeroom where a single kitchen chair had been set in the middle of the floor, crates lined one wall. A couple of mailbags lay empty atop of them. Abe Feldman was tied, shivering and blindfolded in the chair. His mouth taped so he could only gurgle. The only other two people there were Francisco and Aldo Lucci, Guido's brothers. And almost as big.

Irv nodded, just family. Good. He walked over and took the blindfold off the young man. "Abie," Irv said pleasantly, ripping the tape off his mouth.

"Oh Irv," the kid blubbered with pain, blinking his red eyes. "I am so, so, so goddamn sorry."

"I bet you are," Mendel agreed.

"I didn't do it for me," the kid said.

"Didn't do what?" Irv asked.

"You know."

"What?" Mendel asked. "You can't talk about it with Mr. Lowenstein, but you can tell every other snot-nosed pisher that runs the street with ya, right?."

"Who'd you do it for, Abie?" Irv asked quietly.

"My girl," the kid said. "Theresa Wojinski, she's a Polack, came over on a steamship two years ago from Warsaw. She's working in the garment district, payin' off her passage. They put the vigorish on her you know, and it ain't ever gonna pay off, 'cept I help her."

"So you stole from me?" Irv said.

The kid nodded, tears flooding his eyes.

"Abe," Irv said. "Has anybody here ever hurt you?"

The kid looked up. "Huh?"

"Hurt you, you know hit you? Roughed you up?"

"Naw," the kid said. "I mean Guido, he punched me in the gut when he picked me up this morning to get in the car, but I had that coming. I was trying to take it on the lam."

Irv grinned, winked at Guido.

"What do you think about that?" Irv asked Mendel.

"You're the boss. What do you think we should do with this kid?" Mendy asked.

"Well this kid, he's no stranger, you know," Irv said. "I mean his uncle and my Poppa, they go way back. We need to think about that. It counts for somethin'."

The kid looked up, hopeful.

"How much did you take, kid?" Mendel asked.

"Three hunnerd," the kid said.

"How much?"

"Okay, five hunnerd."

Mendy looked at Guido. The Italian shrugged, nodded.

"Okay," Mendy said. "Our people have laws, traditions, you know that? You steal, you pay back five times over. Five times five, you know what that is?"

"Sure," Abie nodded. "It's twenty-five hundred."

"So twenty-five hundred is what you owe Mister Lowenstein," Mendel said. "You understand that?"

The young man nodded. "I'll get it," he said. "I'll pay him."

"Not all at once," Irv warned. "I don't want you robbing banks or something."

"No," the kid said. "I'll work two jobs. Don'cha worry none. I'll get it."

"Okay," Mendel said. "Now you came in here blindfolded, right?"

The kid nodded.

"Know where you are now?"

The kid shook his head, no.

"All right," Mendel said. "We gotta keep it that way. You understand, right?"

Another shake.

Mendy walked over to the far wall, picked up a mailbag, carried it back and pulled it over the kid's head. "You okay in there?" Mendy asked, taking the Smith and Wesson .38 out of the shoulder holster that he wore. Silently, he cocked the gun. "You can breathe and stuff?"

The mailbag nodded.

"Good," Mendy said. "Now let me just fix this." He felt the mailbag, found the kid's eyes, put the gun barrel up to the right eye and pulled the trigger. The bang was muted, and the mailbag slumped over. A small wisp of smoke came out of a little hole in the bag.

"You see that?" Mendy asked Irv. "It's better'n in the back of the head like Bugsy Siegel and Luciano like so much. This way there's not much blood, no blood. You shoot 'em close in the eye like that, and you don't get hardly any blood."

"Good," Irv said. "My suit's brand new and I don't want to chance getting it messed up with blood. Your's too, right?"

"I thought of that," Mendy agreed. "I read the thing about the eye in a dime detective novel, but I didn't know it would work so well."

"And that was decent of you," Irv observed. "To give him hope like that."

"Well," Mendy said. "You said his uncle was a friend of your Poppa's, right?"

"Him?" Irv shrugged. "I was just talking. My Poppa knew his uncle, but hasn't seen him in a few years. He probably wouldn't know him from Mozart now."

"Okay then," Mendy said, as he turned and kicked the corpse once, hard, in the head. "Smack him around," he told the Luccis. "That way he'll have some bruises on him, and it sends a strong message to anybody thinking of robbing us. Then dump his ass down by the river."

"Hey," Irv said. "We'd better get going. The dinner's in two hours, and we've gotta pick up the girls yet."

* * *

It was 10:00 p.m., and the Bar Mitzvah dinner had been exactly what Irving had expected. It wasn't as crowded as the kiddish, but the dinner was just a little over a hundred people, mostly family and close friends of his parents.

Up on the bandstand, the combo – piano, trumpet, drums and saxophone player – was playing all the popular music from Tin Pan Alley, Gershwin, Cole Porter and Sammy Fain. Several couples were already on the dance floor swaying back and forth to the smooth music. Off to the side, four alterkochers had put Herbie on a chair and carried him over their heads in celebration of the new Bar Mitzvah bocher. Herbie was already slightly schnockered from three glasses of wine and so was his younger brother Seymour.

"Well," Irv said. "Mendel and I have to work in the morning, and these ladies need their beauty rest."

Miriam and Elaine giggled in harmony.

It took ten minutes to make the rounds and say the goodbyes, another five to bring the car around. When he came in to get the girls, Irv grabbed a bottle of whiskey and put it under the seat. He took Miriam home first, then drove uptown to drop off Elaine, pretending not to notice as she pressed closer and closer to Mendy in the back seat. After Elaine had been safely seen to her door, Mendy jumped into the front seat and the two men drove off.

"You really want to go home?" Irv asked.

Mendy shook his head. "There's a table of showgirls who want to work in the club, remember? Guido's saving the best two for us before he hires them."

"Two? Is that all?" Irv laughed and reached under the seat bringing up the whiskey bottle. He handed it to Mendy, who opened it and then gave it back to Irving. "Time to get fortified," Irv said.

They had passed the bottle back and forth a few times as Irv drove over to the club, but suddenly he stopped the car at an intersection. "Mendy, you know something? We've only a year left for legal booze in this country; the Volstead Act is gonna pass, sure as hell. They're gonna shut the distilleries down in the next twelve months."

"Not this one," Mendy said. He pointed at the label which read Canadian Club.

"Agreed," Irv said. "We'll buy from a Canadian distiller when we can't get the real stuff in the States anymore. The club has to have the best to keep its customers, agreed?"

"Absolutely! That's exactly what we'll have to do then," Mendy said. "Either that or buy moonshine from Kentucky. But I've tasted moonshine and most of it isn't worth a damn. It tastes like piss. And, that's not gonna win us any customers."

"Just think," Irv said as he continued to drive again. "One year from now, you, me, anybody that wants to drink, he's gonna need to know someone who can get it for him." He turned and looked at Mendy. "That's where the dough is gonna be, you know," he said. "Big dough, too. Not in the nightclubs, but in the booze."

"So you think we ought to get in the booze business?" Mendy asked.

"I know we ought to," Irv replied. "But also keep the Moulin Rouge, the Cavalier Club and the Mirage Club; and, maybe open up two or three more speaks, not quite as classy as the Moulin Rouge but in the same general category like the Cavalier and Mirage. Sort of corner the upper class market. Whaddaya think?"

"Not a bad idea, but how do we get in the whiskey business? The speaks are easy 'cause we already know the business."

Irv drove in silence, thinking.

"I know how we'll do it," he finally said. And, we won't be stepping on the toes of Meyer Lansky, Luciano, Longey Zwillman or even Arnold Rothstein and any of his boys."

"Okay…" Mendy replied, waiting. "So nu? Nu?"

Irv held up the bottle. "We buy fucking Canadian Club," Irv said. "Or, Hiram Walker, or whoever the fuck makes the stuff. Liquor stays legal in Canada, then we buy Canadian Club, sell it up in Canada for a profit, or arrange to have it brought down to the States for even more profit."

"Sounds good," Mendy said. "How much does it cost to buy…" He squinted at the label again. "…How much does it cost to buy Hiram Walker?"

"I don't know," Irv admitted. "A couple million, I'd guess."

"Couple million, huh?" Mendy chuckled. "We've got some money, but we don't have that much, that's for sure."

They pulled up in front of the club. Jazz music spilled out from the windows.

"So we raise it then," Irv said, shaking his head.

"How?"

"I don't have a clue," Irv admitted. "But there's gotta be a way for a coupla enterprising young guys like us. How about going to the boys, Lansky, Siegel and Zwillman to form a little partnership?

"I don't think so, Irv. We aren't big enough for them yet." Mendy moved to get out of the car. Then he stopped, still thinking. "You know," he said, looking at Irving, his head cocked. "But, maybe…just maybe, I do have a way."

Chapter Eleven
The Same Day

Twenty blocks uptown from the Lowenstein Bar Mitzvah kiddish, Lou Kravitz walked down 37th Street, the ruptured duck freshly stitched on the left breast pocket of his officer's uniform, his cap scrunched down low to shield him from the biting early winter wind, his heavy duffel bag tossed over his shoulder and balanced by his left hand. He carried his B-four officer's bag in his other hand. Lou stopped at an intersection, stared up at the street sign, and then looked down at the address scrawled on the paper in his gloved hand. Nearly five blocks to go and his six-foot-three-inch frame was starting to sag as the heavy duffel bag was starting to bother him. He should have taken a cab, he supposed, but cabs cost money and were hard to come by at the noon hour. He shifted the bag up higher on his shoulder and grabbed the B-four even firmer.

After trudging the long five blocks through a steadily increasing blanket of snow, Lou got to the Park Avenue address on the paper, a brownstone with steep stairs leading up to a small landing and a plate glass door. A small round woman in a babushka was sweeping the snow off the landing, and she looked up as he stopped.

"Are you lost, son? Can I help you?"

Lou smiled. It was the uniform, he knew. Everyone was ready to help a returning soldier now that the war in Europe was over. "Does Martha Van Dyke live here?"

The woman straightened up for a moment. "Why you can't be...?"

"Oh no, ma'am," Lou said, taking off his hat despite the cold wind. "I was a friend of Henry's. I've brought his wife some of his personal effects."

"Why, God bless you," the woman said. "She's in 2-B, one floor up. Here, I'll see you up there."

"No, please," Lou replied. The woman was obviously winded just sweeping, and she had ankles as thick as loaves of bread. "I can make it myself."

"No, it's no trouble, sir." She turned and held the door open for him, and then preceded him up the stairs, resting on each riser, leaning with both hands on the banister. The apartment building, which had once been smart and stylish, was now showing its age. The Park Avenue address was the best part of it except for being fairly cheap rent. The carpeting on the stairway needed to be changed and the place generally needed a good painting with some new light fixtures installed in the hallway. "It was such...a tragedy about...poor Major Van Dyke..." The landlady huffed as she mounted the remaining stairs. "Him a...father and...never even seeing...the precious little one." She turned, her eyes misty with tears. "I lost a son too," she said. "To the influenza epidemic. He never even left this country. Imagine that! Spent the entire two years at Fort Riley in Kansas."

Lou said earnestly, "He did his duty, ma'am. Any death in the military service of our country is honorable."

She seemed more than satisfied with his answer and gave Lou a warm smile and then knocked on the door of the apartment at the top of the stairs. A vertical strip of light appeared as the door was opened.

"There's an officer here, a Major, Martha," the landlady said. "a friend of Henry's."

The landlady stepped aside and there she was. Martha Van Dyke, looking as young as she had looked when Lou and Henry had first met her in college as Martha Donovan. She had been a college student then. Her dark auburn-colored hair was still radiant about her face as if the light of heaven itself were falling upon her. She had a baby in her arms and the effect was not unlike the paintings of the Madonna that he had seen at the Louvre in Paris after the Armistice. Lou gripped the banister and steadied himself. What was happening here? He had come to help the widow of his best friend, a friend only a few months in his grave. Yet he found himself totally captivated by her Irish beauty. He swallowed hard and smiled.

"Lou!" Martha swarmed all over him and buried her face in his chest sobbing and laughing at the same time. "Oh God, I've prayed you'd be spared from the horrors of war, and you were."

"I wish that it had been Henry instead of me," he muttered smitten by the fresh smell of her recently washed hair.

She stopped holding him and stepped back. "Don't ever say that," she said sternly. "And I mean it. Don't ever say that again. The Lord takes whom he will, and it does none of us any good to grieve over his choices. My Henry's life was brief, but he had a wife who adored him. And he may never have seen him, but he knew he had a son and believe me, that son will know more about his daddy than most other kids." Her complexion was radiant as she pulled back a slip of blanket to reveal a slumbering six-month-old.

Lou beamed at the child who had a mop of reddish-blond hair and ruddy peach-colored cheeks. "He's a great lookin' kid. He looks just like his mommy. Henry would have been so proud." He turned away from her full of emotion. "Oh, Martha," he whispered with a hoarse voice. "It was a bum war. A bum war. It took our guys, some of them just boys barely eighteen. Henry was killed in action over a year ago, but I can still feel him with me all the time."

She took a deep breath, closed her eyes and held it before reminding him that thanks to God, most of our soldiers returned home at the end of the war. Martha looked down at her robe and hurriedly clutched it together. "My goodness," she blushed. "Would you look at me, here in my dressing gown." She pulled it shut, drawing the fold together on the soft cleft between her breasts.

"I should have let you know I was coming, but the ship just docked this morning. I can wait out here in the kitchen with a cup of coffee while you change."

"Okay," Martha said. "I'll only be a few minutes, so make yourself at home. I'd like to make lunch for you, if you have the time. Think about it while I'm changing clothes." Martha turned to the landlady. "Thank you for bringing him up, Mrs. Dubinski." Then she closed the door to the bedroom.

The landlady smiled and wheezed her way back down the stairs, as Lou took off his trench coat and settled himself in the kitchen. Of course, he had known all along that Martha Van Dyke was a beautiful woman, a desirable woman, the kind of woman that men dreamed of. He could remember her as a student barmaid back when he and Henry had first met her, a small apron wrapped around her waist, a serving tray in her hands, waves of red hair clinging to a sweat-dampened face, as she brought drinks to the table. She earned extra money with tips to help defray college expenses. Even then, Martha Donovan had been an Irish beauty, but she had been Henry's, and he had understood that all along. Henry was the one she loved, and besides, with his family's money, there was no question that he could support her in ways that most men could scarcely imagine. So Lou had given moral support to the misty-eyed couple. In fact, Lou recalled an incident one morning at breakfast in the officer's mess hall after Henry had left, one of the other fellows had made a snide crack about Martha having a great ass, and Lou had decked the man out cold on the dining-hall floor with a single punch, the only time he had ever hit a man in his life. And for what? For verbalizing the exact same thoughts that he had just entertained himself. It had been several weeks now since he had last made love to a woman in London. He reminded himself of why he had come here – friendship. And besides, he had made a promise to Henry and a promise made was a promise kept as far as Lou was concerned. He was doing the right thing for a widow whose young husband had died for his country. He closed his eyes and took a deep breath just as Martha opened the door and came out of her bedroom.

Lou Kravitz smiled and sipped at his cup of coffee, looking around the attractive breakfast nook. At first, he had refused lunch because the cupboards in the little off-beat Park Avenue apartment had looked sparse, and he didn't want to take anything from the young mother and her infant son. But she had insisted, so he joined her for a tuna sandwich, some potatoes chips and a few hermits – brown spice and raisin cookies. Pretty soon he was telling her stories about London and the English countryside, the good parts of the war.

"You sound as if you loved it," Martha surmised. "Did Henry love it too?"

"He did," Lou said enthusiastically. "And he wished you could have been there to see it with us. He kept saying how he wanted to bring you back to England someday soon after the war."

"That would have been nice." Martha smiled. "But now we can take little Henry to see where his father was a hero." She said it without smiling and just a faint touch of tears in her eyes. "Maybe one day we can all go together," she said innocently without thinking about the significance of her words.

The aching in Lou's loins returned. "I brought you his things," he said. He opened a folded cloth and carefully took out a gold Waltham pocket watch, a Waterman pen and a pair of captain's bars, along with the gold oak leaves of a Major. "I told them to bury him with his wedding band," he said. "I hope I wasn't presumptuous?"

"No," Martha shook her head. "I like that, and Henry would have too."

Irv nodded and then took out an envelope. "They didn't pay me for awhile in France," he said. "We were pretty far advanced into the front lines, and there wasn't anything to do with the money anyhow. Nothing but gamble, and I don't play cards or dice. So, well, anyhow…I didn't get paid until they mustered me out this morning, and I got it all at once. My back pay for almost half a year, overseas pay, per diem pay. I want you to have it." He handed her the envelope, and Martha lifted it.

It was thick, and she looked at the penciled notation on the side, Kravitz, L., Major, $1540. "Lou," the young woman whispered. "I get widow's compensation from Henry's death."

"I know," he said. "But it's not much. Not what Henry would have given you."

"Don't worry about us. His family has plenty of money," she murmured with reservation.

"But are they sharing it with you?" Lou stared directly at her, waiting for an honest answer. "Or do they dole it out for the baby and then put the balance into a trust account?"

She shrugged. "Neither."

"Take the money then," he insisted. "Please, I want you to."

She opened up the envelope, counted out seven hundred dollars and put it in a handbag that sat on the kitchen shelf. She put the rest back in the envelope and handed it back to him. "You're swell, Lou," she said. "You really are a good friend. But if you really want to help us, help me to get a job."

Lou sat up puzzled.

"Henry's family really wants nothing to do with me," she explained with a grim face. "Or the baby either. As far as they're concerned, we're both just shanty Irish and not good enough to polish their boots. But, that's okay, we don't need their money even if it's a little hard getting started. Help me get a job, Lou, and we'll show them our heels."

"I will," Lou promised. "Martha, you can count on it too, within two weeks. It'll be a good one, too." He nodded his head vigorously in affirmation.

He stood up, and she stood as well wrapping her arms around him. She had changed from her robe into a black dress to receive him, a dress with a high lace neck, but on her it had a seductive appeal. He hugged her back and then stepped away before more could happen.

"I'll stay in touch," he promised. "You'll hear from me in a few days."

"Thank you," she whispered. "Thank you for coming back from this terrible war."

He went out before anymore could be said, down the stairs and out into the cold. The landlady was there just coming up the stoop from the local market with a bag of groceries.

"Mrs....Mrs. Dubinski?" Lou asked.

"Yes, sir?"

"Mrs. Van Dyke's rent," he asked. "How much is it?"

She looked at him for a moment. "Twenty dollars a month," she said. "Which is quite a lot, I know, but there's many that would want to live here, and the price of coal has gone up."

"I'm sure it has," he said. "Tell me, is she paid up to date?"

"Now, Major..."

As he helped her with the groceries standing in front of the building, Lou blurted out, "Please. Her husband was my best friend, and I want to help her and the baby...You know, help her get her feet on the ground."

"Well," the landlady said, pursing her lips together. "She's two months behind, but not to worry. I won't put her out, not with a little one at her breast."

Lou stepped up, holding out eight twenty-dollar bills.

"Mercy!" the landlady whispered, looking at the wad of green bills.

"The two she's behind and six more," he said. "And tell her it was the Veteran's Benevolent Fund that paid it, will you?"

"Benevolent Fund," she repeated. "Is there really such a thing?"

"There is now." Lou smiled.

* * *

Lou Kravitz walked quickly down the street trying to stay warm in the 40-degree temperature. There was still six hundred and eighty dollars in his pay envelope, and he'd be staying at his uncle's again until he could lease another apartment so he thought maybe he should take a cab. But he decided to keep walking because it helped him to think and right now he had plenty to think about.

He couldn't get Martha Van Dyke out of his mind. He had never met a more beautiful, more desirable woman in his life. Even the French girls in Paris didn't appeal to him like Martha, but he still fucked them all anyways. And with Henry gone, he was thinking of her in an entirely different way. He had to get those thoughts outta his mind, at least for now. It didn't seem right to him. Martha needed time. He needed time, time to mourn, to grieve, to adjust. And when that was over, maybe…just maybe…he would want to see her again, but in a different way. But now he needed to find her that job that she needed so desperately.

Morgenthal, short, balding, thin as a whisper – he had a first name, Nathan, but Mendy had never bothered to learn it – worked as a bookkeeper and dressed like one. He always wore arm garters, an eyeshade and baggy wool pants with a seat so shiny you could almost see yourself in it. Also, it seemed he didn't own a shirt that did not bear the stains of his profession. He was both compulsively disciplined and organized. Morgenthal kept his red inkwell to the left side of his desk, and his black inkwell to the right, and even now at eight in the morning, his left shirt cuff bore faint crimson smudges, while his right spotted black. He was a walking double-entry ledger with notes jammed into his many pockets.

A man who spent the entirety of his life indoors, he had a nearly colorless mouse-of-a-wife who did all the family errands. Morgenthal had a pale complexion by nature, but he was even paler than usual this Monday morning as he sat in the back room of the Moulin Rouge Club and went over the books with Mendel Goldblatt. Mr. Goldblatt could be a difficult man at times.

"That," Mendy said, tapping impatiently with a freshly manicured finger on a ledger entry. "That, right there. It says right there that we paid two hunnerd and seventy-three bucks for food for the kitchen last week. Am I right?"

Morgenthal's adam's apple pumped up and down twice.

"Yes sir," he said. "Two seventy-three for food costs. That's what the figures add up to."

"But!" Mendy's eyebrows shot up. "When I asked ya, a few months ago, how much ya figured we would spend per week for the rest of the year, on food, you told me no more than a hunnerd and fifty."

"But that was over four months ago," Morgenthal whined. "And based on the business the club did over the summer, averaging the weeks out, it was correct."

"What?" Mendy said, exasperated. "You don't know that joints like this do more business during cold weather than they do when it's hot?"

"No," Morgenthal shrugged. "I have never been to a nightclub, 'cept this one during the day when it's closed. Gosh, Mr. Goldblatt, I've never been to a real restaurant with my wife, Irene."

"Oh, for crying out loud," Mendy paced back and forth, then wheeled and jabbed a finger into Morgenthal's chest. "I find out you're cheatin' me, I will cut your nuts off and shove 'em down your throat, you understand me?"

Morgenthal looked at him wide-eyed with fear.

Mendy jabbed again. "I will put that little skinny wife of yours out on the street corner and sell her white ass to the highest bidder every night until she earns back what you took from me," he said. "I'm warning you," he said poking at his chest again.

Morgenthal rubbed his arms nervously. The black and blue marks had just begun to fade from his last meeting with Goldblatt. If the Moulin Rouge Club didn't pay him nearly three times as much as the best of his other clients, he wouldn't have come within a city block of the place, not with a powder keg like Mendel Goldblatt running the show.

"But I'm not robbin' you, Mister Goldblatt," Morgenthal protested. "I don't even touch the money. I just keep the books. I take the receipts from the night tallies from the till, enter them into the books and then add up the numbers. That's all."

"Don't try to bullshit me," Mendy warned. "I know how guys in the restaurant business can get together on a scam with other guys. I know how it works, and if you're fuckin' me..."

"I wouldn't cheat you," Morgenthal swore. "Honest. Of all the people on earth, believe me, I wouldn't cheat you, Mister Goldblatt."

"You'd better not." Mendy turned and stormed out of the club, wondering now if the chef was getting a kickback from the purveyors. He had heard all about the horror stories from other restaurant owners about the various scams that the employees dream up to cheat the house. The backdoor of the club shut behind him with such a bang, it rattled the window.

* * *

He was still fuming when he sat down with Irv for breakfast at a mid-town diner about fifteen minutes later.

"What's with you this morning, you're so quiet?" Irv asked over his New York Times. "Margie Hauser cross her legs on you or something?" Irv kidded Mendy about his new girlfriend that he had met about ten days ago.

"Huh?" Mendy looked up from his coffee. "Naw, it's nothing like that." He told him about the morning's conversation with Morgenthal.

"Mendy," Irv laughed. "The guy's a bookkeeper. A bean counter who writes numbers. He gave you a projection based on the numbers he had and estimated what the business would do based on past performance. What you really wanted was a financial analysis, and that takes a guy with more on the ball than an ordinary bookkeeper, for Chrissakes. Like you're talking about a CPA with management experience or even an MBA, Master's of Business Administration, degree."

"Shit," Goldblatt sighed. "Maybe we should hire one of those guys."

"That'd be risky," Irv said, turning a page of the business section. "Somebody like that would figure out right away that we're running a helluva lot more money through the club than you could ever make with a regular bar and restaurant. It wouldn't take too long for him to figure out the gambling operation in the back room. But a guy good enough to do the job right…shit, they're all working down at the banks and the big corporations downtown. Hard to picture them getting into our business."

Mendy nodded. "You turn in your resignation with the D.A.'s office yet?"

Irv nodded in return. "Yesterday," he said. "Just as we discussed. The old man squawked a little about me staying on, but not much. He thinks I'm opening a private practice, and can make a helluva lot more money that way, than I can working for the city. Besides there's a snitch down at the office who has it in for me and has been bendin' the D.A.'s ear for the past several months." Irv told Mendy about Milton Blackman's jealousy fits ever since law school. And, his growing file on Irv, motivated out of pure envy.

"This file," Mendy asked. "You've seen it?"

"Sure," Irv nodded. "The little dipshit keeps it locked in a file cabinet in his office. And the file is…you know the kind that you can pull away from the wall, tilt back, and then pop that bar on the bottom to open it?"

Mendy nodded. He'd opened a few of those locked file cabinets in his day. "So what's he got on ya, anything?" Mendy asked.

"Naw, nothing but little chickenshit stuff," Irv said. "He's been trying to involve me in several questionable plea bargain cases that I helped the boys out with, if you catch my drift. But we got no worries. I had one of Guido's cousins pinch Blackman's briefcase one Friday while he was waiting for his train. It didn't have anything in it but a newspaper and what was left of his lunch, which means his only files are at the office, and I can handle that just fine."

"And you're planning an accident?" Mendy smiled.

"Oh yeah!" Irv nodded. "He smokes a pipe, like all day long. I've already arranged for a little fire in his office. Nothin' …like burning down the joint, or anything like that. He'll lose the file cabinet, maybe his desk. And with any luck, the D.A.'ll make him pay for the cost of the furniture and repainting the office. Everybody's always warnin' him about spillin' ashes all over the place."

"Think that'll stop him?" Mendy asked.

Irv shook his head. "It'll slow him down though," he said. "But I'll have to keep an eye on him as long as he's with the District Attorney's Office. He's a pain in the ass, but he always has been, even in law school."

The buxom waitress came and set plates of salami and eggs and hash browns down in front of the two men. Mendy smiled up at her, giving her a slight wink. She blushed and then smiled back. He had that sort of effect on women and would probably have her in bed by the end of the week.

"So what's on for today?" Irv asked his partner.

"A meeting with our money guy, just like we planned for the liquor business," Mendy said. "I'm gonna stop down on Wall Street where he works, feel him out."

"Well call me if he's interested," Irv said. "I'd like to meet him."

"He's a good guy," Mendy nodded as he buttered his toasted bagel. "Not like you and me though," he grinned. "A real straight shooter."

* * *

Lou Kravitz sat, feet up on his desk, and stared out his window at the smoke and smudge of the downtown Manhattan rooftops. He knew Abe Solomon didn't like his feet on the desk, and just about now he was for doing anything that Abe Solomon didn't like. He could recall with clarity the past conversation that he and his uncle had with the senior partner of the firm back when Lou had decided to apply for a commission in the Army.

"There'll be a place for you here when you return, Louis," Solomon had solemnly promised him. "Not only that but you'll keep your seniority. You'll get an increase in pay when you come back, just as if you'd been here all along, and we'll reassign all your old clients back to you. Don't worry, son. We'll take good care of you."

He'd been taken care of all right. Solomon & Sons had given him his job back, but at a salary that was actually less than what he'd made when he went off to war. And as for his accounts, other men in the office had them, men who'd sat in a nice safe New York office during the war, making money and having a good time while Lou was sleeping in trenches, dodging bullets, and breathing through a gas mask.

"The country's sliding into a recession," Solomon had told him with a knowing shrug. "You're lucky we have a job to give you at all. As for your old clients – why, Louis, the men on those accounts have been serving them faithfully for better than two years now. You were here only a year or so when you left, and it wouldn't be fair to take that business away from them now when times are so hard, would it?"

"Not unless you'd promised it to me like you did," Lou had solemnly answered the white-haired partner.

"Well," Solomon had shook his head. "Sometimes promises can't be kept, Louis. Circumstances do change you know."

Sometime promises can't be kept. Oh yeah! Not as far as Lou Kravitz was concerned. Lou kept his promises.

He remembered the meeting with Martha Van Dyke that first day he'd gotten home from the war. Her natural Irish beauty, long auburn hair loose around her shoulders, flawless cream-white skin and her rounded buttocks with those sleek long legs. He remembered her touch, with hands so delicate and gentle that even now just thinking about it, he still trembled. And he thought about her last words, "...If you really want to do something for me, help me get a job."

And since he told her that he would, he now had to make it one of his top priorities. Even in a city where jobs were scarce now that the great monster of the war had died, along with its insatiable appetite for bodies, he would not only find her a job, but he would find something damn good for a woman with her personality and ambition. But right now he didn't have the foggiest idea as to how he was gonna accomplish that promise.

"Mister Kravitz," Florence Krell, an elderly secretary called from his doorway. The rumpled woman, a long-time employee of the office, didn't bother to hide her displeasure with seeing Lou's feet up on the desk. "There is a gentleman here to see you. A Mr. Goldblatt," she frowned.

"Goldblatt?" Lou puzzled over the name. It sounded Jewish, but the firm had very few Jewish clients. He had even heard Solomon telling his assistant to order a Christmas tree for the lobby, an idea that seemed hypocritical to Louis Kravitz since the senior partners of the firm were all Jewish. "Oh...Goldblatt!" Suddenly it came back to him, the candy store, the union hall, the help with the uniforms during the war. "Yes, Florence, please show him in."

Lou's feet were off the desk when the secretary returned with Mendel Goldblatt, a fact that pleased the old functionary immensely. In fact, Lou was standing, his suit jacket buttoned, and a smile on his face for the first time in days.

"Hello, Mister Kravitz."

"Lou, please."

"Yeah," Mendy said. "Sweet Lou, right?"

"Right," Lou laughed. "But I haven't been called that in years. Please Mendy, have a seat. Would you care for some coffee?"

"No thanks, Lou," Mendy said. His memory was proving him correct. He liked this guy. "I'm great, just fine thank you."

"It's good to see you again," Lou said. "How did you know where to find me?"

"Your uncle," Mendy told him. "He knows a man who knows my father. Delancey Street, you know how it is, it's a small world."

"And thank goodness for it," Lou agreed. "I've always wanted to thank you for your help with the uniforms. They were a Godsend."

"It was the least I could do," Mendy said frankly. "You fellows were over there fighting a war after all, and we were parked in cushy New York City."

"Well, we would have been fighting the war naked without your help."

They both laughed at the thought of this. Then Lou cleared his throat and sat up straighter in his big leather chair. "I hope," he said, "That you've come to see me today asking for something that I can do for you and return the favor."

Something so that I can return the favor, Mendy thought. He was impressed with Louis Kravitz's intelligence, his polish, and his memory in returning favors because, after all, that's the way the game is played, a system of debits and credits. But most people forget the rules. "I have," Mendy said, nodding. "My partner and I are looking for investors to help bankroll a solid business proposition."

He explained their idea of buying Hiram Walter, Ltd.

"Well," Lou said after Mendy had finished talking. "Obviously there are some ethical considerations here."

"Ethical?" Mendy asked. He wasn't sure if he'd even heard the word before.

"Sure," Lou said. "With the passage of the Volstead Act and it's effective date in a few months, the sale of spirits will be illegal in the United States, and the States are, after all, the most important market for Canadian Club whiskey. Anyone buying into a distillery today would have to be doing so under the present knowledge that continued sales in the States would be illegal – not illegal in

Canada where the distillery is based, but certainly in its largest market. In fact, if I remember correctly, the Walker family is American, and they put their business in Canada purposefully to escape harsh American revenue regulations."

"Yeah?" Mendy said. He wasn't sure he even followed most of what Lou had just said.

"So it creates a pretty hazardous situation," Lou explained. "As investors in a Canadian business, the shareholders would be on perfectly solid footing in selling their whiskey in every country but the United States. However, buying into such a company right now…well, if one intended to operate and conduct the business with complete respect for the laws of the United States, it would be a dubious investment, to say the least. But if one intended to sell whiskey to people who would then smuggle it into American markets, well then the return on the investment becomes considerably brighter. One could almost say that it would be a gold mine. But it would be a gold mine that would run contrary to the prohibition laws of the United States government."

"But not illegal for us," Mendy pointed out. "only illegal for the bootleggers."

"That's right," Lou agreed. "Unethical for you, especially if you knew they were going to bootleg liquor into the U.S., but not illegal, per se." Lou opened a cigarette package on his desk and nodded for Mendy to help himself, as he lit his own Chesterfield and mused over the business opportunity that such an investment might create, if one was willing to take a few risks.

"An interesting situation," Lou said half to himself. "A little speculative, but filled with great opportunities." He picked up the telephone and asked the switchboard operator to connect him to the firm's research department. After half a minute's wait, he said, "Yes, Kravitz here. Please get me the fair market value, net worth and estimated sales for Hiram Walker, Limited, of Windsor, Ontario, for the year 1917."

The two men talked about the war and sports until the phone rang again, ten minutes later. Lou answered it, took down some figures, and hung up.

"Okay," he said. "Net worth…"

"Net worth…?" Mendy repeated uncertainly.

"The total amount the company is worth – assets minus the liabilities," Lou explained.

"Oh! How much is it?"

"Well, it's just an estimate, as the firm is privately owned. But as of their last fiscal year, it was estimated the net worth was about twenty-six million dollars."

"Twenty-six, huh?" Mendy did his best to hide his astonishment. He'd figured one million, maybe two would be enough to buy just about anything. He'd never dreamed that there were things in the world that were worth that kind of a price tag. "So that's what it would sell for?"

"Oh no," Lou shook his head. "That's just the net worth. The fair market value is different. Let's say that prohibition finally goes through, the fair market value might be significantly less because of the potential loss of business in the States."

"So what would it sell for?"

"It would probably sell for around eighteen million on the open market," Lou said. "But if you were to buy it and operate it as a business, you would probably have to put an additional figure on the good will of the company as well."

"Good will?"

"Yes," Lou nodded. "The value of the reputation of the company in the general market place. Canadian Club is, after all, a very well-known brand of whiskey."

"So what's good will worth?" Mendy asked.

"In this case," Lou ruminated, scratching out figures on a notepad. "They have had fairly consistent revenues, I would say maybe another few million dollars." Mendy did the math in his head. "That's about twenty million dollars."

"Yes," Lou grinned. "Plus give or take a few hundred thousand dollars for inventory and such."

"So you'd have to raise maybe more than twenty million dollars just to buy a business like that," Mendy said mostly to himself.

"Only two," Lou said.

"Huh?" Now Mendy was really confused.

"Two million is probably what it would take to make a bona-fide down payment on an offer to purchase."

"Make..."

"Sure!" Lou leaned forward. "You see if you buy a larger business like this, it's pretty much assumed that you won't have all the cash in your bank account necessary to close the purchase, but will have to make arrangements with a bank or someone else to finance the balance of the transaction. And even then, you will have to raise additional monies for operating cash and contingencies. So nobody really pays cash these days for the purchase of a large company. Either you have a stock swap or do a progressive buy out over a period of years, starting with ten percent down."

"Like General Motors!" Mendy said. Just that year, GM had opened a new company, the General Motors Acceptance Corporation, that would finance a buyer's new vehicle if he – the idea of a woman buying a car was practically unthinkable – would put as little as ten percent down on the purchase.

"Exactly," Lou smiled.

"But even the two million, you must figure that Solomon & Sons would hesitate at participating in this kind of deal because of the..."

"...The ethical considerations," Lou finished for him.

"Yeah," Mendy said. He started to get to his feet. "Well, Lou, it was great to see you again, even if you can't help us."

Lou hesitated. What was he thinking? This was a great chance for him. He had always assumed that Abraham Solomon would be a man of his word, and he had turned out to be anything but. Solomon was an opportunist and now it was Lou's turn to be the same.

He looked at Mendy Goldblatt, a nice young guy, who had done Lou a big favor in the past. And even though the two men were barely acquaintances, Lou realized with a start that Mendy was, outside of Martha, probably the closest thing he had to a friend in New York City.

"What's say we take a walk?" he asked. "Maybe we can work up a little appetite for ourselves before lunch."

Lou reached to the coat rack and got both of their hats and coats. An hour later, the two men had walked in the brisk, early, winter weather all the way to Central Park, and Lou had astounded himself with how much he'd shared with Mendy about his life for the past three years. Mendy heard about his agreement with Solomon before he enlisted, his friendship with Henry VanDyke, Jr., the war, VanDyke's death, his visit to Hank's widow, his promise to her, how Solomon had broken their agreement…it all came flooding out like a swollen river breaking through a dam. The only thing he did not disclose was his feelings for Martha. Those were his alone, and besides even he was not sure what to do about them.

As for Mendy, he had carefully listened to everything Lou said, nodding, asking brief questions, encouraging him to go on and not minding that the two of them were trudging through the chilled streets. It was as if they were old school chums or something, and shared a friendship that went back for years.

"So," Mendy said when Lou had finished. "If you'll excuse my French, it sounds to me as if this Abe Solomon really put the screws to you, fucked you over good."

"Exactly," Lou nodded.

Mendy bought two hot coffees from a street vendor and handed one to Lou. "So whaddaya do about it?"

"Well, you know how the saying goes, don'cha? Don't get mad, get even." Lou's eyes grew hard.

"Yeah," Mendy said, "I'd put the fucking screws back on him, but I'd turn them a lot tighter believe me. I'd really make Solomon feel the pain. The putz!" As a flock of pigeons suddenly fluttered upwards to get out of their way, the mobster continued. "Do him worse than he did you. Send a message to the old man, make him think real hard about fucking with you twice."

Lou gasped with surprise. He'd never used such language before, and in the service he'd disciplined subordinates who spoke in such a fashion. But when he heard Mendy say it, it seemed to make a lotta sense. "My thoughts exactly," Lou nodded wisely, looking down at the cracked sidewalk.

"How're you gonna do it?"

"Well," Lou said, looking up. "I've always figured that if you're going to get somebody, you'd better get him where it will hurt the most."

"Good idea," Mendy grinned. He sipped his coffee.

"And with Solomon, there are only two places like that."

"What're they?" Mendy asked.

"His reputation," Lou told him. "And his wallet."

Mendy nodded. They walked on in silence, drinking their coffee.

"Tell me something, Lou," Mendy said. "Let's say you had a restaurant and you were spending, I don't know, say three hundred bucks a week for kitchen supplies, food and that kind of stuff. And let's say you wanna figure how much you'll have to spend for a particular week in December. How are you gonna do that?"

"Well," Lou began as they started to walk around the park. "A restaurant can be a very seasonable business, especially if it's one that's in a location that draws more people during certain months. A restaurant in the theater district, for instance, is going to draw many more people during October through May than it will during the summer. And the best way, of course, is to do monthly cash flow comparisons. Over the course of three or four months in a row, it would be logical to assume that there would be a ten percent growth in the coming months, compared to the same month the year before. But generally, restaurants are busier during the winter than they are during the summer. After all, they might have ceiling fans and everything, but who wants to put on a suit and tie and go out for dinner and then sweat through the evening? So my gut feeling is, if it's three hundred dollars during the summer, you'd be looking at between four hundred and four fifty a week during December. It's sorta complicated, a lot more than you might imagine. Why?"

"Oh, just wondering," Mendy said smiling. He stopped outside a drugstore and tossed his empty cup into a wire trash basket. "Hey, do you mind if I go in for a minute? I gotta make a quick phone call. If you got time for lunch, I got a guy I'd like you to meet."

"Sure," Lou smiled back. "I've got plenty of time."

Twenty minutes later, the two men were climbing out of a Ford cab at Junior's Deli in mid-town. A light snow had begun to fall clouding the rooflines on the tops of the taller buildings around them.

"Wait up a minute, Lou," Mendy said as he handed a half dollar to the cabbie. The driver tipped his hat and drove away.

"If I tell you something, can you promise to keep it between us?"

Lou looked him in the eye. "I give you my solemn word," he said, offering his hand.

Mendy shook it, looked around, and then when he was sure no one else was listening, "One, you're a pretty good guy, Lou, a little square but that's okay too. However, there's something I want'cha to know about us before we even start a discussion with my friend. Now listen to me good! And I want you to completely understand something, going in. And two, the business my partner and I are in…it's…well not all kosher, and it's important to us that you know all the facts before ya commit yourself."

"I appreciate your concern, Mendy," Lou smiled. "Actually, I'd already guessed that."

"And you don't have any problem with it?"

"Put it this way," Lou said. "Have you or your partner ever been arrested?"

"For anything that stuck? No, never."

"That's what I thought," Lou nodded as the swirling snow flakes were beginning to stick to his eyebrows. "You're a smart guy. I'm assuming that your partner's a smart guy too…"

"That's putting it mildly. He's the real brains."

"…And smart guys usually don't get busted," Lou said. "Meaning that if we're careful, we won't either. To be frank, two years ago the very thought of doing anything that broke a rule, let alone a law, would have shocked me. But, I've played the game according to the rules for awhile now, and I've seen where it's gotten me. So no, I don't have a problem with it. Not anymore, not at all."

Mendy grinned again. "Let's get some lunch," he said with a big relieved grin on his face.

* * *

Several minutes later, Lou was surprised when he learned the identity of Mendy's friend and partner.

"Sure," he told Irv, shaking his hand. "I've heard of you. My father talks about you all the time... 'a Delancey Street boy dat makes good with all the important momzers downtown,'" he mimicked.

"Well now, I don't know all about that," Irv said smiling. "But thank your father for the kind words. They're much appreciated."

"Well it's a pleasure anyhow," Lou told him. "I've even read about a few of your cases while I was overseas. My aunt would send me cookies wrapped in several pages of The New York Mirror. By the time they made it to England, sometimes the news was considerably fresher than the cookies. I never told her, of course."

"Of course," Irv grinned.

A beefy Jewish waiter in a starched white apron, his curly hair parted in the middle, took their orders and returned in about ten minutes, his pockets jingling with the sound of his tips from early luncheon customers.

"So Lou," Irv said as he bit into a kosher hot dog, "Mendy tells me that he's told you about our plans to get into the whiskey business, huh?"

"He has," Lou told him. "And I think it has great possibilities."

Irv leaned forward, his hands on the white tablecloth. "How would you put something like this together?

"Well," Lou said, jotting some figures on the back of a menu. "I think we would need about twenty investors, each one contributing one hundred ten thousand dollars. That's two million, two hundred thousand dollars."

Mendy let out a low whistle.

"Don't worry," Lou told him. "There are thousands of men in mid-Manhattan alone that could write a check like that in the wink of an eye, and several hundred of them have accounts with Solomon & Sons. And besides, we don't ask them for the hundred ten thousand all at once, just thirty-five thousand a piece for the purchase escrow."

"Seven hundred thousand," Mendy calculated swiftly in his head.

Lou slowly explained. "That's right, but we only use five hundred thousand as good faith monies. The balance goes to our new corporation as seed money, or if you prefer, initial capitalization. You could even think of it in terms of a syndication fee. You see, as you haven't yet approached Hiram Walker regarding the purchase of the company, we don't know what their response will be. They may say no, in which case we really don't want to tie the bulk of the investors' money up any longer than necessary. Or they may ask us to restructure it differently than we'd intended, in which case we would have to advise our investors to see how they felt."

Lowenstein agreed.

Lou cleared his throat, continuing. "So, from the total amount of good faith monies collected, we simply take five hundred thousand, twenty-five percent of the total purchase price up front, put it in an interest-bearing escrow account and use the account to show Hiram Walker that we are serious. The investors would all then sign guaranteed promissory notes for the balance of their seventy-five thousand dollars which they would make good upon demand. The three of us get a combined equity of sixty percent in the issued stock, which would give us majority control. And we have the guaranteed option to buy them out in three years for their original investment plus fifty percent. A generous return on their money, right?"

The boys nodded their agreement.

"In other words, it's almost like a three-year loan, but it has some subtle differences. In the meantime, they would get their proportionate share of the dividends from the stock earnings. Good for us, good for them."

"The interest-bearing account?" Irv asked. "Where would that be?"

"Canada," Lou suggested instantly. "The Bank of Toronto would be my first choice for a particular reason. It's easier to buy a Canadian corporation with Canadian funds, and besides, I imagine that you would like all of this to happen some place that isn't right under the nose of the American authorities. Secondly, over a period of time we could develop a healthy line of credit with a large Canadian bank."

"That's right," both Mendy and Irv chimed together, causing them to break up in a gale of laughter.

"We would need to create a Canadian limited liability corporation to act for our business interests north of the border," Lou cautioned.

"I can take care of that," Irv said. "I have a Canadian barrister in Toronto on retainer with the law firm I'm using for some other matters. It would be good to see him earn his keep for a little while. Anything else you need?

"Well," Lou said hesitantly. "The downside risk if the entire deal goes mahoola – down the drain – would be the advance for the syndication fee. The investors lose the sum of ten thousand dollars each, which admittedly is a good amount of money, but well within the limits that they can afford to lose. Most of them have made huge profits from the war. So they're now in a position to step up and take a risk for some damn good potential profits in the future. But I want to make sure that the ten thousand is all that they are risking."

"How so?" Irv asked.

"Distribution," Lou said. "For this to work, the whiskey has to get over to the States after the border is closed because of Volstead. That's a must if the investors hope to see any large return on their capital. But the investors don't want to know about bringing the liquor from Canada into the U.S.A., because it will be illegal. Therefore, we have to sell the whiskey in Canada and as part of the investment agreement, the corporation has to agree that it will operate only outside the United States and that the shareholders will be held harmless for any deviation from the agreement. We'll need a clause affirmatively stating that."

"Doesn't Solomon & Sons have a legal department to handle that sort of thing?" Irv asked, the first hint of a smile on his face. He already knew what the answer would be.

"They do," Lou agreed. "A very good one too, in fact. But I…wasn't planning on using them on this syndication agreement."

"Because you aren't planning on going through the office, right?" Mendy said with a grin.

"That's right," Lou admitted. "Old Man Solomon will blow a gasket when he finds out about this. An investor can only write so many hundred-thousand-dollar checks a year, if you follow me. And every dollar that gets put into this pot is a dollar he loses for something else that he's trying to put together. And when he finds out that his firm's name was used to put together the deal, he'll have fourteen conniption fits."

"Okay," Irv said. "I get the picture. So I'll draft the agreement for us. While contracts were not my favorite subject in law school, I'll still be able to handle it okay. But level with me, Lou. How much trouble will you get into over this when the old man finds out that you used the firm and its client's facilities to put the deal together?"

"Well," Lou mused. "There's an unwritten rule in the firm that when one hundred thousand dollars or more is being put together in the house's name, Abe and his partners are supposed to have the last word on it. But it's just that, an unwritten rule, sort of a tradition. As far as state and federal regulations go, I am a registered member of the firm, period. There's not a damn thing they can do about it so long as I don't blatantly make a representation that this is a firm syndication, and I'll just be damn careful of my choice of words as I call potential investors, minimizing the importance of our office."

"But they can sack you," Irv said.

"Oh yes," Lou agreed. "We can depend on that. But it will be worth it just to see the expression on Solomon's face when he hears about the ten-percent syndication fee on two million dollars. And besides, I intend to resign just as soon as the investment group comes together."

"Well," Irv said. "If you put this deal together for us, you'll be our partner. And that's a promise, so don't worry about it."

"Actually," Lou said quickly. "It wasn't me I was so worried about right now. It's a special friend of mine that's been looking for a decent job for over two months, and she needs it badly."

Irv's eyebrows went up.

"Lou's got a girl," Mendy explained.

"Not my girl," Lou objected. "Not a girl, really. A lady, Martha Van Dyke, she's a widow. My best friend's wife and smart as a whip. Hank Van Dyke got killed in the war. She has a baby, and she needs employment. She's very bright, a wonderful person, really."

"Smart, huh!" Irv mused. "Does she know all the right people? Celebrities? Business types?"

"She knows them all," Lou said nodding. "Her husband was Major Henry Van Dyke. You know the Van Dyke family. Christ, they're worth millions, but they're pushing Henry's wife out because they never approved of him marrying an Irish girl."

"Classy looking?"

"She's gorgeous!" Lou blurted. Then his face reddened.

"Well, we could use a smart hostess at the Moulin Rouge Club," Irv said, thinking aloud. "Especially someone that knows lots of good people. A person like that could make the club the place to be, you know. And that's great for our business too since once booze dries up, that makes it harder for the cops to bust us since they wouldn't want to embarrass any big shots. So yeah, I could give this lady a job. But what about you, Lou? What are you planning to do on a daily basis once Solomon throws your ass out? You'll have some money from the liquor deal, but that won't keep a bright guy like you busy enough, will it?"

Lou shrugged and shook his head. "I haven't thought that far ahead other than being part of our new company."

Irv looked at Mendy, nodded, and said, "Tell you what, we'll take care of both of you. Your lady friend is our new hostess, and as for you…well, I'm sure our business has all kinds of uses for a financial man that's good with money. You'll be our partner."

Lou grabbed the two men in a bear hug. "Thank you guys. It looks like we're in this business together for the long haul, and that suits me fine. You don't know how much this means to me. You won't regret it. I've got to tell Martha Van Dyke about her new job." And with that, he left the restaurant in a big hurry.

"Poor guy," Irv said to Mendy, watching Lou go through the incoming lunchtime crowd. "I wonder if he knows what he's getting into."

"With the dame?" Mendy asked, "Or with us?"

Irv shrugged. "Both," he said.

"Let's finish our lunch," Mendy said nodding his head.

* * *

The evening was still young. At the Moulin Rouge Club, a tuxedoed pianist played a medley of the ragtime music of Scott Joplin, who had died in his late forties two years before. A few couples danced, most sat in the leather booths and at the candle lit tables…talking, laughing and smoking cigarettes.

"Good evening, Mister Cantor, and how are you?"

Eddie Cantor, already famous on the vaudeville circuit as Banjo Eyes turned at the sound of a familiar voice. He took in a vision in a red chiffon dress that marvelously accented the dark auburn of the beautiful woman's hair cascading down past her creamy shoulders. "Martha!" Cantor exclaimed. "Who are you calling Mister Cantor? That's my father, you know."

"Just teasing Eddie," Martha Van Dyke said, giving the Broadway star her warmest smile. "You're looking great. Still playing with Mister Jolson over at Ziegfelds?"

"Al Jolson?" Cantor asked her. "Naw, Will Rogers' in the show now. Al's out in California. Got his head spinning about talking pictures. I dunno, movies that talk? I think that just distracts from the real purpose of going to the picture show, which is trying to put your hand on your girl's knee."

"Well you better watch it when you do that," Martha warned. "Or her big brothers will come lookin' for you."

"Hey," Cantor smiled. "That's good! Can I use it?"

"You'll use it anyways, even if I say no, right?"

"Absolutely!" Cantor grinned.

"Then consider it a gift."

"So how is this working out for you, here at the club?" Cantor asked seriously. "Now that you've been here for several months, are the boys taking good care of you?"

"They sure are. It's worked out even better than I thought it would when I first started. I needed to get out of the house and earn some money," Martha shrugged. "And the boys here needed some help. So here I am." She smiled like she meant it.

"And I'm glad for you, Marty," Cantor said. "Grief has a purpose, but then reality sets in and you have to go on living especially for the little one, right?"

"Absolutely and thanks, Eddie," Martha said in a husky voice, gladly accepting his hug and a five-dollar tip for his favorite booth.

"Now don't tell me you're eating by yourself this evening?" she whispered quietly to the little Broadway star, moving toward the booth.

"No, Fanny said she'd meet me here after rehearsal," Cantor said looking around. "She here yet?"

"Look behind you."

Cantor turned and was kissed, smack dab on the forehead by a small, dark-haired woman draped in mink.

"I'm sorry I'm late," Fanny Brice told Cantor. The famous Jewish comedienne's voice didn't have a hint of the Yiddish accent that she affected on stage. It was one of vaudeville's most well-kept secrets that, prior to starting her tour of performances around the Catskill resorts, known as the borscht circuit, and winding up as one of the big stars in the Ziegfeld Follies, Fannie Brice had not known a single word of Yiddish. "My putz of a conductor couldn't get the downbeat right for any of my entrances during the entire show. He must have had another fight with his girlfriend while his wife was outta town."

"Fanny...please," Cantor said in mock seriousness. "There's a lady present."

"Who?" Brice looked past Cantor and shrieked. "Marty is that you? Honey, you look absolutely divine!"

The two women kissed and beamed.

"Eddie's heading out to California to do a movie tomorrow," Brice explained. "This is his fare-thee-well-till-we-meet-again exit. Isn't that right, Eddie?"

"Oh, yeah," Martha scolded Cantor. "Jolson's got his head spinning about pictures, huh? And what's yours doing, Mr. Cantor?"

"Appearing above him in the poster, God willing." Cantor laughed.

"Martha, it's great to see you. What a pleasant surprise. We'll tell our friends you're here for good now. They'll be so pleased."

"Thank you, and please do. We'll take real good care of them, Eddie. That's a promise too."

Just inside the street door to the club, Lou Kravitz stood in the shadows, watching the entire performance. If he'd been smitten by Martha in her bathrobe, without lipstick, he was ready to be hung on the wall by a hook at the sight of her in an evening gown. Wow! And the easy banter she had with people left most folks speechless. He admired her ability to do that.

"I owe you," Mendy Goldblatt said, looking at Martha easily handling the crowds.

Lou turned. He whistled. He had never seen his new friend in a tuxedo before.

"Like it?" Mendy said. "I think it makes me look like an undertaker, but it's required dress for the staff, and it wouldn't look good for me to break my own rules."

"So why do you owe me?" Lou asked.

"Martha," Mendy said. "I thought we were doing you a favor when we hired her, but it's clearly the other way around. Our door is up more than twenty percent in the last three months, and the take is up over forty. Not only does she bring people in, but she brings in the right people who have serious money to spend on the tables, and a good class of folks too. Our bouncers are getting fat and lazy."

"Well I'm glad this worked out, Mendy," Lou said.

"Pal, we're amazed at how fast everything is coming together. It seemed like only a few months and you had the money for the deal all put together in a nice package."

"It didn't take that long," Lou told Mendy frankly. "A couple hours on the phone and five, maybe six personal visits. Everybody smelled the money in this one, and I think they're kinda excited about the idea of being bootleggers without incurring any of the negatives."

"Abe Solomon know about this yet?" Mendy asked.

"Not yet, amazingly enough," Lou told him. "But it won't be too much longer now. The Canadian monies went into the Toronto bank today, and so did our fee. I'm giving notice next week so when he sees that, he's gonna suspect something for sure. After I officially resign from the firm is when the shit will hit the fan. But then, it'll be too late. The rest of the monies will already be in our Toronto bank escrow account."

"Well, when you decide to make a move," Mendy told him, "we've already fixed up an office for you. I'm serious, you've got no idea how many different deals we got going for us."

"I hope you're serious, because I sure am."

"So are we and don't forget to say hello to Martha for us. She hasn't even been here a year and she's already indispensible."

* * *

Lou left Mendy and looked around for Martha. He stepped into the light, and Martha Van Dyke's eyes widened happily as soon as she saw him.

"Lou," Martha mouthed in a low voice as she walked quickly over to him. She made his name sound like music. "I love being at this place. It's so…exciting."

"I'm glad you're feeling better," Lou told her earnestly as they moved over to a private corner of the Club.

"I'm really happy now," she said. "And it's all because of you. You saved little Henry and me, you really did. I was almost ready to give in, to send him off to live with his grandparents so he could have some kind of stable life. But now… Oh! It's just great! Why last night I made fifty dollars alone in tips, can you believe that?" She kissed him on the cheek and took the handkerchief out of his breast pocket to dab at her eyes. "I'm sorry, Lou," she said. "But it's just that…you're my hero and always will be."

Her hero. Lou's world almost spun out of orbit at the sound of those words. And they stayed with him for the rest of the evening.

* * *

It had been a long night, one that ended with Lou having a late dinner that was more like breakfast with Mendy and Irv. He overslept, missed his first train, and then his second, and it was nearly ten in the morning when he finally arrived at Solomon & Son's offices on Wall Street.

"Morning, Mister K," the doorman said. "I got an envelope here for you."

"Oh! Thanks, Billy."

Lou accepted the envelope and noted the embossed return address: The Moulin Rouge Club. Smiling, he got into the elevator, gave the operator his floor, and nearly keeled over when he opened the envelope. Inside were fifty one-hundred dollar bills secured with a paper band, and a folded note. Lou opened it. The bold script read, *It never hurts to have a little extra spending money in your pocket for confidence.* The note was signed, *Your partners.* Lou peeked at the money again to make sure it was real.

"You okay, sir?" the uniformed operator asked.

"Me?" Lou repeated. "Sure. These new elevators just make me a little queasy."

"Lotta folks get that way, I understand."

Lou rode the next two floors in silence. The elevator came to a halt. He stepped out, pushed open the frosted glass front door to Solomon & Sons, and was immediately confronted by Florence Krell, Solomon's officious elderly secretary. She looked red in the face, as if she had been personally offended.

"Mr. Kravitz," the old gray-haired thin woman hissed. "Mister Solomon instructed me to take you to him just as soon as you got here."

"Oh," Lou smiled. "He did?"

Lou brushed past Miss Krell and walked down the hall to his own office. Agitated with him, she quickly followed Lou into his office. Keeping his hat and coat on, Lou looked around the little room. The basketball, his trophies – all of these had gone home, one at a time, to his apartment over the past week. The only photograph that was left was a team picture on the wall and his framed varsity letter. Lou took both of these down and tucked them under his arm.

"Mister Kravitz," she repeated. "Mr. Solomon is waiting."

"Yes," Lou agreed. "I would imagine that he is."

He pushed past the secretary again and walked back down the hall to the front door. He had it half open when he felt a brisk tap, low on his shoulder.

"This is most unacceptable." Florence Krell was nearly trembling.

"Is it?" Lou asked pleasantly. He stepped out into the hall and heard her footsteps behind him.

"Well, what am I supposed to tell Mister Solomon?" the amazed secretary asked nervously.

"Mr. Solomon?" Lou turned and smiled, touching the five thousand dollars in his coat pocket. "Tell him to go fuck himself!"

The elevator arrived, and he stepped in. As the wire cage sank down to the street level, the last thing he saw was the old biddy's wide-eyed stare and nervous twitch in her cheek.

Chapter Thirteen
November 1919

Irving Lowenstein stopped in front of the Brooklyn storefront wearing a newly purchased fedora, his hands buried deep in the pockets of his camel hair overcoat. The neat lettering on the glass of the front door announced proudly, B'NAI DAVID SYNAGOGUE. Whoever had painted the sign had done a classy job. It was clear and distinct but not in the least gaudy. Just last week the lettering had still read, Silverstein's Fashions. Not that Silverstein had been there all that long, maybe only two years at the most.

Silverstein, a Russian Jew, a dress designer by profession, had come to New York by way of Paris with all the right instincts for a solid haute couture. He purchased literally dozens of bolts of fabric for fine dresses suitable for the best party, wedding, Bar Mitzvah or funeral, but had realized his mistake practically after the first month that he had opened. His Parisian friends had told him about New York City's insatiable female appetite for fine linens, velvet, chiffon and silk dresses but neglected to mention to him that there were only a few Jewish women with money enough to buy such expensive things. And of those gentiles who did buy such things, not many would deal with a Jewish merchant, and especially if they had to venture across the river to Brooklyn.

The few neighborhood women who had wandered into his shop were, to his chagrin, all wearing dresses sewn from those floral-printed flour and sugar sacks so popular with the chronically poor, and none had bought more than a few dollars worth of an expensive fabric or several other inexpensive items like spools of thread and the like. Selling in the garment district had been out of the question since the workshops bought their fabrics wholesale, same as Silverstein, but cheaper because of the quantity discount.

Silverstein had been out of business for almost eight months now and was presently working at a brewery, loading beer wagons and trying to scrape together enough cash to buy him and his family steerage passage back to France. At least in Paris, a man could make a reasonable living working inside, out of the wet and snow, and not have to step in horseshit all day long loading beer wagons.

In the meantime, the storefront had sat empty, and when seven months had become eight, Irv heard about the vacant store from some of Lucci's numbers runners and traveled across the bridge to Brooklyn and reasoned with the landlord, explaining to him exactly how dangerous unoccupied buildings could be. They were, under the best of circumstances, prone to fire and vandalism. And, that's not to mention the pipes that could freeze during the winter if someone, God forbid, were to hurl a brick through a plate-glass window on a cold January evening and let in the frigid night air.

So the owner, Leonard Rosenbaum, had reluctantly followed Irv's logic and agreed to rent the storefront on a year-to-year basis for practically a song. The storefront and the apartment above it were part of the package that was now leased to the newly ordained Rabbi Barney Green. And Irv had gotten friends of his to spread the word about the new conservative synagogue that had just opened up near Hicks Street and Clark Place. At least forty families promised to attend services as a favor to him, so that Barney could at least get the place up and running on a break-even basis. Then Irv had sweetened the pot by offering a two-dollar a week premium to the new forty family members on condition they would pledge a minimum of seventy-five dollars annually. That would leave them a little over twenty-five dollars for their family. All this information was sent to the women of the household, the ones who collected the weekly paychecks for their pushke, and all forty women, furious that their husbands had gotten them in debt over craps games or cards, had accepted Irv's offer immediately with much gratitude. An extra fifty cents per week, after all, was not to be sneezed at.

Then Irv had sent word to the men of the household that not only had they better show up in Barney's new synagogue, B'nai David, but also their families, right down to every last child – and there were dozens of them – or legs would be broken and their debts would be enforced. Threats of enforced debts would encourage the wrath of the wives, which Irv knew was even more of an inducement than the prospect of a broken leg or even the extra fifty cents each week.

And all of this had been done in a quiet manner without a word of it getting back to Barney. While Mendy, Irv's partner, knew about their organization's occasional generous gifts to the synagogue, Irv had kept mum on how he'd personally funded it and guaranteed its financial success. Irv had done it with clean money, money he'd saved from the Assistant District Attorney's job; and besides, he hadn't liked what Mendy had said about him going soft. Sometimes it was better not to tell a partner everything because they'll worry too much. So Irv had kept the financial arrangements of Barney's new synagogue his own business.

It was about 9:30 a.m., and Irving had been standing out on the sidewalk in front of the newly painted synagogue for about fifteen minutes looking the place over with a sense of pride. He hadn't seen the schul since the store had been completely remodeled and opened nearly three months earlier. It had been recently decorated and sparkled with freshness. The door and front windows were covered with new drapes so that the services conducted inside were private from the general passersby. In the center of the front window was an ornate menorah that had originally come from the Holy Land years ago and was a subject of many "ohs and ahs" from members of the congregation.

The windows had been washed that morning, and the sidewalk in front of the schul was exceptionally clean, evidence that someone had been at work during the past hour or so with a hose, broom and a dustpan.

Irv stepped up to the door, raised his hand to knock, and then stopped. After all, this was a synagogue, wasn't it? And who knocked on the door of a schul during the daytime? Maybe the Rabbi's study but certainly not the front door. Following tradition, he lightly touched, for good luck, the small slanted brass mezuzah mounted on the right doorframe, opened the door and stepped inside.

The place looked larger on the inside than it did from the street. Although all the walls were freshly painted and the floors covered with new carpet, you could still see where Silverstein's storage room had ended and the sales floor had begun. A new wall partition in the back hid, Irving supposed, the broom closet and the cleaning supplies. And, it was easy to guess that the door behind the pot-bellied stove was the entrance to the synagogue's coal bin.

At the far wall, a stained-glass lamp hung by a gilded brass chain from the ceiling, the candle-flame within it keeping vigil over the velvet-curtained wooden cabinet where the sacred scrolls of the Torah were kept safe. Wooden folding chairs were stacked on metal carts near the doorway, making the open space look even larger. There was a chin-high fabric partition that blocked off a third of the space to make up the women's section, and off to the left, cooking smells drifted down from an enclosed stairway, while under the stairway, light spilled from the doorway of a cubbyhole office.

"Is that you, Yitzak?" The familiar voice of Rabbi Barney Green came from within the recesses of the small office. "Coming before lunch? I think your father must have bribed you to be so early for your Hebrew lesson."

"I don't think so," Irv chuckled back, easily slipping into his childhood Eastside accent. "I don't speak any Hebrew except for 'Mogen David' and 'matzos,' but that seems to be enough to get me through the day."

Barney Green, his yarmulke perched atop his head, craned his neck around the doorpost of the little office and a huge smile bloomed beneath the reading glasses perched on his nose. His thick, curly, black hair was already sprinkled with gray, even at the young age of twenty-six. "Mister Irving Lowenstein. What an honor to see you here. I thought you were Yitzak Levin, one of my Bar Mitzvah bochers."

The Rabbi hurried out of the office, his coat removed to keep it from wrinkling, Irv assumed, and his sleeves were rolled up exposing the ropy, heavily muscled forearms that Irv remembered from the boxing ring.

"The name's Irv, Rabbi. Remember?"

"Of course," Green replied, nodding vigorously. And, I'm Barney to you, Irv. Welcome. Please come in…come in," he said, taking Irving's warm handshake in both of his calloused hands.

Barney showed Irv into his office and hung his topcoat and hat on a hook behind the door, all the while chattering away. "What an unexpected pleasure, Irving. You've made my day. Please sit down. Sit down, relax, make yourself comfortable."

"I…I didn't bring a yarmulke," Irv realized suddenly.

"Do you normally wear one?"

"Not since I was a boy."

Barney laughed. "Then don't worry about it. Between me and you, I think the custom was dreamed up years ago by the Rabbis that made them." The Rabbi then turned toward the back wall and pulled a cord that disappeared through a small hole that had been drilled into the ceiling. After a moment, a female voice called from somewhere behind the desk, "Yes dear, what can I do for you? And, it better be different than last night."

Blushing furiously, Barney reached into an obscure crevice next to his bookcase and pulled out a tin funnel clamped to the end of a black garden-hose that also disappeared into its own hole in the ceiling. "We have a visitor, Natalie," Barney emphatically said into the funnel. "Could you come down and meet him? And, please bring us some coffee at the same time." He didn't wait for her answer, but put the funnel back into his hiding place and shrugged as if to say, *Women? What can you do with them?* Then he turned back towards the funnel. "It's a little like one of those devices that would be drawn by what's his name, that new cartoonist?"

"Rube Goldberg," Irv suggested.

"Yes! That's it, Rube Goldberg. But it works, and it saves Natalie and me a whole lot of shoe leather."

"I didn't even know that you were married, Barney."

"Oh yes, for three years now. Natalie first met me while I was still in the ring, and then at the synagogue with her parents. I think she saw more in me at the time than I did in myself. She never came to one of my fights though, but rather stayed home and prayed that I wouldn't get hurt. I married a wonderful woman, Irv. And, you know what? Her family really likes me too. Her father is Samuel Holtzman, the one who manufactures barrels. He's a little tight-fisted with his money but is an all right guy."

"Sounds like she's exactly what any good man would want for a wife."

Barney waved away the compliment and smiled.

"And nu, what about you? The beautiful young lady that I saw at your brother's Bar Mitzvah? Was I looking at the future Mrs. Irving Lowenstein?"

"Miriam Levine?" Irv was surprised to feel himself blushing. "Maybe, Barney. She might be a keeper, but I don't know for sure yet. There are a lot of Jewish girls in New York City. And, I really haven't made up my mind yet. We'll see how it goes."

Barney looked at him, one eyebrow raised. "Two weeks ago, I took some of the children across the bridge to the Museum of Natural History," he said. "Of course, all they wanted to see was the dinosaur bones, but I made sure they saw everything, geology, biology, botany. And I learned something in the agriculture section. You can't live on wild oats. Did you know that? They'll choke you."

"No kidding!"

"No kidding indeed." Barney smiled again. "You were right about your Miriam, Irv. She looked like a keeper to me, too. You'd be wise not to let that one get away or at least seriously think about it."

"We'll see," Irv repeated. "I'm in no hurry to make that kind of commitment, at least not yet. But, time will tell."

Just then, there was a succession of light creaks from the staircase just over Irv's head. In a moment, a pretty, slim, high cheek-boned woman with a warm smile, her head capped with a mass of dark curls with natural light streaks, had come down the back stairs and appeared in the doorway holding a tray with a silver coffee pot, two cups and a plateful of warm shnecken.

"Thank you, sweetheart," Barney said, taking the tray from her and setting it on the desk. Intense feelings for her filled his eyes whenever he looked at her. It was obvious that this was a true love affair. "Natalie, meet Mister Irving Lowenstein."

"The famous Mister Lowenstein who is always mentioned in the newspapers?" Her eyes were a wonderful deep ocean-blue color, and when she realized that she was meeting an important man like Irving Lowenstein, her hands flew to her mouth in surprise. She quickly recovered and shook his hand. "You honor our house, Mister Lowenstein."

"It's Irv," he smiled warmly. "And I'm honored to be here."

"Please have some home-baked cinnamon-raisin shnecken," Natalie offered, still a little flustered by Irving's presence. "There is still plenty of time before our noontime dinner. They're really good too. Barney's already had two pieces and he's gonna ruin his appetite," she fussed.

"Okay, but how about joining us for a quick cup of coffee now," Irv replied, his eyes fairly dancing over her slim hips and well-formed legs.

"For men talk?" She laughed, warming up now. "No, I don't think I'd fit in too well. Besides, I have some brisket in the oven upstairs, and if I don't watch it carefully, it'll get overcooked. Naturally, you'll stay for dinner, won't you, Irv?"

"I don't think so, but thanks anyways. I don't want to impose. I was just dropping by and..."

"It would be a real shanda not to taste Natalie's brisket," Barney interrupted. "Trust me, I'm a Rabbi. It's the best in town. So yes, Natalie, Irving will be joining us for dinner."

"Wonderful! I'll go set a place," and then she admonished them. "Now don't go spoiling your appetite," she reminded them again like they were little boys. "Noon dinner will be ready in forty-five minutes."

As Natalie hurried up the stairs, Irv smiled at the Rabbi. "You know, most people usually go along with me when I suggest something."

"Well, my boss carries an even bigger stick than you, when I suggest something, Mister Irving Lowenstein."

And at that, both men laughed.

"So, Irv," Barney said, pouring a cup of coffee and handing it to him. "What brings you over here today?"

"I had some business in this area, so I thought I'd stop in for a little chat. You know, see how you're doing with the new schul."

"It's doing just fine. Thank you for asking. The congregation seems to be growing each week and the membership director seems more than pleased. But enough of me, now how about you?" Barney nodded. "I read in the paper that you were leaving the District Attorney's office, much to Murphy's chagrin."

"That's right. I've gone into private practice, and I'm really looking forward to it."

"Hmm, you already have enough clients to open your own office? I'm surprised that anyone in this neighborhood can afford you, but I assume you also have clients from all over the city."

"Well that's true; and, I also have other business too. They're uh..."

"I know." Barney smiled, handing Irv a bowl of sugar cubes and a creamer, part of a sterling silver serving set. "I'm not so far out of the fight game that I don't hear things, Irv. I know all about your nightclubs, the punch boards, and the craps games."

"And still you welcome me here with open arms and warm hospitality?"

"I also know how there happens to be a synagogue here at all. I have forty families as part of the congregation, each making only five or six dollars a week, and yet they are able to give a dollar a week to the schul. And this building? The rent's only ten dollars a month for Natalie and me. Am I to think such wonderful things just happen? It must be God's will, yes?"

"Well, the Lord works in mysterious ways. That's in the Torah, isn't it?" Irv said as he threw up his hands in mock despair.

"Actually it isn't. And it isn't in the New or the Old Testament either. But I do agree with the sentiment."

"But I never..."

"Three weeks ago," Barney interrupted. "One of the families in our congregation, it doesn't matter who, got their rent raised so high that they wouldn't have been able to feed their children. And the landlord was a Jew, not a member here or any other schul as far as I know, but a landsmen nonetheless. So epus, I went to see this person and asked him if he was so strapped for cash that he had to make children go hungry? He lowered the rent, of course. And when I told the family, the lady of the house blurts out, 'Oh Rabbi, thank you. You know we'd go to your schul even if Mr. Lowenstein didn't give us the money.' Of course, as soon as she said it, she blushed with embarrassment. But it was too late. She had already let the cat out of the bag."

Irv set his coffee down. "You must think I'm a real schnook, don'tcha, Barney?"

"For what? For helping me set up a schul in a community that badly needed one? For convincing families that didn't follow God that they needed God? For giving a man a chance to turn his life around and use it to help others, rather than spending every Saturday night over at Madison Square Garden beating some poor shlemiel's brains out? No, Irv, if Jews believed in saints, you might be thought of as one."

"I'm no saint, Rabbi. Not the way I make my living."

"The brothels, the girls on the street corners. They're not yours, are they?"

"Hookers? Not us. The Dutchman is the one that runs the hookers. You know, Dutch Schultz? I'm strictly gambling and speakeasy clubs, and a little money lending. Maybe some other things too, like labor unions, but no girls."

"Well that's good because even though the Lord frowns on all of these activities, he especially condemns the taking of a man's daughter and selling her to other men for pleasure...that would be taken as an abomination."

I'd never do that, Irv thought. "So, what're you saying, Rabbi? That you think there's still some hope for me?"

"I think that the Lord feels about man the way that water erodes a huge rock, little by little. One drop at a time. I know that was certainly the way that he worked on me, and now, by the grace of God...and the good will of Irving Lowenstein, I'm a man of God, an established Rabbi. So yes, Irv. I know there's hope. I know that there's a corner there that you will be able to turn, if you want to, when the time is right. And I don't say this just because I know that it's your money that started this synagogue. I believe that God wanted it here and that, if you hadn't started it, someone else would have."

Irv sipped his coffee and said nothing, looking down at the desk while he slowly munched the last of the shnecken.

"In fact," Barney added. "Maybe God is closing a door for you right now, letting you out of this business. With the Volstead Act passing and Prohibition becoming the country's new law, after all, you'll be out of business in the nightclubs soon, won't you?"

"I don't think so."

"But who will go to a nightclub with no liquor?"

"I think there'll still be booze," Irv said. "Plenty of booze. As a matter of fact, I'm talking with some...some friends now. We're putting together a deal to buy out the Canadian Company, Hiram Walker. We're thinking of..." Irv paused, amazed that he had told him as much as he had.

"It's all right," Barney said softly. "What you tell me stays between you, me and God."

The two men drank coffee, silent for the moment.

"This Hiram Walker, it's a good company?" Barney asked.

Irv nodded.

"Bringing what it makes..." Barney deliberately avoided naming the product. "...across the border into America, that will be risky will it not?"

Lowenstein laughed. "Everything's risky today, Rabbi."

Barney nodded silent.

"I think..." he finally said, "...that God would breathe much easier, if you were just a lawyer."

"You're probably right," Irv said. "But I'm in..."

"...So deeply that you don't see anyway out?" Barney finished for him.

Irv nodded.

"Irving, if you want out, God will find a way for you."

Irv nodded. "I don't know, Barney. Maybe I don't really want out, you know?"

Barney nodded. "I know. Believe me, from my days in the ring, I know. But my time came. I will pray that yours will come as well. And now..." He pulled out a silver pocket watch. "...It's 12:30, time for dinner. Lets go upstairs before Natalie's brisket is ruined."

The noon dinner was a real pleasure in Irving Lowenstein's hectic day. The tiny upstairs apartment lacked a dining room, so they ate at a sturdy wooden kitchen table from China that Natalie told Lowenstein was reserved for special occasions. And the warmth of the Rabbi and his wife matched that of the freshly cooked brisket, and Irving Lowenstein eagerly helped himself to several slices of the tantalizing roasted meat with the oven-browned potatoes. An hour later, after they had finished the freshly baked apple strudel, Natalie had refused a last cup of coffee and an offer for help to clear the table while the two men went back downstairs for Irving's hat and coat.

"Thank you, Barney. I really mean it. And here…" Reaching into his wallet, Irv brought out a fifty dollar bill, the equivalent of ten weeks' wages for a typical Brooklyn workingman.

"Irv," Barney protested throwing up his hands. "We never accept money for hospitality to our friends. And if we did, well that's more money than most Rabbis see in three months."

"Then it's for the schul."

"Well," Barney shrugged. "The schul is the Lord's house, and on behalf of him, I accept with much gratitude." Barney then gave Irving Lowenstein a big hug. He took the money and put it into a drawer of his desk, which he then locked with a small key. "Are you familiar with Yom Kippur, Irv?"

"Of course, Rabbi. I'm still a Jew, maybe not very religious but still a Jew, why?"

"Now don't let me put you on the spot here, but do you remember what the holiday is all about?"

"Well, yes. It's the Day of Atonement following Rosh Hashanah."

"Which means?"

Irv smiled and shrugged, not knowing exactly what to say.

"Thousands of year ago," Barney explained. "When the children of Israel had a homeland and a temple, there came one day a year when sacrifices were offered in payment for sins. Is that what you are doing here, Irving? Trying to pay for your sins?"

Irv shrugged and silently shook his head.

"Well, I feel that I need to tell you something," Barney said. "The bulls and the calves that were sacrificed to God centuries ago on Yom Kippur? Well, they may not seem like much to us now, but they were really meaningful to the people who gave them thousands of years ago. You gave a cow as part of the dowry, because it was less expensive than a bull. But God required nothing less than a bull on the Day of Atonement because to the people who offered a bull, it was something that was hard to give up for them. And in giving it, they showed God that nothing was more important to them than Him."

Irv said nothing, listening in earnest.

"I'm not saying that you are anything less than generous to the congregation of this schul," Barney said. "Quite the contrary. There are widows who have roofs over their heads and food in their pantries because of you. Young men are learning Hebrew from texts purchased through your generosity. This place, none of it would exist if it weren't for you. And believe me, I pray daily for God to bless you a thousand fold, as you have blessed us. But, Irving, if you want to show God that you are ready to make amends, then you have to show Him that there's nothing more important to you than repenting for your sins. And you have to be sincere about it."

"Like how does the Big Guy feel about easy money," Irv scoffed flatly.

"Irving, not for even one little second do I think of it as that. You may not be lifting barrels or shoveling coal for your living as some of my members of my congregation, but I am certain that you mind your business and worry over it as much as any banker or industrialist, probably more. But, Irv, if you're making your living in any manner other than one that you'd be happy to tell your mother about or in front of the entire synagogue on a Shabbas morning… well, I think you see what I'm getting at."

Irv nodded wearily and put on his hat.

"Irving, don't look so dejected," Barney said smiling. "God is using you here, as his instrument. I am certain that counts for something. Everything's gonna be all right. You'll see."

"Think so?"

"I know so! There you have it, right from the horse's mouth or in this instance, a Rabbi's mouth…and, Irving!"

"Yes, Barney?"

"Don't be a stranger, eh? Natalie and I will always have a place for you at our table. And I can't tell you what a thrill it is for me to have someone sitting in my office besides a woman who thinks her husband has a dance-hall girlfriend or some kid trying to bluff his way through cheder. Promise you'll come back?"

Now it was Irv's turn to grin. "Sure, Barney. I'll be back with bells on."

"There you go!"

Barney Green saw his friend to the door and stood there with the door open and the winter air creeping in, watching him drive off down the street in a brand new Cadillac. As Barney watched, he felt a touch on his shoulder, a touch so familiar that he did not even need to turn to recognize that Natalie was at his side and had gently slipped her arm through his.

"You know what they say about him?" Natalie said, her voice a husky whisper so soft he could barely hear it.

"I know," Barney said pulling on his lower lip with a concerned look on his face. He did not add that Irv Lowenstein had pretty much confirmed some of the rumors about himself that had floated around the neighborhood for months. It might scare her.

"Do you think this is good, you being so friendly with him?"

"Natalie, my love, remember when you first met me, I was involved in the fight game controlled by men much worse than Irving Lowenstein, and beating poor dumb kids senseless for prize money and a piece of the gate. Yet you married me, right? And now look at us, a rebbe and his beautiful young rebbitsin. Who would have thought that you practically shoved me into our wedding bed, tearing off your clothes on the first night of our honeymoon, hmm?"

"You naughty boy!" Natalie slapped his arm in a mild reproach. "You loved every minute of it, and you know it," she said with a grin.

Checking to make certain no one was looking in from the street, Barney turned and kissed his wife deeply, his hands on her perfectly rounded, firm tuchas. "I have to go," he said. "Young Bennie Holtzman will be here any minute for his Hebrew lesson, and I've not quite prepared." He stepped back, looked at his wife, and smiled lovingly at the most important person in his life. "And don't worry about poor Irving," he added. "I was redeemable, and so is he."

He walked back to the office as Natalie shut the front door. Then after she'd shut it, she stood there looking back at the open door to

Barney's study. "You were redeemable, sweetheart," she said in a whisper so low that he couldn't have heard it. "But your Mister Lowenstein? Him, I'm not so sure."

Chapter Fourteen
Detroit – November 1919

The three New York gangsters left Grand Central Station in Manhattan at 7:15 p.m., and the Wolverine was scheduled to arrive in downtown Detroit at 7:00 a.m., the next morning. The trip had been long and, for Mendy, an eye-opener. Except for occasional forays into New Jersey, the ride on the lavishly furnished train was the young gangster's first trip outside the five boroughs of New York City. The Wolverine had first crossed over to Canada from Buffalo and traveled directly to Detroit through the Windsor train tunnel named after the Michigan Central Railroad Station. After boarding, they sat in the dining car of one of the most famous trains in America, sipping bourbon after a delicious dinner. As the train had rolled through the grayish-brown Canadian countryside, Mendy had stared out the velvet-draped window for several minutes before finally muttering out loud, "A big country. This is one big country, isn't it? Plenty of farmland here."

Lou Kravitz laughed. "It's fall," Lou remarked. "The fields have just been harvested. It was a bumper crop and the farmers are all smiles."

Mendy shrugged. "Who cares?" he murmured. "Well, these Canadians sure have plenty of land for crops, but not many people. And, the folks that do live here don't dress too good, do they? Look at their clothes. They look like something before World War I."

"You've turned into a real snob, my friend." Irv Lowenstein had smiled.

"Oh sure," Mendy returned. "I'm the snob and you're still the one with the expensive blue Wedgewood cuff links from England, right?"

"Well, my family settled in England for several years after leaving Berlin, and these cuff links belonged to my grandfather over seventy-five years ago."

"They sure look expensive to me. I've never seen anything like them before."

"There's lots you haven't seen before, Mendy, my boy. Just keep your eyes open."

And with that, all three men, arm in arm, had laughed, walked through several Pullman cars to their staterooms, tipped the porter five dollars to make up their compartments and went to bed. After a restful night in their private staterooms, they finally arrived in Detroit about 7:30 a.m. the next morning.

A Rolls Royce was waiting for them at Michigan Central Station. The chauffeur, a uniformed Englishman who introduced himself as Phillips, confirmed their early morning breakfast appointment with the president of Hiram Walker the following day, and then drove them in near-silence to the Book-Cadillac Hotel at the head of Washington Boulevard. Each of the men found in his room a basket of fruit and a bottle of Canadian Club whiskey with a note explaining that the refreshments, as well as the hotel expenses were compliments of Hiram Walker.

They cleaned up some, shaved and for the next several hours walked around Washington Boulevard, Woodward Avenue and the rest of downtown Detroit, the automotive capital of the world. It was something to see, a city on the move with new buildings dotting the horizon wherever the eye could follow.

They grabbed a quick lunch at Bowles Diner on Lafayette Street, right behind the hotel, and then went back to their rooms for a nap. But on the way, they stopped off for a few minutes at the renowned J. L. Hudson department store to look around at the new menswear section. They marveled at the Detroit waterfront directly across the river from Canada, looking to see if they could spot either the smoke stacks or the illuminated sign of Hiram Walker & Sons, Limited.

After their nap, around 6:30 p.m., they had a sumptuous dinner in the Book Casino, one of the hotel's prestigious dining rooms. Following dinner, they again took a slow stroll down Washington Boulevard, on the same street as their hotel, an elegant shopping area for men and women, casually looking into the fashionable windows of stores like Walter's, Higgens & Frank and Capper & Capper. After checking out the Statler Hotel at the other end of the street, they retired for the evening with instructions to the front desk to wake them at 6:45 a.m., in time for their 7:30 early breakfast meeting with Harrington Walker, the grandson of Hiram Walker and the president of the distillery.

The same stuffy British chauffeur was waiting patiently at the curb the next morning as the elevator operator opened the set of highly polished chrome doors and the three gangsters headed into the spacious lobby and then down a dozen steps to the main entrance.

"How ya doin', Phillips?" Mendy asked the uniformed driver.

"Would you care to look at a newspaper as we drive, sir?" he responded, touching his cap and completely ignoring the more familiar greeting.

"Sure. You got a Post?"

"Not 'til the morning train comes in from New York, sir. Until then we have the Detroit Free Press and the Detroit Times. The News comes out in the afternoon with the Toledo Blade."

"Nah, that's okay," Mendy told him. Then, turning to Irv, he whispered, "This guy needs his shiny brass buttons shoved up his ass."

Irv pointed his finger up to his pursed lips, indicating that Mendy should be quiet.

The Rolls transported them in smooth comfort to a reddish-brown masonry building on Cass Avenue off Fort Street that looked remarkably like a stately private mansion.

"This is the Detroit Club," Lou told his companions in a half-whisper. "I heard about this place at Wharton. They said there that the people who *run* Detroit business belong to the Detroit Athletic Club, a few blocks away off Grand Circus Park, but the people who *own* Detroit business belong to the Detroit Club."

The chauffeur opened the back door for them and the heavy oak front door of the Detroit Club was swung open by a smartly uniformed doorman. He smiled, but the look in his eyes was pure challenge as to their membership in the club.

"I'm Henry Louis, and these are my colleagues, Mr. Irving and Mr. Mann," Louis Kravitz told the doorman. "We're expected for a breakfast meeting with Mr. Harrington Edward Walker and his brother, Hiram." He turned to the boys and gave them a quick wink.

The doorman's eyes brightened with the mention of Harrington Walker. "Of course, sir," he said, his voice now warm and kindly. "The Walkers should be along shortly. Please follow Jonathan, here. He'll take you upstairs to our private dining room."

An elderly colored man in a freshly pressed black tuxedo bobbed his head in deference, snapped a crisp white towel over his arm and led the three men up a polished wooden stairway and through a room-size landing on the second floor into a lavishly wallpapered dining room with elaborate wood carvings fringing its ceiling. "I'll be takin' care of you fine gentlemen this morning, so anything ya'll want, jus' be askin' Jonathan, and it'll be takin' care of." With that he poured them some fresh hot coffee and left the room.

"What's with the fancy goyischa names?" Mendy whispered to Irv as he sipped his coffee heavily laced with cream. "Whatssa matter with our own names?"

"Walker's secretary asked us to use them," Irv answered quietly. "He said he wanted to keep the meeting private, but the way I figure it, he wanted something that sounded a little more goyischa than Goldblatt, Kravitz and Lowenstein. This is a pretty exclusive club; I doubt that many Jews have ever gotten past the front door."

Mendy looked at the richly paneled walls around. He appeared to be studying the surroundings for nearly a minute, but when he looked up, his eyes were still smoldering. "Not with that momzer downstairs guarding it," he finally remarked in an exasperated manner.

"Easy old sport," Irv smiled. He took his old friend's elbow and led him toward the table, where the elderly waiter had pulled out chairs for the three of them. Coffee, freshly squeezed orange juice and buttered toast were produced in short order. Then they sat and waited.

After fifteen minutes, Mendy looked at his watch and glanced at the other two, his face screwed up in a frown. "Whaddaya think? Any chance this guy is going to show up before Prohibition actually takes effect?"

But before Irv or Lou could say anything in return, a figure loomed in the doorway and in a full deep voice addressed the three men.

"Gentlemen! A thousand apologies for my tardiness!"

Harrington Edward Walker, a portly man with mutton chop sideburns and a vested suit buttoned across his considerable girth, approached the three of them with outstretched hands. With him was a gaunt man with thinning gray hair who looked to Irv like pictures he'd seen of the young, unbearded Abraham Lincoln.

"Gentlemen," Walker said warmly. "Say hello to Henry Ford. Henry these are Mr. Irving, Mr. Louis and Mr. Mann, business associates of mine from New York. They're in…"

"The import and export business from Europe," Lou covered quickly, smiling and shaking Ford's hand.

"You don't say," Henry Ford said with a thin smile. "Give me a call when you get a chance. I'm always looking for new overseas sale outlets for my automobiles."

"Right!" Walker chuckled. "Henry's afraid that there might still be a rural area or two in Europe that doesn't have a dealership for his Model T's. He's the reason I'm late. I ran into him in the lobby, and I've been trying to talk him into producing an automobile more appropriate for…people such as us. That is, those of us that have been more fortunate with life's vicissitudes and have accumulated some financial resources and want something more distinctive, not like the Model T for the masses."

"And, I've been telling him there's no need for me to design such a thing," Ford quipped. "Mark my words. With the economy the way it is, flat after the war, I'll be able to pick up a company in financial trouble that offers such richly designed and fancy equipped automobiles for pennies on the dollar, and I won't need to spend any additional funds on new designs, styling or tools – not at first, anyways."

"That's our Henry," Walker quipped. "He can squeeze a nickel until the Indian is riding the buffalo."

"And not only have I made you late, but I'm also late for an engineers' meeting at our River Rouge plant," Ford said. "So if you'll excuse me, gentlemen, it's been a pleasure meeting you.

Give me a call next week about that export business of yours. If I'm not in, ask my secretary, Helen, to connect you with my son, Edsel. It could be profitable for both of us."

Walker watched until the slender industrialist had left, and then he chuckled again. "I wouldn't set a great deal of stock in doing business with Mr. Henry Ford," he said.

"I've heard he's no great friend of the Jews," Lou said.

"That's right," Walker agreed. "Oh, he'll deal with Jews if they have what he needs or takes a particular liking to them. But by and large, he has no love for them. I've heard stories that his engineers have to paint brass black if they use it on cars, because he won't allow it since he thinks it's a Jew metal."

"What about you, Mr. Walker?" Mendy asked coolly. "Does Hiram Walker & Son's Company deal with Jewish people?"

"Both my brother, Hiram, and I have no religious prejudice of any kind. We're only prejudiced against folks who try to finagle us out of money – or don't keep their word. By the end of the day," Walker said, his eyes twinkling, "we'll see if we're able to work out an appropriate business arrangement with your group. But please, no business right now, Mr...," he hesitated.

"Mann," Mendy said with a slight grin. "The name is Mann."

"So you would be Mr. Goldblatt," Walker said, his hand extended. "I've heard that you are a bright and resourceful man, as you all are. So I trust you'll be bright enough not to judge us until you've gotten to know me and my brother, Hiram, who is Executive Vice President of the company. Incidentally, brother Hiram has the flu or something, so regretfully, he couldn't be here this morning. But perhaps he'll be feeling better later on in the day and can join us."

Mendy's expression softened. "Fair enough," he said, shaking the distiller's hand with a firm grip.

Breakfast began arriving as soon as Harrington Walker had spread a linen napkin on his ample lap. Sweet yellow Crenshaw melons brought in by train from California. Omelets as light as air, then, Delmonico steaks, Canadian bacon, grilled tomatoes, crisp hash browns, all came to the table in a barrage of waiters who did their jobs so efficiently that the food seemed to appear from thin air.

Walker was the perfect host, asking about his guests' families, inquiring about the construction of new buildings in New York City, and displaying an extraordinary depth of knowledge about Lou's basketball career.

"I'm surprised that papers back here reported the games in such detail," Lou said.

"You forgot that my family is originally from back east," Walker said. "I attended Boston University myself and personally saw you play – at least twice – when Pennsylvania played us while I was back for homecoming games and fraternity alumni weekends for the Sigma Chi's. Seeing your moves on the basketball court was the highlight of those trips."

Irv chuckled to see that Lou actually blushed at the compliment.

Finally, when all the dishes had been cleared away, Walker rubbed his hands together and said, "All right. The time has come."

"Time to discuss business?" Mendy asked, hopefully.

"Lord, no," Harrington Walker said. He nodded to Jonathan, the head waiter, who came forward with a bottle and four small shot glasses on a silver salver.

"I know that the sun is nowhere near over the yardarm, yet, gentlemen," Walker said, as he poured four shots of an amber liquor himself. "But I want you to try this." He handed the glasses around and, following his example, the three gangsters sipped at the whiskey, rather than simply tossing it down.

Lou whistled. "That's smooth, really smooth."

"That's Canadian Club, my personal old reserve stock," Walker, the president of Hiram Walker & Sons smiled with pleasure. "It's still in barrels where it was personally distilled by my grandfather, the original Hiram Walker, himself." Jonathan, the colored maitre'd, with a head full of distinguished white kinky hair, closely cropped, at Walker's instructions had decanted it into a bottle just before he served it. "The story is that my grandfather was a teetotaler, but I find that hard to believe. Not that he was an alcoholic, but to make a product such as this without ever tasting it? No, I find that hard to believe."

They slowly sipped the rest of the whiskey in their shot glasses, and then Walker slapped the table. "All right, gentlemen!" he boomed. "Now's the time."

"To discuss business?" Mendy asked, again, anxious to get started.

"Nosiree! To take a boat ride, a wonderful boat ride, to our plant outside of Windsor in Walkerville." And with that he led them down to the lobby and out the front door of the club on Cass Avenue where the Rolls Royce and a Cadillac were waiting for them.

"Mr. Lowenstein?" Walker asked, having correctly deduced that Irv was the spokesman for the group. "Would you care to join me in my car? The other gentlemen can ride in the Cadillac. That way we'll all be more comfortable."

Irv nodded and got in the Rolls while Mendy and Lou got into the back of the new black Cadillac.

"So you live here in the city, but the distillery's across the river?"

"In Windsor," Walker agreed. "In Canada and, the family actually lives in Grosse Pointe, on the eastside of Detroit."

"So why live here?"

"I'm an American," Walker said simply. "My grandfather came from Boston years ago and started in the grocery business. After a few years, he decided to switch to the liquor business, figuring there was more profit in it."

"But why is the distillery in Canada?"

"My grandfather put it there," Walker explained simply, "because the tax situation for whiskey was better in Canada than in the states. Canada never had a whiskey rebellion, so their taxes on liquor were considerably lower at the time. But so much of our market is here that we actually have plans to open a distillery in the States as well sometime in the near future. As a matter of fact, we've already started construction but are holding back our progress now since Prohibition seems imminent. My grandfather and the entire family have always commuted by speedboat or the Walkerville ferry from Grosse Pointe here in Michigan to Windsor each day. Actually, we even built a private dock for the trip since we decided a few years back that we like the States for living, but Canada for the liquor business."

"So you don't think Volstead will last?" Irv asked interestedly when he heard about their plans for building a plant in the States.

"It cannot," Walker said simply. "Oh it may take five years, even ten, for common sense to overturn the Billy Sundays and Carrie Nations of this world, but it will happen. And until it does, well, thank God for Canada."

Irv nodded.

In moments they had made their way north to a well-equipped private dock on the banks of the Detroit River near Grosse Pointe, where an immaculately varnished and polished steam power launch waited, its engine chugging and puffing black smoke into the clear November sky.

"She's a beautiful boat," Irv said admiringly as the chauffeur opened the doors for the two of them.

"Thank you," Walker told him. "Actually, I'm replacing it next year. I have a twin-engine, gasoline-powered powerboat on order from Chris-Craft, here in Michigan, and it should be considerably faster. But until then, this will do."

All four men climbed aboard the boat, and the two-man crew cast off immediately. The boat swung into the current and began to kick up a gentle white rooster tail. Just a few yards from the boat dock, the men saw a small ferry boat winding its way across the river on its way to Boblo Island, an amusement park about an hour from the city.

"We have a company ferry too, just about the same size as the Boblo boat. That's probably its last trip of the season." Walker mused and then continued. "We have a few Americans working for us, and we get our parts – machine supplies and the like – shipped over that way, as well. But most of our employees live in Walkerville, the community next to the distillery."

The launch aimed itself at a group of tall concrete structures with a lighted sign atop the roof that advertised – CANADIAN CLUB WHISKEY. It was the largest illuminated sign in the world, designed by Albert Kahn, the renowned Detroit architect who had also designed the General Motors Building and some of the most prestigious buildings in the country, including the Detroit Athletic Club in downtown Detroit. Then the boat turned upriver, and that was when the three gangsters realized that the buildings, which they'd thought was the entire distillery, was really nothing but the grain elevators, only a small part of the Walker facilities. The distillery was actually a complex of buildings stretched out for more than a mile along the riverbank. Irv saw the size of the place and began to have doubts about buying such a complex. It would be too expensive!

Ten minutes later, the captain had turned the launch expertly into the current and drifted neatly into a mooring at the foot of a path leading to a two-story brick, Italian designed building overlooking a neat green lawn.

"My offices," Walker said simply as a stocky, middle-age man with a neatly-trimmed graying beard came trotting down the steps of the office building and waited on the dock while the crew tied the boat up to the ballard's.

"Gentlemen, this is Angus Ferguson, my product developer," Walker said. "I'm going to put you in his hands for the next hour or two, if you don't mind. I have several lengthy telephone calls scheduled to make for our representatives in Montreal and Toronto. The Joseph Seagram Company is our largest competitor and are giving us fits over their aggressive activities!" With that, the distillery owner took his leave.

Ferguson stood silently while a small yard engine chugged by, pulling a pair of tank cars down to the distillery. Then he turned. "Mind your steps over the tracks, gentlemen," he said in a thick Scottish brogue. "And then if you won't be minding, we'll be going off to the grain bins first."

Mendy looked at Irv and the two men shrugged and followed the Scotsman, with Lou Kravitz falling in behind.

Mendy nudged Irv, his nose wrinkled in disgust. "What the hell," he murmured, "is that fucking smell?"

Irv shrugged, but he knew what Mendy was talking about. The air was sickeningly sweet with the rank smell of decay, like the stench of the streets back in New York on the days when the garbage hadn't been picked up for a day or so. They followed the Scotsman into a low building at the foot of the tall bins where the smell changed to something more like what Mendy had originally expected – a warm smell like toast, or bread baking. They heard a low roar, like a train passing.

"Tis here we dry the grains – hops, oats and barley – before the fermenting process begins. That noise you hear is the auger that transports the grains along a tunnel between here and the distillery. The grain comes off ships and trains from all over Canada, and then we dry it in a standard humidity, which is different for each grain. And only after it's at the correct humidity do we move it into the fermenting vats."

The three gangsters nodded, none of them really understanding what the Scotsman had just said. Then they followed him back out of the building. They walked back along the river, Ferguson explaining that the auger system had recently replaced a series of railway cars that had shuttled the grain between buildings.

"Not that we've abandoned the railway entirely," he said, "but moving the grain underground is faster and more dependable, you understand. Especially in the fierce Canadian winter."

They passed the offices and walked into another building. Now the sweet, thick smell was almost overpowering.

"What's rotten?" Mendy asked.

"Rotten?" Ferguson asked. "Nothing. At least nothing had better be rotten. What you're smelling is fermentation. Bonnie fermentation! It's yeast, bein' grown in the mash above us. It's the bacteria that produce the alcohol, which you understand is the point of it all. Up we go…"

They followed the stocky Scotsman up six flights of stairs, coming out onto a floor full of what appeared to be huge, low washtubs. "What you see before you are the tops of the mash vats, which reach to the ground floor, three stories below us and are sixty thousand gallons each," Ferguson said. "And we won't run out because we have 39 of these vats. They are all in different stages of fermentation. Have a wee look."

They went to the top of the nearest one, looked in, and Mendy almost retched. The vats looked full of what looked like oatmeal stirred into beer, and the smell of the fermentation was almost overwhelming.

"Now, most important is your even temperature!" Ferguson said. "You have to keep it constant within one-and-a-half degrees. Too low and your yeast goes dormant, and too high, it will sour. And then your acidity is important too; that has a tremendous effect on the rate of fermentation."

Mendy looked at Irv and Lou. "This is way too fucking complicated," he mouthed in a whispered voice.

They made their way back down to the ground floor and walked along a spotlessly clean passageway into an area that was full of shining stainless steel tanks and the roar of furnaces.

"Now this is your actual distilling process," Ferguson explained patiently to the men.

"I thought you said the mash couldn't get too hot," Lou said.

"That's during fermentation," Ferguson explained. "In distilling, we bring it to a low boil, because the alcohol will evaporate before the water does. That's all we use in the process of distillation is the alcohol."

"What happens to the mash?" Irv asked.

"By chance, have you gentlemen had a steak for breakfast this morning with your eggs?" Ferguson asked.

Irv nodded.

"The beef was probably fattened on our mash," Ferguson said. "We ship the mash out to several farms about a mile or so away. Cattle mostly. Some hogs too. The finest feed there is for livestock."

At last they came to a room where new charred oak barrels were being filled with whiskey. Ferguson excused himself and came back with a beaker full of clear liquid.

"Here's your end product," he said.

"That's it?" Mendy asked. He sniffed at the beaker. "It doesn't smell like anything. I think that's water, pal."

Ferguson smiled.

"Then have a sip, friend," he said. "Of water."

Mendy accepted the beaker and took a sip. He erupted in a fit of coughing and Ferguson laughed.

"That's 160 proof grain alcohol, my friend," he explained. "It doesn't get its color and aroma until it's barreled. Those it picks up from the wood. And we dilute it one-to-one with water when we bottle it."

The men walked out of the distillery and across a street. Ferguson motioned toward a building that seemed more secure than the others. "Barrels are constantly being moved there into our bonded warehouse," he said. "I can't take you there – it's restricted for revenue purposes. But then, once it's aged, we go here…" He led them into a building alive with the noise of clinking glass. Bottles of whiskey jostled down a conveyer belt to a labeling area, and then moved further to a crating dock where men put twelve bottles into wooden cases.

"How long does the process take, start to finish?" Lou shouted over the noise.

"Let's see," Ferguson mused. "Two weeks to dry the grain, then three to ferment it. Distilling just takes a day. So does bottling. And the time in the warehouse is six years for the regular stock, and twelve for the very old."

"Wait," Irving yelled over the noise. All three gangsters stopped walking.

"You mean to tell me that what we saw being made today doesn't get sold for six years?"

Ferguson nodded, adding, "Twelve for the better product."

All three men just shook their heads in disbelief. They followed Ferguson back to the office building and down a long corridor to Walker's office, where the president himself was waiting for them.

"Thank you, Angus," he said, dismissing the master distiller. Then he turned to the three gangsters.

"So, gentlemen," he said. "What did you think? A little more complicated than running wood alcohol through an old Whippet radiator, eh? Of course, our quality is a little better. And as far as I know, no one has ever gone blind drinking Canadian Club."

He offered them cigars from a humidor and then handed a set of cutters around to snip off the end. "So, gentlemen," Walker said. "What do I owe the privilege of this meeting?"

The three men puffed on their cigars, and no one said a word, but they all had heard the rumor that old man Walker had become quite friendly with Al Capone... even had his photo taken with his arm around him.

"Well, let me take a guess," Walker said. "Sweet Lou, here, I know was in the investment business on Wall Street. Mr. Lowenstein, my sources tell me that you were a brilliant prosecuting attorney, until you decided to start your own law firm. And Mr. Goldblatt, I had to hire a private detective to learn about you, sir. And it appears that trade unions either fall into line or their bosses have terrible accidents when they meet you. So I assume that you are what our papers call a mobster. And that Irv is your lawyer and Lou is your source of investment capital. Unless all three of you are gangsters, and two of you just do a better job of hiding it. Either way, my guess is that you are here looking to buy a liquor business, and you just discovered that the investment is far more than you originally anticipated. Am I correct in that assumption?"

The three still remained silent.

"And the reason that I know this is because a gentleman named Alfonse Capone from Chicago, as well a couple of his Italian cousins from New York, and a fellow named Arnold Rothstein, and a punk from here in Detroit, a two-bit Jewish gangster – no offense intended..."

"None taken," Irv said evenly.

"...named Abe Bernstein," Walker continued. "They've all tried to come over here with dreams about buying Hiram Walker."

"And did you meet with any of them?" Irv asked.

"Not a one, personally," Walker said. "But it's rumored that my father did some business with Capone a few years ago. Whether that's true or not, we really don't know."

"So why did you decide to see us?"

"Sweet Lou," Walker smiled. "This guy was a real classy ballplayer at the University of Pennsylvania, and I've always wanted to meet him in person. I liked the way he played the game," he said with a knowing smile.

"But you don't have any intention of selling to us," Lou said. "And, never did have? Is that correct?"

"Well, that's academic," Walker replied. "As I'm certain you wouldn't dream of buying now since it would be beyond your financial capabilities, at a price of twenty-five or thirty million dollars. But Volstead Act or not, I don't see Hiram Walker & Sons, Limited being for sale in the immediate future."

"But what if we weren't here to buy?" Irv said. "What if we only wanted to distribute your Canadian Club in the states, but with an exclusive distribution agreement for only certain areas – something like that. I'm not exactly sure what you would call it?"

"A distribution agreement, that's what it's called. So you're exactly right!" Walker said.

"Well, I'm just thinking out loud, but my guess here is that at least seventy-five percent of your Canadian Club booze is sold in the USA…"

"More like ninety…"

"And come Prohibition next January, that's all over…"

"That's occurred to us, too."

"However, we can keep it going for you."

Walker laughed. "Mr. Lowenstein, if I wanted to violate a federal law by assisting someone to circumvent prohibition, don't you think I would have already enlisted the help of Capone or Rothstein, or some of these other wealthy people whose names make the papers regularly?"

"I'm not asking you to break the law," Irv said. "I'm asking you to give us an exclusive distributorship to certain parts of the United States and other areas not even affected by the Volstead Act, like the Caribbean."

"Those areas would be limited."

"Real limited," Irv nodded. "But the point is, you sell to us, and we could form a…"

"Holding company," Lou offered.

"Exactly," Irv agreed. "A holding company. You sell to us in Canada, and then what we do with the booze from that point on is our concern, okay? So how many cases do you sell to the United States in a month?"

Walker shrugged. "We produce about fifty thousand cases each month so that means we probably sell, more or less, forty-five thousand cases in the States. But the American authorities could put a great deal of pressure on us not to make Canadian Club available in the States, either directly or indirectly, since all the members of our family are U.S. citizens."

"We'll take care of that somehow, don't worry about it. The important thing is that we can agree to take one third of that output, about fifteen thousand cases, starting next January – and build our inventory from there. And between now and then, we'll buy ten thousand cases a month, about $500,000 each month, if I'm figuring correctly."

"Yes, your figures are accurate, but why would I want to do any of this?"

"To make money."

"I'll make money, one way or another. So why would I want to do this with you?"

Irv reached into his jacket pocket and took out a piece of newsprint. He opened it up. "ACCEPT NO SUBSTITUTES," he read aloud. "Hiram Walker Limited will pay a $500 dollar reward for information leading to the apprehension of persons counterfeiting Canadian Club whiskey…"

"Yes," Walker said. "I paid for those newspaper advertisements. I'm familiar with them."

"So you have a significant problem with people passing off a cheap imitation of Canadian Club as your stuff, right?"

"The price of fame I guess," he responded somewhat matter-of-factly.

"Well, don't you think that will pick up considerably when Prohibition goes into effect?"

Walker said nothing.

"You know about my associate's reputation," Irv said, nodding at Mendy. "What would you say if we put him to work… uh, dismantling any bogus operations trying to fake Canadian Club?"

"And we will pay you $200,000 up front as earnest money for all deliveries," Lou added.

"I've already given considerable thought to the upcoming situation," Walker said. "There's an island off Newfoundland called Ste. Pierre. It's a treaty holdover, technically part of France. So the East Coast is easy to cover. We ship to Ste. Pierre, and that makes it an export, and it's all legal – the French will never go dry – and schooners can take it from there and run blockades into the East Coast. But how would you get booze into the rest of the country?"

"Do you really want to know?" Irv asked.

"I suppose not," Walker said. "Maybe it's better that I don't know all the details."

"Don't worry," Irv assured him. "It's a long coastline. We'll find a way."

All four men smoked their cigars in silence for a moment.

"Well, Mr. Walker," Lou asked. "What do you think?"

Walker looked out his window at the Detroit River and at the skyline of Detroit, down the river towards Belle Isle.

"Gentlemen, I'm pleased with your enthusiasm. Angus will take you back to the launch, and then have my car meet you across the river and take you back to your hotel," he said.

Irv tried to keep calm but was extremely pleased with the outcome of their meeting… at least so far, he was optimistic.

"That way, you can relax and rest up," Walker continued. "And then I'll have my driver come back and pick you gentlemen up at six tonight, and bring you to my house for dinner. I'll give you my answer then. Agreed?"

"That's fine – sure, it's perfect," Irving Lowenstein said.

"Good," Walker said. "Don't bother to dress. It will be a rather informal evening."

Chapter Fifteen
Detroit – November 1919

Not bothering to dress formally appealed to the three gangsters perfectly, as none had thought to pack their tuxedos for the trip. Back East, they knew that a formal dinner party always meant tails or at the minimum black tie attire. However, informal still meant a tie and jacket.

They wore their best dark suits out to Walker's place in Detroit's fashionable Grosse Pointe, suits that were remarkably unwrinkled, as Lou had shown the other two a trick he'd learned in England during the war. They'd packed their suits around newspaper pages before setting them into the suitcases that were fast replacing trunks for travelers. And room service had done the rest.

"That's the way a proper English valet would do their clothes if he was packing you for a trip," Lou had observed back in New York.

To which Irving had replied, "Well, if things work out in Detroit, we can all have ourselves one of them fancy butlers or valets – whatever you call them – by this time next year."

They'd known that the Hiram Walker family was rich. But they hadn't known how rich until Phillips had pulled up under the portico of Harrington Walker's white columned mansion on Lake Shore Drive. Three stories high, it was part of a five-acre estate which included tennis courts, a putting green, and a stable for riding horses, badminton courts, and a carriage house large enough for a family of six. His home was directly on Lake St. Clair and had a perfectly marvelous view of the Great Lakes freighters passing in front of the beautifully manicured lawn.

"Holy shit!" Mendy had whispered. And for that exclamation, Phillips had shown the barest hint of a smile.

Dinner was roasted prime rib of beef with Yorkshire pudding and served in one of the smaller dining areas. Other than the three men from New York, only Harrington Walker and his wife, Helen Cathcort Walker of London, Ontario, a graying, heavy-set, but attractive woman shared the table. Mrs. Walker took no pains to hide her disdain at having three Jewish gangsters at her table for dinner guests. She kept the conversation light and to a minimum, so the dinner went quickly, finishing with a French chocolate mousse dessert covered with rich whipped cream with shaved curls of chocolate. Shortly after the dessert was finished, Walker announced, "Gentlemen, if Mrs. Walker will excuse us, why don't we retire to the study for some Grand Marnier and cigars?"

Mrs. Walker breathed a noticeable sigh of relief and went upstairs to attend to her three children.

The cigars were Cuban, the liqueur – Grand Marnier, French and the better part of a century old, and the atmosphere several degrees warmer in Walker's oak-paneled study with a roaring fireplace. After his guests were seated in lounge chairs and had sipped the exquisite aromatic liqueur, Walker handed around a heavy silver table-lighter and said, "My associates in Montreal tell me that Arnold Rothstein may have to cut a deal of some sort with Sam Bronfman of Seagram's."

Irv said nothing, but looked up from his cigar.

"That makes your visit timely," Walker continued. "Still, as you may know, the size of our family is considerable. I may be the principal in our business, but I have a brother, several cousins and a few nephews or two whose interests I have to watch out for."

"I admire a man who puts his family first," Mendy said.

Walker looked at him with a cool stare for a moment, as if to determine whether the gangster was joking with him. Then, seeing not even the hint of a smile on Mendy's face, Walker nodded agreeably and suggested, "…One, you've guaranteed me a minimum purchase of 5,000 cases each month at $50 a case; two, we grant you exclusive distribution rights for Detroit, Cleveland, Chicago, Philadelphia, Pittsburgh, New York and New Jersey for five years with a renewal five-year option at basically the same terms but with a 5% increase in price; three, you pay cash on delivery here in Canada; and four, you'll use your best efforts to protect the integrity of Canadian Club Whiskey. That's all I'm interested in, and if that's agreeable to you gentlemen, then we're in complete accord," he said.

They nodded in agreement.

Walker continued, now in a good mood. "Here's to a prosperous partnership," he said as they all lifted their drinks in a toast.

Irv, Mendy and Lou had big smiles on their faces.

"These are odd times," Walker said. "And even in the best of times, the whiskey business makes for odd bedfellows. Still, if I have to deal with gangsters to get along in my business, I suppose it is in my best interest to deal with the best gangsters I can find. And I liked what you had to say about protecting the integrity of my product, Mr. Lowenstein. And I must admit that I am intrigued at the prospect of having a partnership that involves Sweet Lou Kravitz, whatever form that partnership may be."

"So we have a deal?" Mendy asked again.

"Absolutely," he said. "But I sure don't want to be in the middle of a jurisdictional war," Walker said, "…between you boys, and Al Capone in Chicago and the Purple Gang in Detroit. You'll make sure that you have all your bases properly covered?"

"Both Capone and George "Bugs" Moran; and, the Purples will be part of our operation," Irv promised. "This is business. As long as they pay up, we won't play favorites."

"Then we have a deal," Walker said. "My Canadian lawyers will contact you, Mr. Lowenstein, with the necessary papers. But my handshake seals it."

They shook hands all around.

"Who are these guys again?" Lou asked.

"They're called the Purple Gang," Irv said. "But you don't want to call them that to their face. They got the name because a shopkeeper they were hitting on for protection said they were purple, like rotten meat and should be thrown away; or maybe their first boss was Sammy Purple Cohen. Either way it's a pretty good assessment. They're punks – fresh kids who started a few years ago doing petty burglaries and puttin' the arm on little old men. Now they're into protection and contract hits for the big boys in New York and Chicago. But they're Jews like us, and I know a guy, who knows a guy. I think we can do business with them. We need their muscle to make our liquor deal work like we want it to without any trouble from Meyer Lansky, Bugsy Siegel and Luciano or the other

Italian goombahs. And, that includes Longy Zwillman from New Jersey and Arnold Rothstein, king of the bootleggers."

* * *

The Woodbridge Tavern on East Jefferson Avenue in downtown Detroit was dark. The lights were turned way down, but the white-aproned proprietor showed them to the backroom where two guys, younger than the New Yorkers, were sitting with a couple of pretty girls with bobbed hair. The girls, with voluptuous figures, looked really young.

"You Lowenstein?"

The guy who asked didn't get up. He just sat there with one hand on his beer, the other around the shoulder of the girl.

"I am," Irv nodded.

"Abe Bernstein," the seated gangster said, holding out his hand. "This here's Izzy, my kid brother."

Irv made introductions all around, and the three men sat down.

"So let's talk business," Bernstein said, as three more beers arrived at the table.

Irv looked at the girls.

"Don't mind the broads," Bernstein said. "They won't talk. And even if they did, they're too fucking stupid to understand anything more complicated than given' a good blow job and orderin' dinner."

The blonde with Bernstein's arm around her smiled reluctantly.

"Okay," Irv said. "It's like this. We've got a business arrangement with the Hiram Walker Company. We're gonna run whiskey in from Canada. We need some guys to get it across the river for us. Rothstein, Zwillman and some of the other boys around New York, New Jersey and Chicago could give us a rough time. You interested?"

"What do I look like?" Bernstein laughed. "A fuckin' admiral? I ain't got no boat. Besides why should we tangle assholes with those guys? They're our friends and we do some contract jobs for them."

"You can find some boats, though," Irv said. "And guys to run them."

"So why don't you find them yourself?"

"We could do the job ourselves, that's right. But from what I hear, if we try that, you'll hijack our trucks and make off with our whiskey. This way, I figure we won't lose so much. And Mendy here won't have to come back, set fire to your homes and maybe do even worse to you personally. You don't want to see his work unless you're on the right side of the table. Get my meaning?"

Bernstein studied Mendy and laughed again.

"You've got balls, Irving Lowenstein. I'll give ya that. Not too many folks would dare talk to us like that. Okay, let's talk dollars and not bullshit, eh!" he said. "What are you willing to pay for the transportation and our protection?"

"A thousand a week," Irv said. "Starting now. You can get your boats, and your guys lined up. The booze doesn't have to start coming across until next January. Until then, we can bring it across legal."

"It's risky business," Bernstein observed, "because you'll also need to take care of Big Al outta Chicago and the boys in New York. We can do it but it'll cost ya a lot more than a thousand a week."

"Okay then, fifteen hundred a week should more than pay for the risk and your time," Irv countered.

"You understand risk?" Bernstein asked.

"Sure!"

"That's what I heard," the Purple Gang leader said. "A pretty smart guy. I understand that you got the percentages figured pretty good with the risk of floating craps games, punch boards and numbers, right?" With that Abe Bernstein laughed again and pulled a pair of dice from his pocket and put them on the table. "What say we toss some craps?"

Irv picked up the dice, rolled them a couple of times, making sure they weren't loaded. "Okay," he said. "What are we tossing for?"

"Fifteen hunnerd dollars."

Mendy and Lou looked incredulous at Irv, who simply nodded.

"High roller," he said. "You go first."

Bernstein rolled and chortled as the dice came up eight.

"Your turn."

Irv rolled. The dice came up doubles – two sixes.

"Shit," Bernstein muttered. "I ain't got the dough on me." He brightened. "Tell you what," he said. "Take the shiksah, instead. Molly, go with the gentleman. She's worth more than fifteen hunnerd, aincha baby? Honest, Irving, you'll see."

The girl came around the table and sat close to Irv, sliding her hand onto his lap.

"How old are you, doll?"

"Eighteen!"

"When?" Irv asked.

She scowled. "Next April."

He moved her hand away. "Tell you what," he said to Bernstein. "You'll owe me. You're good for it, right Abe? Now do we have a deal or not? What's the story?"

Bernstein shrugged.

"We need $1500 a week to take care of everyone, okay?"

Irving looked at Mendy and Lou. Both of them shrugged and then nodded. "Deal."

"Then I guess we're in the Navy," he said turning to his brother. "Izzy, tell the Keywells and the Fleisher boys to meet with us tomorrow for dinner at Boesky's, and we'll work out the details."

* * *

By the time the three gangsters got back to the Book-Cadillac, they were on cloud nine.

"We're in business. Two deals in one day," Lou said. "This couldn't have worked out better."

"And then some," Irv agreed. "Hey, how about we move into the bar to celebrate?"

"Sure," Mendy agreed. Just at that moment, the desk clerk came around the counter and handed him a note.

Mendy looked at it and said, "Where's the phone?"

The clerk showed him to a phone on a table in the lobby, and Mendy said, "I gotta call New York. This won't take but a minute."

Irv and Lou clapped one another on the back and got some expensive Cuban cigars from the smoke shop next to the desk. Irv looked at his watch. "Come on," he mouthed impatiently to Mendy.

Mendy held up his hand and nodded. Then he put his hand over the phone. "Irv, come on over here," he said. "You'd better take this call."

"Who is it?"

"Just take the call, Irv, okay?"

Scowling, Irv picked up the receiver. "This is Irv Lowenstein," he said. "Who's this?"

"Irv," the voice said over the scratchy long-distance connection. "It's Rabbi Barney...Barney Green. I've got some bad news, old friend. It's your brother Herbie, Irv. He's dead."

"Dead..." Irv muttered. "But how..."

"Irv," Barney said. "They killed him."

Chapter Sixteen
November 1919

Shock and dismay. Irv Lowenstein had both, but only for a few moments. After that, he moved on to deal with the business at hand, his brother Herbie's funeral.

His Jewish faith left him no choice. There were certain, traditional customs to be followed, laws to be observed, and one of those required that his brother, Herbie, would have to be in the ground by sunset the next day. It was the way such things were done in conservative Judaism. As the oldest brother, he had to make all the arrangements since his parents were overwhelmed with grief.

"I've started the arrangements," Barney told him during his phone call to Irving in Detroit, "I talked to your old friends at the District Attorney's Office and got the body released from the morgue, and Herbie's down at Messinger's funeral parlor.

"No," Irv told him immediately. "Not Messinger's. I'm not having my brother's funeral at that schlock joint. I want it uptown. Fifth Avenue. Park Avenue. The Goldman Brothers, the best. I want my mother sitting on a new sofa, not that piece of dreck at Messinger's with the stuffing coming out of the corners. I want the best casket money can buy. I want people to know that my kid brother Herbie was gonna be somebody important one day. I want an uptown funeral…"

"Irv," Barney told him softly. "Your Poppa's friends, most of them are so tightly budgeted that the carfare would almost prohibit them from attending services."

"Then we'll hire cars…"

"And they wouldn't take them. Not in a time of grief. They've got pride, you know, and will only spend what they can afford."

"But," Irv said, his voice breaking. "I want the best. He's my kid brother. You understand? I want the best."

There was silence on the line.

"All right," Barney finally said. "There's a funeral parlor uptown called Nussbaum's on Fifth near 38th street. They've had a number of prominent Jewish clients before. I'll call them, soon as we hang up here, and have them work with Messinger's. They'll bring down their best casket, furniture and their own people. Everything you'd have uptown. But they'll bring it to Messinger's. You have my word on it. I'll get it done, and it will be done right." He didn't need to add that it would cost a mint; Irv knew that already.

"That's good," Irv said. "That'll be just as it should be for the kid." Then, with the details out of the way, he was concerned about his family.

"How's Momma? How's she holding up? Poppa? Sarah?"

"I'm at your folks' house now," Barney told him. "Everyone's doing as well as can be expected under the circumstances. I brought Dr. James Relle with me, and he just gave your mother a sedative, something to calm her down. She's lying on the couch downstairs. Your Poppa's in the parlor with the neighbors, they brought over a bottle of schnapps, and they're sitting around kibitzing and having a drink or two. And Sarah's down at Messinger's. She took them the new suit you bought for Herbie last month. I told her that she could wait until morning, but she wanted to do it tonight while it was on her mind, so I sent my wife with her for company."

"Rabbi, thank you," Irv told his friend. Then, he thought for a moment and asked, "Where's Seymour?"

"Nobody knows," Barney told him, "Your Poppa said that he sometimes stays at a friend's house when they're working on music projects at school."

"Yeah," Irv agreed. "That pal of his, Johnson, Kevin Johnson....Kevin Johnson, that's it. He lives somewhere in Midtown. But I don't know his phone number."

"Neither does your Poppa nor your sister. Of course, he might not have one."

That made sense to Irv since students usually watched their pennies carefully.

"I'll go by Julliard and pick him up in the morning," Irv told the Rabbi.

"I'll go with you."

Irv almost refused the suggestion. Then he thought about how emotional Seymour was, almost given to tears over a lower score than what he'd expected on a musical composition. He was a very sensitive kid and needed special treatment most of the time. He would be really upset with his brother Herbie's death

"I'd appreciate that," he finally said.

"I haven't talked to your folks yet about the service," Barney said. "But I'll go see their Rabbi next, and make sure he can be there to do it."

"No," Irv told him, insistent this time. "Not Rabbi Ashbaum. Not him. He always thought Herbie was a nogoodnik. I won't let him bury him. I want you, Barney. You, please."

"But Irv. Your family…"

"Please. Please, Rabbi. I want Herbie buried by somebody that loved him."

More silence.

"Fine," Barney finally told him. "I'd be honored. Now, I've got some more arrangements to make, then. So you call me as soon as you can when you get home. I'll be staying here for the night with your family."

Irv put the black telephone back into its cradle and turned towards the door. Lou was standing there with all three of their bags.

"I checked us out already," Lou told him. "Mendy's out front, getting a taxi. There's no train from here until morning, but there's one from Toledo in three hours and then a night train from Chicago, and I've already reserved a couple of sleeping compartments for us. So we'll take a taxi down to Toledo from here, and then in Chicago catch the sleeper to New York at six this evening. They'll have us at Penn Station by mid-morning."

* * *

"Tell me this again," Salvatore Provolone said to the man who nervously stood before him with a crestfallen face. "My Paulie did what?"

The man swallowed. Even if you didn't take into account the fact that Provolone was capo de capo, the "chief of chiefs," of all New York, the man's sheer size was overwhelming to the average person. Only five foot eight at 240 pounds, "Little Sal" had shoulders so broad that he had to turn a little to fit through most doorways, and there had been a day several years ago when all of that mass had been solid muscle. Now softness had crept onto his giant frame, but not much. And even if he had been as small as his name suggested, Little Sal wielded huge power. Men who simply looked admiringly at one of his many mistresses were frequently found the next day in the East river with their pricks cut off.

"Paulie had decided to take down the Jews' bank run… grab their black bag," he said, first hemming and hawing before spitting it out.

"Paulie did this?"

"Yes, Don Salvatore," he replied, not looking him in the eyes.

Little Sal nodded, with sadness. It was good that this man showed him respect, even when it was obvious that the stoop-shouldered henchman was about to shit in his pants.

"And the boys just did this on their own, huh? Nobody asked me? Nobody says, 'Hey Paulie wants to start a war with the Jews over on Delancey, that okay with you, Don Salvatore?'"

The man began to make excuses. Then he stopped himself and simply said, "You're right, Don Salvatore."

"And both of Lowenstein's people are dead, is that correct?"

"Yes, Don Salvatore, that's right."

"And one was his younger brother, Herbie?"

"Yes, Don Salvatore."

"Fuck it!" Little Sal smacked the arm of his big leather chair. "Who did this? Who else was there?"

His hand shaking, the man handed his capo a list with three names on it.

"The last two are in the hospital," he added. "But they'll be okay after a few days."

"And, Paulie was there, too?"

"Paulie was driving, Don Salvatore."

The capo nodded, then shook his head.

"Maybe the Jews won't figure out who did it," the man suggested. "Maybe they won't know."

"Won't know!" Provolone roared. "How the fuck would they not know? Who the fuck else would do such a stupid thing? And even if it were somebody else, no one would even dream of doing something like this on my turf unless they asked me first. No one except my worthless fucking shithead of a son."

The man before him actually began to physically shake with fear as urine slowly dribbled down his leg.

"All right," Little Sal told him. "It is good you bring this news to me first. Bad that you bring it so late, but good that you bring it at all. You are a brave man! And you know as well as I know what Paulie has done is going to point like a trail of shit straight back to our family. There is no damn way it can't. The Jews are going to know who did this within days, at least Mendy Goldblatt will know. He knows everything! So this is what we are going to have to do…".

* * *

Now that he was here in Messinger's, Irv couldn't shake the feeling that he was in the midst of a bad dream. Barney had been true to his word. The drab little Delancey Street funeral parlor had become a first-class funeral home overnight. The shabby chairs had all been replaced by new ones. His mother sat on a new couch worthy of the maternal head of the family. The casket Barney had chosen for Herbie was solid mahogany, and it gleamed under the soft glow of the lighting fixtures that Nussbaum's had brought in from uptown. But the finishing touch was that the funeral director, Wallace Nussbaum, and his staff were all morning-coated and perfectly groomed. They all spoke without a trace of a Yiddish accent and seemed to anticipate every need before it arose. They had transformed the Delancey funeral parlor into one from Fifth Avenue with all the appropriate finishing touches. Irv's associates from uptown, the attorneys, a few socialites, politicians and city officials, seemed relaxed in their surroundings. And the people from the neighborhood were all shocked into quiet respect by the amazing transformation that had taken place in less than twenty-four hours.

A garden had sprung up around Herbie's casket. When Irv had stood there and seen his brother for the first time since he'd left him three days before, that was the first thing that had struck him was the wonderful colors of those flowers. Then he had looked at Herbie and remembered the good times they had when growing up together. So he'd just stood there, for fifteen full minutes, looking at his brother in the open casket, tears running down his face.

It had been an aborted attempt to steal the evening's "take" from the Moulin Rouge Club as Herbie and one of Mendy's soldiers had carried the black bag down to the night depository at the bank.

Of course, Irv had given the Luccis hell. But, he had known that Herbie had probably tried to throw his weight around acting like a big shot, insisting that, since he was a Lowenstein, he was the guy who would carry the bag full of cash down the darkened street to the bank – just so he could brag to his buddies that he had walked down the street with three thousand dollars in his hands.

The Luccis had done right in sending one of their guys, Bobby Frazzoni, with him, and the man had done his job. He'd been killed as well, but not before shooting two of Herbie's attackers. They hadn't even gotten away with the cash. The Luccis had found it and had taken out all but two hundred dollars, so the police wouldn't question where such a bundle of money had come from. The other guy's funeral would be the next day as he was Italian and Catholic, and the Catholics had to have a funeral with a wake following it.

Now Irv was sitting in the side parlor at Messinger's with Mendy and Lou. His chin with a light beard scratched against his collar as he rubbed it. He'd get used to it in a couple of days, he supposed, but right now it felt peculiar not to have shaved. He was sitting shiva now, and he couldn't shave for the next thirty days.

Irv was dressed immaculately, in his best-tailored suit, and Mendy and Lou were as well, all shined up and smelling of Bay Rum aftershave lotion. The two of them were talking quietly with him when Irv had suddenly looked up to see one of Nussbaum's assistants carrying the largest bouquet of flowers that he had ever seen, and placing it next to the casket.

Curious, Irv got up, and Lou and Mendy went with him. There, bending over the sofa and shaking his mother's hand, was Vito Benucci, consigliere to Salvatore Provolone.

"Motherfu…" Mendy muttered. Irv could hear the .38, snub-nosed revolver being cocked in Mendy's pocket.

"Mendy, Irv…"

They turned to see a worried Rabbi Barney. "Remember where we are," he said. "And, what we're here for."

"Exactly," Mendy said, beginning to draw the gun from his pocket. But Barney put a hand out and stopped him.

"Be respectful," he said, "remember that we have a grieving family here. A family whose loved one recently died because of violence. What are you going to do, refresh their memory for them?"

Mendy slipped the revolver back into his pocket.

"Bring him here," Irv told Mendy.

"No need," Lou observed. "Here he comes."

The swarthy Italian was a six-foot-three giant, around 250 pounds and dressed in a navy blue pinstriped suit with patent leather shoes. His bowler hat and coat had been left at the door.

"Such a nice man…" Irv could hear his mother commenting to someone behind Benucci. "A friend of Irving's," she smiled.

Benucci paused before the casket, crossed himself, bowed his head for a moment, and then crossed himself again. As he approached Irv, he slid his hand under his coat.

Instantly, Mendy had fingered his gun, holding it in his pocket, but pointing it at the man's stomach.

Ignoring him, Benucci pulled a thick envelope out of his inside breast pocket. Bowing his head slightly, he began, "Irving Lowenstein…"

"What can we do for you, Benucci?" Irv asked him in a subdued tone of voice.

The man bowed his head again.

"Mr. Lowenstein," he intoned again in a formal manner. "Don Salvatore Provolone is saddened by your loss. He asked me to give you this to help with the family's… with your expenses."

Irv hefted the envelope and then, without looking inside, he opened it upside down and shook it. Hundred dollar bills fell out on the carpet and covered the Mafioso's shiny black shoes.

"What is this?" Irv sputtered angrily, "You think that you can waltz in here and pay me for my brother's life? You'll pay me, but not with this."

"Mister Lowenstein," Benucci said. "Don Salvatore had no part in this, on my mother's grave. I swear to the Almighty that I'm telling you the truth," he urged.

"You expect us to believe that?" Mendy asked. "Three people saw the car that drove away. Two of your people were put in St. James' hospital last night with severe gunshot wounds. Don't insult us!"

"Everything you say is true," Benucci agreed, "but Don Salvatore had nothing to do with it."

"Then he's lost control of his people," Irv growled.

"There were... well, unusual circumstances."

"No shit," Irv whispered, not wanting to attract any more stares than they were already attracting. "My kid brother is dead in a box. I'd say that that was pretty fucking unusual, you pompous dago prick."

The consigliere's eyes glowered with hatred for a moment. Then he lowered them.

"Listen," he began hesitantly, "The guys that did this are going to pay. I'll see to that, personally."

"No," Mendy interrupted. "I'll see to that."

Benucci nodded to him.

"As you wish," he said. "But before you do anything, Don Salvatore would like you to permit him to visit you tomorrow at 3:00 in the afternoon but only out of respect for your family."

"Tomorrow," Irv said, "We are sitting shiva. No one comes into our house but friends and family. That's respect."

"But, we are your friends," Benucci assured him.

Irv looked pointedly at the coffin, and then just as pointedly back at the consigliere.

"All right," Benucci said. "If your mourning will allow you then, would you come to see Don Salvatore...at his home? Benucci hoped that the significance of the invitation would make an impression on the three of them."

The head of the New York Cosa Nostra was notoriously reclusive and when he met anyone on business, which was rare, the meetings were, without exception, at his office on Park Avenue. The capo's house and family had always been an absolute, inviolable sanctum, up until now, so the invitation had special significance. "We can send a car for you," Benucci offered.

"We'll drive ourselves," Irv responded.

"And we'll be bringing two others, our driver and one of our boys, Moe Greenbaum," Mendy added.

Benucci started to object, and then caught himself.

"Of course," he said. "That will be just fine with the Don, I'm sure." He paused. "So can I tell Don Salvatore to expect you tomorrow promptly at 3:00 p.m.?"

"We'll be there," Mendy told him, "and on time."

The Italian's eyes smoldered again with resentment, but again he caught himself.

"Of course," he repeated. "Thank you. The Don will be waiting for you," he added hastily with a condescending tone.

He turned back to Irv.

"Until tomorrow, then," Benucci told them.

He turned and walked away, his shoes shuffling through the hundred-dollar bills like so many autumn leaves.

Just at that moment, Seymour Lowenstein hurried into the funeral parlor, looked for his mother and threw himself into her arms, sobbing uncontrollably.

"Momma," Irv Lowenstein said in compassionate whisper, glancing at his watch. "I know what you're saying, but now is just not the time to discuss it."

"And the time to discuss it is when?" Esther Lowenstein sobbed into a lace-edged handkerchief. "When these animals kill you and Seymour, too? When your father and I are sitting shiva for two more sons with no Lowenstein grandchildren to comfort us? My heart! May God strike me dead before I have to face such a thing!"

"Momma…"

Esther Lowenstein wailed on, ignoring her eldest son's hand on her shoulder. Irv looked up, hoping for some help from the rest of his family. But Sarah was out of the room, tidying the kitchen, and Seymour's hand suddenly froze in one of the numerous bowls of nuts that dotted Esther Lowenstein's immaculate parlor.

Irv looked to his father.

Moishe Lowenstein nodded, his eyes hooded and red-rimmed.

"Listen to your mother, Irving," the old man said. "Maybe in one way, this tragedy is Hashem telling us that our sons need wives. After all, the Scriptures tell us that the sound of children's feet in a household is a consolation to an old man's heart."

Irv wondered quietly where in the Tanaach it said that, and privately assumed that it did not say it anywhere at all. It had long been one of his father's habits – inventing a platitude to fit a given situation, and then he attributed it to Scripture so that it would have the added weight of divine admonition.

And that "Hashem", which was Hebrew, not Yiddish, meant "the name." Normally, only Rabbis and Chassidim used it. Everybody else just said, "God." So Morris Lowenstein was definitely exaggerating so as to appear pious.

Still, it broke Irv's heart to see his mother sobbing that way.

"We'll get married, Momma," he promised her, noticing that Seymour's face got even paler as he said it. "Both of us. We just haven't found the right girls yet. After all, they're going to have a high standard to live up to since our family grew up in a household run by the best wife that any man could ever have."

Esther Lowenstein's face brightened for a moment, then it clouded again and she again buried her face in the handkerchief.

"You're just saying that," she sobbed, "to make me stop crying. You don't mean it."

"Of course we do, Momma," Irv assured her, as he glanced at his watch again.

"So nu?" Esther Lowenstein looked up at her son, her face seeming decades older than it had been before he'd left for Detroit. "Where are the girls that you bring home so your father and I can see if you are doing right by yourself? How many have I had at our table on *Shabbas*? Not a single one!"

She sobbed again and Irv looked at his watch for a third time.

"But…" Seymour added weakly from the sofa. "But, I'm still in school…"

A muted knock sounded at the front door.

"I'll bring a girl home soon," Irv promised his mother. "Really, Momma. But right now, I've got to go out for a little while. That's Mendel at the door."

"Out?" Now it was his father who looked horrified. "Herbie is barely in the ground, and you are going *out*? We are sitting *shiva* for your brother. The Rabbi has not even come by yet. How can you be going out? We may need you for a minyan."

"It's a business, thing, Poppa," Irv apologized. "The meeting was set up weeks ago. I couldn't change it. Really."

Moishe Lowenstein huffed.

"And what kind of businessmen do you deal with," he scolded, "that would call a man away from a household during the shiva period?"

"He's goyische, Poppa."

"A goy! God help us!" Esther Lowenstein wailed again but this time with more strength.

For the briefest of moments, Irv considered reminding his mother that his father had been cooking up his cockamamie schemes with Lucci, a staunch Roman Catholic, for decades now, but he didn't. The situation was far beyond anything that could be salvaged by logic and reason.

"Really," Irv said, edging toward the door, taking his hat and coat from the clothes tree in the hallway. "I'll be back in just a little while. Before the Rabbi gets here, I promise."

He rubbed his bristled chin, wondering idly what he looked like. There was no telling in the house since every mirror had been draped with black fabric, although he suspected Sarah kept a hand mirror in her room that she sneaked off to for facial repairs every hour or so. His beard felt stiff. He was used to shaving every day and having a smooth face. From the living room, a fresh sob erupted.

His lips set thinly; Irv put his hat on and stepped out into the gray chill of a New York winter.

* * *

"You carrying?" Irv asked Mendel as their driver, Morry Levy, drove steadily across the Brooklyn Bridge, the river steaming darkly below them.

"Are you nuts? Of course I'm carrying. Not that Provolone's apes are going to let me get two feet into the door with a piece in my pocket."

"And Lou?" Irv asked, ignoring the remarks. "He's safe, with the Luccis?"

"Two of them," Mendel nodded. "The third Lucci is going to be down the street from Little Sal's with two carloads of guys. If we don't come out in fifteen minutes, they're coming in."

Irv nodded. Everything he had ever heard about the Italians told him that they should be okay. A capo de capo like Salvatore Provolone would not invite them into his home and then let harm come to his guests. Still, it hadn't escaped him that this could all be a trap, a way to get the leadership of his boys in one place and then do away with them once and for all. That was why he'd had Lou stay away. It gave them all a measure of safety, since Provolone was unlikely to kill two of them if one survived to seek revenge.

"This is the place."

Irv sat up. The Heights were in the better part of Brooklyn, and Salvatore Provolone's house was located in the better part of the Heights. It was a three-story, resembling an English-looking Tudor mansion, set back from the street. The drive was guarded by a gate with two stocky, swarthy men in overcoats. The one on the left looked inside the car and tipped his hat, while his companion opened the gate. Morry drove into a courtyard shared by the mansion and a carriage house, and Vito Benucci stepped from an alcove at the side of the house, his hat over his heart.

"Mister Lowenstein," the Italian said as he opened Irv's door. "Welcome. Thank you for coming on such short notice, and at such a difficult time."

Irv really wanted to tell Sal's henchman to go fuck himself. He didn't. This had to be as difficult for Provolone as it was for him; having the Jews over to his house and eating crow in front of his own people. Irv decided to respect that, a little.

He nodded, and he and Mendy got out of the car with Moe Greenbaum. The three of them were escorted into the house, where a pair of men – the twins of the ones at the gate – relieved them of their coats and hats. Morry had stayed in the car. One of the goons looked at Mendy, his eyebrows arched, and Irv nodded. Shrugging, Mendy reached under his suit jacket and handed the man his gun, a Smith & Wesson .38 with a taped grip.

"A good piece," the Italian said, hefting the weapon. "I'll keep it safe for you."

That was it! There was no frisking, no shakedown. Vito Benucci led the three gangsters down a short hall, past a sunny parlor where a young girl was practicing her piano, to a heavy, oak-paneled door. Benucci knocked once and then turned to Irv.

"I'll leave you now," he said. "Don Provolone asked to meet with you three in private."

"Avante," called a gruff voice from within.

Irv looked at Mendy and Moe, shrugged, and opened the door.

"Mister Lowenstein."

Salvatore Provolone stood to meet them. He was half a head shorter than Irving, but the Italian's bulk weight more than made up for the difference. He came from around the desk in the book-lined study, his suit jacket buttoned. Shaking hands with him was like shaking hands with a tank.

"Don Provolone," Irv said with a slight bow.

"'Sallie,' please," the Italian protested. "My friends call me Sallie or Sal."

Mendy bristled, but Irv simply smiled and said, "Then I'm Irv."

Provolone set four snifters on his desk and produced a bottle of 20-year-old cognac. He started to pour, and then stopped.

"The glasses," he asked. "They are okay?"

"They're fine," Irving said. "We don't keep kosher."

Provolone nodded and poured, handing one glass each to Irv, Mendy and one to Moe, who pointedly set it down on Provolone's desk.

Ignoring the slight, the Italian nodded at a sofa and three wingback chairs in an alcove.

"Please," he said. "Be comfortable."

The three Jews each took a chair and Provolone settled his muscled girth on the sofa. He waited until Irv had sipped his cognac, and then he said, "Mr. Lowenstein, Irv... my heart grieves at your loss. My heart and the heart of my family."

"Thank you," Irv said flatly. "But I must tell you, Sal, that I know your boys were more than just observers in this matter."

The Italian nodded curtly.

"It shames me," he said softly, "but you're right."

Irv looked around at the library, the books, and the desk.

"Sal, may I speak frankly?"

"Please!"

"Our people," Irv said. "They're different. A tough Jew wakes up in the morning, the first thing he does is go look for another tough Jew so he can piss down his leg in disrespect. You know? That's what makes our guys so different. We've got three top honchos that get along like one family."

"So I've heard," Provolone nodded.

"But your people, they tend to fall in line better. This whole 'Don' thing – no disrespect intended…"

"…And none taken…"

"This whole 'Don' thing, the recognition, respect and the cooperation. There seems to be more discipline among the Italians."

"Sicilians," Provolone corrected him. "My people, their families, they're from Sicily. And it's an island, capiche? A little place. You have to get along, so we do."

"That's why," Irv said, "I think the Italians, the Sicilians, are going to wind up running New York when this all washes out. You all get along, more or less. After all, Manhattan, it's an island too, capiche?"

Provolone grinned, displaying one gold tooth in an even mouth of whiteness.

"So how is it?" Irv asked, "that your people kill my kid brother and you say you knew nothing about it?"

The grin dropped from Provolone's face.

"It is the truth," he said. "I swear on the Virgin Mary, on my mother's grave."

The clock ticked on the library mantle.

"The men who did this," Provolone told Irv in a low voice. "I cannot kill them. It is not our way, they did not kill one of ours. But I can mark them, and I have. There are five of them, and each one is wearing a bandage on his left hand."

Irv looked at the Don, a question in his face.

"Their fingers," Provolone explained. "They each cut off a finger. The small one, on the left hand. I required them to do it in front of me. As a mark of their penitence."

He paused and took a breath.

"I cannot kill them," he repeated. "They are all 'made men'. It would cause… trouble among my people. But, on the other hand, you may do with them as you will. I will not object."

Moe remained silent, but Mendy could not restrain himself any longer and spoke up. "And what about your son?" His voice was barely a whisper. "Is your son missing a finger, as well?"

The Italian mobster paled visibly.

"We know," Irv told Provolone. "Your kid was shootin' his mouth off over in Queens, not an hour after the robbery. How he rolled some kike on the Lower East Side."

"Irv," Provolone said. "Mister Lowenstein. Please. My Paulie is young."

"My Herbie was younger."

"Then you know the love that I feel."

The ticking of the clock seemed louder.

"And it is not just that," Provolone said, hastily. "If I allowed my Paulie to be harmed, and I did nothing, the other families would never understand. There would be chaos. Wars. I would be toppled. The people who would take my place, they would not be your friends."

"My brother is dead," Irv told him. "A friend like this is something I need?"

Provolone sighed.

"Tell me, Mister Lowenstein, you are not married, are you?"

Irv shook his head.

"But you will be," Provolone said. "A man like you, of course you will take a wife. And when you do, and she gives you a son... it makes your life complete. I cannot explain it to you. And then everything you do, you will do for that boy of yours. Giving him chances you never had. Taking care of him. Protecting him."

He looked up at Irving.

"Tell me," the Sicilian asked him. "What would you have done to protect your brother?"

"Anything," Irv said immediately.

Provolone nodded. Moe started to add something, but Irv shook him off.

"Then you know," the capo said, "that I will not stand idly by while you harm my son. I would protect him with my blood, with the blood of my house. Wars would erupt here that would make the old battles at the Five Points look like a lovers' quarrel. It would destroy us all."

"I didn't start this," Irv pointed out.

"Nor did I," Provolone said. "But you can finish it, by agreeing to end your vengeance with the five men I have marked. My Paulie only drove the car."

"It was his idea!" Mendy nearly shouted back at the crafty Italian boss.

"I will deal with him," Provolone said. "He is marrying at Easter. After that, I am sending him away, to Miami. We have a hotel there. I will make him work on something small, not too important, for many years before I let him come back to New York."

"And if I end it with the five men you have marked," Irv asked, "then what will you have for me?"

Provolone smiled.

"Protection," he said. "Real protection. I will get the word out on the street that your clubs are under my protection and that you and your people are not to be harmed. That your enemies are my enemies."

"For how long?"

Provolone smiled more broadly.

"When I do this, I will, of course, have to be able to justify it to my associates, you realize this, don't you?" The Siciliano continued. "So I would ask for just a small piece of the take from your games. So it seems right to those around me."

"A piece of the take..." Mendy repeated incredulously.

Provolone nodded.

"Maybe ten percent," he suggested.

"Maybe five," Irv countered reluctantly.

"Done," the mob boss, said, offering his hand in friendship. Then he called for Vito Benucci. The three Jews got up and left.

"What the fuck..." Mendy's face was flushed as they drove out of Provolone's gate. "These dago bastards killed your brother, your baby brother, and now you're offering them five percent of our take? Why not just send them flowers, maybe let them fuck your sister on top of it?"

Irv glared at his partner but Mendy just shook his head in disbelief.

"Sorry," Mendy said. "But... shit, Irv."

He sighed and turned to Moe Greenbaum with a flushed face. Moe nodded his head in agreement with Mendy.

"One," Irv told him after a moment of silence, "Herbie is dead, and that is a fact, a final and absolute fact, and nothing on earth that you, or I, or Sal Provolone is going to do will ever bring him back. We just can't change that. Two, you've got a kid brother too, Mendy. What do you want, a war, and a chance to maybe go to his funeral? And three, Provolone's right, he may be the boss in his organization, but you can bet that the five or six capos under him are watching him like a fucking hawk, just waiting for him to slip up. So yes, sure, I'd like to slit his kid's throat right there in front of the paisano bastard, let him bleed all over Provolone's fancy oriental rug. But if I did that, there'd be families sitting shiva all over Delancey Street by Friday. So this is the best way."

"Well, it stinks," Mendy told him.

"Life stinks," Irv agreed. "Now, you just make sure those five guys are all dead before the end of the year. And I don't mean just dead. I mean dead in a spectacular fashion."

"Don't worry," Mendy said, turning the car back toward the Brooklyn Bridge. "You just keep an eye on the newspaper headlines during the next few weeks."

Chapter Eighteen
December 1919

"That shanty-Irish bitch…."

Three years had passed since Martha Van Dyke had overheard her father-in-law's crude diatribe on her Irish background, but the words still hurt. She was a scandal and an outrage to Henry's old-New York social clan and, the only way, in their opinion, he could have done worse would have been to marry a Jew.

Scandal and outrage…. Martha shook her head not really fully understanding their prejudice against the Irish as she got into her shiny little red Jackson runabout and pressed the self-starter. The engine caught on the first turn, and she pulled out the knob for the headlights.

"You gonna be okay now, Miss Van Dyke?"

Martha smiled at Guiseppe Lucci – "Scrappy Joe" everyone called him – the little Italian, looking every bit of his name with his cap placed at a jaunty angle.

"Sure, Joey," she smiled. "I'll be fine."

"I could start up the beer truck, you know," he said, looking up and down the darkened street. "Follow you home, wait until you get inside the door."

"Really," Martha repeated with a warm smile. "I'll be just fine."

The Italian's face darkened.

"Jesus, Miss Van Dyke," he said, eyes wide. "I hope ya don't think I was suggesting nothin' out of line. I mean, I just want to make sure ya get home safe. I wasn't thinkin' of no funny stuff."

Martha laughed and wondered to herself silently if there was such a thing as a man on the face of God's green earth who "wasn't thinkin' of no funny stuff."

"I know that, Joey," she told him nonetheless. Leaning over the little car's side-curtain, she kissed the little Italian on the cheek and saw him blush in the backwash from her headlights.

"Well," he said flustered. "Anybody tries to pull any shit, 'scuse my French, ma'am, you drive back here and honk the horn. I'll be here until eight, makin' sure them Polacks we got sweepin' up don't try to sneak no steak or booze out the back door with the garbage."

"You worry, too much, Joey."

"Hey," the Italian smiled, tipping his cap. "I'm paid to worry."

Martha put the car into gear and drove away from the Moulin Rouge. So she was a scandal and an outrage to Hank's parents, eh? The mere fact that she drove her own car would probably be enough to give Henry's blueblood mother a nervous rash over most of her body. That she not only drove her own car but worked in a nightclub? And recently got promoted to assistant manager too. That would be enough to take a few years off the old biddy's life too, or at minimum, a few conniption fits. Secretly, Martha hoped it would too, a wish that did not sit easily with her guilt-ridden Catholic background.

Pulling her beaver fur coat more closely around her throat, Martha drove to the corner and turned uptown. As she did, she had a shadowed glimpse of a man getting out of a black Model T Ford to crank it up. A few seconds later, she glanced back and saw the Ford's lights come on. Martha pressed down on the gas pedal and hurried along, driving just as quickly as she could without attracting undue attention to herself.

The man wasn't trying to hide from her. It was always a Model T with the same driver in a tan hat and black topcoat. He didn't follow her home every night, but he did it often enough that she'd notice him in the past few evenings.

At first, Martha had thought it might be a masher, one of those creeps who followed women around pestering them, maybe hoping to peep into her windows as she undressed, or worse. But then, the third night, he'd followed her back to her apartment and she'd turned and seen him in the streetlight, a mustachioed man in his early thirties, looking at a wristwatch and writing something down in a small notebook.

Then she understood the situation. The Van Dykes were having her followed by a private detective. While they had no use for Martha whatsoever, her son was another matter. Little Henry was the only child his father would ever have, and Henry, Jr. had been the Van Dykes' only son. That made little Henry III – called Trip –

the Van Dykes' only hope for carrying their old-New Amsterdam family name into succeeding generations. There were cousins and nephews, but when it came to direction succession, Trip was the only one left of the male Van Dykes. He was treated as a valuable commodity in his grandparents' eyes, and therefore, their dislike of Martha increased daily. It was improbable that the heir to the Dykes' steel and railroads fortune should be the son of some-redheaded-Irish-hussy-of-a-barmaid whose only connection to their precious 500-Fortune-society family was that she had spread her legs for their young and hot-blooded son. Martha knew that their marriage had driven them crazy with frustration.

They'd wanted her to give little Trip up and agree to stop using her husband's name, signing over her rights as his mother. And then, leave town with a steamer trunk full of their old-New York money.

When that hadn't worked, dear, sweet Lou Kravitz had shown up and given her the hostessing job at the boys' Moulin Rouge. Then, six weeks later, that's when the shamus, private detective, had first shown up, lurking around the employees' entrance with his bushy moustache, notebook and pencil.

He hadn't come inside the Club yet; hadn't worked up quite that much nerve, not yet anyways. But Martha knew that it was only a matter of time before he, or one of his associates, would be there in the Club with a camera taking photographs of her as the assistant manager of one of the best speakeasies in New York City. The photographs and notebook would eventually wind up in court as evidence in a nasty custody battle for little Henry, filed by the high priced lawyers retained by the paternal grandparents.

Martha parked in front of her building. The Model T went down the block, did a U-turn and then came back and parked on the opposite side of the street, brazen, and not worried if she saw him or not. For one moment, Martha thought about doing what Lucci had suggested, driving back to the club and blowing the horn. But no, Lucci was a hothead, and he'd kill the guy, and then that would just make matters worse. Pulling up her coat collar, Martha switched off the ignition, and then trotted across the sidewalk in her high heels and let herself in the front door with her key, closing it securely behind her.

She raced up the steps, paused at the door of her apartment collecting her wits, and unlocked the door hurrying into the semi-darkened front room. The landlady, Mrs. Dubinski, was asleep in a wing-backed chair, her knitting in a basket at her feet, and her eyes popped open as Martha shut the door.

"Oh, it's you," the old chubby Polish woman said kindly. "I put the baby to bed at eight, and he's not made a peep since."

"Did he eat?"

"Did he?" Mrs. Dubinski's kindly face beamed. "Two bowls of stewed meat and dumplings that little one put down. I swear, you're going to have yourself the next Jack Dempsey, if he keeps eating like that."

"Well, thank you Mrs. Dubinski," Martha said laughingly, taking two quarters out of her purse.

"Now, there's no sense in you paying me," Mrs. Dubinski insisted. "What are neighbors for?"

But she put the fifty cents in the babysitter's apron pocket, nonetheless. After all, she'd been with little Hank for almost nine hours.

"Well, I'd best be off," the old woman said. "Stanley will be home from the foundry in an hour when his shift ends. And, he still has a few chores to finish around this apartment building before I'll give him his nightly bottle of beer," she laughed.

"Take care, Mrs. Dubinski," Martha said as she followed the cherub woman to the door and latched it behind her.

Martha went, as she always did, to Tripper's open doorway and stood there, looking down on his small form and waiting patiently until she felt comfortable that she had heard the sound of his regular breathing. Then she went to the front window and parted the curtains.

The Model T was still there. In the driver's seat, she saw the man had struck a match to light a cigarette.

Martha knew that things were going well for her financially because of the money the boys were now paying her and the tips from good customers, she'd put aside enough money at the

Chemical Bank that she would soon have enough for a down payment on a little house, maybe someplace in Brooklyn. But, if the Van Dykes came and took little Trip from her, she wasn't sure she wanted to go on living. She lit a cigarette, took a puff, and angrily stabbed it out. Then she walked into the kitchen and cranked the phone on the wall.

"Operator?" Martha asked. "Yes. Give me Broadway eight, four, three, three please."

The phone rang four times before a sleepy male voice answered.

"Lou?" Martha asked, her voice soft and timid. "Lou, I'm so sorry to bother you at this hour. But there's this man, Lou, and he's been following me around for awhile now...."

* * *

"You sure this is the place?" Solly asked nervously.

Mendy looked sideways at Solly Gerber, a big muscular black-haired Jewish kid with a boxer's busted face. Solly hadn't been his first choice for this work, or even his second, but it hadn't seemed kosher to bring any of the Luccis along on this job. After all, the guy they were looking for was an Italian and, while the Luccis were straight-up guys, loyal as hell under normal circumstances, you never could tell, with Italians, how one would feel about whacking another dago.

"Yeah," Mendy finally told Gerber. "This is the place."

"Well, maybe he ain't comin'. I mean, the guy's lost a fuckin' finger. Maybe he don't feel like gettin' laid tonight."

"He feels like it," Mendy grunted.

"How d'ya know?"

Mendy looked at the kid, a rugged twenty-year-old with a stubborn cowlick. He thought about ignoring the remark, but the kid had to learn sometime, and now was as good a time as any.

"When a guy gets taken down a peg or two, like this guy did," Mendy shrugged, "it sure hurts, and I'm not sure how he feels about himself, right about now. Maybe he doesn't feel like he's still a man or worse, he feels like a big schmuck for letting someone talk him into a stupid move. And, now he's gotta prove to himself that he's still got a set of balls, you know?"

"Maybe the fucker's married, and he's banging his old lady regularly, so he doesn't give a shit."

Mendy sighed and pushed his hat back, leaning back in the darkened driver's seat of the big, wide-fendered Packard touring car.

"You don't prove to yourself that you still got a three-piece-set by banging your own wife," he carefully explained to Gerber. "Trust me, he'll go for the girlfriend."

Suddenly, a Cadillac, too fancy a car for the neighborhood, pulled under the streetlight at the end of the block, it's headlamps going dark. A husky man in a topcoat got out. Even from half a block away, they could still see the white gauze on his left hand.

"Bingo," Gerber breathed, reaching for the door.

"Wait," Mendy said, putting his hand on the big kid's chest. "Let him go inside. It'll be easier."

They waited five minutes, Mendy smoking a cigarette slowly. Then he nodded and they got out of the car and walked down the street. The front door of the building was glass, so Mendy took his hat off, put it over his fist and punched sharply, once. The window broke with surprisingly little noise and Mendy shook the glass slivers off his hat and set it back on his head. He reached inside, turned the knob and opened the door.

"Step on the outside of the stairs," he whispered to Gerber. "They'll squeak less."

Second door on the left at the top of the stairs. That's what the snitch had told them, although they would have guessed the same because of the familiar sounds coming from the apartment. There was a steady thumping five feet before they'd even gotten to the door. Mendy grinned. He took out a ring of a dozen keys he'd gotten at the hardware store years before, and kept trying them until he found one that turned the lock. Nodding at Gerber, he eased the door open.

* * *

Irv hadn't answered his phone after several rings, but that hadn't surprised Lou. Irv slept most afternoons, and rarely got home before 6:30 in the morning, what with closing up the club at 5 a.m. and then meeting with Mendy for an early breakfast.

Still, Lou had hoped that his other partner, Mendy Goldblatt, would be there. He would know what to do in a case like this.

Lou sat in his Chevy around the corner from Martha's apartment, in a darkened alleyway from which he could just barely see the Model T parked across the street from her place.

What to do? Go knock on the guy's window? Show him the stubby, blued .38 automatic gun that Mendy had given him on the way to Detroit and was now in his jacket pocket? Lou sure knew how to use it too. He had been trained in the army to use most weapons and was an excellent shot, but had never killed a man, even in the war. After all, he had been in the Quartermaster Corps, and an officer at that.

But, Lou thought about it for a few seconds. The man was just a hired detective by the Van Dykes, some poor working slob trying to make a living the hard way.

And what if this joker has a gun of his own? What if he panicked and pulled it out? What then? Lou didn't want to kill the guy, he just wanted to scare him off from bothering Martha.

He was just about to get out of his car and walk across the street when he saw the driver of the Model T get out, crank up his engine, and step back into the car. The Ford's lights came on, and Lou let the detective get halfway down the street before he put his own car into gear to follow him.

* * *

"Oh, Jesus. Oh yes. Yes, Joey. Oh, give it to me. Oh, God. You're so big."

The bedroom was dark except for a single table lamp, dimmed by a red silk scarf draped over the shade. In the crimson shadows on the bed, a buxom and naked dark-haired girl no more than eighteen was on her knees and elbows. Kneeling behind her rounded ass, was the Italian, wearing nothing but his undershirt and his socks as he gripped her slim waist with his one good hand, grunted and thrust. Every time his hairy buttocks lurched forward, the brass bedstead banged against the wall, and the girl gasped in pleasure.

Mendy would have found it hilarious, had he not known what this guy had done. He stepped silently into the room and then stopped behind the foot of the bed, suddenly aware that Gerber was no longer with him.

The kid was standing behind him, still in the doorway, looking at the couple making love on the bed.

"Get in here," Mendy mouthed wordlessly and the kid slowly crept into the bedroom.

Shaking his head, Mendy pointed at the girl and pantomimed a grabbing motion with his hands. The kid shook his head, and Mendy closed in until his gun barrel was no more than six inches behind the Italian mobster's head.

Nodding once, Mendy cocked the gun. The sound of the hammer clicking back was clear and unmistakable.

The banging against the headboard stopped.

"Stand up," Mendy told the Italian, and the guy released the girl and backed away to the side of the bed, where he stood up without turning around.

"What?" the Italian grumbled aloud. "You could have waited another five fuckin' minutes, ya know." On the mattress, the naked girl lunged for the nightstand but, Gerber quickly grabbed her, ending up sitting on the mattress, and pinning the girl on his lap. It only took the big kid one hand to do that. With his other hand, he reached into the drawer of the nightstand and came out with a nickel-plated revolver, which he held up so Mendy could see it. The young girl squirmed, her sweaty breasts shiny in the light, her nipples large and erect.

"You assholes," the Italian growled. "You assholes are in such deep shit. You know who I am? You know who the fuck I work for? What I do?"

"Turn around," Mendy said quietly, ignoring the man's questions.

The Italian turned around. His hair was slicked back, and he had a nose and cheekbones that looked as if they could have come straight off the Indian on the nickel. Tufts of hair, black and gray, hung out the scooped neck of his undershirt, and his uncircumcised cock was drooping like a wax candle in a hothouse.

"Hands on top of your head," Mendy said.

"Let me pull my pants on," the Italian said.

As he reached for his trousers, Mendy growled, "No. Leave 'em, off."

Grimacing, the Italian straightened back up, putting his hands on his head.

"Joey". The girl whimpered. "Joey." This guy's getting' a hard-on, Joey." The Italian ignored her.

Mendy glanced at Gerber. "Leave the shiksah alone," he said. "You want one, we'll get you one later, after the job's done. Now, let's get the cuffs on Mister Goombah, here."

The kid stood up and handcuffed the Italian from behind. The front of the kid's trousers were sticking out like he had a tent pole in his pants, and when he noticed that Mendy had seen his hard-on, his face reddened even further in the crimson light.

"Whattsa deal with the bracelets?" The Italian looked at Mendy as he asked it. "You guys cops?"

"Yeah," Mendy said flatly. "We're cops. Let's go."

"What? Like this?"

"That's right. We've got a new policy down at the precinct house. It's come-as-you-are."

"Well, fuck you. I ain't goin' nowhere without my pants and my shoes."

Mendy nodded once, thin lipped. Then he suddenly whipped the pistol across the Italian's face, his right hand moving so fast that the gun was just a blur. The Italian staggered while Solly Gerber got behind him and jacked his arms up until they looked like chicken-wings. The Italian just stared at Mendy, blood streaming down his white undershirt from his broken nose.

"You're fuckin' dead," the Italian mumbled through the thick blood. "You know how fuckin' dead you are?"

"Yeah," Mendy said. "I know."

He motioned with the gun to the bloodied man.
"Come on," he said. "Let's go."

* * *

The Ford did not go far, just a few blocks down the street to a commercial building in that fringe area between Chinatown and little Italy. The guy got out and went in, and a few minutes later a light went on in a second-story office.

Lou parked, got out and tried the front door to the building. It pushed open easily since the lock hadn't caught behind the detective. Lou went in, padded slowly up the stairs, and easily found the one office with a light on. He found that the door wasn't even locked as he turned the doorknob stealthily and gently pushed the door open a few inches.

The detective had his coat off and was standing behind a desk, facing the windows, his back to the door. There was a whisky bottle on the desk, and the guy had a tumbler in his hand, drinking from it as he looked at the notebook in his hand. Slipping his gun out of his waistband, Lou slipped the door open and crept into the room. He covered the four steps to the desk silently and raised the gun.

"Don't turn around," he said, his voice low.

The man dropped the glass full of whiskey. It hit the steam radiator in front of the window and shattered, filling the room with the smell of liquor. But the detective did as he was told.

"We, uh, we ain't got no money in here," he said in a reedy voice.

"I'm not here to rob you," Lou told him. "Now take off your tie."

"I got a partner," the guy told him. "He's gonna be back here any minute."

Lou glanced around the office. There was only one desk, and a couple of hooks on the wall. One of the hooks held the detective's coat, the other one his hat.

"Your necktie," Lou repeated. "Take it off and, if you lie to me again, I'll kill you. We're not playing around here."

"Just calm down," the detective said in a voice that sounded anything but calm. He fumbled with his white collar and took off his four-in-hand tie.

"There," he said, holding it up. "You want it? Take it."

"I don't want it," Lou said. "Put it over your eyes. Make a blindfold, then take off your belt and sit down."

The guy did as he was told, sitting at the wooden desk chair and setting a new black leather belt on the blotter in front of him. Stepping around the desk, Lou put the gun barrel against the man's temple, provoking a quiet shudder from him. Lou then passed the belt around him one-handed, buckled it behind the chair back and, tied the man to the chair.

"What's this about?" You could tell the man was frightened. His voice sounded on the verge of tears.

"Martha Van Dyke."

"That Irish cunt?"

Lou cocked his .38.

"Shit," the guy said at the sound. "I didn't mean nothing, pal. No disrespect, it just sorta slipped out. Whaddaya want with this Van Dyke woman, anyways?" the detective said with fear in his voice.

"Where are your files on her?"

"On the desk. There's only the one folder."

Lou picked up the manila file folder, glanced at it, and then tossed it and the note pad into a metal wastebasket. He lit a match from a box on the desk and dropped it into the basket as well. In a few moments bright flames were licking up from the metal can.

"You understand that you're through following this woman, right?" Lou asked.

"Shit," the man said. "These people got money. Right now, they're my main source of income."

"And I," Lou said, "am your main source of oxygen. If you want to keep breathing, you will stop following her."

"They'll just hire somebody else."

"Then it will be somebody else's problem. But, I'll tell you right now, if I have to, I will kill every private investigator in New York City. Do you understand me? I'm that serious about this whole business of digging into other people's lives."

"Yeah," the guy answered. "Sure, so who are you? Her boyfriend?"

Lou put the Colt's muzzle back against the man's temple.

"You aren't listening to me," he whispered sinisterly. "You are done asking questions about Martha Van Dyke, you understand? Tell your clients you had a death in the family. Tell them you're going in the hospital. I don't care what you tell them, but get off this case, or next time I see you, all you're going to hear from me is the explosion of this .38 automatic against your ear, got it?"

The man gulped and nodded.

Lou glanced down at the trashcan. There was nothing left in there but flimsy gray ashes. He stepped quickly around the side of the desk and slipped out the office door. He was all the way to the stairs when he heard the guy back in the office, talking to himself as though he just had had a bad dream, a nightmare.

Lou crept down the stairs and out into the night. There was a cold breeze coming in off the East River, and he needed it. He was all in a sweat.

* * *

"Aw shit. Come on. Not the fuckin' church. Not like this."

Mendy ignored the Italian and pulled him out of the back of the Packard. St. Paul's Cathedral, the largest Catholic Church in Brooklyn, was dark, but Mendy wasn't worried about getting in. He and the kid had left a door unlocked when they'd been there earlier in the evening.

His dark penis swinging like a sock full of quarters, the Italian shuffled along on bare feet between the two Jews. His face was a mass of clotted blood and his undershirt was soaked with it, black in the dim light from a distant streetlamp. The three men walked to a chapel entrance where Mendy stopped, checked the empty street behind them, and then opened the door.

Inside, the Italian stopped.

"Hey," he said, not looking up. "How about takin' off the cuffs?"

He nodded at the stone basin of holy water next to the door.

"So I can bless myself," the Italian explained.

Solly Gerber looked at Mendy and shrugged. Mendy shrugged back and then, stepping behind the Italian, kicked him in the naked ass. Unable to break his fall with his hands, the man stumbled face-first into the marble floor.

"We ain't here to bless you," Mendy said evenly as he and the kid picked the Italian up by the elbows and dragged him out, into the nave of the cathedral. They pulled the Italian to his feet and walked up to the altar, passing through the low, wooden communion gate.

"This is where I got married," the Italian mumbled, looking around, dazed.

"Mazel tov," Mendy muttered. He and Gerber dragged the Italian around the linen-draped altar stone. Behind it, resting on four low sawhorses, a crude cross had been bolted together from a pair of wooden beams.

Mendy nodded at it.

"Get on," he told the Italian.

The man glowered through the clotting blood.

"Fuck you," he said.

Mendy buried the toe of his immaculate black Florsheim shoe into the Italian's shaggy testicles.

The man gasped, turned pale and doubled over in pain as Gerber picked him up and set him like a sack of potatoes on the cross. Working together, Mendy and Gerber used a coil of baling wire to bind the man's ankles to the wooden beam. Then Mendy slugged him in the side of the head with the gun barrel, dazing him enough that they could take off the handcuffs, lay him back and wire his wrists to the cross as well.

The Italian's head lolled to the side. He couldn't seem to keep his tongue in his mouth.

"Wha' the fuck?" He asked thickly. "Wha'sis about?"

Mendy looked down on him.

"It's about a sixteen-year-old boy that you whacked a few days ago, and left to die on the street," he said.

"Sixteen..." the Italian muttered. He came around. "You mean that Jew kid? Shit, the guy with him shot at us first."

"Of course he did," Mendy said, opening a carpenter's canvas workbag and taking out a hammer, a box of ten-penny nails and a handful of fender washers. "You were trying to rob them."

"But I already paid for that," the Italian protested. "With this."

He moved his bandaged left hand as much as he could with it wired to the beam.

Mendy smiled thinly.

"You think," he said, his voice barely a whisper, "that you can take a young boy's life and then pay for it with a finger? A fucking finger? You stupid cocksucker. I ought to break the other one off and shove it up your ass."

He slipped a metal washer over one of the ten-penny nails and nodded to Gerber, who held the fingers of the Italian's wounded hand straight while Mendy lined the nail up with the center of his palm.

"Listen," the Italian said quickly, glancing around. "You guys are making an awful big fuckin' mistake, I mean it! I work for Don Provolone. Little Sal Provolone. You know? You don't want to be fucking with one of Little Sal's people. He'll hunt you down to the ends of the fuckin' earth. But you let me go now, we'll forget all about this whole mess, capiche?"

"Little Sal?" Mendy smirked. "Little Sal? You dumb, fucking wop. Who the hell do you think fingered you for us?"

And for the first time that evening, the Italian looked scared.

Mendy raised the hammer, high above his head.

"Aw, shit," the Italian screamed in fear, squeezing his eyes shut.

* * *

"I'm sorry to call you so late," Lou said on the phone.

"It's all right," Martha told him, holding her nightgown gathered at the neck. "I wasn't asleep yet."

"I just wanted to let you know that the private detective won't be bothering you anymore."

"You didn't..."

"Kill him?" Lou laughed. "No, Martha. I got out of that business when the war ended. We just... had a little friendly talk, that's all. He finally saw the light."

"Well, that's good news," Martha said. "Thank you, Lou."

"Okay then," Lou said. "Good night."

"Wait!" Martha said, leaning toward the phone. "Wait! Lou? Are you still there?"

"Yes," his voice came back over the phone. "I'm still here."

"Can you come over to the club tomorrow night?"

"Uh – sure."

"That's great. I've been wanting to talk with you."

"Gee whiz. I've been wanting to talk with you too, Martha."

"Great," Martha said. "Tomorrow night, then."

"Tomorrow night."

·

Chapter Nineteen
December 1919 – April 1920

"Mendy, for crying out loud. The cathedral? Saint Iggy's? That's Little Sal Provolone's fucking church."

Irv kept his voice low. They were standing on the front stoop of his parent's house, ostensibly having a cigarette while they waited for the rest of Irv's family to arrive for Shabbas dinner.

"Do you know who found the body?" Irv asked him. "I'll tell you who, a nun, Mendy. An eighty-year-old fucking nun. She was about to change the altar cloth or something, and what's the first thing she sees? A naked, dead wop nailed to a cross, hoisted up with a rope, twenty feet over the damn altar. That's outrageous!"

"He wasn't naked," Mendy said as he gazed down the street.

"What?"

"He wasn't naked. He had on an undershirt."

Irv rolled his eyes.

"Well, that changes everything," he said disdainfully. "He had an undershirt on. But the fact remains, Mendy, that the first guy this old biddy's ever seen in her life in the raw, was dead and dripping blood on the frigging altar. On the altar, Mendy. Provolone was steamed. He tells me they might have to bring somebody in to reconsecrate the church, whatever that means. What the hell were you thinking? Where was your head, Mendy fer Chrissakes, up someone's ass?"

Mendy took one last drag off his cigarette and then flicked it out into the gutter. He blew the smoke in one long stream and then turned to face Irv, his eyes dark and brooding, the way they looked when he was very serious.

"What was I thinking?" Mendy answered. "I'll tell you what I was thinking, Irv. Little Sal Provolone's kid decides to flex his muscles by robbing us and then just out of pure meanness has his guys kill your kid brother. And Sal's going, 'Okay, you can hit these guys, but you can't touch my kid, and I will put the word out that your clubs are under my protection; and by the way, I'm taking five percent of the action.'"

"He wanted ten," Irv pointed out.

"So what?" Mendy glanced up and down the street as he said it. "It looks the same, Irv. It looks like Little Sal Provolone has reached out from Brooklyn, and picked up these nickel-and-dime lower East Side Jews and put them in their place, right into his hip pocket. Like he can bust our balls any fuckin' time he wants. That's bullshit Irv, and you know it too."

Irv drew on his cigarette.

"So your answer to this is to deliberately embarrass him?"

"No." Mendy shook his head. "My answer to this is to take this first guy out in a way that Sal Provolone would never order – not in a thousand years. My answer is to show the other families that this was done by somebody outside Provolone's family, doing it this way, and without his consent. It's our answer to show everyone that we aren't in his pocket. And by the way, before we hoisted this dago up on the cross, I whacked him, a big old .45-caliber hole, right between the eyes. Because that's something else Little Sal would never do to one of his own either, spoil the corpse so they can't have an open casket."

Mendy lit another cigarette.

"Well," Irv mused. "At least you killed him before you strung him up like that."

"Of course I did" Mendy said, tossing the match out into the street. "We're not animals, ya know."

* * *

The sound of conversation drifted down the quiet street and the two men glanced towards the noise. Just turning the corner was a group of three teenagers: Seymour Lowenstein; Kevin Johnson, a slender, freckled-faced, carrot-topped youngster in a brown overcoat; and a smiling young woman bundled in a blue overcoat and scarf. They stepped out into a patch of sunlight, and Irving almost stopped breathing, because the woman, long-legged, and high-breasted with bright blue eyes set off by raven-black hair tied back in a bow, was the most beautiful girl he had ever seen, Rebecca Schumacher.

* * *

Dishes, glasses and flatware clinked as the waiters set the tables, but other than that, the Moulin Rouge was quiet, an odd contrast to the usual hubbub of jazz music and the cocophony of a hundred separate conversations. In a far corner of the club, Martha Van Dyke sat at a table, a cup of coffee at her elbow as she checked the evening's menu and the table assignments. A shadow crossed the paper in front of her, and she looked up.

"Hey, handsome." She smiled at Lou Kravitz, got to her feet, and gave him a peck on the cheek. "What are you doing here so early? I thought we were gonna have a little talk tonight but a little later."

"We are, if you have the time now," Lou told her, setting his hat on a chair close to him as he sat down. "Since, I've got an early dinner with my uncle tonight."

"Oh, right. It's your Sabbath, isn't it?"

"We say 'Shabbas.' Yeah. Starts at sundown. I don't get to a schul, a synagogue, too often anymore. Not unless somebody's getting married or having a Bar Mitzvah or something. But I like the Shabbas dinners. They… I don't know…sorta keep you in touch with yourself, ya know what I mean?"

Martha looked at him in a puzzled manner, her head cocked to one side.

"What?" Lou asked.

"Nothing," Martha said, waving her hand. "It's just, well, the better I get to know you, the more complicated you become, Lou Kravitz."

Lou felt himself redden at the remark. "Listen. The reason I stopped by? I just wanted you to know, again, that the guy who's been following you, won't be doing that anymore. He won't bother you ever again."

Martha's eyes widened and her face visibly paled. "But Lou, last night you said…"

"No, no," Lou hurriedly added, "It's not what you're thinking. Nobody laid so much as a hand on him. I just reasoned with him, that's all. And he's off the case. We burned your file, right there in his office."

"My file? What was in it?"

"I don't know. I didn't look. It's none of my business."

Martha reached across the table and gave his hand a quick squeeze.

"Thank you, Lou. You're...you're like the big brother I never had." Lou tried to hide his disappointment at her patronizing words as Martha tapped her pencil on the menu again, thinking about the evening.

"Listen," she said, biting her bottom lip in concentration. "Mary Pickford and John Gilbert are coming in tonight. Will you be coming back? I'd like for you to meet them. They're good customers."

"No," Lou told her, reaching for his hat. "I can't leave early or my uncle gets upset. Once you get in his house on Shabbas, it's like you slammed the door shut on one of them new washing machines. He'll want me to stay forever."

"Oh," Martha nodded, frowning slightly.

"Why?" Lou asked.

"Well," Martha looked down at the table. "It's just that – well, Henry's been gone for awhile now, and he was a swell husband, Lou, really swell. But he's not coming back, and little Tripper is going to need a man in his life and so do I..."

"Go on," Lou urged in a hushed voice, his heart starting to come alive with increased pounding.

Martha looked up, her face suddenly brightened. "And there's this guy that's been coming in, H. Wellington Brown, Jr., and he's asked me out to dinner a couple of times. I haven't said yes, yet. I wanted to ask you about him. He says he's an investment banker on Wall Street."

"Bud Brown?" Lou fumbled, his heart plummeting down to his knees. "Yes. He's an investment banker, just about the most successful one in the city, at least among men his age. But, Martha – H. Wellington Brown, Jr.'s married."

"I know," Martha said earnestly. "Bud told me that right away, the first time we met. But he says he's getting a divorce."

Lou scowled.

"Divorce? I hadn't heard that on the street. But even if he is, why give yourself that sort of trouble? You know how people talk about divorce, and Martha, you're Catholic. Isn't that a big problem?"

"It is," Martha nodded. "But I also have a little baby boy, and there aren't that many men who want that sort of baggage, you know? And that might be a bigger problem. I mean, sure, there's any number of men who want… well, you know what I'm talking about. But Bud seems sincere. I like that."

Lou took a deep breath, composing his thoughts. And then, just when he was about to speak his heart, the bartender was there, tapping Martha on the shoulder and showing her an invoice.

She turned back to Lou.

"You've been a dear," she said. "But I've got to run and take care of business. Love to your uncle, okay? We'll talk more later on in the week, right?"

She kissed him again on the cheek, and then she was gone and Lou was sitting there, fingers frozen to his cheek, touching that place where her lips had grazed him.

* * *

Her name was Rebecca Schumacher, and she was friends with his sister Sarah. She also studied piano at Julliard and frequently played recitals with Irving's younger brother, Seymour. Irv got that much right away, and no more, because, just then, Morris Lowenstein came striding down the block, smiling, "A welcoming committee! What a mitzvah!" he beamed with pride.

Introductions were made all around, and this time Irv caught that the young man's name was Kevin Johnson.

"Nu Seymour?" Morris Lowenstein said, his eyes happy. "This beauty, she is Sarah's friend and your girl?"

But before Seymour could answer, Rabbi Barney, got out of a taxi at the curb, and hurried introductions were made once again, by which time Morris Lowenstein pulled out his Elgin pocket watch, squinted at it, and said, "It's time! Momma's gonna be getting shpilkes if we're late five minutes." Let's go in."

Everyone started up the stoop. Everyone, that is, except Mendy, who lightly touched the Rabbi's arm. "Rabbi? May I have a word with you?"

Then, turning to Irv he added, "You'd better stay, too, Irv."

Barney's face immediately got serious.

"Certainly, Mendel," he said. "What's up?"

"I was wondering," the gangster said, looking up and down the street. "If I could get married at your schul. And Irv, I was wondering if you would be my best man."

"Sure," both men stammered at the same time, but Irv regaining his composure first said, "Mendy, you old rascal. Who's the lucky girl?"

"Margie Hauser," Mendy said, stepping on a cigarette he'd already put out. "The baker's daughter."

"Margie?" Irving nodded. "A pretty girl. I knew you dated her a few times back several months ago. But, I didn't know you were still seeing her."

"Yeah. It's something sorta recent. We started up again about six weeks ago and just started talking about getting married, sudden like."

"Well," Barney said, "I would want to meet with her and you beforehand, of course. But yes, Mendy. It would be my pleasure. When's the date?"

"I don't know. Maybe in a month or so. We'll have just a few people. Maybe my folks and hers. Irv here, and a maid of honor for Margie. I don't know, about eight to ten people in all."

Barney's face clouded. He put his hand on Mendy's shoulder.

"Mendel," he asked. "This girl, is she in trouble?"

"Not if I marry her, she isn't."

Barney pursed his lips.

"It's good," he said, "that you are doing the right thing. The honorable thing, something a real mensch would do. But Mendel… a quick wedding. Is that what you want to remember for the rest of your life?"

"It's not so quick, Rabbi," Mendy said. "Nobody's forcing me into this. Her folks don't even know she's …you know, having a baby. It's something I want to do."

"Fine," Barney nodded. "Call me at the schul when I have my calendar in front of me, and we'll set the date and have a meeting with both parents."

The three men turned to enter the house, but Irv put his hand out, stopping his friend. He waited until the door had closed behind Barney, and then whispered in a hoarse voice, "Mendy, what the fuck? There's doctors for this sort of thing, you know? And no coat-hanger amateurs. We could send Margie to a good Park Avenue O.B. doctor, a first-rate surgeon, and get this thing fixed up for a few hundred bucks. And ship her up to the Catskills to recuperate. You don't have to go marrying her just because she's got a bun in the oven. How do you know it's even yours?"

"She said I was the first, and only," Mendy shrugged. "And I did some checking around. She's really a nice girl, and I believe her."

"So she tells the truth. Is that any reason to marry her?"

"Listen," Mendy said. "For two years, now, my parents have been haking mir in tsheinick, driving me crazy, every time I have dinner with them. 'When are you going to marry? When do we get grandchildren? You're not getting any younger." I figure this way, I'll kill two birds with one stone. And, I like her besides. She's really pretty and…a good girl too…appreciates me and all that kinda stuff."

Irv rubbed his chin in thought.

"The situation could be better," he muttered. "I don't know, Mendy. You might want to think about this a little more. I mean, it's not like buying a car, you know?"

"No," Mendy agreed. "It's more like buying a pair of shoes."

"Shoes?"

"You buy a car," Mendy explained, his hand on the doorknob, "and that's what you're driving, every week, every month. You're stuck with it, you know? But shoes? Hey, you can change them every day," he said, grinning at Irv.

"C'mon," Irv said, giving Mendy a push towards the front steps. "Momma's already nervous that her dinner will be ruined."

* * *

Lou nervously played with the door handle of his Oldsmobile, debating whether he should go back inside the club.

Big brother, indeed. Couldn't Martha see how he felt? Didn't she understand that there was only one reason why a man would go out in the streets for her at three in the morning, a loaded gun in his hand, risking his life for her?

He thought about it for a moment. Obviously, she didn't understand. And as he looked back on it, he could see why. He wasn't her lover or even a boyfriend in the real sense of the word. He was Henry's best friend, Lou Kravitz, the pal who looked after his widow, like a glorified brother-in-law. The shlemiel who was always there. The pal who looked after the widow, like a real schmuck. No wonder she thought of him as a brother. He'd never given her any reason to think of him any differently.

Well, he could easily fix that. He opened the car door, took a few steps toward the club, and then stopped again.

Maybe, he thought, it was more than that. Lou pictured himself as he had looked in the mirror that morning. He was a good-looking guy with a muscular build, not movie-star handsome, but better than most. No question about that! Lots of girls had told him how handsome he was for the past few years. And while his business with the guys was making him a good living, he had just recently paid off the last of his business-school loans, so he wasn't rich yet, although he was headed that way.

Bud Brown, on the other hand, was wildly successful, with one house in the city and another in the Hamptons. He was on the board of the Metropolitan Opera, and a past president of the Harvard Club. He had that little pencil-thin moustache that women seemed to like.

Lou touched his bare upper lip and thought about that.

There was also the fact, he mused, that H. Wellington Brown, Jr. was a goy – the son of a Presbyterian family, and their roots stretched all the way back to Scotland and the 1500's. And, while that wasn't Catholic, it wasn't Jewish either, not by a long shot. And maybe that was part of it too. The old cliché, "I like those Jews, but I sure wouldn't want my daughter to marry one."

We come from different worlds, don't we Martha? Was that it? Was he deluding himself, thinking it could ever be anything else? Shaking his head, Lou turned and got back into his car.

* * *

"Poppa may be wearing a yarmulke, but this meal isn't strictly kosher," Irv told Rebecca Schumacher as they made their way to the dinner table. "Is that okay with you?"

"That's fine," she smiled. "My family's observant on Saturdays, but that's about it. And with me away at school, now, I eat just about anything I feel like, even on Saturdays."

"Where are you from?"

"Originally upstate, Rochester, but the family moved into Manhattan three years ago," Rebecca said, adding thoughtfully, "My father pulled a few strings to get me into Julliard; he knew a man on the board. Normally, it helps if you're from the city, you know."

"Hey, if you've got connections, you'd be crazy not to use them."

Rebecca relaxed noticeably.

"So," Irv asked, pulling out a chair for her. "How long have you known my brother?"

"Seymour? Not long. Maybe a few weeks. He was just awfully nice to invite me over for Shabbas dinner."

"I'm impressed. You practically know the whole family."

"Don't be!" Rebecca laughed. "Actually, I've known your sister, Sarah, almost two months now, much longer than I've known Seymour. He's a friend of Kevin Johnson's, and once in awhile, Kevin and I will play a piano duet, but he's not my real recital partner, only at the spring concert, sometimes."

"So you're Kevin's girl then, right?"

"Kevin Johnson?" Rebecca laughed again. "Hardly. I don't think Kevin even has a girl. I don't think he's ever had a girl. At least, I've never seen him with one. We're just good friends. That's all! Just friends, our music is what we have in common."

"Well then," Irv smiled, pulling out the chair next to hers. "Do you mind if I sit between you and Sarah?"

* * *

"Irving..." Rebecca Schumacher looked up at him, her eyes full and dark in her apartment doorway.

"This," she continued, "was a wonderful evening. Thank you."

"Thank you," Irving responded, and tipped her chin up gently with his fingertips, brought his face down to hers and gently kissed her.

"Hmmm," she purred pleasantly. "You can do that again, if you'd like."

So he did, his tongue caressing hers, and he slipped his right hand up easily from her waist, resting it on her breast, where he kneaded her nipple gently with his thumb and forefinger. He felt Rebecca respond even through her bra and the thin silk dress.

She reached up and held his hand there for a moment, and then gently slid his hand away, back to her waist.

"I'm sorry," Irv whispered. "Am I going too fast?" Rebecca smiled.

"I don't know," she said. "I've never let a man touch me there before."

Irv straightened up.

"Never?"

Rebecca smiled again and nodded, his hand still cradled in hers.

"It was very... nice," she said. "Really nice. And I'd like you to do it again. Soon. Really soon. But only if we're sure we're right for each other."

"Right for each other?"

"For always, not just one or two nights."

Irv looked down into her eyes. A virgin. He'd never suspected that anyone so beautiful could possibly be a virgin.

"I understand," he finally said. "And Rebecca?"

"Yes?"

"I'd like to do it again, too."

She giggled and kissed him once again, gently, on his lips. Then she opened her door with her key and she was gone, leaving him with his thoughts.

A virgin. And the funny thing was, that thing that she'd said, about always, not just an evening or so. With most girls, that would have sent Irv Lowenstein running for the nearest exit. But with this girl, it sounded pretty damn good.

* * *

Martha stood in the foyer of H. Wellington Brown, Jr.'s penthouse, the beginnings of a smile on her face. The evening was young and the spring air was cool, but even in the simple sleeveless dress that she wore, Martha was not the slightest bit chilly.

It had been a few months since Bud had started asking her out, and she'd finally accepted his offer. She had been contemplating over Lou's comments, but now she couldn't even remember why she had waited so long. The dark-haired, athletically trim Bud had been the most perfect gentleman all evening. He'd ordered for her at dinner, selected the wine, hung on her every word as they'd chatted, risen respectfully from his chair and helped her up with the slightest touch of his hand as she had gone to the ladies' room to powder her nose.

And he'd asked about little Henry, as well. That was something she hadn't expected. Bud seemed definitely interested in her son's welfare, his future.

The man was so...graceful. That was the word. He was graceful which was why it had seemed so paradoxical when he'd reached for the check and spilled a half-empty glass of wine on his dinner jacket. But that could have happened to anyone, Martha mused. And his apartment had been on the way to the jazz club they were planning on going to next, uptown, in Harlem.

She stepped a little farther into the entryway and looked into the apartment's small living room. It looked rather austere, and tidy, too, far tidier than she would have expected for a man, living alone, who was not expecting company. It looked temporary, like a place where nobody actually lived at all.

"Uhm – Martha?" Bud's voice drifted up the hallway from the bedroom. "Could you come here for a minute? I always have trouble with these ties."

Martha smiled. Henry had been that way as well, she remembered. A four-in hand tie had been something he could put on without even thinking about it, but the formal bow-tie he'd worn when they went out for dinner had always been mostly a mystery to him.

She went down the darkened hallway and hesitated at the bedroom door. There was no light showing, only the dim lights of the street below, drifting in through the windows.

"Bud?"

"In here," he said, his voice very near.

Martha walked into the shadowed bedroom, her eyes not adjusted to the darkness. She jumped slightly, as his hand slid around her waist.

"I'm sorry," Bud said, his mouth very close to her ear. "Did I startle you, Marty?"

"A bit," she admitted. "It's so dark..."

She turned, her eyes adjusting to the low light, and inhaled sharply. He was standing there naked from the waist up, his nipples showing darkly through a haze of curly chest hair.

"Goodness," Martha said. "Bud..."

"Oh, I'm sorry," he said, moving closer. "The wine soaked through the shirt as well, I'm afraid. What are you looking around for?"

"The tie," she said. "I thought you said something about a bow-tie."

"Forget the tie," Brown told her, stepping right up to her and slipping his other hand around her slender waist. He tilted his head towards her and brought his lips to hers, kissing her.

Martha kissed back, her tongue exploring his, her fingers caressing his naked back. She sighed and relaxed in his arms, and then hesitated as she felt him unbuttoning the back of her dress. Through the thin lined dress and his trousers, she could feel him getting hard, rubbing against her slightly, rhythmically.

"Bud..." she said, and he kissed her again, her dress all the way unbuttoned now. He was starting to slip it from her shoulders. "Bud, no. This is too fast."

He kept slipping the dress off.

"I like it fast," he said. His voice had changed. Harsh.

"No," Martha repeated and she stepped back.

She was not at all prepared for what he did next.

Little more than a fleeting shadow in the darkened room, his hand flicked up and slapped her hard, backhand, across the face. Martha saw stars for an instant, and tasted a hint of warm blood.

"What..." she asked weakly, and then he hit her again, an open-handed slap this time, and he stripped her dress down, restraining her arms. She kept trying to step back, and she was against the armoire when he pulled her brassiere and her slip down as well. Her damp, full breasts were bathed in the dim, blue light from the windows.

"You little shanty, Irish tramp," Brown hissed, the remark reminding Martha oddly of her father-in-law. "You sit there and flirt and make eyes at everything in pants down at that Jews' night club, and you think you'll say 'no' to me? I'll show you 'no.'"

"No, Bud," Martha begged, "Please..."

He picked her up and tossed her roughly onto the bed, where she struggled to free her arms. In an instant he was atop her, hands under her thin panties, leaving her garters where they were. His fingers were inside her in an instant.

"No!" Martha yelled it now, loudly, and then moaned as he hit her again, this time with his closed fist. He was fully erect now, rock hard, and she gasped through tears as he forced himself into her. He did it easily, and she realized with horror that she was as wet as she would have been if he'd gently seduced her.

"No," she protested again, a whimper this time, and he grabbed a handful of her hair as he jerked her head back.

"Yell if you want," he hissed as he shoved himself into her further. "But if you wake my neighbors, bitch, I swear, I'll really hurt you..."

* * *

"Hey, Joey. Where's Martha?"

Guiseppe Lucci looked up from the crate of glassware he was

inspecting and smiled at Lou Kravitz.

"Hi, Lou," he replied. "She called in this afternoon. Wants to take off a day or two. Said her kid's sick. So I said sure. Poor girl's been working six days a week for months now. I was surprised, she took off last Saturday night too."

"Saturday night?"

"Yeah. She had a date with that guy. That big wheel, H. Wellington Brown, Jr. He's been chasing after her for months."

Lou turned his head slightly to hide his disappointment. "So what's wrong with little Henry?"

Lucci shrugged at Lou's question. "I dunno," he said. "Mumps? Flu? Chicken pox? Kids get sick. Y'know?"

"Sure," Lou said.

He left the club, toying with his keys as he walked out to his Oldsmobile. He looked up at the sky, thought for a moment, and then got into the car and drove over to Martha's apartment only ten minutes away.

* * *

He was surprised when she answered his knock, not by opening the door, but by calling, "Who's there?"

"It's Lou," he said through the oak door.

"Oh, Lou..." There was silence for a moment. Then Martha's voice came back again. "Go away, Lou."

"Martha?"

No reply.

"Martha. Come on. It's me. Open the door."

The neighbor lady across the way opened her door, looked at him inquisitively, and then closed it.

"Come on, Martha," Lou said, his voice lower now. "I'm disturbing your neighbors."

There was the click of the lock being opened. The door opened an inch and stayed that way. Lou pushed it tentatively, and it swung open. He stepped into the tidy, bright apartment, and Martha was standing at a far window, looking down at the street.

"Hi," he told her. "How's Henry?"

"He's fine." She stayed at the window and did not turn around. "He's down at the park with a neighbor lady and her kids. Playing."

"He's better then?"

"Better?"

"Joey said he was sick."

"Oh. Martha kept her back to him. "Yeah. That's what I told him."

Lou crossed the room until he was standing right behind her.

"Martha? What's going on?"

She kept her back to him and her body shook slightly. He heard her sob.

"Martha?"

Lou reached out gently, touched her waist that he so longed to hold, and turned her around. He gasped at what he saw. Her right eye was black, almost swollen shut. And her lower lip was bluish yellowed, split and puffy.

"Brown did this?"

She nodded slightly.

Lou turned and started for the door.

"Lou! No!" Martha caught him by the wrist. She was crying now. "No. You can't do anything to him!"

"Like hell I can't."

"Lou!" Martha sobbed. "Please! I don't want you doing anything to him."

Lou thought for a moment.

"Then we're calling the police," he said, reaching for the phone.

"No!" She pushed the receiver back into its cradle and looked up at him, tears streaming down her face. "You can't do that either! Don't you understand? The Van Dykes, Henry's parents, they've just been looking for a way to get little Henry away from me. If something like this gets out? That I was alone with a man at his apartment? That I was... that he did this to me? That's all the scandal they'd need to get a court order. They'll take Henry away from me, Lou. They will. Bud would tell them the worst lies about me, if I caused any trouble over this. He told me so, and I believe him."

Lou set the phone down.

"Lou," Martha said. "You're a great guy. And I know you want to help me. But the only way you can help me this time is to leave it alone. Do you understand? Just leave it be!"

Lou nodded.

"Tell me," she insisted. "Promise me that you'll leave it alone. You and Mendy and Joey, everybody. That you'll just forget about it like I have to."

"I promise," he finally said.

"Okay," Martha told him, leading him to the door. "Now leave, Lou. I don't like you seeing me like this."

"You're still beautiful," he insisted.

Martha shrugged.

"Maybe beautiful is the source of all my problems," she said. She opened the door and he stepped out.

"Don't forget," she told him. "You promised."

"I won't forget," he told her, and the door closed.

He stood there for a moment on the landing, thinking. It was true, he wouldn't forget. He'd never forget. After all, it was the first time that he had ever lied to her.

* * *

Morris Lowenstein looked up from his newspaper, the yarmulke still covering the bald spot on the back of his head, despite the warmth of the evening. The early spring sounds of children playing in the street drifted in through the open living-room windows, and the aroma of the fine brisket dinner they had just eaten still lingered throughout the house. He watched his wife pick up her needlepoint, set it back down, and then fidget with the doily on the arm of her chair.

"Neshomeleh," Morris said gently. "You are like a little kitten tonight. Why so restless?"

"It's this," Esther Lowenstein sniffed. She reached into her apron pocket and took out a linen envelope, a fine piece of stationery with an engraved wedding invitation from Ben and Shirley Rotenberg inviting them to the nuptials of their son, Max.

"Leibschen?" Morris asked suspiciously. "And the son of our best friend has found his bride? For that you have shpilkes? It's a great blessing, Esther."

"But both of our sons are still bachelors," she sobbed. "Why not them?"

Morris rolled his eyes heavenward.

"And you would begrudge this young man his blessing because of that? God forbid!"

Esther sniffed and put the envelope away.

"Seymour is still young," she said in a small voice. "But Irving? He's a professional man, a lawyer. He should be married by now with children...our grandchildren. And, Sarah, she needs a husband and a family, too." Esther moaned.

"Shhh," Morris said from behind his paper. "Maybe it's not so terrible."

"All those girls Irving sees," Esther wailed with her hands clapped to her head. She looked around, and whispered hoarsely, "You know, I think he takes them to bed..."

The paper stayed up between her and her husband. Scowling, she crossed the room and peered over the top of it.

"Morris Lowenstein, are you listening to me?"

Morris blushed, embarrassed that she'd caught him grinning. But before the conversation could go any further, there was the sound of the front door opening. Both of them turned towards the entry hall, and smiled broadly when they saw that it was Irving.

Irving came into the room and they saw that he was not alone. Rebecca Schumacher, Sarah's friend, was with him, a corsage on her dress, a smile lighting up her beautiful blue eyes. She had her hair down, despite the unusual warmth of the spring evening, and she was absolutely radiant.

"Home so early?" Morris asked. "Young people like you?"

"Just stopping by to say 'hello' for a minute, Poppa" Irv said. "We just had dinner and we're on our way to the symphony."

Esther smiled at the thought of her son attending the symphony.

"But we wanted to stop here first," Rebecca said warmly, "to tell you the good news."

"News?" Esther asked.

"Yes," Irving smiled knowing he was about to make his parents extremely happy. He looked at them both.

"Poppa," he said. "Momma… We're here to ask your blessing."

Esther Lowenstein's mouth dropped.

"You mean…" Morris whispered.

"Yes, Poppa," Irving said as he and Rebecca crossed the room to be close to his parents. "I've asked Rebecca to marry me…"

"And," Rebecca added, with tears in her eyes, "I've said, 'Yes!'"

* * *

The gilded lettering on the door said, "Wellington Investments," and the knob turned easily at Lou Kravitz's touch. He'd heard through the grapevine that Bud Brown was an aggressive businessman and kept his staff late, even until six o'clock on Friday nights. This was done to plan their stock trades for the opening of the Monday market, and then, after everyone else had gone home, he stayed even later to check their work.

Like Midas counting his gold, Lou thought bitterly.

The gun in his coat pocket brushed against the door and he silenced it with his hand.

The gun had been Mendy's idea. When he'd heard that Lou was planning to go to Brown's office and scare him off, Mendy had asked him whether he was gonna carry a gun. Lou had nodded and showed him the Colt .45 automatic.

"Your army pistol?" Mendy had asked, and when Lou had nodded, Mendy had simply said, "No way. That can be traced back to you."

He'd opened a drawer and pulled out a Smith & Wesson .38 Special.

"Take this instead," he'd told Lou. "The serial number's filed off, and it's absolutely untraceable."

Lou took the gun, but, when he'd opened the cylinder to remove the bullets, Mendy had stopped him.

"What the hell ya doin'?" Mendy asked with a frown.

"I don't want to kill the son of a bitch," Lou had said. "Just scare him."

Mendy shook his head.

"You never carry an empty gun," he'd told Lou. "Not ever. You go heavy, you be ready to use it."

He walked back through the outer office, found the door slightly open with Wellington Investments on it, and quietly pushed it with his elbow. It swung open easily. He found Brown sitting at his desk, jacket off, windows open behind him to let in the evening air and a sheaf of papers before him on the desk. He looked up as the door squeaked.

"Hello?" He scowled for a moment and then smiled. "Oh, it's Lou Kravitz, isn't it?"

Lou nodded.

"I'd heard you left Wall Street," Bud Brown said, as he tapped his desk with a pencil. "We're not looking for anyone at the moment. But if you come back on Monday, you can talk to our personnel director. Name's Harley. Elizabeth Harley."

"I'm not here to apply for a job," Lou said gruffly.

"Really?" Brown pushed his seat back slightly. "Then what's your business?"

"No business," Lou said. "This is personal."

Brown stood up, his brow furrowed.

"Martha Van Dyke," Lou said. "She's a friend of mine."

Brown looked at him for a moment. Then he laughed.

"She is, is she? And what kind of bullshit has she been telling you about me?"

Lou felt the heat rising in his face.

"She doesn't lie," he said simply.

"Well," Brown said angrily, hands on his hips. "If she's told you anything other than that she spread her legs for me, then she's a fuckin' liar."

Lou moved closer. "And that's how she got her eye blackened?"

Brown shrugged.

"She likes it rough," he said. "I don't, but if that's what a woman wants, then…"

He looked up at Lou. "Were you in the war, Kravitz?"

Lou nodded.

"France?"

Lou nodded again. "Let's cut the conversation, you prick!"

"Then you know how some of these broads can be," Brown smiled. "Sick bitches."

Lou reached into his pocket, found the gun, pulled it out and aimed it at Brown's head.

Brown laughed.

"Oh, I see," he said. "So you're the avenging hero, now? Okay. Fine. Go back and tell that little shanty Irish slut that I just pissed down my leg, I was so afraid of you."

"You're walkin' a thin line, Brown. Believe me when I say it." Lou warned him.

"Really?" Brown smirked. "I'm so scared, I'm shaking."

"You'd better stay away from Martha," Lou told him, his eyes cold.

"Kravitz," Bud Brown said. "What are you doing here? You're defending a woman who works in a nightclub. You think I'm the only one who's had her? You think she doesn't like it rough? Get serious, man. She's the best blow job in town."

Lou hesitated for a moment. Could it be true? No, he knew it was Brown's bravado and bullshit excuses.

Brown rounded the desk.

"Go home," he told Lou softly. "You're a good man, Kravitz. I won't call the police. We'll just forget this little incident. You'll get nowhere killing me, except a lifetime in jail." Brown continued. "Now… go get yourself a good stiff drink."

He put a hand on Lou's shoulder and steered him toward the door.

"Oh, and Kravitz?" Bud Brown called after him with an evil grin.

Lou turned and looked over his shoulder.

"Tell the little slut that I'll be looking forward to the next time. Maybe by then she'll learn to give a better fuck."

Blind rage flooded Lou's mind. He turned and crossed the room in three strides, grabbing Brown's shirt in both hands, his temples pounding. Lou lifted the man from the floor and hurled him deliberately out the tenth floor window.

He left the empty office feeling good for the first time in twenty-four hours.

"Shit, Lou, no kidding? You threw him out the fucking window?"

"I did, but I didn't go to his office with the intention of heaving him out the window. I just lost my temper…blew a fuse."

"Good for you Lou. I wasn't sure you'd have the chutzpah to take care of Mr. H. Wellington Brown, Jr. properly. But, sometimes in our business ya gotta fight fire with fire."

Outside the office door, a piano was playing new ragtime songs as early evening guests began to filter into the Moulin Rouge.

"I know how that can be," Mendy said calmly, feet up on the desk as he lit a cigarette.

"No, you don't!" Lou shook his head wondering how anyone in the world could be so calm after hearing what he had done, then he remembered that Mendy had a long history of violence, just like Bugsy Siegel and Dutch Schultz.

"And that's not a bad thing," Mendy shrugged. "You went to keep Martha from being bothered by this putz, right? And now he doesn't bother her or anyone else anymore. He was a bad guy!"

"But I killed him!"

Mendy looked at Lou, his head cocked.

"Lou," he said softly. "Over there, in Europe. You ever fire your gun?"

"In the Army?" Lou asked. "Well, sure. I had to. After all, the Krauts tried to overrun our lines. Several times."

"Ever kill any of them?'

"Maybe, probably. I'm not sure. But do I have to talk about it?"

Mendy shrugged.

"So what's the difference?" The gangster held his palms up. "Over there. Here in New York. What's the difference?"

Lou sat down and solemnly nodded his head.

"Yeh, I guess you're right but, that was war," he said. "We had no choice."

"And so's this," Mendy told him. "It's a war between us and every son-of-a-bitch that wants to keep guys like you and me in tailor shops and behind pushcarts. It's a war between the crooks in Tammany Hall and the guys on the street like us that got enough chutzpah to fight back. So tell me, this Bud Brown…you're sure he's dead?"

"Mendy, the man fell out of a tenth floor window."

"Okay," Mendy nodded. "He's dead."

"Did you touch anything while you were in the office?"

Lou thought for a moment.

"Just the doorknob, going in and coming out. And Bud, of course. I grabbed him by the lapels."

Mendy waved his hand dismissively. "The coat won't hold no fingerprints," he said.

Lou looked at him blankly.

"Fingerprints," Mendy explained. "Something the cops use for identification purposes.."

"Shit. Yeah. I've heard about that. But no, other than the doorknob, I didn't touch a thing."

"Then I'm proud of you, Lou. You got balls and I like that!"

Outside the office door, the piano stopped playing and a jazz band struck up. Without thinking, Lou checked his watch. Nine-thirty. Dinner hour at the Moulin Rouge.

"How'd you tear your jacket pocket?" Mendy asked, noticing that the right pocket was slightly torn, "Trying to pull the piece out?"

Lou nodded.

"Carry it in your waistband next time," Mendy said. "Now empty your jacket pockets."

Lou did as Mendy suggested, putting a Waterman fountain pen, a handkerchief, a money clip stuffed with bills and some change on the table.

"Now give me your jacket."

Lou took the suit coat off and handed it to Mendy, perplexed. Then his mouth dropped as Mendy stood, walked across the room to a pot-bellied stove, opened the door and shoved the coat into the stove.

"What are you doing?" Lou asked.

"That was evidence that you were in a scuffle. You got another coat here?"

"Just my topcoat."

Mendy nodded.

"Put that on, go home, change clothes, and come straight back. Bring more money, lots of it. You've been playing poker for the last three hours if anyone should ask."

Lou stared.

"Alibi," Mendy said. "If I'm asked, I'll get six guys to say you were here since four this afternoon, playing seven-card stud. That you're up probably $2500 or more. Now what was this Bud's office address?"

Lou told him and then Mendy asked about the home address.

"He lives at The Dakota," Lou said. "Across from the Park. Always tries to impress people with how much money his family's got. I don't know the apartment number."

"Won't need it," Mendy said. "That's easy to get."

The gangster walked around the desk and put his hand on Lou's shoulder.

"Go out the back way," he said. "Go home, change clothes and come back. We've got the rest of this handled." Lou nodded and moved toward the door.

"And Lou?"

Lou turned.

"What you did for Martha? That was a mitzvah to her. A real mitzvah. You're a mensch. Think about whadda good guy you are, not about that useless fuck, Bud Brown."

Lou stepped out of the office and stood there for a moment, brushing off Mendy's compliment and taking in the Moulin Rouge. The band finished a number and there was a splatter of polite applause. It was going on ten, but that was still early for the club. The real players didn't show up until after eleven. By then, the theaters had closed for the night, and the high rollers usually started to show up for some action around midnight.

He started for the side door and then, on a hunch, decided to go out the front entrance. This would take him past Martha and, while he couldn't tell her what had happened earlier that evening, as Mendy had said, "you weren't there..." – just seeing her would be enough to make Lou feel good for the rest of the night.

* * *

"This is bunk. I know you got a goddamn game going on in back."

Lou heard the disagreement before he rounded the corner and came up on Martha, politely arguing with some man standing in front of her wearing a pinstriped gray suit and a black bowler, berating her. He had never seen him before, and instantly, the hair rose on the back of Lou's neck, but he deliberately took a deep breath and calmed himself down before approaching the pale-skinned stranger. Lou smelled "cop".

"Can I help?" Lou asked in his friendliest customer voice, offering his hand as he stepped in, close enough that he would tower over the stranger.

"Who the hell are you?" The stranger ignored Lou's hand.

"I'm Lou Kravitz, one of the partners, and I would appreciate it if you would watch your language in front of the lady, friend."

The man smirked, looked as if he was about to say something, and then thought better of it. He looked up at Lou.

"She won't let me in the poker game," the man said.

Lou looked at Martha. She'd put her makeup on expertly, covering the shiner. The only sign of her struggle the previous evening was a touch of swelling under the one eye, and Lou wouldn't have noticed that, except for the fact that he dreamed about her face every night. Her black dress set off her auburn hair perfectly, and she was showing just enough cleavage to excite him.

"What's he talking about?" Lou asked.

"I don't know," Martha answered. "I offered to find this gentleman a dinner table, but he keeps talking about cards."

"No card game here," Lou told the stranger cheerfully. "Gambling's against the law in New York City, and so is booze since Prohibition was passed a few months ago." This is an exclusive club for members only, a gourmet-dining club, and that's about it.

"Get off it," the man said roughly. "You got a card game goin' on in the back. I was here last Tuesday with one of your members, and got cleaned out. Now I'm here to win back what's mine."

He reached into his breast pocket and came out with a roll of hundred dollar bills, waving them in front of Lou's face and smirking.

"That's a lot of money, friend," Lou said. "Better put it away before some bad guys get the wrong idea and decide to relieve you of your wallet."

"But Mr. Lucci invited me as his guest," the stranger said, looking confused. He had also mispronounced Lucci.

Lou shrugged.

"I don't know what you're trying to pull, friend, but there's no game here. Not Tuesday. Not now, not ever. Now either you leave peacefully or …"

"Or what?" The man pulled his shoulders back, a belligerent look in his eyes.

Lou started to get pissed. "Or I will have to summon the police," Lou said without emotion.

"Fat chance!" The man looked at Martha, then at Lou, then back at Martha.

"Oh, fuck it," he finally said. "I'll go spend my money somewhere else!"

He pulled his hat low, over his eyes, straightened his lapels, and walked briskly to the front door.

"Who was that?" Lou asked, as Joey Lucci had materialized out of nowhere lurking around, waiting for trouble. Joey had a talent for showing up at the right time, discouraging any customer problems. His oiled hair was parted neatly in the center, and his dark suit was impeccable. He smelled slightly of Bay Rum.

"Nobody I know," Lucci told Lou, his face frowning.

"Said he knew you, and you had personally invited him to be your guest," Lou added. "But he couldn't pronounce your name worth a damn."

Lucci nodded.

"That's because the dumb cop wasn't thinking right and remembered some name he had seen on a sheet. I never saw him before in my life," Lucci sneered.

Lou turned to face Lucci. "You mean he was a cop? I could almost smell it on that guy."

Lucci laughed.

"Hell yes. You seen his shoes? Big, thick soles for walking a beat. And, that suit fit like shit, I'll lay you fifty to one he's never seen it before tonight. Yeah, somebody dressed up a beat cop in a fancy suit and sent him in here to try and make us do something stupid. But he ain't putting nothing over on Martha."

"That's right," Martha said. "If he doesn't show up with somebody I know, he stays in the front room. Besides, a few hundred dollars doesn't hack it in our games. The stake for any of our poker games is twice that much."

"That's my girl," Lucci grinned. "Forget the flatfoot. Police are probably just checkin' out all the clubs, that's all. Oh yeah, didja get your invitations to Irv's wedding?"

Martha nodded, and Lou noted the way her eyes lit up at the word, "wedding."

"Hard to believe, isn't it?" Lou asked, deliberately covering up the fact that he was staring at Martha again. "New York's most eligible bachelor finally takes the big plunge with Rebecca Schumacher."

"It'll be good for Irving," Lucci shrugged. "God knows, a man needs a wife to raise his children and take care of the house."

"Yes," Lou agreed. "God knows."

And suddenly he became aware that Martha was staring at him.

* * *

Milton Blackman bashed his derby against the door panel of the Ford in frustration, denting in the crown. This is what he got for using a beat cop instead of a detective. But the D.A. had refused to allow the Chief to assign a detective to the matter, saying that casing the Moulin Rouge was a waste of time and money. So Blackman had taken what the desk sergeant could find for him and wound up with nothing, absolutely nothing. "But, how could you mispronounce his name, officer?" Blackman asked sarcastically.

"Because Lucci is an Italian name." The Irish cop shrugged. "I ain't never had much to do with no dagoes."

Blackman fumed. "Okay," he said. "What's the layout of the club like? We know how large the building is on the outside. Did you pace out the back room area, like I asked?"

The cop shook his head.

"Naw, I didn't have a chance, since I blew the joint after they told me there weren't no poker."

Blackman rolled his eyes.

"But you said this Kravitz fellow offered to buy you dinner!"

"Yeah, but I didn't take him up on it, though."

Blackman stared at him.

"Why not?"

"I was on duty," the cop said pointedly. "And besides, I wasn't hungry."

Blackman leaned back in his seat, his hands clasping his head, the exhaust of the Ford rumbling softly somewhere below him.

"If… you… didn't measure, pace… off… the… club," Blackman said slowly, stressing each word, "we won't know how big the back room is or how many people will be in there. And, then we can't figure on how many police officers to bring along for the bust. And if we don't know how many police officers to bring, we can't very well raid it, can we?"

"I dunno," the cop shrugged. "I only been on one of these raids once before and all I did then was drive the paddy wagon. Whatssa difference how big the room is?"

Blackman looked at the cop in disgust, finally realizing the mentality of the policeman and that he would never understand that the dimensions of the room frequently indicated the size of the crowd. He just shook his head in frustration. No wonder characters like Lowenstein were allowed to run all over New York City. Teddy Roosevelt may have overhauled the New York City Police Department in his day, but absolutely no one was minding the store now. The average New York cop couldn't find his ass with both hands and a flashlight. He waved dismissively.

"Forget it," he ordered. "And just drive."

"Where to?" The cop put the Ford in gear.

"Back to the station." Blackman said wearily. "Where do you think? We're done here, at least for the night. But, there'll be other days, believe me!"

Chapter Twenty-One
Spring 1922

After much discussion, Irv and Rebecca had finally set a date for their wedding in the spring of 1923. Now that the commitment was made, Irv was getting anxious to have it over already.

Irv had had the apartment for only a month. On Central Park West, the best address in New York, it looked over the park and had a uniformed doorman, an elevator boy, and a garage that ran into a courtyard where one could enter or leave a car without being seen. It had four bedrooms, three baths, a sitting room as well as a living room, and a terrace where one could take breakfast or enjoy a cocktail, twelve floors above the cacophony of taxis blowing their horns and the other sounds of the city.

"I love this place," Rebecca cooed as Irv unbuttoned the back of her dress.

She complimented the place perfectly, he thought to himself. Rebecca had decorated it magnificently with the added assistance of her cousin, Charlotte Greenberg, an up-and-coming interior decorator. Generally speaking, Jewish girls would go so far sexually with a man before they were married and then their legs would snap shut like a steel trap. Irv had reached that place with Rebecca, and although frustrated and aching each night they were together, he played by her rules.

He would have to wait until their wedding night and, like most Jewish men before that special night, he would have to find himself a pretty shiksah to relieve his misery.

Irv wasn't cheap. He already spent some $5,000 on the apartment and figured that enough was enough. He wasn't sorry, though, because he'd decided it was worth it the first time they had a session necking, and she had allowed him to partially undress her. She was okay with that since they had announced their wedding date, and she had the diamond ring on her finger. But now, he unbuttoned the next button, thinking of Rebecca's milk-white breasts.

"Darling," she said, turning to face him. "Can that wait for a few minutes? I wanted to talk to you about our wedding plans. I've already discussed it with my parents, and they've really given us carte blanche. Isn't that great? "

Inwardly, Irv groaned. But, he smiled and nodded.

"Sure," he told Rebecca, running his hand lightly through her long, black hair. "What's on your mind?"

"The bridesmaid's dresses," Rebecca said, the slightest bit of a furrow on her brow as she spoke. "I mean, your sister will look darling in that yellow chintz, but I'm just not sure it's the right color for my cousin."

"As I've told you," he smiled. "You have the best taste about those things. Do what you think looks the best."

Rebecca frowned.

"The shop said they would have to charge us for the fabric if I changed my mind again, since they've already ordered it, and honey, we should watch our expenses, because its already costing my parents and us more than we had originally planned.

"Never mind that," Irv smiled anxious to get back to her wonderful breasts. "It's your day…"

"Our day."

"That's what I meant. Get what you want."

His fingers went back to the blouse's buttons, and started to fondle her almost perfect white breasts with rosy nipples that stood erect when he sucked them.

She reached behind her back and took his hand, holding it gently and stopping him.

"Now," she said. "About the flowers…"

Irv was getting impatient. This seemed like a lot of nonsense to go through to get something he was already getting on a regular basis from other women. But then again, she was a fantastic girl. And his mother was deliriously happy with her.

Rebecca talked on about the flowers, and Irv thought about Mendy's comment about changing girls the way you changed shoes. True to his word, Mendy had been showing up at the club almost nightly with a different chorus girl from one of the musicals uptown, while his wife sat home alone. Irv couldn't imagine treating Rebecca that way.

"Now for your mother, I think pink would be a nice color, don't you?" Rebecca continued.

Irv wondered how much longer this was going to last. He had to get to the Moulin Rouge in an hour. And then, he wanted to take a trip to a new club they were thinking of buying, the Versailles Club. But he thought of Rebecca's young, tight body, and he smiled because he had a huge hard-on.

"Enough already, Rebecca. The wedding plans are coming along just fine. Let the party planner do her stuff."

Chapter Twenty-Two
Spring 1923

Irv stepped down solidly on the napkin-wrapped wineglass, smashing it while the crowd erupted in shouts of "Mazel tov!" Even though it was not his schul since the little Delancey Street building could not have accommodated the crowd gathered for the nuptials, Barney Green smiled as proudly as if it were him who had just taken a bride. He stepped forward and announced, "Ladies and gentlemen, it is my esteemed honor to present to you for the first time…Mr. and Mrs. Irving Lowenstein. Mr. Lowenstein, you may now kiss the bride."

The joyous crowd gathered at the most fashionable hotel in New York City, the Plaza, after the ceremony as Irving's mother sobbed into a white Irish linen handkerchief that a friend had given her. Morris had rented for the occasion a meticulously tailored tuxedo and looked the part of a happy father who had just married off his son. The newly married Goldblatts, Lou Kravitz and the Lucci brothers smiled for the wedding photographer, as he roamed the room snapping different groups. And, a young woman, Rebecca Schumacher, beautiful enough to pose on a Vogue magazine cover, pledged forever her perfect body to Irving Lowenstein, a goddamned gangster.

Milton Blackman took it all in, the lavish cost of the wedding, the political biggies present – the Mayor, Lt. Governor, Congressmen and Judges – the table full of expensive wedding presents, envelopes stuffed with cash, the lavish trays of appetizers being passed by white gloved waiters and the expensive arrangement of flowers on each of the fifty tables made Milton Blackman want to retch.

He touched the small white silk yarmulke on the back of his head just to make sure it was still there. It offended him that Lowenstein called himself a Jew. He wondered if the slick, manicured attorney, owner of the most successful speakeasy in town, with his easy smile and his social pretensions, had even been in a schul since his Bar Mitzvah. Blackman doubted it. It also made him furious that the rumor around town was that Lowenstein had worked out a deal to buy the Versailles Club for less than 25 cents on the dollar. It seemed that everything Lowenstein touched turned to gold.

Blackman loathed the fact that several of the men present at the wedding were being treated here today as if they were part of New York society rather than part of the New York Crime Syndicate. He was also jealous that the party cost more than the home his family had recently purchased over in Brooklyn. He hated the fact that Lowenstein had the chutzpah to send every attorney on the D.A.'s staff an engraved invitation, and that he had actually found himself standing in the housewares department at Saks buying the miserable son of a bitch a set of expensive linen dinner napkins in exactly the color for which the bride had registered. Life wasn't fair but, he already knew that. He was so jealous, his entire body ached with the pain.

Blackman glanced around and realized that out of all the wedding guests, his was the only face not smiling. He forced himself to grin. He hoped the Plaza Hotel had a good janitorial staff, because it would take days to clean the mess up and get rid of the cigar odor after the affair was over and everybody had gone home with a piece of wedding cake.

Blackman looked quickly over to the newly married couple. Lowenstein and his bride were posing for newspaper photographers from the media. Flashbulbs now popped all over the place.

Blackman looked at the sea of yarmulkes and wondered if he was the only righteous man among them. He had always hurried home from work every Friday afternoon to wash and change clothes for dinner and the evening service. He spent his Saturday mornings reading the Torah and took elaborate pains to live his life as God intended. For this devotion, he was rewarded with a twenty-six-hundred-dollar-a-year position in the Manhattan District attorney's office. He wondered if there was really a God at all!

Lowenstein's parents circulated around the crowd urging each person to eat more appetizers before the five-course meal, sweet table and fresh fruit were offered to the guests. How Blackman longed to see his own mother so happy. But the only prospect he had for making her that happy was Ruth Greenblatt, the twenty-five year old daughter of a baker, as plump as her father's Kaiser Rolls. He had been dating her for seven years now and still hadn't set a wedding date. He had been with her just the night before, and when he had tried, through the layers of her clothing, to place his hand on her breast, she actually had the nerve to move his hand away and say, "Now, Milton, I'm saving these for my *husband*."

The guests were lining up now at the back of the banquet room to congratulate the newlyweds and the rest of the wedding party. He would have to smile and congratulate the gangster's whole family, including his pale, thin, brother, Seymour, the piano player at Julliard and his sister, who was decent-looking in her own right. Blackman had heard rumors, for several months now, that the brother was as queer as a three-dollar-bill. Nothing concrete, but plenty of gossip, and Blackman needed a weakness to puncture Lowenstein's coat of armor, and that just might be enough to bring about the downfall of Mr. Irving Lowenstein. He hoped to God the rumors were true!

New York City had strict anti-sodomy laws, a legacy from the Dutch reform Protestants who had founded this city on the Hudson. And New York newspapers were like newspapers everywhere else. They would happily exploit a scandal involving celebrity types, just like a weekly tabloid.

Not that Blackman had any hard information on Lowenstein's brother, but he thought with his connections, he might get it. He just needed time. And, he doubted that Irving Lowenstein's political friends could protect his kid brother if the rumors were true. All Blackman had at the moment was the smoke but, maybe it was time for him to go looking for the fire.

* * *

Wrapped in mink, topped with a fashionable women's hat that had attractive black netting covering the top half of her face, Rebecca touched her wedding ring for perhaps the hundredth time that day and watched as the porter placed her trunks on the luggage cart. She noticed Irving tipping the red cap two dollars and saw the black patron's eyes grow wide at the size of the gratuity.

A locomotive hissed white steam, blowing pressure out of its brake system, and Rebecca jumped at the sound, despite herself. Irving's friends, she thought, that nice and well-educated Lou Kravitz and the dark brooding one called Mendy with the Lucci brothers, had just joined them. They were milling around on the other side of the platform laughing at the performance of an organ grinder and his little, brown monkey scampering around the crowd looking for coins to fill his tin cup.

"Happy?" Irv asked her, putting an arm around her shoulder.

"Very much so," she told him snuggling into his shoulder. "Irving, these men aren't all going with us to Niagara Falls, are they?" she asked looking up into his eyes.

"On our honeymoon?" Irv choked back a laugh. "No, sweetheart, not hardly. Lou's just come down to see us off. And Mendel and the Luccis, well, yes, they'll be riding on the same train with us as far as Buffalo, but then they're going on to Detroit. We've got some business there to take care of."

"Oh? Are you opening another club? I heard that you just took over ownership of some new place called the Versailles Club in Brooklyn, the Upper East Side or somewhere, I just can't remember."

"We're working out the details on that," Lou said, shaking his head. "This is some other business."

"I see," Rebecca mused, thinking to herself. *What kind of business could my husband have in Detroit?*

"All 'board!" It was 8 p.m. and the Wolverine train was ready to depart from the station on time. It was seldom late and that was part of its good reputation.

Irv smiled and offered her his hand as Rebecca stepped up into the Pullman car, glad to see that Irv's friends were walking down to the club car at the other end of the train. The conductor showed the newlyweds into a deluxe compartment, where a bed was already turned down from the wall, and a bottle of Veuve Clicquot, French champagne, nestled in an ice bucket. More bills exchanged hands, and then she and Irv were alone. Slowly the train moved forward and Irv opened the champagne, holding it and turning the bottle expertly like a man who had opened several bottles of champagne before. He poured two glasses and handed her one.

"Well, Mister Lowenstein," she said, sipping the wonderfully smooth French champagne. "Niagara Falls, here we come."

"Indeed, Mrs. Lowenstein," he smiled. "And how shall we pass the time between here and there?"

"Well," she teased, sitting on the bed. "I'm gonna try and get some rest."

"And I," Irv told her, setting his glass on the table, "am going to do my best to interrupt that rest…but, in a pleasurable manner."

With that, he was on one knee next to the bed, expertly undoing her garters and then reaching up and sliding her bloomers down and off of her legs. She was still wearing her mink, and she thought for a moment to protest, but then Irv's fingers gently parted her legs and he began to lick her with his probing tongue with soft, slow licks that sent shivers through her whole body. She felt totally wet already.

"Oh, Irving," she said, burying her fingers in his hair and pulling him closer.

She closed her eyes and moaned as the train picked up speed.

* * *

Mendy opened his eyes as the train slowed. Joey Lucci, sitting in the seat opposite him, had a hand cupped to the train window, peering out into the early-morning darkness.

"We almost there?" Mendy asked.

Lucci nodded. "Windsor, Ontario," he told his boss. "that's the end of the line."

Sam Abramowitz and Harry Fleisher, two lieutenants from the Purple Gang, were waiting for them on the platform when they got off. Mendy had to restrain himself from laughing, because the two were wearing dark pin stripe suits, spats and snap-brim fedoras. It was like holding up a sign that said, "Hey – look Ma, I'm a gangster!"

Then again, Mendy thought to himself, what else would you expect from the Detroit mob? They might make the best cars in the world there, but the fact remained that if you drove just two miles outside the city limits, you'd be knee-deep in cows' shit and cornfields. The Purples were something else!

"You got luggage?" Fleisher asked him.

"Just these," Mendy said. He and Lucci each had a salesman's sample case and a Gladstone bag. Harry Fleisher nodded, but didn't offer to help them.

The four men piled into a waiting Packard and set off driving towards Walkerville, home of Hiram Walker. The Detroit River was on their left, reflecting the lights of the still-sleeping city. Sam Abramowitz turned and looked back at Mendy.

"We parked the truck in a warehouse and had some guys unload it, just like ya said."

"And the guy you think is your stoolie, you let him know that the truck's coming in this mornin'?"

"Just like ya said," Abramowitz told him. He shook his head. "Now listen to me you guys. I wouldn't want you thinkin' this ain't somethin' we couldn't handle ourselves. We get nothing' but respect from the Chicago and New York boys."

"Oh yeah? Then, how come we've had so many of our trucks hijacked in the last several months?" Lucci said with an icy stare.

"What the fuck you sayin'?" Fleisher asked.

"These guys have been hitting you pretty hard lately, but it's with our booze. And, now we know that the main snitch is a cousin to Capone's right-hand man, Frank Nitti. Am I right?"

Abramowitz nodded.

"So how much respect is that? If you whack him, Alphonse would wipe you right off the face of the mother-fuckin' earth. No questions asked. So don't try to make us think you don't owe us big time for getting' rid of the problem, because you sure as hell do." Lucci said it matter-of-factly without any emotion.

Fleisher grumbled and turned back to stare out the windshield.

They pulled into a warehouse just down the street from the Canadian Club distillery. A canvas-topped Ford Model TT truck was sitting there, a small stack of whiskey cases piled behind it.

Fleisher looked at Mendy as he took his bags out of the trunk of the car.

"Four guys ain't gonna be enough," the Purple Gang lieutenant said. "You're just askin' to be put in a wooden box."

"Four guys will be plenty," Mendy said quietly. He opened up one of the salesman's sample cases and took out an odd-looking gun with a shoulder stock and a handgrip under the barrel. Opening the Gladstone bag, Mendy took out a round canister-like magazine and snapped it onto the gun, just behind the hand-grip.

"What the fuck is that?" Fleisher asked.

"Thompson .45 machine gun," Mendy said matter-of-factly. "The Colt Company is making them for the Army. Shoots about two hundred rounds a minute."

Harry Fleisher's eyes grew wide as Lucci assembled an identical weapon.

"Okay," Mendy told Abramowitz. "Here's the drill. When your driver here gets back to Detroit from havin' his truck hijacked, you want your whole crew in one place so the cops can round 'em up and book 'em for suspected violation of the Volstead Act."

"Yeah, yeah," Abramowitz said. "I know, I know, we already fixed that. They're gonna take us down to the precinct, book us all for operating after hours, and then my lawyer's gonna spring us loose at noon and get the charges dropped."

"And you're gonna have the newspapers there to cover the raid?" Lucci asked.

"Will Muller, The Detroit News' police beat writer, and a photographer will cover the story. The whole fuckin' town is gonna know that every last one of us was down in the lock-up when the shit hit the fan. That's an airtight alibi that even old Scarface can't dispute."

"Good," Mendy said. "Who's driving the truck?"

"Me, boss." The driver was a red-faced Irishman in a plain cloth cap.

"When they take this truck, you act scared and don't let on we're back there, you understand?" Mendy asked. "You mess up and you ain't coming' home tonight...or any other night, got it, Paddy?"

"Sure, I got it, boss. Don'cha worry none," the driver said in a thick Irish brogue.

Mendy and Lucci climbed into the half-loaded truck with Fleisher and Abramowitz and settled down in the back, whiskey cases piled all around them. The warehousemen quickly placed boards over them and then placed more whisky cases above and around them completely covering them up.

"Hope you guys ain't bothered by small spaces?" Mendy said to the three men.

"Now's a hell of a time to ask," Lucci replied, and the four men laughed.

The truck rumbled under them and the bottles clinked in their cases as they went down the street. They drove for what seemed like forever until they crossed the Ambassador Bridge over to Detroit, and then Mendy heard the screech of brakes outside and the truck lurched to a stop.

"Hey mug, get out of that cab," someone yelled in a hoarse voice.

Mendy heard it as clearly as if the man was standing next to him.

"I'm leavin' boss" the Irish driver whispered over his shoulder as he hurried out of the truck's cab. Then he loudly exclaimed, "This here truck don' mean nothin' to me, and that's the God's truth." He mumbled at the same time under his breath.

Good! The driver sounded scared!

In seconds, the truck was moving again.

They didn't go far this time. They came to a stop within a few miles, and Mendy could hear men's voices and see the yellow glow of a warehouse light through the cracks between the cases of whiskey. He slowly pulled back the cocking lever of the Thompson, and next to him, he heard Lucci doing the same.

Abramowitz and Fleisher loaded their sawed off shotguns at the same time.

"Okay you assholes," Mendy heard a man growl. "I got a guy standin' by to take this truck down to Toledo and sell the entire load of booze. I want all that whiskey offa there in the next ten minutes, You hear me?"

The truck creaked slightly and Mendy heard scraping sounds as men began unloading the truck. They came closer, closer, and then suddenly there was light as the two cases in front of Lucci were removed simultaneously.

"Good morning, you thievin' sons of bitches," Lucci said with a bright grin, and with that, the four men pulled their triggers in a burst of gunfire.

* * *

"Mr. Hugo Lancaster," Irv said warmly. "Good of you to drive downtown so early and meet me this morning. Toronto sure is a beautiful city, nice and quiet."

"It's early," the Canadian grumbled, ignoring Lowenstein's other comments. "I don't know why we are meeting at 8:30 a.m. for breakfast at the hotel."

"Oh," Irving said. "I thought you knew. I'm on my honeymoon, here."

"Well," Lancaster groused some more. "I'm used to doing business at my club, either at lunch, or later on in the afternoon, around cocktail time!"

"I apologize for the inconvenience," Irv said deciding already that he wasn't going to like the man. "But, maybe we can forget breakfast and get right down to business," Irv said as he waved the waiter away but poured himself and Lancaster a cup of coffee.

He set a small leather bag on the empty seat at the side of the table, and opened a leather portfolio, taking out sets of typed papers.

"In the bag is one hundred thousand dollars, American," Irv said. "In addition, there is a proposed agreement setting forth the conditions of our purchase of your distillery company; and, beginning in February of next year, we will make monthly payments of the same amount until the sum of five million dollars is reached. In return, we operate the business, but you hold title to the Lancaster distillery in a bank escrow until you are paid in full, after which the bank will transfer the title to our company, and the deal will be concluded. Are those the basic terms as you recall them?"

"They are indeed," Lancaster admitted. "But I've been thinking, sir, and one hundred thousand dollars is a very small down payment, considering the value of the business. Our attorney tells us that ten percent is the usual minimum in purchases such as this."

Irv opened a legal pad and glanced at it.

"I see here that in the past two years or so, you've diversified your holdings, Mr. Lancaster. You put four hundred thousand dollars into the Jackson Motorcar Company in Michigan just last year, did you not?"

Lancaster nodded unhappily.

"And the Jackson Motorcar Company went bankrupt two months ago, isn't that also correct?"

Lancaster blustered, but finally nodded his head. "See   here," he said. "My distillery is a very valuable piece of property…"

Irving finished the sentence, "…that had sold almost all of its product in the United States, which now has been dry for several years. Therefore, your gross sales are precipitously low and, in the meantime, you have missed the last two mortgage payments on the house you built in Toronto just four years ago. And, in addition," he continued, "you recently sold your summer home in Owen Sound at a loss to raise some cash, eh?"

Lancaster looked up, flushed and angry.

"Don't try to jerk me off, sir," Irv told him with a smile. "If you do, I will drop our negotiations like a bad habit and close the deal with distillery number two on my list, one of your biggest competitors. Let's face it Hugo Lancaster, you need this transaction and need it badly, or else in sixty days, you'll be financially insolvent. You already know that's a fact, and so do I. Now sign the agreement, sir, before I begin to feel less charitable in the terms, especially, the down payment."

* * *

Fifteen minutes later, Irv was unlocking the door to his hotel suite, the signed papers in his briefcase tucked under his arm.

Rebecca was sitting at the table, a glass of tea at her elbow, looking at a newspaper.

"News from the outside world?" Irv smiled.

"Terrible news," Rebecca said, shaking her head. She showed him the paper. "Four men were killed in Detroit this morning. Several others wounded. Nobody knows who did it. The police think it was a mob war, or something."

"What's this world coming to?" Irv asked, glancing at the paper and thankful that the Purple Gang as well as Mendy's and Lucci's names were not mentioned in the story. He set the paper aside. "Well, what shall we do today, my darling?"

"I'd like to go see the Falls," Rebecca said sprightly.

"Good idea," Irv agreed. "Except…"

"Except what?"

"Well," he shrugged. "The guidebook says that the Falls have been there for millions and millions of years…."

"Yes?'

"So certainly," he said, putting his arms around her and unbuttoning the back of her dress, "they will still be there later this afternoon."

"Oh, Irving," she laughed. He undid her brassiere as well, dropping it and her dress, so she stood, encircled in his arms, naked from the waist up. He lowered his head and took one nipple in his mouth, gently kneading the other with his thumb.

"Oh…" Rebecca moaned. "Irving…."

* * *

Manhattan District Attorney's Office
Manhattan, New York

INVESTIGATIVE REPORT

Date: May 10, 1923
Subject: Surveillance: Lowenstein, Seymour

Subject was followed from Delancey Street residence via streetcar to corner of Fourth and Mercer, Greenwich Village, where he was observed entering an apartment building located at 2432 Mercer Street at 9:20 a.m. This officer secured a vantage point on the roof opposite the apartment building, from which he was able to observe subject with binoculars in the apartment of one Kevin Johnson, music student. Johnson was observed from time to time to be completely nude from the waist up. At this point, shades were drawn in the apartment windows. Subject and Johnson left apartment at 11:00 a.m. and proceeded via streetcar to the Julliard School of Music in New York City.

Edward Bruce, Sergeant

Milton Blackman looked up.

"Well, sir," the sergeant beamed at him. "Are you pleased?"

"No, sir," Blackman told him. "I am not."

The sergeant stopped smiling.

"Why – what's wrong, sir?"

"It's all circumstantial," Blackman said. "It would never hold up in a courtroom without photographs or an eye witness to the act itself."

"But you've got to admit that it sure looks bad, doesn't it, Mr. Blackman?"

"Bad is not good enough," Blackman replied through clenched teeth. "I've just explained to you the problem. I need some solid evidence of their shenanigans."

"Why, right here," the sergeant tapped on the document. "This friend of Lowenstein, he had his shirt off."

"And so do, I imagine, half of the officers in the afternoon shift when they change in the locker room at the end of the day," Blackman said. "Do you propose that we prosecute all of them for being fairies, as well?"

The sergeant frowned.

"This Johnson fella, he was smiling like a happy guy," he said. "Mind my word. These two was playin' hide-the-sausage, sure as I'm born."

"Then get me some real evidence of their shenanigans, sergeant," Blackman growled. "Photographs. Witnesses. Medical opinions. Something more substantial than just conjecture."

"Ohhh, Mr. Blackman. You want me to..."

"Yes!" Blackman struck the desk and the big Irish cop jumped. Blackman threw the memorandum at him. "I want you to catch him in the act! And don't give me any more of this crap!"

The big Irish cop left and Blackman went back to his paperwork. The good news was that he was finally getting some decent information from the New Jersey police. It seemed that the word was that the Lowenstein gang had just purchased a Canadian distillery. Soon, very soon, they would be running whiskey over from Canada in huge amounts. And when they did, Milton Blackman was going to be ready for them.

Chapter Twenty-Three
Spring 1923

Milton Blackman had just finished a rather lengthy conversation with the same Irish cop who had the Lowenstein kid under surveillance a week ago. Looking at him disgustedly, Blackman scratched his chin. "Yes!" Blackman yelled, striking the desk with his fist, and the big cop jumped. Blackman threw the memorandum at him. "I would prefer that you catch him in the act! But maybe we can salvage something from your half-assed reports." The two men talked for a few minutes more, and then Blackman picked up the phone, spoke a few words, and another man, a detective in a black suit with worn, shiny pants, came in and joined them. The three men conferred for several minutes and then the two police officers left, leaving Blackman to his paperwork.

On the very top of the stack was a copy of a lease that Louis Kravitz had signed for warehouse space on the East River. There were two warehouses, both of a good size, and they could hold a substantial amount of either pre-Prohibition or smuggled whiskey. The Volstead Act had been in effect for almost two years now, but liquor was still flowing across the Canadian border in abundance. The club owners and gangsters had stockpiled all the Canadian whiskey that they could before Prohibition became effective, and Blackman knew that money was flowing into the police department from the same sources. Club owners and whiskey distributors were paying off cops at all levels to close their eyes as to what was going on at the scores of "supper clubs" that had recently been opened around the city. One of the most successful clubs was the Moulin Rouge owned by the Lowenstein group. And, their Cavalier Club was not far behind in class. Some were even hiring cops in their off duty hours as bouncers. For all he knew, the two who'd just left him were on Lowenstein's payroll.

Blackman shrugged. He'd just have to take things one at a time. Patience was indeed a virtue in the police business. The bootleggers needed a constant new supply of whiskey to quench a thirsty America and Blackman would be waiting for them.

* * *

Kevin Johnson put an egg in boiling water, turned over the hourglass timer and then poured water from the steaming teakettle over the strainer in his cup. Wearing boxer shorts and an undershirt, he padded barefooted back into the bedroom, first stopping off at a floor-length mirror to admire himself, and then to pick out a shirt and a necktie, smiling at the thought of last night's romp with Seymour as he did so. He still hadn't been able to talk Seymour into spending the night with him, because he was afraid that his family might find out. Shaking his head in amusement, Johnson walked back into the kitchen and pulled his egg from the water with a spoon.

Ten minutes later, he was dressed for the day. Checking to make sure he had four subway tokens in his trouser pocket, he put on his jacket and left the apartment, smelling the rich, yeasty smell of baking bread from the bakery next door as he trotted briskly down the stairs.

He stepped out into the morning daylight, the hustle of traffic on the street, and the conversations of neighbor women coming back from their morning shopping. He was just about to turn and walk to the subway station when a large man stepped in front of him.

"Kevin Johnson?"

"Yes. What is it?"

The man flashed him a gold detective's badge.

"New York City Police. I need you down at the station to answer a few questions."

* * *

Barney Green shook hands with the members of his minyan, carefully put away the Zechel, velvet bag, containing his Tafellin, and closed the schul door after the last man had left. For a moment, he debated locking the door since he had recently heard from a friend of a friend that a schul had been robbed over in the Bronx the week before. Pulling his chin in concern, he decided to leave the doors open. Danger or no danger, there was no way that he was going to put a locked door between the members of his congregation and their God.

Touching his head to make sure his yarmulke was in place – an action he repeated so often that he no longer thought about it – the Rabbi walked up the stairs to his apartment, calling, "Natalie, is there any tea made?"

Barney Green's wife, eight months pregnant, met him at the door and smiled.

"I just poured it, sweetheart."

The Rabbi smiled and gently put his arms around her, careful of the life within her, even though she had told him, time and time again, "Our baby will not crack. Believe me Rabbi, it's not an egg." He always laughed when she scolded him with these words; he closed his eyes and smelled the sweetness of her hair, thanking Hashem for the gift of a woman who would love him so much that she would give him a child.

He stepped into the apartment and was just pulling the door shut when she screamed. They both heard it at the same time, the sound of glass shattering downstairs.

"Those children!" Barney regretted his anger as soon as he spoke. He caught himself and took a deep breath. "How many times have I asked them to be careful when they play stickball? Keep the tea warm, love. I'll be right back."

He turned and walked down the steps, certain that there would be a baseball lying there among the shards of his front window.

His first reaction was relief since the glass that had been broken was the glass on the door and much smaller than the big plate-glass windows on either side of it. But when he turned to look for the ball, he saw a short length of iron pipe instead.

The Rabbi scowled. Hate crimes against Jews were very rare in Brooklyn. The Catholics may have viewed his people as Christ-killers, and rarely shopped in Jewish stores, since there was an unwritten code of tolerance. He stepped closer to the pipe. And then he stopped.

Hissing.

What was it that he heard hissing?

He blinked in the dim light of the schul and then he saw it: a short piece of cord, poking out of a hole drilled in the cap of the pipe, and sputtering red sparks as it grew shorter.

"God of Israel, be merciful."

Barney Green turned and raced back up the stairs, horrified to see his wife stepping into the doorway.

"Back! Back! Get back!" He waved his arms as he took the stairs at a run, three at a time, the way he'd run subway steps when he had been in training as a boxer. "Natalie, please…get back!"

But she just stood there, confusion written on her face. So he took the last few steps in one giant stride and threw himself at her, trying to smother her body with his, as the world erupted in yellowish red flame, smoke and noise, and then collapsed around him.

* * *

"You come from a good Catholic Boston family," Milton Blackman said to Kevin Johnson. "Your father's a respectable businessman. His brother, your uncle, is an alderman. His sister… well, she's a nun.

The Assistant D.A. tapped the sheet of paper in his hand.

"Goodness me," Blackman continued. "It says here that your other uncle is an archbishop of the church. Could that be correct?"

Johnson shrank back in his chair, saying nothing. His eyes started to fill up with tears. Blackman shook his head and walked around the table to where the young man sat.

"It's going to kill them," Blackman whispered in his ear. "Do you know that? Just kill them. Their own blood, arrested in the big city for sodomy, for being queer."

The young man shivered, and Blackman smiled. This looked as if it was going to work.

The radiator hissed noisily and the young man looked up. Blackman had chosen this interrogation room, long since scheduled for renovation, because of its flaking walls, the noisy steam pipes, and the suspicious red-brown stain along one baseboard. It was a desolate room, and that was what he wanted Kevin Johnson to feel – Desolation! Solitude! Despair!

"Of course, it might be your death, too," Blackman said. "The Irish don't take it very well when one of their own is a fairy. They're not like the French that way, are they? Then again, your family won't have a chance to deal with you until the state's finished with you. And, from what I hear, there are several strapping gentlemen up at Sing-Sing who just love to see your kind. I've heard reports of fairies having to stuff socks in the backs of their drawers, to keep the blood from soaking through and showing on their trousers."

That worked. The kid definitely looked terrified, and no one had so much as slapped him around. Not once. Blackman turned and nodded at the uniformed policeman at the door.

"Leave us for a minute, will you, officer?"

He waited until the door had closed behind the cop, and then he pulled a chair up next to the young musician and put a hand on his shoulder.

"I can keep this quiet," he said in a low voice. "I can see to it that you get probation...no time in the penitentiary at all. Not a single night."

Johnson turned to him, saying nothing. He didn't need to. The hope was written there all over his face.

"I think you're actually the victim here," Blackman told him. "That Lowenstein boy. He probably slipped something in your drink. Tricked you, didn't he? Now isn't that right?"

"No!"

Blackman shook his head.

"That's very noble of you, Kevin," he said. "But I can't for the life of me see why you're protecting him. He's trouble. His whole family is trouble. Surely you know that. They're criminals of the worst kind – bootleggers and gamblers and pimps. And I want you to know right now that Seymour Lowenstein is going to jail. We already have all the evidence we need. Your testimony is just going to be the icing on the cake. We have enough to send both of you away for at least five years. But why send two to prison when one would do quite nicely and even save the state of New York some bucks?"

Johnson looked up happily, buying Blackman's bullshit.

"That's right," Blackman said, setting the hook even deeper. "In fact, I'm sure your friend Seymour would encourage you to tell us the truth. Only one in jail, instead of two? What good would it do him to have both of you in? They'd split you up you know, different cellblocks, and maybe even different prisons. Seymour would see the sense of sparing one of you that pain. He'd understand why you did it. All you have to do is promise to show up in court next week and say what he did to you – forced you to do – and I will give you my personal guarantee as a man of honor that no harm will come to you, and not a word of this will go on your record."

Johnson wet his lips in nervousness.

"What…" he began.

Blackman leaned closer.

"What," Johnson repeated, "do you want me to say?"

* * *

Barney Green fluttered his eyelids, and got that old, painful feeling – the feeling that he had experienced several times in his early days as a boxer. The feeling of waking up from traumatic unconsciousness. Only it was usually just his jaw that hurt. This time, it was his whole body.

A smell. An awful smell, like sulfur and copper and sewer gas, filled his nostrils, and he coughed. What could possibly stink so much? He blinked his eyelids a few times clearing his eyes and looked, wonderingly, at the massive shards of wood that littered the floor around him. They were his doors, he finally realized. The doors to his apartment. The doors his wife had been standing next to a few minutes ago.

"Natalie, sweetheart? Babe?" The Rabbi's voice was a harsh, choking whisper. He swallowed and called out her name again. "Natalie"?

He forced himself to raise his head and he saw his wife, slumped against the icebox at the far side of the kitchen.

"Natalie, speak to me…please darling."

* * *

It was like an absolute fairyland! Rebecca Lowenstein, she was still savoring the sound of "Mrs. Irving Lowenstein," snuggled next to her husband under the carriage blanket as the old-style two-horse carriage made its way back from the Falls to the hotel. The driver was paying attention to the road ahead so, using the heavy blanket to hide her actions, she crept her hand over onto her husband's lap and then slid her fingers down the inside of his leg toward his crotch.

"Hey," Irving said. "I don't think you should be doing that. This is Canada. That sort of stuff might be illegal up here."

She giggled. "So they can arrest us. I don't care so long as we're together."

Apparently, neither did Irving. He'd become hard as a rock under her touch and she cupped her hand, held him through the English flannel of his trousers and stroked him rhythmically.

"Here's the hotel," he said as the carriage pulled under the portico. "And not a moment too soon."

He paid the driver and Rebecca quietly laughed as Irving held his hat in front of his lap while he helped her to the pavement.

"You will pay for this when we get up to the room," he whispered good naturedly.

"Ooooh, promises, promises," she cooed. The she laughed again as they stepped into the huge, wood-paneled lobby of the Niagara House and walked across the parqueted floor toward the brass-caged elevators.

Rebecca could feel herself getting wet as she walked. Her mother had come to her the evening before the wedding and given her a stern talk about a wife's responsibilities and how she must submit to her husband, distasteful as it may seem.

Distasteful? All Rebecca had to say about that was, *poor mother.* But maybe it wasn't too late. Maybe Irving could sit down and have a cigar and a brandy with Poppa when they got back, give him a few pointers on how to please a lady.

Because Rebecca was very well pleased … and looking forward to being pleased again.

"Mr. Lowenstein? Mr. Lowenstein! Telegram for you, sir!"

Irv turned, smiling, gave the boy a quarter, and opened the Western Union envelope as they stepped into the elevator.

"Top floor, please," Rebecca told the operator, and she smiled again in anticipation.

She heard the rustle of the yellow paper as Irving unfolded the telegram. And, then she could see his face tighten and turn white as he read it.

"Sweetheart? Irving? What is it?"

"Take us back down," Irving told the lift operator.

The uniformed boy nodded as the elevator started to descend.

"Darling? What happened?"

"I've got to see the desk about a train reservation back to the city," Irving told her. "Go back up to the room and start getting us packed, willya sweetheart? I'll be there in a few minutes"

"Packed? But why?"

"We've got tsouris."

"What?"

Rebecca's husband looked at the elevator operator and then whispered into his wife's ear. "My brother, Seymour," he said tersely. "The police picked him up this morning and are holding him in jail."

"Where's my brother?"

Half a dozen excuses flashed through Lou Kravitz's head to put off the meeting between Seymour and his brother Irving. He thought about it carefully; *He's not back from his honeymoon yet. Or, he got held up by business.* But, he finally decided to tell him the truth.

"I don't think Irv's quite ready to see you yet, Seymour," he said quietly. "Right now, I think he'd just as soon forget that you were his brother."

The young man was visibly shaken for a few moments. Then he straightened himself up, wiped his nose and looked directly at Lou Kravitz.

"I'd... I'd expected better of him," he mumbled. "After all, he's still my family."

"That's true. But he's also your mother's son. Your father's son as well."

That did it. The kid started to cry; big, fat tears rolled down his face.

"Seymour," Lou got a handkerchief out of his coat pocket and slid it across the table to the young man. "Seymour, for God's sake, have a little pride. Quit your bawlin'."

The kid took the large, white hankie, dabbing his eyes furiously but to no effect.

"Can Irv... can he get me out of here? I'm really afraid of this place with all these weird people."

"It's already done. I paid your bail just as soon as I got down here. All we're waiting on is for them to finish up the paperwork."

The kid stopped crying almost immediately and seemed to pull himself together.

"What about later? Can Irv keep us from going to prison?"

"Sure." Lou glanced up at the guard standing at the back of the drab visiting room, and kept his voice low. "I mean, they didn't catch you guys, uh, doing anything to each other, did they?"

Seymour straightened up.

"No." He shook his head. "No. Nothing like that. But they told me that Kevin's confessed."

"That's bullshit. They tell you garbage like that all the time to make you break down."

"Oh, are you sure?" he said with new hope in his voice.

Seymour fell silent for a moment. Then he spoke again.

"So, do you think they told Kevin that I confessed?"

Lou didn't say anything. He was thinking. He looked up and smiled at Seymour.

"Tell you what," he said. "Maybe I'd better make another call. See about getting another bondsman down here to make bail for your friend, too, okay? Would you like that?"

Seymour smiled and nodded his head.

* * *

"Yeah," Irv Lowenstein said into the phone. "Yeah, Lou, that's good thinking. Why don't you bail Seymour out and then I'll send Mendy down in about fifteen minutes with bail for the other kid too. That should ease the pressure on both of them considerably."

He hung up and set the phone back on the table. He was still in the clothes he'd traveled in and, hadn't even taken his topcoat off yet.

* * *

Later, in his office at the Moulin Rouge Club, Irv met with Joey Lucci.

"Four nights," he told Joey, grimacing. "Four fucking nights. That's how long my honeymoon lasted. Do you know that? And what's this deal with Barney's schul? What's that all about? Charlie Luciano and his boys, including our good friends Bugsy and Meyer Lansky? Are they still pissed off that we wouldn't cut them into our booze business since they had already turned us down almost two years ago?"

"They might be, boss, but I'm not quite sure." Lucci shook his head. "Those assholes weren't that organized. They was just street gangsters from out of town, I think; part of a mob. The ones that weren't killed are probably still running, or hiding out. Don't think the big guys downtown had anything to do with it."

"Well, I want their names, then. And I mean now."

"We already got guys askin' questions on the street," Lucci assured him. "We'll find out! It won't be long, maybe just a few days."

Irv stood up.

"You goin' home?" Lucci asked him. "I mean, no offense, boss, but you look like shit."

Irv wiped his face with his hands.

"I'm going down to the hospital," he said.

"I'll drive you."

"Okay." Irv nodded. "But give me a minute, all right? I've gotta find Mendy and talk to him. If we find out that the boys were on orders from Charlie, it's gonna be a whole different ballgame, right Joey?"

* * *

Seymour Lowenstein reached into the brown envelope the sergeant had handed him, and took out his belt and slipped it into the loops on his trousers, cinching it tightly. He put on the wristwatch his brother had gotten him for high school graduation, and slipped his wallet into his pant's pocket. Then he looked around.

"Where's Kevin? I thought you said Irv was going to bail Kevin out, too?"

"He is." Lou nodded. "But, the Bail Bondsman only brought enough dough down to make bail for one guy. He's sending Mendy down to spring Kevin Johnson later on."

Seymour hesitated.

"You're sure?" His eyes searched Lou's face.

"I'm positive," Lou told him, looking him straight in the eyes. "Don't you worry, kid. We'll take care of Kevin Johnson."

* * *

Stefano "Steve Banana" Lucci, another Lucci cousin, straddled a chair turned backwards and listened to the club's latest find, an octoroon singer named Sissy Phillips, as she ran through her numbers for that evening's entertainment.

The girl had pipes. He had to give her that! And she had more than that. Even in the red simple dress that she'd worn to the late-morning rehearsal, she looked pretty damn good with high, firm titties and slim, muscular legs that went all the way up to her asshole.

Steve had been married for two years now, and had one son at home and another bun in the oven. That's what the doctor had told his wife, Maria, and him last Wednesday. And the doctor had also told them too, that it would still be okay to have sex for awhile. But, Steve wasn't buying that. You knock your old lady up, you don't keep on banging her. That kind of shit was sick, like coming in your unborn child's mouth. You did that kind of shit, you fathered fairies and whores. He wondered if that was what had happened with Seymour Lowenstein. At the same time he wondered how long it would take him to get Sissy Phillips in the sack; he didn't mind coffee with cream. She sure looked good to him."

"Hey, Banana?" It was one of the Green Hats, the Irish toughs that Mendy had hired to help keep things in order. "There's a guy here to see Irving. Says he's the Assistant District Attorney."

"Fuck." Steve Lucci turned around and made sure that the bar was concealed behind its false wall. It was the same kind of liquor storeroom that the 21 Club had built at the beginning of Prohibition. And, he knew that once the liquor storeroom was closed, you'd have to be awfully damn lucky to find it. Lucci then swung the door closed. "Send him on back. I'll talk to him."

Three minutes later, the Green Hat was back with a fairly, tall, portly guy wearing a cheap, worn-out suit, thick-soled shoes, and with thinning black hair. He looked like a D.A.!

"Hey." Lucci smiled. "I'm Steve Lucci. Can I offer you anything? Coffee? A coke? Maybe an egg cream?" He nodded toward the back, where the old bar had once stood. "I'd offer something stronger." He grinned. "But that would take an act of Congress."

Cheap suit didn't crack a smile. "I'm Milton Blackman," he said. "Assistant District Attorney for Manhattan. "I'm here to ask Irving Lowenstein some questions. He knows me quite well. Tell him that we need him for about 20 minutes… just a chat, nothing formal."

Milton Blackman had gained about 40 pounds over the last few years and didn't look good at all. He had an unhealthy pallor to him, like a stuffed animal.

Steve shrugged.

"He ain't here. He just left to go to the hospital. Rabbi friend of his got a pipe-bomb tossed into his synagogue yesterday morning. You'd think the police would keep that kind of shit from happening, wouldn't you?"

The cheap suit's face reddened, his prominent Adam's apple moved up and down as he swallowed.

"Tell him I was here," he said, handing Steve a card. "Tell him I still want to talk with him… about the embarrassing situation involving his brother."

"Oh yeah?" Steve took the card and flicked at it with his fingertip. "His brother in some kind of trouble?"

"Just tell him," Blackman said. "He'll know what I mean! Lowenstein's a smart guy. We went to law school together. We were also in the District Attorney's office. He'll remember!"

And he left.

* * *

"God, Barney." Irv Lowenstein looked at his old friend and felt his pain. The Rabbi's head was bandaged, one arm was in a cast, and his left leg was raised in traction. "Man, I am so very sorry."

"Sorry? Irv, why should you be sorry? You were away with your wife on your honeymoon."

Irv shook his head. "Rabbi… Barney. Let's not pretend. The guys that did this to you, well it was their way of getting to me and we both know it. I'd bet my life on it!"

Barney shook his head slightly. "It was probably some Irish hooligans. Anti-Semitics. Meshugeneh goys with hate in their hearts."

"I don't think so. It sounds more organized than that to me. It could have been ordered from downtown to keep our guys in line."

Barney managed a weak smile. "You don't know that for a fact, do you?" he asked. "Not one way or the other. Hashem is the only one who knows for sure. The Lord, he knows and he will punish them. Not us, it's not our place."

Irv ran his hand back through his thick hair. "Barney. Natalie lost the – "

"– Our baby," the Rabbi's eyes grew moist. "Yes. I know. They told me this morning..." His face brightened, just a little. "But she is alive and well," he said. "Just bumps, and a few bruises. And if Hashem is willing, perhaps he will give us other children, if it is his will."

Irv's face flushed with a flash of anger in his eyes. "Damn it to hell, Barney, none of this shit was God's will, and you know it. It was the will of some asshole trying to get to me through you. And he's not going to get away with it. He's – "

"– He hasn't gotten away with a thing," Barney corrected him firmly. "Do you forget your Hebrew so quickly, Irv? Don't you remember that the word for 'God' and the word for 'Judge' are one and the same? This will be handled in a much higher court than you could ever convene. On the head of our dead baby, I swear that to you. It's the truth."

Irv just looked at him in disbelief.

The Rabbi tried to sit up a little, and then gave up on the effort.

"Don't be stupid, Irv," he whispered. "If someone tried your patience, you don't go off half-cocked because that's exactly what they want to happen. That would be wrong, you know that. We are basically a gentle and forgiving people... most of the time. That is unless continuously threatened, then we respond."

Irv picked up his hat and smoothed the sheet over the Rabbi's broken body.

"You are a better man than I am, Barney," he said. "You're much better than I'll ever be."

* * *

Irv left the hospital, and straightened up. There was Joey Lucci, waiting with the car, the long, black Lincoln that Irv had bought before the wedding. And standing next to Joey was a cop, and someone Irving didn't recognize at first.

Milton Blackman.

"A word with you, Irv?" The words were polite, but came out arrogantly, the way Blackman said them.

"Sure." Irv turned and began walking quickly down the sidewalk, making the Assistant D.A. trot to catch up with him. Irv took out a cigarette case, lit a cigarette, and put the case away without offering one to Blackman.

"It's a terrible thing that happened to your brother," Blackman said.

Irving didn't reply.

"If your parents hear about this, it's going to kill them!"

Irv stopped walking and turned to face Blackman. "What are you trying to say, Miltie?"

The A.D.A. shrugged. "If you want to, you can plead guilty to a simple bootlegging charge, nothing big, nothing that would make you do any time. That, and resign from the State Bar. Maybe, then, I could get this whole matter dropped."

Irv smiled thinly. "That's blackmail, Miltie. You know that, and I'm not buying it."

Blackman shrugged and looked around. "I don't see any witnesses, Irving. Think about it."

Irving looked around pensively for a moment.

"I'd say…" he began.

Blackman leaned closer.

"I'd say," Irv whispered. "Go fuck yourself, you big, fat schmuck."

* * *

"It was awfully good of you to come down here and bail me out like this," Kevin Johnson said.

Mendy shrugged. "Don't mention it, kid." He grinned. "Friends of the family get special treatment."

The young musician grinned back as they stepped out of the police station into the sunlight of a New York afternoon.

"Well, I appreciate it." The young man looked at the curb, where there was nothing parked but police cars.

"Oh," Mendy said, as if he'd just remembered something. "I had a flat. Second one this week. Had to leave my car over at the Moulin Rouge. You mind taking the subway?"

"Not at all," Johnson grinned. "I do it all the time. Don't even own a car, myself. Still going to school you know."

He reached into his pocket, but Mendy handed him a token.

"Here, kid," he said. "My treat."

They walked down the block, the kid babbling on about how glad he was not having to miss a rehearsal at Julliard the next morning or something. Mendy nodded, pretending to listen. They walked through the turnstiles, dropping their tokens, the kid looking surprised when Mendy turned with him to head for the uptown lines.

"Yeah," Mendy grinned. "I figure I might as well. I got a suit I have to pick up from a tailor up there."

"Well, maybe we can ride together a little ways."

"Sure kid," Mendy smiled "A little ways."

They walked to the tiled platform and joined the crowd gathering at the station's edge. A light breeze began blowing out of the tunnel and a light was showing far away. Train coming.

"That our train, kid?"

Kevin Johnson leaned and looked down the track. Mendy put his hand on the kid's shoulder, gave it a pat.

The train was less than a hundred feet away now.

"Sorry kid," Mendy whispered.

And he gave Johnson a push.

Chapter Twenty-Five
Spring 1923

"Son of a bitch!" Milton Blackman hurled a clipboard across the length of his small office as papers fluttered to the ground.

"Son… of a bitch…" Blackman snarled again, and now secretaries and other lawyers were starting to peer out of their offices to learn the cause of the commotion. He got up and slammed the door shut.

"What precinct was the subway station in?" he asked sarcastically.

The cop standing at Blackman's desk had not been invited to sit down and glanced uncomfortably at his notes.

"The eleventh precinct, sir, over on Hobart Street."

"Shit!" Blackman picked up an inkwell, set it back down, and threw the Black's Law Dictionary instead. "That's practically at our front door. Any witnesses?"

"Hundreds," the cop said. "But all they saw was him landing on the track. The coroner says that if there'd been a note, it would have been perfect suicide, real obvious-like. The thought was that maybe this Kevin Johnson lad was despondent about his arrest, you know, that he took the big plunge, rather than face up to the consequences."

"Despondent, my ass. He was shoved into the train, and you know it."

"Well, if he was, whoever did it got away with it. No witnesses for identification purposes. And no other evidence to work with. The lad wasn't just hit, the fuckin' train ran over him, sir. Body looks like a fuckin' side of beef."

"Shit!" Blackman threw another book and regretted it immediately. It wasn't good to have a display of temper in front of subordinates. He looked at his desk, and found the several warehouse leases that he had been pouring over just a few minutes before the cop entered his office.

"Call the Inspector from the precinct where these buildings are located," he said "and let him know that we'll need a truck and five, make it ten, men. Tonight at midnight."

* * *

Mendy cut the ignition and let the big, black Lincoln coast the length of the alley, stopping under the shadow of a fire escape. It was half past ten, and only a few lights were showing from the kitchens and back rooms of the old brick apartment building.

"You sure about this, Irv?"

Irv Lowenstein looked back at him, his face shadowed under the snap-brim fedora.

"You tell me, Mendy. Are you certain that this is the guy who threw the pipe bomb into Barney's house?"

"He's the guy who led the crew for Lansky and Luciano. Our snitch don't screw things like that up since he would have to answer to me."

"Okay, then, that's good enough for me pal."

The two men got out and Mendy took a long-handled grappling hook out of the back seat, snagged the lowest rung of the fire-escape ladder and pulled. The ladder made remarkably little noise as it slid to the ground, and the two men started climbing.

"Third floor," Mendy whispered. "Right off the fire exit stairs."

When they got there, the window was open a few inches and there was a faint aroma of tomatoes and garlic. Mendy opened the window and the two men stepped into a small kitchen, dishes drying in a rack next to the sink.

It didn't take long to locate the guy. They just followed the sound of the snoring and found him, sleeping on top of the covers in boxer shorts and an undershirt, an empty wine bottle, a Colt revolver and a telephone on the bed stand.

There was no woman. Not that Mendy had expected one since the information he had was that this guy was still single, but he was relieved that he was alone because another person would only complicate the situation.

Irv picked up the Colt, pocketed it and then nodded. Mendy took out a long-barreled Smith & Wesson .38, put the barrel next to the sleeping man's temple and cocked the gun. Instantly, the Italian's eyes were open, his hand reaching for the nightstand and knocking over the bottle, which fell to the hardwood floor with a hollow thud.

"Quiet, now," Mendy whispered to the man in the bed. "No need to wake the neighbors." Mendy looked up at Irv. "Where you want him?"

"Right here's fine." Irv took out a pair of handcuffs and cuffed the guy's wrists to the iron head of the bed. He looked around, found the guy's trousers, took the belt out, and used it to bind his feet to the footboard.

"You guys are wasting your fucking time," the Italian said. "I ain't saying a fuckin' word."

"Then shut up," Irv told him, back-handing him across the face. He picked up the telephone and whispered, "Gramacy 7103."

The other end of the line rang twice and then was picked up.

"Lansky." Mendy could clearly hear the man's voice on the phone, even across the room.

"Meyer?" Irv paused a moment. "Meyer, you fucked up big time. You shouldn't have put a contract out on the Rabbi." He hesitated for a few seconds before continuing. "Lucky for all of us Meyer, that the Rabbi is still alive, right?"

"Rabbi? What Rabbi?"

"The guy that did it," Irv said. "You know where he lives, right?"

"Why're you asking?"

"Because he needs an ambulance over at his place. Right away."

And with that, Irv pulled the Colt out of his pocket, cocked it, stuck the barrel in the fly of the Italian's boxers, and pulled the trigger.

The Italian was screaming, writhing in pain, even before the sound of the gunshot had died, and Irv held the phone to the injured man's mouth so Lansky could hear his agony.

"Who is this?" Mendy could hear it over the phone, even with the guy screaming like that. "Lowenstein, you crazy putz, is that you?"

"That's good," Irv said, hanging the phone up. "We can go now, Mendy."

"Go where?" Mendy asked wearily. "You just shot one of Luciano's top soldiers. The world ain't big enough for us to find a hole to hide in over the next few weeks, now."

"Oh yeah, don't worry about it. Ya fight fire with fire, Mendy. You know that, don'cha?"

* * *

"Okay. Ram the truck through the door."

"Through it? Don't we bother to knock, first?"

Blackman looked up at the policeman sitting behind the wheel of the idling Mack truck and shook his head.

"Why not send them a Western Union and give them time to pour out the whiskey? No, sergeant. I've got a warrant, and we don't have to knock first. Now ram the truck through the goddamn door."

"It won't be good for the truck."

"It won't be good for your next promotion with the department either if you argue with me. Now do it."

The cop nodded and ground the truck into first gear. The stout, heavy truck crept up to the warehouse door, nudged it, and rolled back.

"Not like that! Hit it, you stupid putz!"

The cop backed up the truck, revved up the engine, and drove into the door at a good fifteen miles an hour. The door cracked like a falling tree and crumbled as the truck, steam jetting from its radiator, rolled into a well-lighted warehouse. Cops poured down from the back of the truck, and raced around to the front of it, where they stopped.

"What are you waiting for?" Blackman threw his hands up. "Get in there. Arrest them!"

"Arrest who?"

Blackman walked up, past the crumpled fenders of the truck, elbowed his way through the line of uniformed police offices, and gaped in surprise.

Except for a small pile of wooden crates at the far wall, the warehouse was empty. A single watchman, an old man in blue, bib overalls, was sitting in a rocker under a bare light bulb, previously read newspaper pages curled around his feet.

"Well, there's a few crates aren't there?" Blackman turned to a cop holding a crowbar. "Go open them, damnit."

The cop picked his way across the greasy cement floor, and set his bar into one of the crates. Nails screeched hollowly in the big, empty warehouse as he pulled the top off the wooden box.

"Mr. Blackman, sir?" He waved his arm. "You'd better see this, sir."

Blackman trudged across the floor and the cop stepped away from the crate. Excelsior was packed around dozens of teapots.

Teapots. Cheap, china teapots made in Japan. He moved them aside and rummaged around, finding nothing but pots.

Fuming, Blackman turned and found the watchman, still sitting in his rocker.

"Where is it?" The Assistant D.A.'s voice rang across the empty space.

"Where's what?" The old man's voice was weak, and he breathed heavily with traces of asthma.

"The stuff that was here. All the crates."

"Oh. That? Hell, they came and got that a good week ago. Don't know where they took it. I just watch the place. Say, who's going to pay for fixing that door?"

* * *

"Go? Go where?"

"Saratoga," Irv said as he grabbed clothes out of Rebecca's closet and threw them into steamer trunks. "You like Saratoga, don'cha? And it'll be a nice little change for both you and Margie."

"Be careful with those!" Rebecca took over the packing herself. "What's in Saratoga this time of year?"

"There's three nice cabins together that we just bought up there a few months ago. It's beautiful country and you'll be staying there a few days with Mendy's wife and kids. The Luccis will go along and keep an eye on things for you."

"The Lucci's. You mean you're not going?"

"No." Irv looked at his watch. "I've got an important meeting in Chicago."

"Chicago? But why Chicago? And why do I have to leave?"

Irv looked at his watch again and set his own Gladstone bag, already packed, next to the door.

"Rebecca, I haven't got time for this. We've got tsouris, okay? This place isn't safe anymore."

"Safe? Safe from what?" she replied.

"Fire. Bombs. Bullets. Kidnapping. I don't know. Now will you please quit askin' so many questions and finish packing so we can go?"

"Bombs? Bullets? Kidnapping?"

Lowenstein closed his wife's trunks and went to the door.

"Okay, guys. Come get it."

The Luccis and a few of the Irish Green Hats came in, doffed their caps to the lady of the house, and took the luggage out to four Cadillacs idling at the curb.

"Listen," he told his astonished wife. "I know you got questions, but Margie Goldblatt will explain everything to you sweetheart. Now I got a train to catch. I'll see ya in a week or so."

And with that, he was gone, leaving Rebecca alone in a room full of Italians and Irishmen.

"If we leave now," one of the Lucci's told her. "We can have you in the cabin and unpacked in time for dinner."

Feeling completely numb, she moved hesitantly toward the door.

* * *

"So you're Lowenstein," Capone said smirking, his chief enforcer, Frank Nitti, sitting at his side filing his fingernails.

Irv had never met the man before, but he knew the face from the newspapers and the weekly newsreels at the movies. The round, almost cherubic face, the neatly combed, black hair, and the thin, white scar on his left cheek.

Alphonse Capone.

"You like a smoke, Mr. Lowenstein?"

Irv nodded and the other man snipped the end off a fat, well-rolled Cuban cigar, handed it to Irv and then held out a table lighter, keeping the flame a proper inch beneath the expensive cigar's tip until Irv had it going.

Capone lit a cigar of his own, and Irv leaned back, looking out the window at the ornate Chicago Water Tower and the bustle of The Loop. Capone had recently moved his office from Cicero, a suburb of Chicago, to a hotel in the downtown area for convenience.

It had taken Irving all night to get here, and although he'd had a sleeper, he had not slept a wink. He'd stayed awake, thinking of what Mendy had said to him when he saw him off at the station; *You know, they call me 'Whacko,' but you're the one that slipped a gear here, Irv. Lucky Luciano, Bugsy Siegel and Meyer Lansky? After they have a "sit-down" with us and ask for twenty percent of our booze business, we say, we'll think about it. And, then they bomb Barney Green's and we muscle one of their guys! You just declared war on the biggest Italian gang in New York. I'm closing the clubs until you get back. I just hope we still have a club by then.*

Capone sat back in his own chair and blew a ring of smoke. "Meet Frank Nitti," he growled nodding in the direction of the feared mobster.

"Oh yeah, Irving," Capone said. "We already heard about the trouble you boys had in New York. Somebody shot the nuts offa Charlie Lucky's top triggerman. That your work, my friend?"

Irv didn't say a thing.

"I like it because you ain't sayin' nottin' about it. It's good, you're keeping your mouth shut." Capone glanced at the tight-lipped Nitti sitting by his side and the goombah standing behind them.

"That's one for the books," Capone continued nodding his head and smiling. "More of my boys learn to work like that, I wouldn't have to hire new guys as often as I do. You know what I mean? The guy died, you know."

"Excuse me?"

"The guy what got his balls blown off. He died in the hospital three days ago.

"Oh." Irv lowered his cigar. "I'm sorry to hear that."

"Just as well. You lose your balls, you're no longer a man. Might as well be dead, know what I mean?"

Irv nodded, so did Nitti.

"Well," Capone leaned forward in his chair. "Why are we here? Because, you need some muscle to pull your ass outta the fire, right? You got a good thing going for you and don't wanna see it to see go down the toilet, huh, Irving?"

Irv nodded.

"Right, and why would I want to help you and get my good friends, Lansky and Luciano, pissed off at me," Capone shrugged. "You know, you ain't the only guy in the room from New York. I'm from New York, too. I was born there." Lowenstein looked surprised. "And, no offense, Lowenstein, but you're a fuckin' kike, just like Lansky and Bugsy Siegel. Charlie Lucky, he's a Siciliano, just like me, a crazy fucking wop. People think I'm nuts, but he makes me look like an altar boy. Now why do I want to help you against somebody like that?"

"Because I've also got a deal with the Purple Gang. You won't be alone with just our boys if there's an all out war," Irving replied.

"You and me both. I got a deal with them, too. And, I don't think Luciano and Bugsy want to take on all three of us. But what can you do for us that we can't do for ourselves? This has gotta be a two-way street or it ain't gonna work, right?"

"I can get you your liquor at my cost for the next three months."

Capone cupped his hand to his ear.

"Whaddaya say?" My hearing's all fucked up. You say booze at cost for nine months?"

Irv shook his head, thin-lipped. "Six months sounds better."

"That might work," Capone said. "But why do I want to get into bed with you, when that would make Charlie Lucky sore? You know us Sicilianos, right? We got this pride. Don't like the taste of eatin' crow in any form."

"Because I'm loyal," Irv told him.

"How's that?"

"You're my friend?" Irv asked. "Then, I'm a loyal friend. I'll do shit, crazy shit for you if it's necessary. Like shoot the balls offa Lucky Luciano's top triggerman. Plus you'll make plenty of money with me. We can be partners in lots of things."

Capone stared at Irv for ten long seconds. Then he smiled, a gold tooth sparkling in the morning sun coming through the tall office windows.

"Now," he said. "You're talking."

Capone had made the call while Irv was still in his office. Not that he'd overheard much since Capone and Luciano had spoken an Italian dialect, and even though Irv knew some Italian from his lifelong friendship with the Lucci brothers, he hadn't understood much more than the occasional "capiche?"

His cigar was almost burned down to nothing when Capone hung up the phone, and the Chicago mobster looked at Irv and shook his head, smiling.

"Well," Capone said, "that went about the way I thought it'd go. Charlie Lucky is one pissed-off wop. Turns out the guy you popped was going to be his brother-in-law or something. He had plans for you that included a welding torch, but I reminded him that he stepped over a line. In our business, we got rules. We don't kill cops, we don't fuck with a guy's family, we don't touch people protected by our own, and we never, ever, fuck with the church."

Capone paused, letting his last remarks sink in. Irv knew full well that the story about Provolone's man being crucified in the cathedral had made it all the way to Chicago.

"So, we now have two wrongs," Capone said. And before Irv could protest that he had not, in his eyes, done anything wrong, Capone continued, "That don't make it right, but it does cancel one another out. And hey, there ain't no dough to be made in going to war with each other, is there? So, if you got a few minutes, maybe I can get Ray Bernstein from the Detroit Purples on the phone and talk about the next whiskey shipment. The Purples like a few days notice before the delivery. Incidentally, you did say our cost for the booze will be the same as your cost for the next nine months, right?"

"I agreed to six months." Irv said in a low, even voice without flinching.

Capone smiled, knowingly.

"That's good," he said. "Don't take no shit from anyone. I like that in a guy. Irv, you've got some balls! So let's do a little business...."

* * *

The white gulls soared high above the lake, moving their wings lazily to occasionally catch the rising air and move up, up, up until they were mere specks in the air; then again circled Lake Saranac until they were only just a hundred feet above the surface of the sun-dappled lake. They suddenly broke formation, opened their wings and split into two, swooping dives, claws almost skimming the water for lurking fish as they leveled out and began to climb back up into the blue skies to repeat the drill for food all over again until their appetites were fully satisfied.

Rebecca Lowenstein, from the porch of their spacious Adirondack cabin, was fascinated by the determination of the birds in their search for food. The sun warmed her breasts through the thin cotton dress, a sensation that would ordinarily have pleased her if she hadn't felt so trapped, like such a... such a what? A victim? A prisoner? Yes. Yes, on both counts.

She turned and walked back into the cabin, where Marjorie Goldblatt, her belly large in the end of her sixth month with her second pregnancy, was scrambling eggs in an iron skillet.

"Good morning," Margie told her cheerfully. "I made enough for two. We've got eggs, bagels, lox and cream cheese. How's that sound?"

"Thank you, but no. I don't have any appetite."

Concern clouded Margie's face. She had the dark beauty of a Sephardic Jew, with her thick black hair down past her shoulders, and, her full figure, even though she was going into her seventh month of pregnancy, men still found her deeply sensual.

"What's the matter? You feeling under the weather?"

Rebecca shook her head and then stopped, staring at the other woman.

"'Under the weather?'" She shook her head. "Is that what you think? That I've got the sniffles or something? My God, Margie, our husbands packed us up and moved us out here to the middle of nowhere with not so much as a tearful good-bye. We've got men with guns protecting us from other men with guns out by the road. Do you think that's normal?"

Marjorie Goldblatt scooped two equal helpings of eggs out of the skillet and set the plates on the plank log table.

"I thought," she said as she spread cream cheese on her bagel, "at one time that I was going to live and die on Delancey Street, maybe marry a baker like my Poppa if I got lucky, and wear dresses that I sewed myself out of those floral-printed flour-sacks. And, probably have three or four kids. That was what my life was going to be. But now that I have Mendel, I have a good house, buy my clothes ready-made, and my babelahs will all grow up healthy and cared for; and, my life will be better than I ever had a right to expect. Here, she said, pouring two cups of coffee. "Drink this, you'll feel better."

"Better?" Rebecca could feel her eyes growing wide. "You think this is better? Our husbands are talking about bullets and bombs? And your husband...."

She caught herself.

"What?" Margie shrugged as she sat down at the table. "You were going to say that my Mendy sleeps with other women? I know that. A man like Mendy will never stop running around with other women. But ya know something? It doesn't mean anything cause he only loves the children and me and that's what's important. He'll always come home, and after all, that's what counts. And, when he does come home, he takes wonderful care of me, and little Abraham, because he loves us both. No man is perfect. But the one I've got, all things considered, is pretty darn good."

"Pretty darn good? Margie, our husbands shoot people – they're gangsters, break the law and run around with other women."

Margie took a bite of the scrambled eggs and then added salt and some pepper to the rest. She looked up at Rebecca and nodded her head knowingly.

"Just what business did you think Irv was in when you agreed to marry him?"

"I knew he was a lawyer and had broken up a few months before with Miriam Levine. His sister, Sarah, was a friend of mine and he had night clubs –"

"– that serve illegal booze and have gambling in the back rooms," Margie added impatiently. "But that's no big deal, because the whole country hates that damn Prohibition law, and besides, everybody gambles at one time or another. Look at the punchboards, numbers and horse races. That's all gambling, too." Margie looked at Rebecca incredulously and took another bite of eggs.

"Everybody may break the law – even hate it, Margie, but it's still the law. You break it, get caught, and busted, you can't very well call the cops, tell them you're sorry and then they let you go with a wink."

"My Mendy says you've got to make your own law... become the law. It's like our guys have to be the cops and the judges too, but only in their own world."

"'*Their own world*'... Margie, that's crazy."

Margie took a bite of her bagel. "Maybe so," she agreed. "But listen, sweetheart, you married 'crazy,' and that's the way it is. You're stuck with it now! And, you don't really have it so bad with Irving. He takes real good care of you, and he's good lookin' too, a real sharp dresser. Now you'd better eat your eggs before they get cold."

The front door opened and Joey Lucci walked in and hung his suit coat on a coat rack by the door.

"Wow." He smiled. "It's really warming up out there. You girls okay? I'm just gonna go in the other room and use the phone for a minute."

Rebecca smiled faintly. She looked at the table where Marjorie Goldblatt was eating calmly, and then got up and went over to Lucci's coat and patted down the pockets. She heard the jingle of keys and took a deep breath. Fishing the keys out of his pocket, she opened the front door, and darted over to where the black Cadillac was parked in the shade of a huge oak tree. Down by the road, a man was calling out to her, but she ignored him, put the key in the ignition and turned on the big engine.

Lucci was running out the front door yelling for her to stop, but she ignored him as well. Grinding the big car into first gear, she floored the gas pedal and aimed the sleek automobile down the aisle of trees toward the main road. She was doing forty miles an hour as she rushed past the guards at the gate and skidded, spewing gravel, onto the county road out in front of the cabin. Glancing up at the rear-view mirror, she could still see the two guards gaping at one another, shotguns in their hands, as she moved into third gear and aimed the big, expensive car onto the open road.

* * *

"She what? And you let her? Aw, son of a bitch, Joey, whaddaya doin' there? Sittin' around with your thumb up your tuchas? Three guys with Thompsons, and you can't keep a skirt in a cabin. No, you stay there and keep an eye on Margie. This thing is pretty well calmed down now but we still have to give it enough time to make sure that Luciano and Bugsy have the word out to all their soldiers. Irv listened for a few minutes to Joey Lucci on the other end of the phone: "Nah, don't apologize. Forget about it! After all, she's my problem."

Irv Lowenstein hung up the phone and shook his head. He'd just gotten back from Chicago, and hadn't even taken his coat off before he already heard about the tsouris up at the lodge with his wife. Shaking his head, he started for the door.

"Where're you headed?"

Irv stopped and looked at Mendy Goldblatt, who was sitting with his feet up on a desk, smoking a cigarette. Completely calm. No problem. After all, his wife was still up at the cabin, behaving herself like she should. Only Rebecca was acting up. Dammit, he didn't have time now for this kind of bullshit.

"Rebecca," Irv growled. "She took off. Probably drove over to her mother's house. I'm gonna go get her."

Mendy shook his head.

"What?" Irv asked.

"The first rule in the book," Mendy told him. "Never chase a woman. You do that, she'll have you running after her the rest of your life."

"But she took off."

"Well, suppose Sarah took off from her husband…"

"Sarah ain't married."

"As her big brother, you oughta do something about that. But if she was married, and she took off, what do you think your mother would do?"

Irv thought about that for a moment.

"Maybe let her stay a couple of nights," he said. "And then tell her to get her tuchas back where she belongs, with her husband."

"There you go."

When Mendy was right, he was right. Irv nodded and hung his coat back on the hook. He left the office and walked out into the club where a zaftig new singer, a bobbed blonde who couldn't have been a day over twenty, had just finished her rehearsal number. He waited until she'd left the club's small stage and then walked over to the piano player.

"Who's the new singer, Bill?"

The old negro smiled.

"Notice her, did ya, boss? Hell, I'm half blind, and I noticed her, too. Name's Cassie somethin'. Girl from over Jersey way. Got a good set of pipes on her, thass' fer sure."

"Got a good set of everything else, too."

The old man laughed.

"Well, I wouldn't notice that, boss. I'm too old to notice shit like that, he laughed shaking his grayish-white hair."

"Well," Irv muttered, "I'm not."

Patting the old man on the shoulder, Irv walked past the stage, back toward the dressing rooms.

* * *

Irving came back to his Park Avenue apartment early Friday morning, making a minimum of noise so as not to disturb Rebecca. Her luggage was back in the closet, so Mendy had been right after all. She was home waiting for him... but was she? The apartment was empty. Sullenly, Irving made himself a pot of coffee, lit a cigarette and opened the Times.

He was almost all the way through the sports section when the front door opened. He held his temper in check and smiled at Rebecca.

"Hey baby," he said. "Where've you been?"

"Well, I guess, Irving, that I should be asking you the same thing."

"Business," he said curtly. "Important business! So, where've you been?"

"The doctor's."

"The doctor's?" Irv set the paper down. "Whatssa matter? You sick or somethin'?"

She just looked at him. Then her face clouded up in anger, and she walked out of the room.

Irv scowled. He put out his cigarette, stood up, and walked into the bedroom, where Rebecca was sitting in front of the vanity, dabbing at her eyes.

"Hey, Toots." He put his hand on her shoulder and she quickly brushed it away. "What is it?" He turned her chin so he could look her in the eyes. "This doctor thing, is it something serious?"

"No." She squeezed her eyes shut. "I mean, yes it is! And, don't call me Toots like I was one of your chippie girlfriends."

"Come on, baby? What is it? Tell me."

She opened her eyes.

"You bastard," she said quietly. "I'm pregnant."

Chapter Twenty-Seven
Summer 1923

The three friends, all rumpled, and still wearing their evening clothes from the previous night, sat in the hospital waiting room making idle conversation, and talking about basketball, baseball or old times. All three men looked tired. Next to them was a sand-filled canister with dozens of cigarette butts. When the door at the far end of the room finally opened, all three men stopped talking and looked up at the doctor, still wearing his scrubs and surgical mask.

"Mr. Goldblatt?"

Mendy Goldblatt got to his feet, wiping the sweaty palms of his hands on his suit coat and looked anxiously at the doctor. He said nothing, but waited expectantly.

The doctor slipped his mask down and his face broke into a grin.

"You have a son, sir," he said. "Eight pounds, three ounces and mother and child are both doing well."

Mendy's face softened.

"A son..." His face clouded for a moment. "Ten fingers and ten toes?"

The doctor laughed.

"All of the usual equipment," he said. "He's perfect, sir. Congratulations! You can see them both in a few minutes."

Mendy sat back down, a look of sheer relief on his face, as the doctor hurried back into the delivery room. The gangster was quiet for a few minutes, and then took a leather case out of his jacket pocket, and handed an expensive Cuban cigar to each of his friends.

"Mazel tov, Mendy," Irv grinned as he bit the small end off his cigar. "A son! You've been blessed, kain ein horeh! Whaddaya gonna call the little guy?" Irv asked.

"I think Margie wants to call the baby Harold, after her grandfather, and that's fine with me."

"That's a good solid name," Lou agreed.

Mendy closed his eyes and took his friends, Irv and Lou, in his arms, bear-hugging them both, simultaneously. He glanced up at the clock on the waiting-room wall.

"Now you guys go home and get to bed," he said. "It's four o'clock in the morning."

"Shit, we can wait with you, Mendel," Lou said. "Just to make sure that Marjorie and the new baby are fine."

Mendy laughed and shook his head.

"And see Margie without her face on? Uh-uh. She'd have a conniption fit and bawl the hell out of me. She wouldn't talk to me for at least a week."

The other two men laughed. The idea of Mendy's wife even thinking about getting angry with Mendy was ludicrous. But they got the message.

"Okay," Irv agreed. "But we don't want to see your face around the office any time this week or next, you hear me, you big putz?"

Mendy laughed and clapped him on the back.

"Give Margie and little Herschel our love," they said almost together, already giving the baby a Yiddish nickname.

"All right then." Irv grabbed his hat. "Let's go."

Irv and Lou made their way through the pristine, white corridors, out the tall front doors of Mt. Sinai hospital and down a broad set of marble steps to the street. The sky was still dark, but birds were beginning to chirp away. Other than that, the city was unusually quiet.

Irv struck a match and lit Lou's cigar and then his own.

"So Mendy has a son," he mused. "That's just great, a real blessing from God. We'll have to let Rabbi Barney know to expect a call from Mendy so he can get ready for the Bris, and then twenty-two days later the Pigyon Ha-Ben"

"And you and Rebecca have a baby on the way too!"

"Yeh," Irv agreed. "So when do you plan on catching up, Louie? We can't have you a bachelor forever, you know. We're all in our late twenties and not gettin' any younger"

"You sound like my mother," Lou said as they walked slowly down the street, and both men laughed.

Then, after a moment's silence, Lou added, "Martha says she met some real nice guy. A lawyer, and he's also a state senator up in Albany. The Democratic party may run him for Governor. Thomas Rourke," Lou continued. "Good man. Never married, good Irish stock, squeaky clean. I guess some old friends introduced her and now it looks like a good match. He really appreciates Marty and little Hank and that's real important."

Irv nodded. "Louie," Irv said softly. "Why don't you tell her?"

Lou looked up. "Tell her what?"

Irv laughed. "Man, the only one in this town who's carrying a bigger torch than you is standing out in New York harbor welcoming all the immigrants! So why don't you do something about that?"

Lou shook his head. "No," he said. "She was my best friend's wife. I can't look at her without thinking of him. I couldn't imagine… you know…being with her, in bed and all. Or, actually, I can. I think about it all the time, but I know that, if push came to shove, I'd be thinking of Hank. It'd be like there were three of us in the bed, you know what I mean? For Chrissakes, little Trip is Hank's son. And besides, she's not Jewish and my folks would really be upset if I married a shiksah."

Irv nodded in agreement.

"Then what you gotta do," Irv said, "is get over her. Meet yourself a nice Jewish girl."

"Kind of hard to do in our business," Lou replied.

"My sister Sarah is a nice girl, 22-years-old and she's a real looker too!"

Lou suddenly looked Irv's way.

"Sarah? Yeah… Sarah's a real nice girl and good lookin, too, but what would she want with a guy like me?"

"Are you kiddin? She's already sweet on you."

Lou laughed. "Get outta here…"

"I'm not kiddin' ya, Louie. She asks me about you every time I'm back at the house. And she's a good girl too. Hasn't been around much. Matter of fact, nobody has ever touched her, not when she's got me for a big brother."

Lou felt his face reddening. He hoped his friend didn't see it.

"Geez, Irv… that doesn't matter."

Irv Lowenstein stopped walking.

"Yes it does, Louie. It matters a whole bunch. Especially in our business. You can schtup whoever you want, but when you marry, that girl had better be a virgin. The very last thing you ever want is to meet some drunk one night and have him tell you he was hiding the salami between your old lady's legs long before you were. And, she was great in the sack. Uh-uh, that wouldn't be so good, Louie!"

Lou shrugged and they started walking again. In a minute, they had reached Irv's new black Packard V8.

"So Louie... think you can get outta Shabbas dinner at your uncle's this Friday, maybe come over and have dinner at my folks' place?"

Lou thought about it.

"Well, I suppose. Will Sarah –"

"– Be there?" Irv interrupted, then laughed. "If I tell her you're coming, you can bet your sweet tuchas she'll be there."

"Well then..." Lou grinned. "So will I."

Chapter Twenty-Eight
1924 – 1932

Steven O'Neil stuck a finger down the stiff collar of his dark-blue, woolen New York Police Department "blouse" and pulled the garment away from his neck, letting in some cooler air. His father had been upset when he'd enrolled in the Police Academy and said that being a police officer was an occupation unworthy of a family that could trace their lineage back to the ancient kings of Ireland.

But Steven thought the stuff about "ancient kings" was nothing more than so much bullshit. Lot's of people were named "O'Neil," and not all of them could be related to kings. And besides, claiming lineage to Irish kings was like getting a big inheritance in Confederate money. If Ireland still had kings, O'Neil doubted that his father would ever have come to America. And besides, the family needed the money, and the Police Department was one of the few places in New York where an Irishman could make a decent wage – that and being a bartender, and he didn't much care for standing behind a bar serving beer and whiskey half the night. Lord knew, his dad had given up on that long ago. Now all the old man did was sit around the house and suck up beer that he got from God knows where. The situation had made Steven O'Neil a true rarity in New York City – an Irishman who hated the smell of liquor.

O'Neil walked over to the black box on the light pole at the corner, took the key from his blouse, put it in the box and turned it, recording the fact that he was on his beat and on schedule. He turned to go, walking down the street twirling his billy club and glancing at the cars parked at the curb as he did so. Vagrants sometimes got into unlocked cars and slept in them, or worse, so he glanced inside each vehicle as he walked,

He passed a fancy new Cadillac, stopped, backed up, and glanced into the back seat.

He couldn't believe his eyes.

There on the back seat of the Cadillac, out in plain view and not even covered with a blanket, was a case that said, "Canadian

Club." The top was off, and while three of the niches were empty, nine bottles were still in the solid cardboard case.

O'Neil pulled an Elgin pocket watch out of his trousers pocket and glanced at it. He had twenty minutes to go until he was due at his next corner black box, but knew that he could make it there in five if he walked faster.

So he had fifteen minutes to spare.

He stepped back into the dim light of an alleyway and waited. Maybe the silly bugger who owned the Cadillac would come back in the meantime, and he would have himself a "collar." That would look good on his record.

* * *

"The name of the business is Canadian Ace," Lou was saying. "Medium-size distillery up near Toronto. And what with Prohibition, the Canadian owners are on hard times. The government is putting a lot of pressure on them to prevent the deliveries of whiskey in the United States."

Irv nodded. Ever since American authorities had applied pressure and forced the American owners to unload Hiram Walker, the Canadian source of illegal whiskey had been harder and harder to work with. Owning their own distillery made a lot of sense. And, from the papers that Lou had just shown him, Canadian Ace was undervalued and would make a nice addition to the small distillery the boys had purchased a few years ago when Irving was on his honeymoon in Niagara Falls.

"So," he asked Lou, "what's our next step?"

"I think we go up there, take a good look for ourselves, and…"

He stopped talking as the office door opened abruptly. Joey Lucci burst in.

"Sorry for the interruption, guys. But we got more tsouris."

Normally it cracked Irv up when one of the Lucci brothers tried to speak Yiddish. But the look on the little Italian's face kept Irv from laughing.

"What kind of tsouris?" he asked instead.

"Mendy," Lucci said. "The cops pinched him with three quarters of a case of booze in the back of his car."

"Cops?" Irv scowled. "Pay them what they want and tell them to quit fucking around with us."

Lucci shook his head.

"The cop what pinched him? He's not on the pad yet."

Irv rolled his eyes.

"Then put him on."

"We tried," Lucci said, shaking his head. "The dumb mick's a straight arrow. Won't take the dough. What do you want us to do? Whack him?"

Irv shook his head.

"No," he said. "You don't kill a cop. Not ever."

He looked up at Lou.

"This distillery thing is gonna have to wait until we get this straightened out," he told him. "Looks as if I gotta have dinner with the judge again."

* * *

Business had finally exploded upwards during the next several years of Prohibition and the three men prospered like they could never have dreamed possible. The distilleries did very well and they had acquired several new speakeasies. Americans were thirsty and the boys were making millions.

Chapter Twenty-Nine
Spring of 1932

Rebecca could hear the distant laughter of Joey, now 8-years-old, playing with the other children, Harold, Abraham and Trip — Henry III.

Sarah Kravitz beamed.

"I can't believe you and I are pregnant at the same time," she told Rebecca Lowenstein. "It's like we're sisters. I mean we are sisters-in-law…but this makes us even closer, you know?"

Rebecca Lowenstein made a weak attempt to smile as she contemplated her thickened abdomen. Her clothing was already too tight for her, but she was not showing much, not yet anyway, but she soon would be. She hated that part of pregnancy because it made her commitment to her husband even more binding.

Irv had gone reluctantly along with her when she had wanted to sleep in separate beds back when she was pregnant with Joey. She knew Irving had gone to Barney Green about it, and the Rabbi had agreed with her. For medical reasons, he too had suggested separate beds. If they were not extremely careful, there was a strong possibility that she could have had a miscarriage.

But even after Joey had been born, and she could no longer maintain that she was recovering from childbirth, she continued to resist Irving's advances for several years. Occasionally, when she did let Irv have sex with her, she had been secretly using different birth control devices. She knew about his other women, mostly singers or showgirls from the club, that he spent half his nights with. They were little more than nofkes, and who knew whom they'd been with before Irving. She worried about exposure to social diseases and just the thought of it repulsed her. At least, that's the way she rationalized her vehemence, although she would never admit to her jealous tantrums, even to her mother.

And then there'd been that night when Martha had announced her engagement to Tom Rourke. *How was it that Martha could find such a nice, decent, upstanding guy?* They'd announced their engagement, and Rebecca had drunk too much Veuve Clicquot champagne and that night she let Irving sleep with her. The next morning she woke up and found the wet spot on the sheets and realized what had happened. She'd sat on the commode in their beautiful marble bathroom and washed herself again and again, but it was almost as if God had turned against her. Two months later, Rebecca had learned that she was expecting another baby.

Margie and Sarah always talked about how they worried about Mendy and Lou, how they prayed every night that their husbands would come home safe to them. Rebecca, on the other hand, always prayed, although she never mentioned a word of it to her parents or anyone else, that Irv would be killed by some mobster.

No such luck! The bastard was as lucky as could be…and, always at just the right time.

Rebecca forced down a spoonful of cottage cheese as she rubbed her abdomen absent-mindedly and looked out at their hotel veranda on the lake with pine trees and blues skies. The Catskills at Jennie Grossinger's famous hotel were beautiful and in all their glory in the spring of the year.

And even this felt like a prison to her.

"Oh look!" Sarah beamed as she looked at Martha coming down the hotel stairs into the sitting room area. "Here comes the bride-to-be!"

Martha looked radiant in a thin, pale green sundress that set off both her reddish auburn hair and her magnificent figure.

"You've got to be careful," Sarah told her. "I saw Tom peeking around the corner like a kid only a few minutes ago. Now, you know he can't see you before the wedding, because it's bad luck, and you've only got a few hours more before the ceremony."

"He won't see me," Martha laughed. "He and his Democratic State Committee buddies went into a huddle in the hotel's library just a few minutes ago. It's official! We're going to announce right after our honeymoon in California. Thomas Patrick Rourke is going to run for Governor!"

"Politics sounds like a pretty public life to me, are you sure that's what you want, Martha?" Rebecca said, regretting her comment as soon as she'd made it.

"It's very public," Martha agreed solemnly. "But it's the right thing for us. And besides… living in the Governor's mansion for a few years, well Tommy and I can handle that! And, if that's what my man wants, then I'm gonna support him just like you girls support your men."

Both Martha and Sarah began laughing, but Rebecca was strangely silent. She took another spoonful of cottage cheese and thought about birds in gilded cages.

* * *

"So," Irv asked. "How much of this shit was in his suitcase?"
Lou checked his notes.

"About a pound of heroin."

Irv shook his head. "I told those fuckers, no dope. I told them not once but several times. And here's one of our own numbers' runners and he's carrying this stuff while he does our business. And, you know what Luciano and other people are going to think? That he squared it with us first. What'd he say when the boys picked him up?"

"Said it was his," Mendy said. "Said he and his girlfriend got a heavy habit. Pleaded with us to help them clean up."

Irv scowled. "So now he thinks we're what? Fucking stupid? Think some junkie's going to buy a pound just to feed their own monkey? That's a fucking insult. This guy connected, or what? Anybody's brother-in-law, relative or that kind of family tie?

"No," Lou said. "Just a kid that came to us, asked for a job running numbers two years ago. His Poppa's a baker back on Delancey."

"Shit." Irv put both hands atop his head and closed his eyes, thinking about the situation. "Give them both a hot-shot of his own shit. Half an ounce. Then dump them both in the river. The police will find their bodies. We'll pay for the funeral but at least the word will be out that we're in the clear. By the way, is he the baker's only son?"

"Yeah," Lou said. "His older brother died in the war."

"Damn. But that doesn't make any difference. We gotta whack both of them. We can't let this kind of shit get into our business. It would kill us with Luciano and Lansky. Whiskey is fine, gambling's good, and whores are okay as long as they're doing it because they want to and they're shiksahs. But no dope. The guy on the street, he can understand a shot of whiskey, a game of cards and even gettin' his sock yanked. But narcotics? People think we're selling dope, and they'll line up to fink us out to the cops. So this dummy and his broad are kaput! Next order of business."

"Canadian Ace," Lou said. "The Canadian holding company still hasn't attracted any attention from the feds, so we're adding another line that will produce an extra hundred barrels a day at the distillery. It'll increase the total annual output to over a million gallons."

"Good." Irv had gotten up, and he was looking out the window at the lake. Down below him was the hotel's broad patio, and he could see Rebecca feeding his son. He smiled.

"Think it's wise to increase our sales now?" Lou asked thoughtfully. "Congress is really making serious noises about repealing the Volstead Act. The feds are way over budget on enforcement, the country's tax base is down with the economy, and everybody and their brother are drinking. When the gate goes up, we'll have a lot of competition."

"Then we'll just have to make sure we've got the right brand, the people's choice," Irv said. "The economy is so far in the shithouse that it'll have to get better. People will drink more when it's legal and especially if their business is bad or they're without jobs. We have to be prepared to undercut the competition by at least twenty-five cents a bottle once liquor is legal again, no matter how low they go. We got the reserves to outlast anybody in a real price war. And then once we've cornered the market, we can raise the price again."

Lou nodded and made a note in the leather-bound notepad that he always carried in his breast pocket.

"Look at this," Irv said. He motioned the other two men over to the window. Margie Goldblatt had joined Rebecca and Sarah at their table and the women looked like flowers at a distance, their dresses pastel-soft in the sunlight.

As the men watched, the women looked up and Sarah and Margie smiled. Rebecca looked up as well, and Irv imagined that she was smiling at them also. He just couldn't see her frown because she was squinting into the sun.

"We are fortunate men," Irving Lowenstein told his companions. "Fortunate men, indeed."

* * *

My Dear Mr. Senator:

I understand that you are the chairman of the nominating committee for the New York State Democratic party and are considering the nomination of Thomas Patrick Rourke for governor. Mr. Rourke is, insofar as I know, a fine man and of excellent reputation. But, I further understand that he is engaged to be married to Martha Van Dyke, the widow of Henry Van Dyke, and that does raise concerns with me.

Please be aware that Mrs. Van Dyke has been employed for nearly a decade by the Moulin Rouge Club, a notorious speakeasy owned by Irving Lowenstein, Louis Kravitz and Mendel Goldblatt. These men are alleged to have underworld connections and are rumored to be involved in crimes ranging from violation of the Volstead Act to extortion, labor racketeering, numbers and even several unsolved murders.

If you contact me, I can give you all the details that I have in my files on these three men. Being a lifelong Democrat, I would never want to see the party make a mistake such as the one it is apparently contemplating in the nomination of Mr. Rourke for governor.

Your obedient public servant,
Milton Blackman, Esq.
Assistant District Attorney for Manhattan

"Murder?" Ernie Romano, the Congressman from the heavily Italian district of Buffalo cocked his head and looked at the senior Democratic United States Senator from New York. He kept his voice low, as Tommy Rourke was standing on the far side of the banquet room, being congratulated by members of the nominating committee. "Well gentlemen, is that true?" he softly asked other Congressmen huddled around him.

"I checked it out as soon as I got this letter," Congressman Thornton Greely said, "And none of the men mentioned in this letter has ever been successfully prosecuted for so much as even a parking ticket. Goldblatt has been arrested several times, but always at the instigation of this Blackman fellow. And, as far as a speakeasy goes, hell, most of my relatives either owned one or at least worked in one. So what's the big deal? I've been to the Moulin Rouge myself with the missus and it's a first-class club."

"But Blackman's a policeman?" another man, Congressman Jimmy Farrow, Chairman of the U.S. House Appropriation Committee, asked mildly.

"He's an Assistant District Attorney," Greely said scoffingly. "Or at least he was. Been on disability for several years now. His heart. Our folks at Tammany Hall, who are in the know with local politics, say that it's mostly sour grapes. He and Lowenstein have been rivals ever since law school, and Lowenstein has always been the big man. He was in the D.A.'s office himself, you know, years ago."

"So..." The Congressman glanced over at the men lighting cigars on the far side of the room. "What do we do about this letter?"

Congressman Joe Kowalski then took the letter out of Greely's hands, tore it into little strips and dropped it into the spittoon at his feet.

"Nothing," he said. "This Blackman is a nobody and sounds like a royal pain in the ass. Come on, let's join the others."

Chapter Thirty
Brooklyn Receiving Hospital – June 1933

"For Pete's sake, Barney, what were you thinking?" Irv Lowenstein laughed and shook his head. "Five years in the ring and you never so much as broke a fingernail. And now you go to change a light bulb, fall off a ladder and break your ankle?"

"The ladder broke," Barney protested. "And I'm glad it was me, because the wife was thinking of doing it. And she's pregnant again, you know."

"Mazel Tov," Lou Kravitz said as he reached over to shake his hand.

"So Rabbi…" Mendy Goldblatt looked down the corridor of the hospital ward. "How long they keeping you here? Last time you were here, five or six years ago, I thought they'd never let you out. We can get you a private room and –"

"No, no, no," Barney protested. "Honestly, I'll only be in here today, and then I'll be headed home tomorrow before noon."

"Correction." Irv smiled. "We'll be back here to take you home tomorrow morning about eleven o'clock, if that's okay with you." You rest up until then. But until then… well, we were gonna wait to give this to your missus this weekend, but we figure now is even a better time."

He took a folded check out of his pocket and handed it to Barney.

The Rabbi looked at it and his jaw dropped.

"Fifty thousand dollars…" He stared at the three men.

"For your new synagogue," Lou said. "From us to you. And we have one other thing…" Lou opened his briefcase and took out a manila envelope tied with a red cord.

"Here's a few shares of Canadian Ace distillery," Irv explained. "Only five hundred but with dividends and stock splits, it should be enough to give your family a little puskeh, a nest egg, in the years to come. Liquor's legal in Canada, you know, and it will be again here in the states in a few months. Perfectly respectable."

"That is, if you don't have a problem with living the good life off of booze," Mendy laughed.

"Are you kidding?" Barney accepted the envelope. "I was at an orthodox wedding last week. Nobody is more conservative than they are, and the mechutonim, relatives, were all shikkur."

The men smiled. Then Barney looked up at Lou. "How's Danny, your first-born, coming along?

"He's my pride and joy," Lou replied, beaming as he proudly presented a photograph to Barney.

"And, your children?" Barney said to the other two men. "Photographs, please. I want to see family pictures."

Irv and Mendy both grinned and opened their wallets, showing the Rabbi snapshots of the four smiling children. Barney touched the images as if they were something sacred. Then he looked up at the men again, his face sober.

"You know," he said. "The Depression looks like it's finally easing off some throughout the country. The Volstead Act, as you said, will soon be history. It's almost as if we are all being given a new beginning. For your children, it really is the beginning."

Irv nodded.

"So," Barney continued. "Why don't you fellas begin a new life too?"

He tapped the envelope containing the stock certificates.

"This distillery," he said, "is doing very well. I read the financial columns in the paper. And in a few months, everything associated with it will be completely legal. Perfectly respectable, just as you said."

"That's right," Lou agreed.

"So..." Barney suddenly sat up in bed. "Why not just stick with this liquor business and forget all about your other activities? You know, I've never discussed this with you before. It was...well...your business. We're friends, for good or bad, so I turned my head. I didn't want to know from anything, except that I felt part of your families. But now you are all family men. And there are children involved, right? Why not give them a family background they can all be proud of and hold their heads up high wherever they go?"

Far down the hospital corridor, there was a clink of trays as nurses began to serve lunch.

"I say this as a friend," Barney added.

"I know you do, Rabbi," Irv told him, his hand on his shoulder. "Tell you what, we'll think about it, but in the meantime, we'll be back tomorrow morning to get you out of here. Okay?"

Barney Green nodded, the hope written in his face, tears flooding down his cheeks as he again looked at the $50,000.00 check.

* * *

"So..." Irv lit a cigarette as the three men walked down the front steps of the hospital. "Whaddaya think of that?"

The big black Cadillac was standing at the curb a few feet away, its engine idling, one of Mendy's "soldiers" standing next to it looking around, alert.

"The Rabbi made sense," Lou admitted.

"He did," Irv said. "Mendy?"

Mendy looked up at the sky, scowled, and then turned to his friends.

"I gotta guy out in California," he said. "A union guy. One of our people out in Hollywood. He says the movie business is gonna boom, and we could be doing a lot more out on the West Coast making lots of money providing loans to the film studios – loans with no risk. Also, we keep involved with the unions because they really control the studios. Not a bad idea," Mendy pursed his lips, frowned some and then continued. "And, you know the gambling action that Meyer Lansky and the boys have in Cuba...well, now they're thinking of starting up in Las Vegas, Nevada. It's legal out there."

"Well, I been thinking, too," Irv said seriously. "And while we don't want to knock heads with the big machers downtown, you know, the big shots, there's another spot in Nevada near the California border called Lake Tahoe. It sounds really good. And, it's wide open, guys. And, something else too. Rebecca's been getting a little feisty lately, and it might do us both some good if we get away from her parents. You know, spending some time in Nevada or California could do us both some good."

Lou and Mendy were silent and understood his thoughts completely.

Lou thought some more and finally looked at Mendy. "And don't forget, big guy, we could use some of the money from Tahoe to start our financing operation for the studios. Maybe even go completely legit and start a small bank. Between having the unions control film production and the studios into us for big lines of credit, well gentlemen, I see a bright future for us out on the West Coast, and we'll be completely respectable, my friends."

Irv smiled as he realized that both Mendy and Lou hadn't commented on his personal problems. He grabbed them both by their arms and affectionately pushed them in front of him. "I think," he said, "that we have some time before we pick up the Rabbi tomorrow. Maybe, we should do some serious talking while it's on our minds. Let's take a ride to the Moulin Rouge Club and have some dinner. After all, no use owning one of the most popular speakeasies in town unless you can enjoy it."

#

Printed in the United States
103567LV00002B/187-246/P